RETURN
TO
DAWN

RETURN TO DAWN

a novel on three stages

by

Hoyt Rogers

with

Artemisia Vento
and
Frank Báez

SPUYTEN DUYVIL
NEW YORK CITY

ACKNOWLEDGMENTS

Return to Dawn is the third volume of *The Caribbean Trilogy*. In different versions, passages of the trilogy have appeared in *The New England Review, AGNI, Eunoia Review, The Summerset Review, The Writing Disorder, Axon, The Bitter Oleander Review, Off-course, The Dillydoun Review, The Courtship of Winds, Mudlark, The Fortnightly Review, Isla Abierta, The Raven's Perch, spoKe, The Light Ekphrastic,* and *The Literary Review.* My sincere thanks to the editors of these publications for supporting my work over the years. I also owe a debt of gratitude to Jonathan Galassi, Siri Hustvedt, Edmund White, Paul Auster, Marco Genovesi, Robin Saikia, Frank Báez, Nicholas Callaway, Ricardo Bernardo, Anne Davenport, Nellie Barletta, Pablo Báez, Amy Bernstein, Michele Casagrande, Lena Papadaki, Peter Bernstein, Annalyn Swan, Esther Allen, Bishan Samaddar, Marc Vincenz, and Anthony Seidman, who encouraged me along the way. For information about my other books, please visit hoytrogers.com.

Library of Congress Control Number : 2026006707

This is a work of fiction. All names, characters, places, and incidents are figments of the imagination. Any resemblance to actual persons, living or dead—or to entities, events, or locales—is entirely fortuitous.

Published by Spuyten Duyvil; maps and cover images by Mary Heebner; book and jacket design by John Balkwill, Isa Benedetti, and T Thilleman; supplemental editing for volume one by Joan Tapper.

Return to Dawn, first edition, ISBN 978-1-969900-00-6, printed in the United States. Available directly from the publisher, or through Ingram, Amazon, and bookshop.org.

For S, N, and all the voyagers
who seek their 'untold want' on the open sea

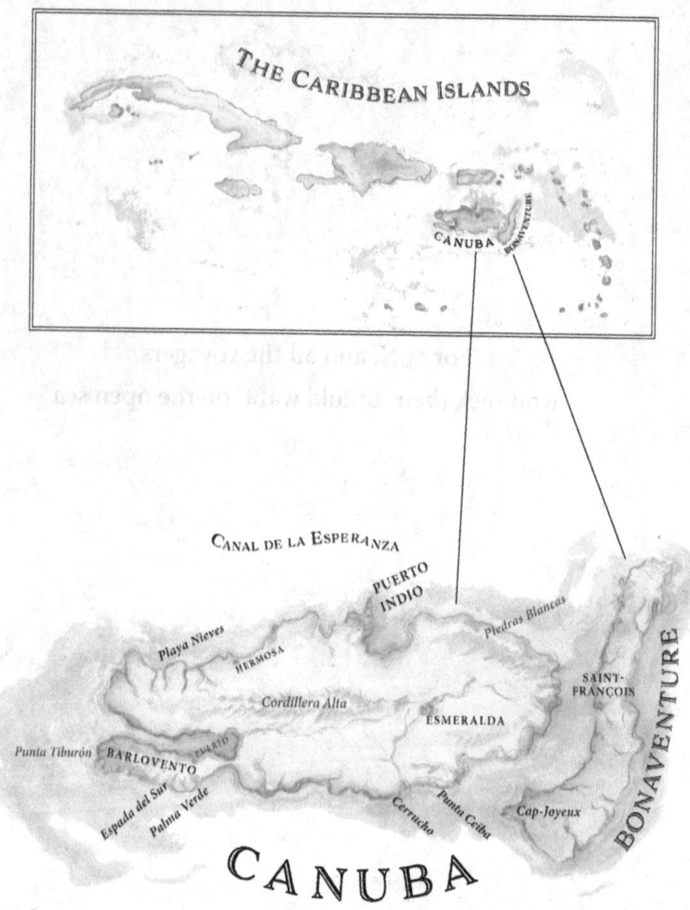

THE CARIBBEAN ISLANDS
CANUBA
BONAVENTURE
CANAL DE LA ESPERANZA
PUERTO INDIO
Playa Nieves
Piedras Blancas
HERMOSA
Cordillera Alta
SAINT-FRANÇOIS
ESMERALDA
Punta Tiburón
BARLOVENTO
PUERTO
Espada del Sur
Palma Verde
Cerrucho
Punta Ceiba
Cap-Joyeux
BONAVENTURE
CANUBA

*T*hough *it stands fully on its own,* Return to Dawn *is the third volume of* The Caribbean Trilogy. *Like its predecessors,* Sailing to Noon *and* Midnight at Sea, Return to Dawn *draws on notebooks I received from a Sicilian journalist, Artemisia Vento, on the eve of her departure for an unnamed country in Asia. She was determined to live out the rest of her days in a cloistered retreat—whether Buddhist, Christian, Vedic, interfaith, or secular, she wouldn't reveal. Discrepantly, she also spoke of an 'environmental hermitage,' far from any contact with mankind. 'You're a translator and editor,' she said. 'These scribbles are a farewell gift to you. Make of them what you will.'*

Among her jottings, I found a lengthy narration. When pressed, she claimed it wasn't autobiographical, merely a re-cord of 'wayward fantasies' she now disowned. In the pages that follow, various actors and puppet-masters 'perform' a story on three stages. 'Tragedies and comedies take place in the course of time,' she explained; 'at some point, they happen to us all. But they're never the final chord: we constantly revise and transform the past. Our dead survive within us in the present. Memory is the surest form of resurrection.'

If readers choose to adopt a counter-linear chronology, they could start with the last of the segments, and thread their way back to the first. Or they could skip from episode to episode, as in the randomness of passing thoughts. In that sense, this foreword might be an afterword—or simply an 'interword.' Where germane, I have reprised certain portions of the prologue and the epilogue from the previous volumes of the trilogy—though in large part, the framing texts in Return to Dawn *are entirely new.*

Artemisia urged me to emend her writings as I saw fit, or throw them away; in any case, she asked me to destroy them in the end. If I recycled them as fiction, she told me to use my own 'byline'—an allusion to her former career. She also wanted me to retain the copyright; she sincerely wished to 'vanish from the world once and for all.' I've preferred to acknowledge her by a pseudonym, 'Artemisia Vento.' Vento, or 'Wind,' is a traditional Sicilian surname. The painter she most admired was Artemisia Gentileschi; the wind was what she wanted to become.

—HR

RETURN TO DAWN

In these flashing revelations of grief's wonderful fire, we see all things as they are; and though the shadows once more descend, and the false outlines of objects again return, yet not with their former power to deceive.

—Melville

The curtain rises to reveal three stages, ascending in a curve from left to right: a forestage with a proscenium, where conventional actors appear; six feet above it, a mid-stage, where scenes are silently acted out as in bunraku, but using limp, life-size dummies instead of puppets; and six feet further up, a marionette stage, also voiceless. At the center of the proscenium is a lectern, to be employed by The Trans Reader, The Female Reader, and The Male Reader, successively. Around the lectern, a jester mutely engages in various antics, sometimes dangling his legs from the proscenium. Below the marionette stage, on the right, a trio of sitar, gamelan, and Native American flute plays between the scenes, or accentuates climactic moments; at times, the musicians should add Tibetan bells of various pitches to their improvisations. Along the bottom of the mid-stage, a simple signage—framed in black, with dark-grey letters on white—states the name of each scene; the signs are changed at the beginning of each scene by one of the bunraku puppeteers, who then joins the others on the mid-stage.

After a pause, on the mainstage, three figures dressed in black make their entrance from the left. They resemble the puppeteers of bunraku, except that that they wear no hoods. In their subsequent scenes on the mid-stage, only one of the three will appear without a hood, 'dezukai'-style, and all will mutely manipulate various dummies. Here they speak in turn, from left to right.

Diana: I am Diana.

Leandra: I am Leandra.

Chiara: I am Chiara.

They speak in unison, with a sound-system echo effect: All three of us have watched our friends and self-appointed foes go through the twists and turns, the inner and outer accidents of life. Here's how we would sum them up: personae in a theatre of vanity, like ourselves, ending in silence on an empty stage. The only solution is to make our exit.

Building 61

In the black rectangle, Diana inserts a sign that reads: Building 61. The three women make their exit to the left, and reappear on the mid-stage, where they will manipulate a dummy on a table. In this case, of the three, only Diana goes without a hood. In the succeeding scenes, whoever inserts the title will reappear on the mid-stage without a hood, whereas the other two will be wearing one. Meanwhile, the Trans Reader makes their entrance from the right and advances to the lectern on the proscenium. As the reader declaims from a large book, actors on the mainstage pantomime the actions described. The same occurs in the subsequent scenes; in longer dialogues, the actors take over from the reader and speak the words themselves, even though the reader continues to voice the surrounding text, like the Evangelist in a Passion Play. The most violent incidents are hidden in shadow on the mainstage; but they're always performed explicitly on the mid-stage by the bunraku-puppeteers, who manipulate limp, life-size dummies under a glaring light. In this episode, a quirky, mocking music accompanies the antics of 'the Beak.' Throughout the work, on the marionette stage, the events are mutely presented as a miniature commedia dell'arte; occasionally, behind a scrim, wayang kulit silhouettes may be substituted for the Western puppets.

The Trans Reader: This is the First Reading.

This morning, Colonel Gilles Annecy reports as usual to San Lorenzo, an army base on the outskirts of Puerto Indio. He parks his jeep in a reserved space, hidden behind the barracks. He's a Frenchman, but with his well-trimmed moustache and stocky build, he easily passes for a senior officer from the Cipango region of Canuba, where many of the inhabitants are of Spanish origin. At sixty-five, he belongs to an earlier generation, and knows the value of prudence: he avoids speaking while on duty, in case his foreign accent gives him away.

Winding through a maze of passageways, he fishes a key out of the breast-pocket of his jacket. He opens an inconspicuous door and slips inside, when no one is looking. In the air-conditioned locker-room, he doffs his Canuban uniform and puts on his work clothes—white coveralls, a matching ski-mask, and rubber gloves. He is now in Edificio 61, Building 61, a squat brown structure without any windows. Judging by its outward appearance, the rank and file assume that it's an ordnance depot.

After punching a series of codes, he emerges into a nondescript room, painted a dull charcoal-grey. In the center sits a man-size slab of cement, raised several feet off the floor and slanted at thirty degrees, with sturdy metal rings screwed into the edges. It's coated with a pristine layer of green foam-rubber, unglued and replaced every week; a stationary helmet, made of steel and lined with plastic cushioning, is affixed to the lower end. A concrete trough with a spigot stands nearby: it contains small aluminum pails and watering cans, spotlessly clean.

On a towel rack, folded squares of blue terrycloth hang in a row, and a tray of medical instruments rests on a glass-topped table. A one-way mirror occupies the upper half of the wall to the right. At first, the Colonel found it disconcerting; but now he enjoys watching his gestures out of the corner of his eye. Further on, another door leads to a holding chamber, managed by his assistants.

The crucial lesson he drums into his trainees is the importance of order—not the Caribbean's strong suit. He likes the sense that his workroom is a space set apart from the hurly-burly of existence, where each operation proceeds according to a ritual. The routine of each movement allows him to daydream, while carrying out his duties without a hitch. During the Algerian campaign, his own superior—whose memory stretched back to the Indochinese War—taught him that interrogators were like pathologists, performing a pre-autopsy, an 'autopsie avant la lettre.'

Or we're like surgeons, Annecy often says to himself. In both cases, the point is to arrive at the greater good, efficiently and unsentimentally. On inspecting the tray, he's gratified to find that everything in its place. The jet-injectors are filled with truth serums, tranquilizers, and—if all else fails—drugs that simulate a heart-attack. Unfortunately, the forceps, scalpels, and sternal saws are merely for show. In the sixties, interrogators proceeded with a freer hand;

they could incise and amputate without any qualms. But times have changed, and his younger Canuban higher-up, a mealy-mouthed civilian, insists on discretion.

'In a democracy,' he preaches in his grainy baritone, 'tactful approaches to the exact same goals can—and must—be found.' Once a prisoner leaves Building 61, he says, the nightmare should be engraved on his memory, but leave no trace of abuse on his flesh.

The Colonel clicks the intercom, speaking in a frigid voice. 'Bring in Subject 527.'

His three husky subalterns wear the same outfits as himself, except that theirs are black; just in case, they carry Beretta M9s in holsters around their waists, and hunting knives buckled to their calves. Luckily, today's prisoner seems to pose no threat: his slight frame hardly warrants such drastic safeguards. But the Frenchman can remember even scrawnier Algerians who turned into spitfires, gnawing his fingers or kneeing him between the legs.

As his aides haul the bound man through the holding-room door, dressed only in his boxer shorts, Annecy whiffs the exalting smell of rancid sweat. A sensation of power sweeps over him, as if he holds a still-throbbing heart in his hands. From the intelligence he's read, he knows that this little pipsqueak—the same left-wing journalist he questioned a year ago—has hardly mended his ways. Recently he even dared to write about his previous experience in Edificio 61, and his lurid account caused problems for the government.

The Colonel detests recidivists; this time, he won't let the muckraker off so lightly.

Through the night, his apprentices have taken turns berating the prisoner, never allowing him to sleep. In their well-furnished quarters, they've developed some techniques of their own. When this subject persisted in talking back, they chained him to a dentist's chair and sprayed him with ice-cold water, every five minutes or so.

Now he's starving and exhausted, and he's almost lost his voice. But as soon as they push him into the inquiry room, he starts bucking and squealing. Two of the trainees hold him firmly in place, careful to leave no marks on his body. From the tray on the glass table, the third selects the jet-injector labeled V. He shoots a dose of valium into the prisoner's neck—enough to subdue him, but not to make him pass out.

When he leaves off thrashing, they lay him feet upward on the slab, and place his head in the stainless-steel helmet. Securing his arms and legs to the rings with padded clamps, they cover his mouth and nose with a piece of cloth. In other circumstances, the Colonel might've allowed one of them to practice his hortatory skills on the captive. But this is no ordinary offender, so he prefers to conduct the interview himself.

He fills one of the pails with a half-gallon of water, and pours the liquid slowly into the fabric. After a minute or two, the man begins to gasp, and his eyes roll back into their sockets. Annecy slides the cloth up just far enough to free the prisoner's tremulous, bluish lips. Now he'll allow him ten minutes to take in some air, and reflect on his behavior. Often a single dousing is enough; but he imagines this journalist will be a tough nut to crack.

While he's waiting, the Colonel's thoughts wander to his wife Verónica, an attractive, mulatto Canuban much younger than himself. He met her on vacation at the Hermosa resort ten years before, and then and there he vowed to transfer to the island as soon as possible. On his retirement in 1998, he leaves the French army with deep satisfaction: he looks forward to an uneventful life in the Caribbean, playing golf and basking in the sun. But it isn't long before his past catches up with him.

One afternoon, an envoy from the country's Joint Chiefs of Staff raps on Annecy's door at the Hermosa Villas. He summons him to Puerto Indio for an appointment with the Chief of Special Operations, General Francisco López, whose CIA contacts have informed him about the Frenchman's special expertise. At the SO headquarters, López greets his guest with a formal salute, as if he were already a member of his team.

Brushing specks of lint from a golden epaulet, he offers Annecy a chair. 'Most Canubans would treat you to a lot of small talk,' he says affably. 'But I don't like to beat around the bush.' He points to a well-worn folder on his desk. 'We've heard a lot about you… You carried out a key mission in the Algerian War.'

Annecy doesn't feel flattered. 'Work is work. But I've left all that behind me.' His upper lip begins to twitch, a nervous tic he's always tried to control.

'As a brother-officer, I know we can't change who we are.' López leans forward and taps him on the wrist, sure of his game. 'We need your help in a training program. It's just for three years, and we're willing to pay.' He nudges a one-page contract across the desk; it vaguely refers to 'wages for services rendered.'

Once he sees the size of the figure, the Frenchman reconsiders. With that kind of money, he could buy one of the better villas in Hermosa, close to the beach. Verónica nags him every day that their bungalow behind the golf course is more like a closet than a home. He takes the pen López holds out to him, and signs with a flourish. 'Like everything you've done in your career,' the General assures him, 'this will remain top secret.'

Several years have gone by since then, and Annecy is reaching the end of his tour of duty. His three novices have already learned about as much as he can teach them...

Zeroing in on the prisoner again, he asks him a single question. 'Are you ready to die?' He gives no marked emphasis to the words, and says them in a Spanish that sounds more Nordic than French. He cultivates it by mimicking Ingmar Bergman films, to conceal his identity from what he calls his 'patients.'

Subject 527 doesn't answer the query. Groggily, he asks a question of his own. 'Why am I here?'

The Colonel continues in a noncommittal tone. 'You know why. You published a defamatory article. And it wasn't the first time.' He spreads the cloth over the prisoner's mouth again. This time he chooses the watering can, in preference to the pail; the alternation makes the task less boring. Once more, he brings the man to the point of drowning, and then lets up. 'Will you ever write something like that again?'

When the cloth is drawn aside, the subject can't even sputter a reply. All he does is whimper 'no, no, no,' like someone pleading with a psychopath.

Annecy presses his chest, and some of the water oozes from his throat. 'That's good, because we'd hate to bring you back to our operating room.'

To his amazement, Subject 527 manages to spit at him. His voice is feeble but defiant, and his eyes burn with hate. 'No, no, no. I have to tell the truth.'

The Frenchman steps over to the mirror on the wall, lifting his hand with an inquisitive flick. Below the rectangle are three small light-bulbs: green, red, and white. As he expected, the green light flashes for a moment: this means he must carry on.

He leans against the tilted platform. 'That was very rude, what you just did.' Then he turns to the tray and picks up a surgical knife. The man's eyes bulge; he starts bleating like an animal. 'It won't do you any good to scream. These rooms are completely soundproofed.' Annecy waves the lancet over the captive's chest. 'Think it over while you take another drink.' Then he holds a pail under the spigot.

As he douses Subject 527 a third time, he urges him to cooperate. 'I'm told we have serious reasons to distrust you. You haven't learned your lesson, and you're only making things worse—for us and for yourself.'

When he pulls the cloth back, the journalist croaks 'no, no, no' once again, almost in a whisper. The Colonel goes over to the mirror and raises his hand questioningly. He knows what will probably happen next…

A few minutes later, a figure dressed in brown and green camouflage strides jauntily through the holding-room door. He sports a red skullcap and a mask with a sharp yellow beak; his pointed, claw-like gloves are bright orange. Annecy hates such garish displays, but he has to put up with them. 'Voici le Bec…' he says to himself, gritting his teeth. 'Here's the Beak.' It's a private nickname he's invented for the clown.

He smacks his lips and flaps his arms—a highly unprofessional approach, in the Frenchman's opinion. He pecks at the captive's face with his beak, and chants a strange, incomprehensible chant. Through the slits in the mask, Subject 527 can see the blue-grey glint of his torturer's steely eyes. An unexpected calmness washes over him. A strange air of complicity envelops them: they seem remote from the room—light years away, in a world apart.

To pass the time, Annecy observes that Subject 527 has crinkly hair and glabrous skin, tinted a pale café-au-lait. The prisoner feels his flesh recede into distant space—an earthly figment of the mind he's already outlived. The Beak presses his vinyl claws over the man's ashen lips. After this nightmare vision, now he's sure he'll keep quiet…

Abruptly, Subject 527 bolts out of his trance. He sinks his teeth into the torturer's hand, biting through the tangerine glove. A thread of red trickles out. 'No, no, no,' he shouts, galvanized by a last surge of energy. The soldiers lash his ankles to the metal rings again. Nonchalant, 'the Beak' leaves the premises as quickly as he arrived.

Annecy is disgusted: the intruder behaved even more ineptly than usual. What can you expect from a civilian boss? The whole platform is splattered with streaks of blood. The clean-up this afternoon will have to be meticulous.

On the other side of the one-way glass, Ángel María stows the mask and skullcap in a blue Formica cabinet. He pulls off the orange gloves and reaches for his first-aid kit. After sterilizing the wound, he sticks a large band-aid on top; nothing to worry about. Now his other hand hovers above the red button. Oh, let's call it quits, he says to himself. He must be terrified by now, no matter how he behaves while he's here.

But then he has second thoughts. He wavers for a moment, moves his finger to the white button, and presses it resolutely. The Colonel sighs with relief. Finally... He makes a slitting gesture across his throat, and one of his subalterns pads over to the tray. Selecting a jet-injector marked PC, he spritzes a heavy dose of potassium chloride into the prisoner's arm. Within minutes, a massive heart attack will finish him off.

Like the earlier whines and bleats, the final rasps and gurgles take Annecy back to his childhood, when he helped his father slaughter pigs, calves, and sheep. He still feels a strong adrenaline rush during his sessions in Building 61, just as he did in those days. His father taught him to channel that sensation—to use it to focus on the matter at hand. It's very stupid of 'the Beak' to let his guard down; what with those distinctive eyes of his, a clever journalist could easily guess his identity.

The Colonel cups the offender's wrist to make sure his pulse has stopped. Then he supervises his trainees as they unstrap the corpse and cart it out of the room. Before rigor mortis sets in, they must scrub the man and dress him in the clothes he was wearing when detained. Cadavers should normally be left on a staircase, in a restroom, behind a bar, at the edge of a park: whatever jives with the captive's habits. As an additional precaution, Annecy will have this one dumped beside an infamous brothel. His family will hush up the story out of shame. The coroners are all Progress Party hacks; at the inquest, they'll determine he died from natural causes—and that will be that.

Once he changes into his street clothes, Ángel María unlocks the door of the observation room. He leaves Building 61 through a labyrinth of hallways, ending at the headquarters of the Joint Chiefs of Staff. At the main entrance, he climbs into the back seat of his limousine, and orders the chauffeur to drive him to Hermosa. He hates it when an uncooperative subject forces him to press the white button; but in certain cases, he has no choice. Thank goodness it doesn't happen too often. After a morning like this, he needs a game of polo to cheer him up. He can hardly wait to shed his Versace suit and Gucci loafers, slip into his jodhpurs and riding boots, and mount his favorite horse, Anything Goes.

Entering from the left, Leandra is hoodless; she slides the title You Only Need One *into the black rectangular frame. Entering from the right, The Female Reader replaces The Trans Reader at the lectern.*

The Female Reader: This is the Second Reading.

Chiara has lived on the island for two decades, when Horacio introduces her to one of his fellow-composers, Alfonso Pérez Berrido. He owns the only other Bösendorfer in all of Canuba. — When it comes to our sublime pianofortes, my Sicilian Minerva, we are a mutual admiration society of two. I am utterly convinced that you will adore him. He is Ángel María's uncle—his boyhood mentor, forsooth. We have inculcated you with our mores, videlicet: in our insula, once you cleave to one of us, you cleave to us all. Besides his compositional abilities, Alfonso is adept at several languages; he is also a superb conversationalist.

A garrulous old codger, you mean. — For the moment, she's tired of her role as everyone's 'sister confessor.'

Do not be churlish, my transcendent goddess! Because of my residence at the monastery, I simply lack the chronology he merits, for the nonce. — Horacio stares at her plaintively, patting down his nimbus of frizzy hair. In his antiquated lingo, inherited from his 'pater,' a pompous diplomat, he pleads: Here is his telephonic codification. Now I pray you, please be a beneficent Athena, and communicate with my amicus posthaste.

Despite her trepidation, Don Alfonso turns out to be a cordial host; he receives Chiara like a long-lost daughter—all the more so, since he's estranged from his own children, too 'contemporary' for his taste. An agronomist by training, he farms an enormous estate on the outskirts of Puerto Indio. In his youth, he produced only chick peas and plantains; but later, he diversified into gourmet vegetables.

His initiative impressed Manfredo Espinosa, the Jefe Supremo of Canuba. In 1952, he succeeded his aging father, an iron-fisted patriarch nicknamed Papito, whose reign was marked by unparalleled terror. The new dictator, Manfredo, is Alfonso's junior by only twelve years: he treats the botanist as an older brother—a mixed blessing, at best. Papito and Manfredo often consult him about their plantations, which cover a third of the island. Dealing with his own cantankerous father as a boy, Alfonso has mastered the art of walking on eggshells. But there's always the danger of falling out of favor, and triggering the Espinosas' greed: they're notorious for expropriating the lands of their former associates.

Chiara's visits to Don Alfonso's farm remind of her upbringing in the Sicilian countryside, where food was also an obsession. Though his wife, Doña Lidia, is confined to the upper floor of the house by a chronic ailment, he insists on preserving her gastronomic standards, which she's conveyed over the years to their cook. After a copious meal with Chiara, once the staff has gone to bed, the elderly man often reminisces about his friendship with Manfredo.

Prematurely, Alfonso has reached the age when the face crumples into a formless mask; his spongy body is even more amorphous. But when he talks about the past, his sunken brown eyes light up with enthusiasm; and when he touches a keyboard, his liver-spotted hands quicken with juvenile grace. Besides their love of music, he and Chiara share a mania for ornithology: along with his wife Lidia, he's been an avid bird-watcher for many years.

The lower reaches of the Río Fernando, silted and green, rope lazily through Alfonso's vast domain. As Chiara listens to him on the terrace, the river seems to imitate his softly meandering voice. — You have no idea how hard it was back then, Chiara. I had to watch out for Papito, Manfredo, and their bodyguards, too.

Why, Don Alfonso? They just followed the Espinosas' orders, didn't they? — She sips a snifter of Armagnac, settling in for the next installment of his memoirs.

If they realized what the orders were... You've probably heard that back in the fifties, Manfredo started posing as the 'Benefactor de la Patria.' He made a point of spending most of his weekends in small towns and villages, listening to people's problems—and even fixing a few, now and then.

Chiara looks at him wryly. — Not by handing out

money, I suppose.

Sometimes he would; but only what for him, was pocket change. Remember, by this time he and his father controlled more than half of the economy. On his forays, Manfredo brought along a doctor—and a couple of brujos, too, with their potions and charms. He would often ask me to join him—especially to visit fields hit by plant-diseases like blue mold.

An invitation you couldn't refuse. — She twirls her dense, auburn mane with a mocking air. — But he only wanted to help the campesinos with 'their' crops…

Exactly, Chiaretta. They were *his* crops, of course: the peasants worked on the lands he'd stolen.

Alfonso told her a chilling tale, a set anecdote in his collection. One day, he'd been driving with Manfredo and his convoy down a primitive road, when they chanced upon one of the tyrant's boyhood friends. Since he hadn't heard from him in over a decade, Espinosa had given him up for dead. But here was his old playmate, sitting in front of a hut beside the road. Manfredo rolled down the window and called out his nickname: Pichipito! What, you still alive? As soon as I look at the bananas in Hatillo, I'll be back… Later, when they halted again before the cabin, a guard was standing outside, his revolver still smoking. He marched toward the limousine, and gave a crisp salute. — Generalísimo, you were surprised this man was still alive. I stayed behind, and killed him on the spot.

Chiara sucks in her breath. — What did Espinosa do?

It was the only time I ever saw him cry. The guard tried to make excuses, but Manfredo had him tied to a tree and shot: his last words were 'Viva el Benefactor'!

Alfonso shuffles to his harpsichord in the adjacent room, and lifts the scarlet lid. While Chiara listens through the open door, he performs a melancholy piece of his own, one of a set of neo-Baroque adagios. For his piano, he composes preludes in the style of Alkan or Anton Rubinstein—though he doesn't play them as well as his solemn sarabandes for cembalo.

Horacio later refers to his works as 'touching pastiches.' He can tolerate the music, he confesses, but he can't put up with the geezer's long-winded recollections. He's grateful Chiara has succeeded him as the melomane's confidante, second only to Ángel María himself.

Sinking back into his armchair on the terrace, Don Alfonso lets out a mournful sigh. — I've never gotten over my mother's death. But my father was so cruel to us both, I was glad to see him go. Not that he could compare to a monster like Papito.

Chiara has read about the coup d'état of 1961. Papito Espinosa, already in his eighties, led a savage revolt against his son. For two months, he gained the upper hand, and went on killing sprees that outdo even Manfredo's. Finally, a band of officers—secretly loyal to the younger man— riddled Papito with bullets. At the time, he was napping on a float in his swimming pool. After the assassination, Espinosa converted his father's house and grounds into the Canuban Military Museum. Wedged among armored tanks and fighter planes, the pool provides a bizarre centerpiece: in imitation of Jayne Mansfield's (Papito's favorite actress), it's shaped like an immense pink heart. Manfredo filled it with blood-red shards of broken glass, as a 'Memorial of Warning to All Rebels.'

When Papito returned to his evil ways, for his son it was a nightmare. Alfonso's hand trembles as he lifts his glass. — I had to help him get rid of his father, if I didn't want to be next.

Startled, Chiara sits up straight. — I thought the men who killed Papito were his own generals.

True. But they had to be armed, in case his bodyguards defended him. The big brass never carry weapons, you know. If their subordinates had gotten wind they'd formed a stockpile, they would've tipped Papito off. That's where I came in.

You mean you gave them the weapons?

Well, I passed them on. Some spooks from the CIA smuggled high-powered machine guns into the country. They found me through one of my former Ag School professors at LSU, and traveled here on a fake DOA trip. They were worried about Papito's 'bad image'—afraid he might cause a communist revolution, like Batista did in Cuba. All I did was stash the guns in my house. I'd always been a harmless civilian, on amicable terms with the tyrant. He never suspected me of being one of his enemies.

You held a personal grudge against him?

Oh, he didn't do me any harm, during those two months. — Alfonso leans back, framed by the door to the music room; the polished contours of his instruments shimmer in the gloom, red and brown. — Papito 'nationalized' most of the larger farms on the island, but he exempted me from the decree. I guess he needed my advice about what to plant, and didn't want me to emigrate. To tell the truth, he'd always showered me with affection.

Affection?

I was close to the Espinosas because I had no choice. I had to protect my wife, my children, my land. — A shadow crosses Alfonso's face. — Papito was Manfredo's father, after all.

And being with him was like being with… your own father? — Chiara hopes she hasn't gone too far; she searches his sagging features with her grey-green eyes.

Alfonso hesitates before answering. — …Yes. But Papito treated me better than my father. And with Manfredo, it was the same, in a fraternal way. When you live with an autocrat, you comply with his whims. But every inch of yourself that you yield adds to your resentment, till the dam finally bursts.

From what I've heard, the whole island was ready to explode.

That's right. Chiara, I know I can count on your discretion.

I have a pet theory. Maybe Manfredo provoked Papito's coup on purpose. Why? So his father would be the scapegoat for all the crimes he'd committed himself. After the bloodbath, Manfredo started mellowing right away: fewer murders, more freedom of speech—up to a limit. Less land-grabbing, too. He even gave some of the big estates back to their owners—especially the ones who were conspiring against him. All just a clerical error, he said.

Life insurance, I'd call it.

You're thinking more and more like a Canuban, Chiaretta. Manfredo's 'change of heart' was due to political expediency. The gringos couldn't afford a hardcore dictatorship on the island anymore—not after Castro. Nowadays, talk-show hosts might link the patricide to some kind of complex. Maybe Manfredo got rid of the poison of his upbringing by killing his father. I don't know. After the 'family incident,' he took his distances from me—to my relief.

He couldn't remain on good terms with you. Even if your role was hushed up, he must've found out.

Probably from the spooks themselves, when they helped him stay on top. The Canuban officers who did the deed were sent abroad for a year: a slap on the wrist—and another propaganda ploy. Espinosa, the Benevolent… By the time he organized our first 'democratic' elections, six years later, he won by a landslide. The CIA poured a lot of dollars into that campaign. Since then, Manfredo has been El Canubano Nuestro, The People's President…

Not the Supreme Chief anymore.

El Jefe Supremo? Not on your life! — Alfonso pauses pensively, rubbing his chin — You're right, Chiara. For me, eliminating Papito had a personal side. They say the CIA isn't as smart as we're led to believe. But maybe this time, they did their homework. You can only get so far by using a man's ideals; you can get a lot further by using his hate.

Refusing her help, he stiffly rises to his feet, and turns toward the river. Through the balustrade, Chiara watches the languid ripple of its glistening shoulders, streaked with mist. The frogs and cicadas strike up a chorus, as insistent as a single voice.

Weren't you afraid? she asks, after a while.

Terrified. I stayed awake all night. When the officers came for the guns, I met them at the southeast gate. I had no way of knowing if they would succeed—but if they didn't, I knew what would happen to me. I'd have to beg for a quick death—not weeks and weeks of torture. — Slowly, he wheels around. — Come, Chiaretta. Follow me.

He leads her to a cubbyhole below the staircase; Chiara has never noticed it before. — Ever since that night, I've always kept this key in my pocket. To bring me luck. See, here's the place.'

It's not very big inside. Room for six or seven guns, at most.

Alfonso nods: To kill a man, you only need one.

Demotatorship

Entering from the left, Chiara is hoodless; she slides the title Demotatorship *into the rectangular black frame. Entering from the right, The Male Reader replaces The Female Reader at the Lectern.*

The Male Reader: This is the Third Reading.

While Espinosa couldn't frequent Alfonso openly—given the part he'd taken in Papito's assassination—he never forgot his boon companion, and did him favors through his nephew, Ángel María. Since Doña Lidia and his mother were sisters, there was no blood-kinship between him and his uncle. Alfonso detested both his parents, and forbade them to cross his threshold; but he was very fond of his nephew, as Manfredo knew. On the surface, the family link seemed so weak that he could patronize Ángel María without raising any eyebrows.

Before long, the young engineer's dark-green truck is replaced by a silver Audi... An astute judge of talent, the 'People's President' converts him into one of his closest advisors: half public-works inspector, half private secretary. With none of Alfonso's reluctance, Ángel María lithely scales the heights of power. He spends many hours each day with the frail but lucid ruler, who's now approaching ninety years of age.

Though he no longer plays duets with Lamia, the

libidinous cellist, Ángel María hasn't given up the piano. His uncle was his earliest teacher, and now they become musical partners again—this time, on an equal footing. They share a predilection for Gibbons and Scarlatti, whose fantasias and sonatas Alfonso has arranged in four-handed versions. Once a week, Chiara provides an appreciative audience of one.

She also listens gladly to their ongoing chats about politics and recent history. They can both speak from an insider's point of view; and in their country retreat, they feel safe to talk freely. With ironic frankness, they explain how Espinosa controls the elections through municipal flunkies, all members of his Progress Party. Thanks to them, he has prolonged his tyranny for several decades, in a milder, more 'democratic' form.

Ángel María comes up with the buzzword one evening, as they sip rum and limeade on the terrace. — Let's just call it a 'demotatura.' — He raises his glass in a rueful toast.

Chiara seconds the gesture. — Hmm. 'Demotatorship.' An accurate term, from what I've heard.

Alfonso agrees: After so many years under the Espinosas, father and son, Canubans couldn't swallow democracy right away. Even today, they still like it spoon-fed. Slightly modernized, Manfredo is still a caudillo—the kind of strongman Latin Americans have always loved.

My uncle must have told you about his excursions with Espinosa in the Stone Age. — Alfonso and Chiara exchange guilty glances, and Ángel María chuckles dryly. — Don't worry, I won't rat on you, if you won't rat on me. I've been on many such trips in the last few years—brujos, healers, magic charms, the whole nine yards. In that respect, the Jefe hasn't changed. He travels with the brass, to impress the country folk: generals to his right, colonels to his left. All his bodyguards are in uniform, too—you'd never see that in Europe or the States. In Latin America, the Secret Service is no secret. The jackboots are buffed to shine like mirrors. The machine guns are right in your face.

Chiara clears her throat uneasily. — Don Alfonso saw people killed right in front of him. Does that ever happen now?

The times have evolved. — Ángel María stares into space. — You can't just gun somebody down. But the threat is there. Now and then, Espinosa has some of his thugs bump off a troublemaker or two. Someone expendable. A professor, a lawyer, a unionist. The bodies always turn up somewhere. A heart attack is easy to simulate, you know.

His matter-of-factness is chilling. Is he trying to bait her? Could the house be bugged? Instinctively, Chiara lowers her voice: Is there still a lot of corruption?

No, no. These days, Espinosa is clean as a whistle. It's part of the new image. He used to be a 'mujeriego,' but he's not a skirt-chaser now. And he's never had any children— no Baby Manfredos. Take it from me, he lives like a monk. He lets his ministers do all the stealing.

Chiara can't help but wonder whether her friend has his own hands in the till.

Alfonso changes the subject hastily. — In my day, Manfredo used to dole out petty gifts in the countryside. I hear he does that in the city now, too.

You're right, Tío Alfonso. So many of the campesinos have moved to town, there's not much difference anymore. Most of the voters live in Puerto Indio. Every morning, there's a line of people asking for handouts, exemptions, cures. The Presidential Palace is a regular Court of Miracles. On the way to my office, I trip over midgets, faith-healers, mambos on the hustle, and beggars who tug at my arm.

Chiara smiles: Your job sounds like a three-ring circus.

Three-hundred-ring, you mean. As Tío can tell you, it's not easy to get along with Espinosa—and it's worse, now that he's so old. Every other night, he wakes me up at three in the morning. I have to drive to the Palace and read to him till dawn. He's nearly blind, poor man.

You should resign! — Don Alfonso is adamant. — You don't want to share a dictator's fate. Manfredo had Papito's body dumped in a truck, and covered with coconuts. Otherwise, the mob would've him strung him up, just like they did with Mussolini.

Ángel María grins. — But Papito's coffin finally made it to New York, where every Canuban wants to go! A lot of trouble, just to get a visa. — He falls silent for a while. — What's happened to Don Manfredo is much worse. At this point, his only way out is to liquidate *himself*.

The cicadas and frogs raise their anthem. Extending her hand like a bishop, Chiara makes the sign of the cross. — Don't worry, time will take care of that. As it does for us all…

Up from a Hill of Beans

Entering from the left, Diana is hoodless; she slides the title Up from a Hill of Beans *into the black frame. Entering from the right, The Trans Reader replaces The Male Reader at the lectern.*

The Trans Reader: This is the Fourth Reading.

Ángel María's quicksilver temperament seems puzzling to Chiara; but his upbringing offers some clues to its source. While his mother, Ramona—Don Alfonso's sister-in-law— belongs to the upper middle-class, she doesn't hail from one of the island's most eminent clans. Her parents once owned a sizeable estate in the mountains near Esmeralda; but they frittered it away till nothing was left but—verbatim—a hill of beans. Like her progenitors, Ramona is a spendthrift creature of pleasure, until the money runs out. Her spouse, Belisario, a second-rate businessman, can barely afford her few remaining luxuries. They're both addicted to all-day soaks in their hot-tub, lackadaisical massages, and dubbed reruns of *I Love Lucy*. Belisario fancies himself a dead ringer for Marlon Brando, and likes to act out the love-scenes from his movies—either with hired floozies or with his frivolous wife. Don Alfonso finds the pair repellent, and never lets them darken his door.

To compensate, he pampers their children, teaching them music, botany, and birding on his farm. Under their uncle's tutelage, Ángel María and his sister, Begonia, regard their parents as little more than wet skeletons in the closet. Like her brother—whom she equals in beauty, though not in charm—Begonia jumps many rungs on the social ladder; but for her, the climb is far more difficult. Though her wealthy Spanish husband adores her, he forces her to reside in Monte Carlo, where no one knows about her seedy origins. They distinguish themselves there as right-wing bigots; devotees of Opus Dei, they spearhead fundraising drives for the 'ultra' causes of the Church.

In June of 1987, Leandra sleepwalks through her wedding on tranquilizers. With a thousand guests—the 'nuptials of the decade,' the newspapers enthuse—it seems as jejune to her as a dog-and-pony show. Once she dozes her way through the honeymoon in Bali, she lies around for months in Ángel María's flat, as passive as a mannequin. Though his affiliation with the Peralta Del Ríos doesn't alter his routine, Leandra's world deflates like a punctured balloon: even her Kultur-Helden, Heidegger and Derrida, lose their talismanic cachet. Ángel María's butler makes all the household decisions. He and the maids never consult the lady of the house, whom they move from room to room like a folding chair.

Don Adalberto Peralta considers his son-in-law a better Ken Doll for his wife, Carolina, than those pesky 'Miranda boys.' Horacio and Catulo got on his nerves with their noxious stream of performing-arts events. While Ángel María's pedigree is meager, the Del Río investment wonks call him 'an asset of tremendous worth.' His government machinations will line the family coffers with thick new layers of profit. Embarrassed by his stables, mistresses, and other self-indulgences, all at the expense of his spouse, Adalberto decides that Paris is worth a Mass. He assumes that given his middle-class roots, Ángel María won't cost much, compared to the millions he'll generate.

Clearly, this is a miscalculation. A few weeks after the honeymoon, Caramela Sosa draws up plans for a mansion overlooking the Río Fernando, complete with multi-level gardens. Ángel María sites the house on land Carolina Del Río already owns: choice acreage she acquired from Don Alfonso. As soon as the blueprints arrive, Ángel María presents them to his mother-in-law; as an amateur architect herself, she can only tip her hat to Sosa's genius. Right away, she enlists her daughter's support.

We owe it to you, darling. This house will be a landmark.

Impassively, Leandra turns her face to the wall. — All

right, Mamá, whatever you say.

When Carolina springs the fait accompli on her husband, he can only submit. He writes a colossal check from their joint account for 'Leandra's wedding gift,' consoling himself with a fundamental fact: the money isn't really his. Since he's pillaged his wife's fortune on a grander scale, he can scarcely reproach his son-in-law for following suit.

Carolina firmly takes charge of the Río Fernando project. As a veteran engineer, Ángel María sagely steers clear of the nitty-gritty; he doesn't lift a finger, least of all to defray the mammoth overruns. The sky is the limit; and to no one's surprise, Sosa's masterpiece is built in record time.

A year later, the spectacular result appears on the cover of *Architectural Digest*. Its swerving terraces and cantilevered walls spill dramatically down the hillside to the riverbank—much to the disgust of Countess Frederica, Carolina's perennial rival. — To think my son could have lived there! Damn it! Verdammt noch mal! Gustavo is such a dummkopf! — She still regrets that he didn't give in to Leandra's overtures, when she doted on him for his intellect.

By the early nineties, Espinosa assigns so many duties to Ángel María that he can't cover them all. Increasingly, the Presidential Advisor delegates his less important roles—such as those of 'Supervisor de Antiguedades' and 'Comisionado de Biología Marina'—to his own faithful minions. His political clout rises steadily, and his retinue grows by leaps and bounds. Employed as deputy ministers, department heads, bodyguards, secretaries, drivers, and so forth, these starry-eyed sycophants—whether female, male, or in between—enhance his status and sate his appetites.

His 'packaging' alters to match his burgeoning prestige. 'Ángel María Cambia Su Look,' the fashion pages trumpet. His stout jowl solidifies with age, but his olive complexion and steel-blue eyes retain their beauty. His finest feature is still his wavy chestnut hair—not unlike Jack Kennedy's, as pundits often remark. He cuts it shorter and shorter, and with less exposure to sea and sun, its golden highlights fade. But his trimmer hairstyle pleases the older generation—particularly his father-in-law, Don Adalberto. In a similar move, he shaves off the captain's beard of his whale-watching years; before long, he clips his moustache as closely as Omar Shariff's.

Over time, Ángel María's sedentary life fattens him up a bit. He's always verged on stockiness, but he's never allowed it to turn to outright flab. He trounces one of his adoring aides at tennis twice a week, just to keep in shape; and though he attends receptions almost nightly, he rarely touches the food. As the years roll by, he appears to subsist only on liquids: the best wines and the finest Scotch. Whenever he graces a party, there's bound to be a grand cru or single malt on hand, even if he has to bring it himself.

Much more than his good looks, his complicity accounts for his effortless sway over others. He never forgets a name or personal detail, and his easy-going banter always sparks an immediate rapport. The classic jack-of-all-trades, who once played football at Texas A & M, he can rehab buildings, tell salty jokes to macho pals, improve shipyards and fisheries, dash off light verse, consult with scientists, select the menu, manage committees, massage the piano keys, balance budgets, flatter the generals' wives, write noncommittal reports—and above all, keep Espinosa happy.

Though his protegé has no training in economics, the 'demotator' declares him the 'Director del Banco Nacional.' In fact, Ángel María is the ideal man for the job, which involves diplomacy more than finance. He can deliver a short speech on any topic and sound convincing; his verve makes up for the lack of substance. At lender conferences, he wins foreign subsidies simply by working the room and flashing his smile. Deftly, he sweeps Canuba's deficits under the carpet, at least until the next round of talks. At home, the National Bank is a major patron of the arts; on this front, he capitalizes on his friendships—and amourettes—with the practitioners themselves. For many starving painters, sculptors, musicians, dancers, or mere aspirants, he is a Maecenas incarnate, a deus ex machina in the flesh.

Angel of the Perverse

Entering from the left, Leandra is hoodless; she slides the title Angel of the Perverse *into the black frame. The last paragraph should be accompanied by the musical ensemble in a casual, flowing tone. Entering from the right, The Female Reader replaces The Trans Reader at the lectern.*

The Female Reader: This is the Fifth Reading.

The fallout from AIDS is late to strike Canuba. By the end of the eighties, the disease has taken a heavy toll in France and the States; but it's still virtually unknown on the island, despite the fact that promiscuity has reached its apogee. Ángel María epitomizes the free-wheeling habits of the Spanish Caribbean. Indiscriminately, males as well as females and she-males hop between the crosshairs of his gun. In industrialized countries, bisexuals often repress their same-sex side as soon as they marry; but like many Canubans, Ángel María does just the opposite.

During their courtship, a scandal might've granted Leandra the perfect excuse to jilt him once and for all. After their titanic nuptials, he feels entitled to spread his raptor's wings to their full span. As the President's right-hand man, allied by marriage to the Peralta Del Ríos, he could have been expected to downplay his mistresses, not to mention his master-mistresses. But perversely, he never denies his many conquests, nor does he affirm them; the list becomes a long, winding chain of question marks. That way, everyone wonders: Will I have the luck to be next? If seduced, they soon find out that their fortune spells misfortune. Ángel María uses foreplay as a trap, and consummation as the coup de grâce. The next stage is blackmail: not the venal kind, but in services quid pro quo. For many eminent figures, exposing him would only bring disgrace on themselves; they have to bend to his demands, or else.

Even Manfredo, the Son of Heaven—as the Miranda brothers used to call him—defers to Ángel María as to a trusted paramour: and there lies the rub. As he morphs from a genial whale-head into a high-bourgeois mover and shaker, his childhood pals lament his transformation. Reading between the lines of his lopped-off remarks, Chiara gathers that Virgilio was hardly flummoxed by the shift, much as he regretted it. According to him, Ángel María was always a double being, as his name implies. Not just half man and half woman, but half angel and half human—a seraph like Lucifer, just before the fall.

The other Miranda brothers were more explicit about their misgivings. Catulo, the choreographer, seethed with righteous indignation—a rarity for him. — That guy is a one-way ticket straight to hell. He brings you to the brink, but never delivers: he's too in love with himself. Horacio is no less scathing, though he couches his critique in more courtly terms. — Of late, our adolescent ludic companion has expanded beyond his britches. To His Majesty, all of us are merely feckless 'Bohemians.'

Lamia lowers the ante, as usual. — Oh, I don't know why everybody wants to get into his pants. Just gold-digging, I guess. He's no fun. Worse than a Mormon missionary.

Beyond the inner circle, the cynics think he's sold out; while the 'Angelistas' believe that one fine day, he'll marshal his political gifts for the greater good.

Over the next few months, Chiara has a chance to shape her own opinion. She observes Ángel María going through his paces at two different parties, as distinct from each other as crack and caviar.

One takes place at Chuchu's 'Colonial Playhouse,' as she dubs it, a sixteenth-century shell she's acquired on the outermost edge of the Old Quarter. Besides her main residence in upscale Loma Linda, the zoned-out heiress maintains several such outposts for her walks on the wild side. The most notorious is the 'Banana Box,' a yellow gingerbread folly, wedged into a crowded slum where Bonaventurans live.

Her Colonial Playhouse is more an opium den than a brothel. It lies on the far side of the Benedictine Abbey, and affords vistas of the poetic ruin from every floor. The oblong courtyard at the back, dotted with broken marble columns, features a twenty-foot waterfall, recycled into travertine pools. Chuchu and her hangers-on spend hours at the Playhouse—sometimes several days—clumped together like newborn kittens. With drug-glazed eyes, they watch the sun as it creeps though the Abbey's Renaissance arches; and once it sets, they gaze at the cascade, as it gushes through a kaleidoscope of artificial lights.

Chuchu has often mounted raves at the Playhouse, to the annoyance of her techno-blasted neighbors. But this year, in an all-embracing mood, she decides to throw a conventional fete, and invite her more 'presentable' friends. Among them is Ángel María, greeting or meeting the assembly with his warm, debonair aplomb. First, he embraces his hostess, practically crushing her anemic frame. In the course of the evening, he slaps Lamia's behind, bows to Horacio, and drapes himself between Arnaud and Fátima Fontaine.

If Ángel María is attractive to others, Chiara concludes, it's because he literally draws them close. Even among touchy-feely Canubans, she's never met anyone more tactile than he. Again and again, he holds an elbow, bestows a kiss, or fondles a shoulder; and with certain interlocutors, his entire body surges into play. His intimacy, never overbearing, is always expertly gauged.

On formal occasions, he displays a different character, as the next party proves: here he metamorphoses into Espinosa's paladin. A month after Chuchu's shindig, a 'cultural tea' is held at the Presidential Palace; it marks the sixtieth anniversary of the dictator's first published work, a brief essay on a minor Honduran poet. Like many tyrants, he dabbles in literature, and his toadies hold his fulsome style in the highest esteem. Generals in gold braid, bureaucrats in black suits, ambassadors in multi-colored sashes—all rub shoulders with the regime's pet 'intellectuals.'

Chiara has been invited by Ángel María as a 'well-known journalist.' Espinosa's lackeys think she might review his books someday in the British, American, or European press. They corral her as soon as she enters the Ninfeo, an anteroom uglified by misbegotten malachite nymphs. 'The splendid writings of our President deserve universal acclaim': variously embroidered, that is their unctuous refrain. Across the hall she spies Lamia and Horacio, 'frenemies' sparring in a corner. Second-class citizens at this affair, they've tagged along with the Minister of Culture and Fine Arts.

When Ángel María appears, there's a pregnant hush. He pauses in the faux-Baroque archway, assaying his subjects. Will he upstage the Son of Heaven? No: to the chagrin of his would-be rivals, he avoids that mistake. After buttering up some lesser nabobs, he confers with Espinosa longest and last. He shoots Chiara a cursory nod, but only because she's trading Teutonic jokes with the Swiss Ambassador. As for Lamia and Horacio, who's adept at receiving occasional leaves from his Abbot, he looks straight through them—a far cry from his caresses at Chuchu's, several weeks before. His whole demeanor has stiffened, even the expression in his eyes. His obsequiousness to the political class has deadened him, as if he wore a wooden mask.

Through the years he adopts many guises: the truck-driving 'good ole boy', the moon-struck lover, the ambitious engineer, the accomplished pianist, the dedicated yachtsman, the hell-bent social climber, the slick banking official—and now more than ever, the President's main man. And these are only the personae Chiara has studied up-close: she suspects the array must be numberless. In the end, who can actually know him? On first approach, he gleams like swiftly flowing water, clear and bright; but the more his surfaces shine, the more his depths turn opaque.

Eagle Roosts

Entering from the left, Chiara is hoodless; she slides the title Eagle Roosts *into the black rectangular frame. Entering from the right, The Male Reader replaces The Female Reader at the lectern.*

The Male Reader: This is the Sixth Reading.

In one department at least, Ángel María does his duty to Leandra to the letter. Before long, she's producing children every eleven to fourteen months, including two sets of twins. As the pregnancies wax and wane, she gladly sinks into an oubliette of nannies, diapers, and preschools. This is heaven at last: dewy faces that coo with unquestioning love, hands that grasp at nothing but their mother's fingers, minds that covet simple things like a cookie or a toy. Now she finds her passion, deeper than any calling as a 'thinker-composer.' She forgets where she stored her thesis on John Cage, and never ferrets it out again.

Ángel María plunges into a dizzying whirl of dinners and other yuppy soirees. Protean as always, he splices them with his government obligations and 'Bohemian' sprees; but he reduces his presence at all venues to a cameo. The strategy makes his advent even more desirable. Typically, the Canuban social pages divide their klatch into three parts: 'before Ángel María arrived,' 'while he was there,' and 'after he left.'

Though dinner hostesses invite Leandra pro forma, she never accepts. They understand Ángel María will swing by on his own, fancy-free. To balance out the table, they add an extra woman—single, separated, or divorced. The President's man seldom leaves alone; it's basic courtesy to give his companion a lift to her door. Who would ever know if he crossed the threshold, to entertain her for an hour or two? No matter when he returns to his wing of the house, in Leandra's apartments the schedule follows its appointed rounds: the baths with rubber ducks, the bed-time stories, and the solitary late-night films.

At the 'Bohemian' revels, a similar rule applies. The only difference is that when Lothario decamps, it's usually with a man. On one such occasion, an opening at the Gallería Caribe, Chiara has her first tête-à-tête with Ángel María in quite a while. At the outset, she met the artist who was showing his works, Brent Cunliffe; they agreed to share a taxi when the wine-soaked do broke up. The bash staggers on, and the young American shanghais her as an interpreter. Sloshed Spanish-speakers want to know whether the flies suspended in Jell-o squirmed when they died, whether the buttocks imprinted on wax were actually Brent's, and whether he smoked grass or sniffed cocaine while he 'created.' The answer to all their queries is YEEES, SIIII.

Toward the end of the vernissage, Ángel María swoops by. He's clearly taken by the sculptor's boyish physique and pretty face—'joli-laid,' to be exact. Adroitly, he snatches at the Ganymede, proposing to drop him off at his hotel. A cup-bearer in point of fact, Brent is tottering after one or three too many. Naively, he sets a condition. 'Oh, could you driiiive Chiara home, too? She's realllly helped me a lot.'

Ángel María has no choice but to acquiesce. — Of course, of course. She's my best friend! — It entertains her to see him a bit flustered for once; but she has no doubt he'll win out in the end. Recovering his nonchalance, he escorts them to the parking lot. His black Jaguar shines among the alley-cat cars of the artistic fringe; shortly after his honeymoon, it replaced the silver Audi, once he felt assured of unlimited wealth. Since he only uses his chauffeur for official engagements, he takes the wheel himself. To Chiara's bemusement, he asks her to sit up front. With ironclad politesse, he consigns Brent to the back seat, where he abruptly conks out. Emboldened by the artist's vinous snores—and his monolingualism—he bears down on Chiara in Spanish as they veer towards the Malecón.

You realize I'm taking you home first, don't you? Though our puppy's kennel lies on the way.

But he's asleep, and you're giving him time for a nap. How diplomatic. Now I see why you're so useful to the government.

Aha, and you think I might even lend a hand to Uncle Sam. Everybody believes you're a spook for the CIA.

Then I hope a fat check is in the mail. I'm Italian, remember? And don't start in on NATO, for heaven's sake. You all overrate me. Or maybe you overrate yourselves. I'm only interested in reading books, writing an article now and then…

And finding out what makes this country tick, particularly Ángel María. All right, maybe I'm not so important. But there must be some reason you hobnob with everyone, everywhere, all the time.

Speak for yourself.

He has to concede. — It's true. You and I can turn up any old place. From a whale-watching trip to a beauty pageant. From an embassy dinner to a palos night: by the way, what a laugh that was last month, when you played drums with the campesinos!

Sure, to call up the dead. What can I say? If I tell you I'm not a spy, that'll convince you all the more. But if I wind up in all those places, maybe it's because they make print-ready copy for Condé Nast. Or because I love this country more than you Canubans do.

Hmmm. When it comes to us, do you prefer Canubanos or Canubanas? Or both? In all this time, I've been too shy to ask.

Chiara shrugs. — Shy? Well, you are—in a way. You're very Latino—outgoing, physically affectionate. But your urge for privacy is like a Swede's. My behavior is consistent: pure Sicilian. Like a Canuban's, but with more tradition— and a heavier focus on food. You're a mystery. I can't put all the parts of you together. So, I'll toss the question back to you.

Ángel María peers at the road ahead, gripping the wheel. Then his fingers relax, and he leans back. — Well, nobody could blackmail me here, since we don't care about such peccadillos. Oh, we like to gossip. But no one ever lost his job, or his position in society, by sleeping with somebody— male, female, or in between. Though he might lose either one by *not* doing it! All we have to do is keep our mouths shut, and then we can do whatever we want. So I agree: the CIA couldn't be following that lead. It's just your own little hobby.

What do you take me for, a peeping Tom-ette? As for

sexual ambiguity, you're no different from most Canubans, as far as I can tell. Anyway, I'm not the only one who's noticed your quirks.

Yes, but not everyone is as thorough as you… or as… omnipresent. — He seems proud of the adjective.

All right. I'll admit I'm always intrigued by what other people are up to. But I'm not a blabbermouth, like your immortal flame, Lamia.

And yours, or so I've heard. All right… I guess I can confide in you… I might as well put you to the test. It's hard to keep things bottled up inside. I'm surrounded by thousands of acquaintances, but not a single friend. There's no one I can feel at home with, and simply be myself. Tomorrow, what say I call you?

To tell me how things went tonight?

Ángel María chuckles. — Why not?

They've reached Plaza Drake, and Brent wakes up, gurgling like a baby. Sleepiness suits him: it gives him bedroom eyes. Yawning and stretching, he straddles the seat and sprawls in Chiara's place up front. Before they drive off, Ángel María pecks him on the cheek—just the maneuver you'd most expect from the king of birds.

Entering from the left, Diana is hoodless; she slides the title Proteus and His Brood *into the black rectangular frame. Entering from the right, The Trans Reader replaces The Male Reader at the lectern.*

The Trans Reader: This is the Seventh Reading.

At eleven the next morning, the telephone rings. Chiara happens to be nearby, so she answers right away.

You must have been sitting by the phone, in suspense.

Not really, Ángel María. I didn't even think you'd call.

I'm not like most Canubans. I always follow up on what I say. I told you I'd report on last night. Everything turned out fine and dandy. An American dessert, sweet as apple pie…

No need to elaborate.

Not to you, Chiara! I'd like to invite you on a little trip. To a place I know you've never seen: the horse ranch at Quiquiricoba. Next Sunday. I'll pick you up at ten AM. All right?

Though Chiara doesn't let on, she's delighted. Don Adalberto's hideaway is the nearest place to Puerto Indio with panoramic views of both the mountains and the sea.

During the two-hour drive, Ángel María opens up as he's never done before. Wistfully, he talks about his childhood, especially his summers in the sierra near Esmeralda, on his grandparents' bean farm. As Chiara knows, they sold most of it off to pay their debts. 'Gone with the wind,' he murmurs. He also reminisces about his engineering studies at Texas A & M. Several miles from campus, he boarded with a family of Mennonites. 'I felt like a Protestant monk. But I made up for lost time, when I got back to our magic island!'

He goes on freely about his countless love-affairs and one-night stands, in every corner of the globe. During his international missions for the Central Bank, he's made untrammeled use of call girls, rent boys, and chance encounters along the way. In the balmy, radiant weather, he lowers the windows. Holding the steering wheel with his right hand, he draws lazy arabesques with the left. His words glide on the breeze, and his chestnut hair sparkles in the sun. The sea frames his profile as the Jaguar purrs, bounding toward the high cordillera. Needless to say, there can be no speeding tickets for him.

Turning right, they climb a steep, hairpin-curved road till they reach a picturesque hamlet, prosperous and neat. The townspeople of Quiquiricoba labor on the huge Hacienda Peralta—expanded and maintained with Del Río funds. Ridge after ridge, its ten thousand acres dip into vales and surge to high crests, as far as the eye can see. Though Don Adalberto calls the estate a 'horse farm,' it's also famous as the premier coffee plantation in the country. He specializes in the Ojo de Oro bean, as prized on the international market as the Blue Mountain strain from Jamaica. But its shade-hungry bushes are hidden from view: above them, blossoming amapola trees carpet the hills, like waves of fire rolling toward the distant peaks.

Chiara can hardly contain her joy. — Mamma mia! This is fabulous!'

Ever the macho, Ángel María takes her down a peg. — Don't worry, Chiara, you'll get over it.

At the end of a long avenue of royal palms, Leandra stands on the top step of the clapboard Victorian house, patrician in its understatement. She's the last person Chiara imagined she'd find here: she assumed Ángel María would swill GlenAllachie all afternoon with his cronies and their girlfriends—plus one or two of his own. Motherhood has softened Leandra's face, and even her pointy chin appears more rounded than before. Old friends, they warmly embrace. Since the wedding, despite her pregnancies, she's slimmed down a bit—from chasing all those children, Chiara supposes. What with the two sets of twins, her brood already includes half a dozen tykes, all of them overactive.

Tucked behind the clapboard house, where Don Adalberto's great-great-grandparents had once lived, a concrete wing surrounds the Olympic-size pool reserved for modern entertaining. The children bounce around like jumping beans, pursued by their nannies. Bantams who rule the roost, they won't take no for an answer, and the grown-ups comply with their every whim. Not to be outdone by their father, they too have amassed a court of sycophants. Chiara tots up twenty other members of the 'infant race'—as Henry James called them—scampering around the deck-chairs, splashing in and out of the kiddie-pool, tumbling through the flower beds, and thwarting any attempt at adult conversation. Chiara dives into the melee, as if she were a toddler herself. Ángel María pitches in, too, romping with the youngsters all afternoon. This is another milieu where he feels at ease, another role he's nailed down: the frolicsome, devoted father.

After a final round of drinks on the terrace, which commands breath-taking views on every side, the two friends leave Quiquiricoba just as they'd arrived—without any members of the family.

On the way home, Ángel María seamlessly picks up where he left off. He ticks off his AC-DC adventures in such scabrous detail, Chiara asks him the question point-blank. — Well, which do you really prefer—women or men?

He doesn't dodge the issue. — Oh, you know how this country is. We improvise as we go along. I seem to pass through phases that last a year or so; right now, I'm mostly attracted to men.

For a Canuban, his statement is clear and unabashed; Chiara thinks back to years before, when she bumped into him and Diana in Rome. By now they've arrived at the edge of Plaza Drake, and she proposes sundowners on her roof.

I'd love to, but the Emperor will probably wake me up in

the middle of the night. And tomorrow is a work day. — He slaps his right cheek, then pops the left one. — That's what I have to do keep myself alert at the office.

Somehow, I can't quite picture you as a masochist.

He breaks into one of his winning smiles. — You know, Chiara, you and I could really make music someday.

'Isn't it pretty to think so?' — Laughing, she waves him off. — No thanks, Don Giovanni. I'd just be one of the thousands—and I've never liked milling around in crowds.

The Roman Spring of Rolling Stones

Entering from the left, Leandra is hoodless; she slides the title The Roman Spring of Rolling Stones *into the black rectangular frame. Entering from the right, The Female Reader replaces The Trans Reader at the lectern.*

The Female Reader: This is the Eighth Reading.

In the mid-nineties, Chiara spends a week with one of her mentors, Monsignor Francis Berthold; at Princeton, she attended his course on 'The Influence of Ovid on Elizabethan Literature.' After several more stints as a visiting professor here and there, with the permission of his order, he's risen through the ranks to the post of Latin Secretary to the Pope. On the face of it, this is an unusual job for a country boy from Minnesota. But instead of having an abortion, his devout, unwed mother left him on the doorstep of the Carmelite monks near White Earth. As an experiment, the clerics brought their foundling up in the language of Cicero; consciously, they were harking back to Montaigne, whose tutors also raised him in Latin. Nowadays, Berthold's mission is to tweak the Holy Father's bulls and encyclicals—though rumor has it that he pens much of the contents himself. This he neither affirms nor denies: when cornered, he wiggles his shaggy eyebrows and harrumpfs.

True to form, the Monsignor assigns Chiara to a cell in the convent of Santa Brigida on the Piazza Farnese, Spartan but pleasant. One day, while he's chaperoning the junior Swiss Guards on a jaunt to the beach, she roams around the city on her own. She never cared much for Rome as a girl, but with all the spring flowers in bloom, she finds herself warming to the garden-strewn hills and scraggly patches of daisies among the ruins. As she ambles through the Piazza Navona, just before twilight, she suddenly comes across… Ángel María.

Of course, this kind of thing happens to anyone who travels widely, and knows other people who do as well. As the Canuban plutocrat, Isabela Burley Luna, observed to Chiara: 'The world isn't small, querida—it's just narrow at the top.' But in this case, Chiara told her friend several times about her upcoming trip to Italy, and he never let on that he would be there, too. Her astonishment deepens when she recognizes his companion: Diana, the Vodou mambo who'd accompanied her to their lover Amado's grave, years before. For her Roman holiday, the priestess has drastically altered her 'look.' She wears a chic grey halter-dress, dotted with minuscule blue beads; her Afro is bound by a silver band, and a choker of fresh-water pearls sets off her black-swan neck. Up till now, Chiara never realized she and Ángel María even knew each other—much less on such intimate terms.

By the time she catches sight of them, seated on the terrace of a trendy café, she's already come too close to retreat. Diana is nibbling at Ángel María's ear, and he's thrown his arm around her waist. Chiara walks on quietly, hoping they won't notice her. But as she skirts the table, they happen to glance up. Ángel María leaps to his feet and calls out her name; he plants several kisses on her cheeks, then squeezes her in a bruising hug.

Diana lets out a nervous gasp. 'Oh! It's you!' Quickly recouping, she holds out her hand. 'So you're the famous Chiara! Ángel María has mentioned you so often. Even your face looks familiar. I must have met you somewhere, but when? Imagine! Running into each other like this, on the streets of Rome… Isn't that odd, Ángel María?' Turning back to Chiara, she rattles on. 'We have more in common than our friendship with him. He tells me you studied in France, and so did I.'

Yes, I went to a convent school there. — Chiara is tempted to add 'as you already know,' but she tactfully holds back.

Breathlessly, while Ángel María collars the waiter for more drinks, Diana switches from Spanish to French, a language their friend can't follow. — Let's just say we chatted at a party in Puerto Indio, and leave it at that, all right? I'll fill you in later.

What is Diana trying to conceal? Chiara speculates. Her Vodou practices, her love affair with Amado, her political activities, her bucolic life near Barlovento Bay—or something else? Jumpy, anxious, she almost seems afraid. Chiara opts for amiable vagueness, implying she hardly remembers Diana at all. Ángel María insists that she join them for dinner in the Piazza; defending her national honor, Chiara steers them to an authentic osteria in Parioli.

Over the next few days, the pair offer only a flimsy account of what has brought them to Rome. Ángel María refers to a banking conference in Zurich; and Diana, to a cousin in Paris. But the pretense they 'chanced on each other' in Italy wouldn't have fooled anyone—Chiara least of all. Not pressing them, she shows them the Caravaggios in San Luigi and the Titians at the Borghese. Thanks to a tip from Monsignor Berthold, on their last evening she takes them to an insiders' restaurant, 'Amore Divino.' Wedged into a crypt under Bernini's colonnade, it caters mainly to Princes of the Church and other high ecclesiastics. The servers are shapely young women from the Third World, whose scant traditional outfits leave little room to fantasy.

Diana finds it piquant that these beauties belonged to a 'lay' order toiling for the faith, especially when Chiara explains the English pun. Glowing in the candlelight against the reddish sheen of Cardinals' robes, their nubile flesh peeks through wafer-thin saris and sarongs. In her double guise as priestess and courtesan—if Chiara's guess holds water—Diana must feel right at home. She's dressed alluringly as well, in pleated greens and golds that complemented her ebony skin. Like schoolboys on the prowl, the clerics ogle the waitresses; and now and then, their glances dart toward her. Proud of their attentions, Ángel María worships his African idol all the more; and after her second glass of Barbaresco, she returns his gazes with equal ardor. Chiara wonders how any female can escape Ángel María when he's 'mostly attracted to women,' and the same must apply to males when he's 'mostly attracted to men.'

Drinks on the Cayo

Entering from the left, Chiara is hoodless; she slides the title Drinks on the Cayo *into the black rectangular frame. Entering from the right, The Male Reader replaces The Female Reader at the lectern.*

The Male Reader: This is the Ninth Reading.

Chiara's mourning for Amado has finally run its course. At last, she feels capable of returning to Cayo Encantado, where she spied on him and Catulo as they made love on the beach, many years before. The much-awaited luxury inn, after thirty years of delay, has been finished at last. Out of curiosity, she wangles a 'comp' weekend on the jewel-like islet, set in the scintillating oblong of Barlovento Bay. Wisely, she doesn't promise the management an article. 'We shall see' is all she pledges.

Late one afternoon, after a ramble through the seaside grounds, she sits on the hotel veranda, reminiscing about her two ill-fated lovers. His trimness softened by alcohol, Amado died in a traffic accident; beset by cruel diseases, Catulo withered away from AIDS. Visions of their splendid, youthful bodies are interspersed with memories of their decline. She's been woolgathering for half an hour when a low, melodic voice interrupts her.

Excuse me, but would you mind if I joined you? Not waiting for an answer, the woman eases herself into a rocking chair, with self-assured grace. Decidedly, Diana is ubiquitous. Instead of hiding her hair under a turban, or clasping it in a rakish topknot, today she's gathered it in a simple pony-tail; and instead of a hieratic robe or a bead-studded gown, today she wears a plain cotton shift. It's been twenty years since Amado introduced them, and she's only grown more beautiful over time. — She strokes

Chiara's arm. — So you haven't forgotten me, then. I love to stroll in this garden, and I saw you up here on the porch. I have news of you, every now and then, from… our mutual friend.

They order piña coladas with paper umbrellas for fun, like a couple of tourists, and switch from Spanish to French. The rum loosens Chiara's tongue. — Have you been back to Europe lately?

A flicker of irritation crosses Diana's face. — No, I never leave the island now. I live in the countryside, not far from here.

I can see why, if it's anything like this.

Oh, I'm a working girl. I hardly have time to notice where I am. The campesinos run me ragged. I manage a big estate for an absentee landlord.

That I've heard, from Horacio Miranda. But do you run the whole place all alone? Isn't that hard?

Anything worth doing is hard. — Diana frowns resentfully. — Gringos always think that all we do is take siestas.

They pause for a while, gazing out to sea. Chiara is dreamily aware of the other woman's skin—black and luminous as a tropical night.

After a while, she leans forward and presses Diana's knee. — Have you read Lezama Lima's *Paradiso*? It's the greatest book ever written about the Caribbean, bar none.

The priestess draws a blank. — Why the Italian title?

Because of Dante. You'll have to read it, if you want to find out where he comes in. Cuba is a lot like our own zany island, Canuba. A cook can talk about medieval theology while she stirs the beans. Believe it or not, in the final pages, a child with a Danish vase, a Roman general, and a musician preserved under glass all converge. A vanishing point, so to speak.

Or a mise-en-abîme.

That too… Anyway, when the main character asks his mother what he should do in life, she answers him with only four words. 'Intentar lo más difícil.' 'Attempt what's most difficult.' That doesn't sound like indolence, does it?

Diana seems mollified. — I've often thought of you since we visited Amado's grave, and even more so since our days in Rome. You're not like other gringos, European or American.

I'm typical of the ones you've never met. The ones with open minds.

Diana flashes a broad smile. — I'm happy we're friends now. I'm over my jealousy, and all that other nonsense Amado put us through. I really wish I had more time today. You must come stay with me at Espada del Sur. — She scribbles a phone number on a strip of paper, then jumps to her feet. The languorous spell is broken. — I have to get back to the farm, right away. The compañeros are waiting for me down at the dock. See you soon. — Wheeling around at the end of the path, she waves to Chiara gaily. — Be sure to get in touch. My comrades will be glad to give you a lift. Just tell them Rebeca is expecting you.

Chiara folds her hands in a namaste. — I'll come, though it may take a while! Thank you for the invitation. — As an afterthought, she calls out again. — By the way, who's 'Rebeca'?' — But Diana has already disappeared behind a tall hibiscus hedge.

The Peaceable Kingdom

Entering from the left, Diana is hoodless; she slides the title The Peaceable Kingdom *into the black rectangular frame. Entering from the right, The Trans Reader replaces The Male Reader at the lectern.*

The Trans Reader: This is the Tenth Reading.

A year or two later, after a flurry of assignments for the travel magazines, Chiara accepts Diana's offer. Recently, she's made many forays to her old cabin on Grandota Beach and her cave at El Silencio, also on the Peninsula of Barlovento. Like Cayo Encantado, visiting Espada del Sur would be a welcome change from her routine. Besides, she's curious to find out about the mambo's connections with Milady Mateo, whose Transformation Party has long opposed Espinosa— much to the peril of her partisans and herself.

She rings the number the priestess wrote down, and says that 'Rebeca' has invited her to the estate. The voice at the other end is polite but succinct: he takes down her name and they set a date. On the appointed day, a peppy 'compañero' collects her at 1 PM in an army-style jeep, and drives her southwest on the familiar route to Barlovento. After they leave the outskirts of town, the four-lane highway bottle-necks by stages to three, then two—and finally, one and a half.

Chiara nods off at intervals during the five-hour ride; she only half-listens to the bubbly chauffeur, who's certain that 'nuestra Milady' will win the next election. They rumble past conical mountains, piebald with shadow and sun; skim through rice-fields—low-lying vats of fluorescent green; and hurtle past coconut palms on lonely, wind-whipped shores. At last they behold the navy-blue Bahía de Barlovento, the liquid trampoline of the humpback whales. But fifteen miles beyond the port, they enter terrain unknown to Chiara. She sits bolt-upright, eager to soak up the novelty.

A rough country track, barely more than a trail, crawls southward through tangled underbrush; without four-wheel drive, they couldn't have advanced very far. They wind through precipitous hills, flanked by low, cave-gouged mountains. Forty minutes later, they arrive at a crescent-shaped inlet; a fishing village straggles along the primeval beach, overgrown with mangroves and sea-grapes. Chiara requests the driver to pause, and take a break.

She's flummoxed: centuries seemed to melt away before her eyes. These round, thatched huts and hand-carved dugouts, much the same as in Taíno times, have survived the successive onslaughts of Western culture. The only signs of 'modernity' are the threadbare shorts and T-shirts of the inhabitants; straight-haired and almond-eyed, they resemble their Arawak cousins, without a trace of Caucasian or African blood.

From the settlement, the track turns east, and steadily worsens. The garrulous compañero falls silent; he's focused on navigating the jagged rocks and mud-holes. As they ford several streams at their shallowest point, Chiara crosses her fingers the jeep won't stall. Abruptly, they come to a halt before a lichen-mottled boulder.

In a few minutes, they'll escort you from here.

How does he know? Chiara never has a chance to ask; he's fallen fast asleep, exhausted by the ordeal.

Sure enough, a wizened campesino appears on horseback, with another mount in tow. Slumped against the steering wheel, the driver is snoring like a bulldog. Chiara leaves him a thank-you note on the dashboard, along with a gift in cash.

The campesino alights from his plump white mare— nimbly, despite his age. Mumbling a few words of welcome, he holds out the reins of a docile little roan. Chiara puts her foot in a primitive rope-stirrup, and swings atop the saddle of cloth and straw. Filing down a horse-path that branches to the right, they thread their way through the woods. The dense shade discourages any undergrowth: the forest floor is quilted by interlocking patches of moss. Majestic ceiba trees, loftier and broader than any she's ever seen, tower into the waning light; their canopy glimmers overhead like a roof of fine-spun, emerald glass. Their upper twigs flute and chirp, as birds rise in waves on the tide of dusk.

Chiara's companion, Diómedes, tells her that when his father was a boy, most of the peninsula was still covered with woods like these. He wags his head scornfully. 'Now there's nothing but yautías and coconuts.'

An odd comment, coming from a campesino… Cynically, Chiara muses that he's probably felled many such trees himself, so he could plant those very same crops.

Darkness has descended when they reach a crystal river, fifty feet across. Without any guidance, the horses cross its shallows, just where they blend with the sea. On the other side, cutting back inland, the riders emerge into a meadow ringed by ficus-trees, almost as imposing as the ceibas and maras they've left behind. The moon is stealing over the horizon, though the woods still block it from view. A disembodied radiance, it catches the fireflies in its spreading net. 'Nimitas,' Diómedes calls them, 'souls of the dead'—a Canuban diminutive for 'anima,' Chiara reflects, akin to the 'animula' of Hadrian's farewell. Their blinks merge with the dim yellow lamps someone is lighting, in the rooms of a low wooden house. Built like a farmer's cabin, only larger, it stands at the end of the clearing.

As they dismount, a lantern bobs forward to meet them; in its peach-colored glow, Chiara recognizes Diana's face. An able-bodied fellow, still in shadow, is walking beside her—a guard, Chiara suspects, to protect her here in the wilds.

After Diómedes leads the horses away, Diana hands the light to her companion. She kisses Chiara's cheeks à la française, right-left-right. — It took you long enough to pay me a visit. I've been rotting away here in the sticks.

Yes, and in wretched resort hotels, and swampy backwaters like Rome. Ah, the peasant life…

Rome? That was years ago… Well, here's the lord of the estate, as you've probably guessed. Meet 'Osorio.'

Chiara scrutinizes the man, who lifts the lamp to his face. He grins as engagingly as ever, even if his steel-blue eyes belie a certain unease. He shifts the lantern back to Diana, and folds Chiara into a bone-cracking embrace. 'Do me a favor,' he whispers. Make sure you call me 'Osorio' at all times. And our compañera's name is 'Rebeca,' not Diana.'

'Yes, that much I already know,' Chiara rejoins. She's just had lunch with Ángel María the week before in Puerto Indio; but in the meantime, his chunky physique has already altered. Such is his mercurial nature, a few days in the country suffice to slim him down and tone him up. As in Italy, he and Diana make a handsome couple. But here in the forest, their movements are suppler, almost as if they were swimming; like slinky, civilized otters, they weave through streams of air.

Inside, dinner is laid out on a rough-hewn table of tropical cedar, as aromatic as the cedars of Lebanon. Homemade candles cast a sensuous gleam on calabash bowls of yucca and yams. A whopping red snapper forms the centerpiece; like most Caribbean islanders, 'Rebeca' and 'Osorio' prefer its white, flaky grain to a grouper's more rubbery flesh. The meal isn't vegetarian, but its arrangement on waxy green fronds brings Horacio to mind.

Our friend at the monastery sends you his greetings.

Diana replies with a mischievous lilt. — You mean Horacio?

Ángel María butts in. — We've been expecting *him* to come here—not you, Chiara. But I guess you women have been plotting behind my back.

She's taken off guard. — Didn't you know I was invited, Osorio?'

No, how could I? Rebeca didn't tell me, for some reason. — He glances at Diana angrily. — Chiara, you have a knack for showing up *everywhere*. We try to keep a low profile out here. This place is a natural fortress. It's almost inaccessible. — He glares at her, too, for a moment. — And we want to keep it that way, understand? — Then he simmers down, assuming his usual bonhomie. — Anyway, I'm glad to see you, now that you're here.

Uncomfortably, Chiara changes the subject. — What about the number you gave me, Rebeca? You can't be that cut off from the world, if you have a phone.

Diana scoffs. — Oh, that's a friend's apartment in Puerto Indio. His job is to send people here. But only if they know to ask for 'Rebeca.' Without phone lines, how could we have a phone?

How about a radio phone?

Now it's Ángel María's turn to shrug. — They're too easy to listen in on. — He catches himself, as if he's gone too far. — To tell the truth, we prefer not to be disturbed.

That's funny. Horacio never mentioned you in connection with this place. Only Rebeca.

He would've been surprised to find me here, too. He has no idea I'm the absentee landowner Rebeca works for. In the capital, nobody knows about my hideaway. Especially foreigners. — He scowls at Diana again. — Then he lowers his voice; from now on, all three of them do, almost to a whisper. — Don't forget: to the locals I'm Osorio. And we call you-know-who the 'Viejo,' so everyone will think we're talking about my father. — After pouring another round of spring-chilled Verdejo, he sits back stiffly. — Chiara, you really take the cake. Try as I may, I can't give you the slip. Now you've cornered me again. It's a good thing I like you… — He sets his jaw. — I might as well come clean. Horacio Miranda, like his brothers before him, has been very loyal to the movement. Rebeca and I have been wanting to let him in on our biggest secret.

It dawns on Chiara before he can let it out. — Let me guess. Even though you're the right-hand man of the 'Viejo,' you're backing Milady behind the scenes…

Ángel María looks relieved she's spoken the truth. — Any right-thinking person has no choice but to support her.

Diana nods. — The tyrannosaur can't last forever; and when he goes, we're going to need younger folks with experience in government. If he dies in office, Osorio can smooth the transition—between the old faction and the new.

Chiara winks. — As President, pro tem? That can be habit-forming.

You're not suggesting I'd like to become the next 'demotator,' are you? — Ángel María bridles. — I don't need to be number one. I'd rather leave that to Milady, the woman we all admire. If the 'Viejo' keeps hanging on by a thread, I may come out openly for the Transformation Party, and run on the ticket as Vice President. I could take enough reactionaries with me to swing the balance in her favor. Though that will certainly take some doing.

Chiara keeps her own counsel: Yes, no doubt.

He strokes Diana's wrist. — Have you heard the latest joke? — He's pushing the mambo's buttons, and he knows it. — Milady wants to make her lips look smaller, and the photographer tells her: Say 'Pepsi' when I snap the shot.

Instead, she says 'Coca-Cola.'

With sudden vehemence, Diana sticks a knife into the table. — Ha, ha, ha. You like those gags too much. White women pay thousands to puff up their lips with collagen, so they'll look as sexy as Africans.

Why are couples always fighting? It helps to pass the time, I suppose. — The two of them take the hint, and calm down. Chiara goes back to where they left off. — Anyway, don't worry—honestly. I know how dangerous the 'Viejo' can be. Your secret is safe with me.

Diana teases her. — Safe from Uncle Sam as well, ma chère amie?

Don't tell me *you* believe all that silliness. I've already found out several secrets about Osorio. And as I've proved, I'll take them with me to my grave.

Ángel María glowers. — Don't tempt me… — Chiara feels queasy, and her face betrays her. He bursts into a beatific smile—though it's quickly succeeded by a thin, wintry smirk. — Don't worry, Chiara, I'm not going to throw you to the sharks. Not tonight, anyway… As you say, I've learned to trust you over the years. Having lived here so long, I'm sure you're on our side, even if the NATO countries aren't. They think a disturbance might hurt their investments.

What makes you assume our governments oppose you? As usual, the progressives will root for change, while the old fogies will champion the status quo—the same as here in Canuba.

We'd rather keep everybody in the dark. For now, at least. — He reaches over and lays his hand on Chiara's, as though sealing a pact.

Their coziness raises Diana's hackles. — Humpf. What are those other secrets you know about our Osorio, ma chère?

Ángel María tries to bridge the prickly hiatus. — Oh, come on, Rebeca. Chiara and I are tremendous pals. She's in on a whole bunch of trivial things. Where I have my shirts made, Central Bank shenanigans, little love affairs I had in high school… long before I met you, corazón.

Chiara could tell he hadn't won her over. Shifting the topic again, she natters with Ángel María about the 'Miranda boys'—the dance extravaganza Catulo staged before his death, and his brothers' contributions to his swan song; Virgilio's ascendency in the art world, before he met a similar fate. Bit by bit, the tension is defused. Soon they turn to the Mirandas' daughter Verbena, agreeing that her entire story—her Bonaventuran origins, her indigent mother, her rare intelligence, and her adoption by a leading Canuban family—inspire hope for the future.

Chiara points out the obvious. — Yes, it's like the harmony between the two of you. Maybe all the conflicts between Bonaventure and Canuba can be resolved.

Over the next few days, Chiara floats on a cloud of pleasure. Espada del Sur, remote and unspoiled, takes her back to her early days with Amado on Playa Grandota. The hotels started moving in shortly after his burial, and now it appalls her to see the desecrated shore swarming with tourists, and lit up at night by halogen lamps. Here, at least, the ecology of Barlovento is still intact: Ángel María's estate embraces the forest she traversed, both banks of the river, a ridge of verdant hills, and three sheltered beaches. Half-moons of beige and golden sand, girdled by coral-stone cliffs, they angle around a flat, narrow key. It rests like a green sword on the foam-flecked blue—the 'espada' of the name 'Espada del Sur.'

'Osorio' maintains a truce with the campesinos: as long as they don't cut any trees, they have free use of his orchards and vegetable gardens. This must be the source of Diómedes's earlier 'tree-hugging' remark. Whatever his faults—and Chiara has only glimpsed the tip of the iceberg, she imagines—Ángel María is a true environmentalist. Torn between sorrow and pride, he tells her that Espada del Sur preserves the last large stand of virgin woods on the entire coast.

From the journals of Columbus, Chiara knows what the Admiral found when he 'discovered' the Caribbean: liana-raddled jungles, lush as the Amazon, loud with the chatter of monkeys, parrots, and giant parakeets. The Spanish and English destroyed enormous forests on Canuba to make room for cattle and coconuts, and the French stripped Bonaventure to sow their sugar-cane plantations. At the turn of the century, the Americans ransacked both islands for rosewood, ebony, and mahogany; and on into the present, the country people continue to slash and burn.

From lookout points on the hills, Ángel María's men keep constant watch to prevent any further depredation, while Diana teaches the campesinos better farming techniques. 'Osorio' also husbands the hydro-resources on his estate. Now that plastic has crept into the local economy, he outlaws the dumping of trash into the streams. He limits fishing around the key, to ensure that all species can complete their spawning cycle and attain full growth.

The results are heartening. The day after Chiara's arrival, 'Osorio' triumphantly displays a gigantic spiny lobster, half as long as the teenage diver who caught it. Spread-eagle on the table, it spans almost two feet from head to tail. At dinner that evening, soused with Diana's beurre blanc and sprinkled with wild herbs, it becomes a dish far too good for a king. The 'Otters'—as Chiara dubs them in their country guise—make a big to-do about abhorring riches and pomp. But like Tolstoy, they ignore a crucial fact: the homespun comforts they enjoy are a feudal privilege, which some might dismiss as a pretense.

Picking her way through the luscious white meat in its scarlet shells, she contemplates the irony. As a rule, they treat their subjects like equals; but when push comes to shove, the 'compañeros' bow to their will—from the chauffeur who fetched her, to Diómedes who led her in, to the boy who's provided their dinner. She wonders how they like being ruled by a 'Bono' from the other island, their age-old enemy. In keeping with the Russian theme, she sometimes alludes to Espinosa as the 'Czar'—without fully explaining the jest to these pseudo-rustic, pampered nobles.

North of Eden

Entering from the left, Leandra is hoodless; she slides the title North of Eden *into the black rectangular frame. Entering from the right, The Female Reader replaces The Trans Reader at the lectern.*

The Female Reader: This is the Eleventh Reading.

Beyond the fiefdom of Espada del Sur, the scene is far from idyllic. One day Chiara hikes to the ridge behind the estate, and what she sees there gives her pause. The effects of deforestation are overwhelming. As soon as she passes through the final gate, she has to trudge up eroded gullies and kick her way through rubbish-clogged streams. Here and there, a few underfed campesinos tend their bony cows; others gawk at her from lopsided door jambs. Their children crowd the yards in front of termite-eaten cabins. Some of the rutted fields have fallen to waste, weed-choked and abandoned.

Luckily, it isn't raining; in a downpour, the path she's taken would turn into a water-chute. At the top of the crest, she spots a better house, made of cement and roofed with painted tin. A gringo lounges beside the door in a rocking chair. In this Afro-Canuban enclave, it's strange to come across a white man; he seems equally caught off guard by Chiara. Jumping up, he lopes down to the fence. 'Hostia! Una extranjera!'

She can tell from his first word that he's Spanish. Somehow, she feels offended that foreigners have invaded even this outpost. But as usual, she chides herself for wanting to be the only one around, as though the airport might've closed as soon as she got off the plane. The man introduces himself as Paco, asks her where she's from, and wonders how she chanced on this forsaken spot. He's been living in the 'neighborhood,' as he calls it, for several years.

A quiet place to retire! — Chiara guesses he must be seventy or so.

Joder! Sometimes it gets too quiet. But I'm no pensioner, amiga... I have to earn my way by farming. — Paco is gangly, and still strong for his age. He looks her up and down with hungry, dark-blue eyes, scratching his chest through his half-open shirt. She instantly dislikes his sleazy, familiar air. She feels relieved when a young mulatto girl appears at the door. Since she's lighter than the other locals, Chiara gathers she must be his daughter.

Out of the blue, a squat, perspiring campesino runs up

the path to join them. 'Señor, señor, come quick! They're burning your yucca again!

The Spaniard whips around, quivering with rage. — Los hijos de puta! The bastards! — As he scrambles to defend his crop, slinging a dented rifle over his shoulder, he calls out to the girl. — Clarita! Take care of our guest. Give her some coffee.

Chiara is glad to see the back of him. She welcomes a caffeine pick-me-up; it's been an arduous climb. Cordially, she waves toward the girl, who's still standing shyly in the doorway. — Clara, that's my name, too, in my language. We're 'tocayas.' How old are you?

Fifteen, I think. — Under her plaited hair, Clarita's face is totally blank. It seems that her personality has never blossomed—or that someone has nipped it in the bud.

Chiara follows her into the spotless, sunny kitchen. While Clarita grinds the home-grown beans with a mortar and pestle, and brews the java on a propane stove, Chiara attempts to make her talk. — What a nice house! You have the best one around.

My parents like it. — Clarita's eyes dull to matte black. — I have to keep busy all the time. I clean, cook, wash the clothes. I don't want any trouble.

It sounds like slavery. Chiara observes some welts on her arms; someone has been beating her. She continues probing. — Paco must be your father, no? Where's your mother today?

Clarita seems confused. — My parents live over the hill.

Paco is my husband, my marido.

Oh, of course. — Chiara hides her disapproval, glossing over her mistake. — Do your mother and father get along with him?

He gives them money. — A spark of self-esteem lights up her face, the first sign of animation she's shown. — He paid a lot when he married me.

Chiara controls her voice. — Oh really, how much?

A thousand escudos. — She sets a pair of chipped cups on a pinewood table, and they hunker on makeshift stools.

Chiara does a quick mental calculation. Paco bought the girl for about one hundred thirty dollars, more cash than her parents had ever seen before. With a shudder, she pictures the wedding night, though she tries to maintain a neutral tone. — It's restful to be out here in the country. Are you happy, Clarita?

There's a troubled silence. — I should be. My mamá says I'm going to have a baby.

Chiara has no choice but to go on faking. — Oh, that's wonderful news. How long from now?

About six months. — She sticks out her lower lip. — I'm afraid. They say it hurts a lot.

Chiara doesn't want to scare her even more. — I wouldn't know. Most women tell me it's well worth it.

The girl stares at her in disbelief. — You mean you've never had a baby?

No, so you'll be luckier than me. — She kisses Clarita on

the cheek. — Thanks for the coffee, 'tocaya.' I've got to start back before the sun goes down.

She doesn't want to be there when the Spaniard returns. Outspoken to a fault, she fears she might lock horns with him—and from the look of things, he could turn violent. As she gingerly retreats down the muddy track, pitching backwards now and then on her rear, she can conjure up his line of reasoning. — It's all part of life in the countryside: to the peasants, you're a woman as soon as you bleed. Plenty of Canubans marry girls who're fifty years younger. Why not me?

Furious retorts well up in her gorge. — But you're not a Canuban, you're a Spaniard. You don't fool me: you're just one more abuser. And you're a pederast. You've robbed this innocent girl of her childhood, and forced her into servitude. You're worse than Columbus and his soldiers. After all these centuries, by now you should finally have a conscience. Aren't you ashamed?

In the early twilight, she passes the hovels again on the periphery of Ángel María's land. Clusters of campesinos stand outside to watch her go by. Elderly men hold hands with girls, or drape their grizzled arms around their shoulders. Are they fathers and daughters, husbands and wives—or both? Diana told her that incest was fairly common in Canuba. As Chiara has often reminded herself: though at times the island seems like an Eden, serpents hang from every other tree.

Entente Cordiale

Entering from the left, Chiara is hoodless; she slides the title Entente Cordiale *into the black rectangular frame. During the dancing passage, the musical ensemble plays an invented 'cambuca' song. Entering from the right, The Male Reader replaces The Female Reader at the lectern.*

The Male Reader: This is the Twelfth Reading.

It's hard for Chiara to purge Clarita's plight from her mind, even if there's nothing she can possibly do to help. The next morning she tells Diana all about her, while they loll side by side on the beach. In detail, she describes the listless girl, her scum-ball 'owner,' and the squalid poverty that has sealed her fate. Like her Italian friend, the priestess is outraged by Paco's behavior—though she ribs her that some might accuse them of being 'age-ist' toward the old man.

Chiara nudges the pinkish bottom of Diana's foot. — Where did you dredge up that word? I haven't heard it since Princeton!

Oh, I'm not as 'out of the loop' as you think… Anyway, I wasn't being sarcastic. There are billions of Pacos in this world—and unlike you, I don't care whether they're foreigners or islanders, old or young.

You're right. Battering is battering, no matter who does it.

Believe me, it's just as bad in Bonaventure. I could tell you stories that would make your hair stand on end.

I said earlier that it's all part of being poor. But an activist I know in Milan tells me rich women suffer, too. They just keep quiet. — Chiara props herself up on one elbow. — Sooner or later, change will have to come.

Cradling her head in her pliant, silky arms, the priestess glances at her defiantly. — I've been working toward that day as long as I can remember…

The more they talk that morning, the deeper their friendship becomes: to Chiara's delight, they agree on every issue. As an ex-academic, she knows the feminist canon from A to Z; but through her Vodou ministry, Diana has put it into practice, encouraging thousands of women to take charge of their lives. Chiara admires the mambo's staunch commitment to human rights—and to a host of other causes, from pacifism to the environment.

She has to admit to herself that she also feels drawn to Diana's physical appeal. In Espada del Sur, her velvety skin, sultry jet eyes, and sisterly hugs keep Chiara in a constant state of mild arousal. The offhand carnality between them is tantalizing, but harmless. They haven't stoked any outbreaks in Ángel María; and so, for now at least, the coast seems clear.

Telepathically, Diana broaches the subject. — Did anyone ever tell how attractive you are?

Not in a long, long time. — Chiara sighs. — I've been out

of circulation, you might say. — She caresses her friend's hand. — If anyone but you had asked me that, I'd chalk it up to my 'good hair,' as Canubans call it.

Well, I'm no Canuban. To me, any kind of hair can be 'good.'

Chiara nods. — Personally, I think yours is much prettier than mine, the way it floats around your head like a halo.

Let's just say we're even-Steven. — Coquettishly, Diana raises her right knee and dribbles sand down her thigh. — Sometimes I wish I were free of it all, like you. Every time I fall in love, all hell breaks loose.

Does she mean Amado, whom they shared long ago? Or Ángel María, their companion of the moment? Or other men—and women—whom Chiara's never met?

Before she can lead the conversation further, Ángel María pops from behind a sea-grape tree. — Boo! You girls can't get rid of me, no matter how hard you try!

We're not 'girls'! Diana objects. They titter complacently; but both of them resent his intrusion. Why did he creep up on them like that? How long was he eavesdropping, and peeping at them through the leaves? Neither of them knows he's an old hand at two-way mirrors. Oddly, Diana's reaction is more extreme than Chiara's: she freezes in place, and goose-bumps stipple her skin.

Chiara tries to ease the strain with Sicilian olive-oil. — What are you, a stalker? 'Girls' like their privacy, Osorio! As a matter of fact, we were just saying how much we love you. In different ways, of course…

Yes, Chiara, you always put me in my place. You're as inscrutable as Rebeca. But we'd make a great trio, if you two would just cooperate. — He sticks out his long, tapered tongue.

Diana is still fuming. — Leave Chiara alone. Believe me, I'm not being jealous. But she deserves more respect.

No domestic quarrels, please. I want to kick up my heels! — Resolutely, Chiara turns the page. — Tonight should be fun. Who's coming to hear the musicians?

Ángel María puckers his lips. — It's not a Vivaldi concert, sweetheart. Country tunes for country people— and yes, they want to dance! I'm going chew up the floor with both my women. You'll have to take turns.

Diana chimes in boldly. — We'd like to dance with each other, too!

Right! — Chiara is embarrassed by her own zeal. — Even if I don't know how to dance the cambuca very well…

Oh, I'll teach you.

So will I. — Ángel María eyes them suggestively. — You two, together… that's right up my alley.

But only on the dance-floor! — They've said the words in unison; and now they laugh, so infectiously that 'Osorio' joins in. But Chiara notes that after this, he doesn't leave them alone with each other again…

It's Saturday, and the week's work is done. That evening,

from miles around, over a hundred campesinos converge on the house at Espada del Sur, gussied up in their best clothes. The backwoods combo—a toothless singer, an accordion-player, a maraca-shaker, a bongo-drummer, and a washboard-scraper—pour out a crackerjack medley of songs. Unlike the canned versions in the city, these folksy cambucas spring from the soil, as freshly as yucca or black beans. When the jamboree kicks off, Diana grabs Chiara by the arm, and won't take no for an answer. — Do this basic step, and don't sway your shoulders. Now lift your head, look me in the eyes, and keep pumping your heels.

In Puerto Indio, Lamia always dismissed the cambuca as 'too common for an Italian,' and so she neglected that facet of Chiara's education. As for Amado, he always assumed a 'gringa' couldn't boogie like a Latina; with her, he favored American rock, a holdover from his high school years in Queens. Exhilarated, Chiara switches back and forth between 'Rebeca' and 'Osorio,' while the farmhands cheer her on. But after a couple of hours, the novelty wears off, and she leaves the stage to her hosts. She can see that Espinosa's protégé has taken a leaf out his book. Like 'El Viejo' in his prime, Ángel María scorches the dance floor with rapid-fire paces, and Diana matches his every whirl. Welded together, the sinuous 'Otters' spin through the humid breeze, as if mating in mid-water and mid-air.

Close to dawn, while 'Rebeca' shimmies on with her unflagging compañeros, 'Osorio' takes Chiara for a stroll along the beach. — We need a breather from all the ruckus. — He murmurs the words casually enough; but in the starlight, as they pad barefoot along the sand, he swings her around and clamps her body forcefully. Now his intentions are all too clear.

He's strong enough that anything might happen. Still, he relaxes his grip as soon as she evades his mouth. She embraces him fondly. — I'm not in the mood for more.

As the darkness recedes, his urgency ebbs. — You never are. — He sounds disappointed—but manfully resigned.

Standing on the shore, locked in each other's arms, they greet the first light. By a quirk of the clouds, a shaft of sun falls on the islet off the coast, and it glitters like a buckle of greenish copper. With disarming sweetness, he whispers in her ear. — We are blessed, we are blessed.

Chiara is not so sanguine. — Yes. For now...

Black Power

Entering from the left, Diana is hoodless; she slides the title Black Power *into the black rectangular frame. Entering from the right, The Trans Reader replaces The Male Reader at the lectern.*

The Trans Reader: This is the Thirteenth Reading.

By 1994, the citizenry is so fed up with Espinosa that the pollsters consider Milady a shoo-in; yet as before, the prospect only seems to rattle her. Rumor has it that beneath her bumptious exterior, she's terrified of the bloodthirsty tyrant. To save her neck, so the story goes, she prefers to 'captain the opposition, but without rocking the Admiral's boat.' Her nastiest detractors prattle about the bribes she receives from him, with the tacit understanding that she'll always yield when push comes to shove. According to the gossipers, she cravenly abets his democratic charade.

In the opinion of the best-informed, the cagey geezer doesn't need to corrupt his rival; he's adept at electoral swindles without any aid from her. His dubious triumph of 1998, when Milady far outstripped him in the Gallup polls, has already betrayed his machinations. But the vote of 2002 denudes Canuba's body-politic once and for all, revealing its gangrenous putrefaction. This time—so the scuttlebutt runs—a traitor monkey-wrenches the regime's ballot-rigging from within.

After Chiara's stay with 'Rebeca' and 'Osorio' at Espada del Sur, she can easily guess the turncoat's identity. Ángel María represents the Progress Party as Co-chairman of the Electoral Commission, along with his counterpart from the Transformation bloc. Unable to glut the boxes with enough forged votes, the government is faced with a rout. Through some pressure on the weaker members of the Commission—using carrots as well as sticks—

Espinosa parleys his defeat into an 'inconclusive outcome.' The murky recount limps on for months, as public outrage steadily mounts.

Finally, panic-stricken at forfeiting the reins of power, he reverts to the blatant methods of his past (and hidden present). One morning, as Milady's cortege is speeding along the highway en route to a rally, two of the tires on her limousine blow out—at precisely the same time. She comes within an inch of losing her life. Extracting her from the wreckage, a team of medics rushes her to Puerto Indio in an ambulance. By a curious coincidence, they just happen to be idling nearby when the 'fluke' occurs.

In a solemn address to the nation, the 'demotator' congratulates himself on saving his adversary from the brink of extinction. With a tear in his eye, he announces that she'll need to undergo a slew of operations. Under these tragic circumstances, he will have to serve his country for a four more years, no matter what the outcome of the recount. Cowed, the Electoral Commission declares him the victor, though only by the skin of his teeth.

While it can't be proven in court—since all the judges are Progress Party appointees—it's self-evident that the strongman meant to polish Milady off, just as he'd snuffed his own father decades before. Presumably, the medics reneged on their lethal task, in a last-minute pang of conscience. Thanks to her narrow escape, Milady now becomes a martyred saint, a symbol of resistance to Espinosa's tyranny. During her lengthy stays in a private clinic, she's guarded day and night by Transformation partisans. She emerges from her convalescence in a wheelchair, paralyzed from the waist down. Her rotund body wasted, her cheery face disfigured, she has little left to relinquish. Her bouncy manner has yielded to granite determination, and her eyes flash the message that Espinosa can bully her no more.

His hold over some of the citizens hasn't diminished, of course. Chiara's housekeeper, Luz Divina, never swerves in her allegiance to the 'Benefactor': he may be a murderer, but at least he's a patriot—and a white supremacist to boot. Mining this double vein, his propagandists step up their mud-slinging onslaught. For example, they argue that since Milady's mother is a Bonaventuran—a falsehood they've fabricated themselves—her bid for president poses a threat to Canuba's sovereignty. If she's elected, they warn, she would join the two islands under a single flag, on the model of Trinidad and Tobago, or Saint Kitts and Nevis. Cleverly, their strategy appeals to racism, but without ever mentioning it—much less 'colorism,' its slippery Canuban form.

Ad nauseam, Espinosa's lackeys debate the pros and cons of uniting the two countries. They often refer to the 'Mateo Plan' for such a merger, no matter how firmly she denies its existence. Meanwhile, for Luz Divina and her ilk, the subtext rings out loud and clear. Milady is 'esa prieta fea'—'that ugly black woman'—who wants to lord it over folks lighter-skinned than herself. By arousing atavistic qualms about another 'African invasion' from Bonaventure, and a further 'pollution of Canuba's Hispanic purity,' the savvy despot exploits his subjects' basest instincts. After six decades of dominance, he knows all too well that if he hits the kneecap of history, the leg will jerk—and kick a 'Bono' in the face.

Luz Divina's contempt for anyone darker than herself—and her adulation of 'whites' of every shade—lays bare how ordinary Canubans have turned colonial prejudice inward. Cunningly, Espinosa riffs on their age-old intolerance like a virtuoso, speeding the tempo and upping the volume at will. In the aftermath of her 'accident,' Milady's courage in defying him energizes her followers all the more.

As these events unreel, Chiara discusses them now and then with Don Alfonso. Increasingly 'tired of this sorry thing called life,' as he phrases it, he never leaves his ayrie anymore, even for musical events.

Seated on the terrace one evening, he surveys the meandering river, as the cicadas and frogs belt out their hymn. 'Milady's saga reminds me of my student years in Louisiana. Chiaretta, I'm sure you've heard Canubans tell you that the racism on our island is 'just a joke,' or 'nationalism by another name.' Well, I hate to accuse my countrymen of a grave defect, but 'colorism,' as you call it, is what their bias really is. At LSU, plenty of 'good ole boys' fed me a similar line, though it was much more rigid.

Segregation? 'We're talking about a cultural difference; people always want to be with their own kind.' Civil rights? 'These Negroes are making a mountain out of a molehill.' And then they'd offer you another glass of Bourbon, and charm you with a slap on the back.

They thought you were taking the issue too seriously, the dolts, Chiara says. — She made an extensive trip through the American South when she was at Princeton. And she's all too familiar with Sicilian animosity towards blacks— even though Northern Italians belittle her fellow-islanders as 'africani' themselves. Like Luz Divina's belief in her 'whiteness,' ethnicity is just a game of smoke and mirrors— now you see it, now you don't… She takes another sip of her Armagnac. — Above all, they wanted you to toe the line.

Ángel María is seldom on hand anymore for the evenings at Alfonso's farm, though he still dashes off duets with his uncle now and then. Regrettably, even these small pleasures come to a sudden end. Shortly after his wife's demise from cancer, the agronomist suffers from a heart attack himself—as often happens when couples have been close. Unlike hers, his disease isn't protracted; and in the autumn of 1999, when Chiara returns from a three-month whirligig of trips, she's shocked to find that he's passed away.

She phones Ángel María immediately to express her grief, her sympathy, her condolences... Cool as a sprig of mint, he assures her that his uncle didn't languish for long, and didn't endure any agonizing pain. — Don't feel sorry for him, Chiara. I was with him at the end, and I have to say I'd never seen him happier. He chattered for hours. The doctors called it delirium, but to me it seemed more like a kind of ecstasy. He reminisced about his childhood, his marriage, his career… and he relived his greatest love.

The Sonata Sonata

Entering from the left, Leandra is hoodless; she slides the title The Sonata Sonata *into the black rectangular frame. Entering from the right, The Female Reader replaces The Trans Reader at the lectern.*

The Female Reader: This is the Fourteenth Reading.

The world vanishes, like the last echo of a closing chord, as soon as she lands on his shoulder. Why the staccato towards the end, not burgundy but red? In the final loop, when she glides down to meet him, Alfonso quickly unwinds all the tunes he's ever written—in reverse, a long crab-canon at breakneck speed. On the verge of blacking out, he sees her boomerang from the horizon: proudly, she snaps free of the rigid kite-string, drawing figure eights across the sky. That enraptured arabesque inspires him. He's tired of his dreary coda—the bland ostinato of tablets and capsules, pumpkin soup and saltine crackers, queasy diapers and blurred TV, tepid sponge-baths and sinking spells.

After three months of hearing his uncle beg for release, Ángel María grabs a goose-down cushion from the bed and presses it firmly across his face, so hard Alfonso can feel the damask pattern on his cheeks. Just before, after whizzing through 'A Reverie of Loss' one last time, presto con brio, his nephew shuts the piano lid with a thud. But Alfonso already foresees what's in store from the terse prelude to the evening, when Ángel María announces: 'Tío, I've given the staff the night off . . . so we can be all alone.'

As the agronomist fades away, his heir's renditions of the 'Sonata Sonata' are his only solace. With almost twice the notes to hit, the version for one keyboard proves fiendishly difficult, and Ángel María has to outdo himself to nail it down. Following the old man's instructions, he's artfully transposed the four-handed score into a piano solo. He owes this much to Alfonso, who's gifted his stocks and bonds to him—wiring them to a shell company in Bermuda, beyond his children's clutches. Not that Ángel María needs the money—far from it—but he agrees with Alfonso that his grasping cousins don't deserve it. After all, he's always been his uncle's true son.

Plying the ivories is only a minor pastime for the 'éminence grise' of Canuban poltics, who prefers to spend his leisure hours on his love affairs. Still, over the years, his duets with Alfonso have become one of his escape valves. The composer's archaic pieces provide a soothing change of pace, a way to hop off the hamster-wheel of creaking bedsprings for a while.

On Alfonso's orders, the farmhands set up his four-poster in the music room, between the harpsichord and the Bösendorfer grand. Ironwood-paneled, almost windowless, the chamber is meant for nighttime use; but even if his eyesight had held up, he wouldn't have peeked outside. By now, the ragged vestiges of Alfonso's farm have spiked in value, as Puerto Indio sprawls toward the east like a lava-flow. The hazy panorama from his terrace—the Fernando River winding through mist-drizzled hills—has succumbed to a crass Legoland of two-car garages and stucco facades. Built of ochre coral-stone a century before, the Berridos mansion, with its flaky balustrades and vine-choked gardens, looms above the intruders like a reproach.

While he lies paralyzed in the shuttered house, his children are exploiting the last remaining lots with ever smaller bungalows, squeezing profits from the parcels he glumly granted them a few years back. In the mid-nineties, carving up adjacent lands he sold in a fit of pique, developers seeded the blight with a hideous suburb, Cuesta India, a chunky excretion of cookie-cutter 'units.' Thank God his strokes have left him purblind, he mutters to himself; thank God he can no longer see how his mother's ancestral estate has been defiled...

Six months earlier, Alfonso's wife, Lidia, brings to term a rare form of snail-paced cancer. But after a decade of her slow enfeeblement, the giggly housekeeper, Parmelia, and the saturnine cook, Aimée, detect no changes in their daily routine. Lidia's commandeering nurses have always kept the patient's room off-limits, even to her husband, and in less than a week they've come back to look after him. Big-boned and sixtyish, Sandra and Heroina are stern professionals—though as long as they reign unchallenged, they condescend to watch the soaps every evening with the maids.

Before he's restricted to bed, Alfonso sometimes joins them in the kitchen for the telenovelas; to his employees, the snickers of their patrón seem churlish—if not blasphemous. They can't guess he's thinking of Ángel María. His scheming has always struck his uncle as a comic satire of those cello-soaked dramas, in which the poor and pious eventually outflank the rich and despicable. In his ruthless nephew's jaded parody, vice has conquered virtue, hands down. He needs truckloads of cash to fuel his costly habits, and he's raked in the loot through a lucrative marriage and heaps of government graft.

When he was younger, Ángel María longed to inherit his Tío's fortune. Gossips always assume he's snowed Alfonso with exactly that in mind, on the pretext of visiting his Tía Lidia—what else? But the cards have been stacked against him, more than they know. For one thing, Alfonso dislikes pretty boys on principle; for another, he despises his nephew's parents, who cadge a monthly allowance from wealthy cousins in Madrid—and not just a few pesetas. In the agronomist's book, Lidia's elder sister and her hirsute husband are nothing but hedonistic leeches. 'They simmer in the jacuzzi so much,' he sneers, 'they look like a poached kiwi and a stewed prune.'

In the end, he overlooks Ángel María's provenance—and Begonia's—due to their startling musical prowess. As children, both of them are pint-size prodigies, though the sour little girl soon gives up on his lessons. Her brother's inborn skill at the piano is close to concert-level, whether he practices or not. In his loneliness—though he won't admit it to himself—Alfonso finds his nephew's 'amoríos' amusing. Will the Lieutenant Colonel shoot him for frigging his wife? Will that vamp Melinda nab him with his latest conquest, a girl whose mother named her 'Madeín Canuba'—lifted from the label of a T-shirt? Would his oblivious wife, the heiress Leandra, get wind of either one?

All this is a jaunty scherzo. But years before, Alfonso's one and only love-affair was a wistful adagio, like the second movement in a Brahms quartet. After Sonata left him, he composed a rambling opus in her memory, a four-handed pastorale for piano and harpsichord. Nimble as spider-monkeys, Ángel María's hands scamper over the ivories, aping Sonata's sudden swoops and dives. Then they hover, almost immobile, while fluting her standard call, *cuácoo-coo-coo*, or the come-hither tones of her bedtime signal, *ooá-oo*. Meanwhile, Alfonso keeps up a dogged basso-continuo on the cembalo.

As his uncle often marvels, plucking the strings at his double manual across the room, Ángel María wrings velvet and chocolate from the keys. What a sumptuous tone... no wonder Bösendorfer was the 'Klavierfabrik' Liszt endorsed, the makers of Leipzig's foremost instrument. To his chagrin, Alfonso's stubby fingers have never attained the subtleties of touch demanded by the piano—as in the Magyar master's 'Unstern,' for example, or his 'Nuages gris.' Besides his love of Scarlatti, this was why he switched to the harpsichord: for its forthright dynamics and phrasing. He purchased his Antunés instrument—lacquered in black and red, and once owned by Domenico himself—at the same Vienna auction where he bought the hulking mahogany grand.

But why does Sonata abandon him? There has to be somebody else: he mulls distraughtly over the mates who might've replaced him. Say what you will, his tender respect must have been a hard act to follow, for any male. Maybe, during her idyll with a human, she develops an eccentric yen for other species. Maybe she's fallen for a Key West or a Zenaida; maybe a ruddy, with that foghorn voice of his. Maybe a crested quail-dove, with his Elvis topknot and garish markings—but is that even conceivable? She'd have to migrate all the way to Jamaica! Then again, maybe... tal vez...

Ángel María is too polite to laugh at his uncle's guileless jealousy, though he often fears the agronomist is losing his grip. 'There, there, Tío, you shouldn't fret so much; she probably just longed for her natural food. You couldn't expect her to stay here forever. She's already shown you how grateful she is.'

But Alfonso only hangs his head and starts all over again. One year with her wasn't enough. Why did she skedaddle so suddenly? Remember how beautiful her plumage was? Toasted brown, burgundy, and cinnamon, aglow with health. Oh, and her rosy feet, her tapered tail! She was such a good girl at first—who would've thought she could be so heartless? Or in the younger man's tacit translation: Sonata, the bitch, she seduced me with malice of forethought.

Ángel María is the only pianist ever invited to perform the 'Sonata Sonata' with Don Alfonso—and he often allows Chiara to listen in. He originally christens the work with that droll title; but true to his melancholy bent, he soon revises it to 'A Reverie of Loss.' Sententiously, he boasts to his nephew that it 'weds two biological classes in an overarching harmony—threatened but triumphant.' Throwing humility to the winds, he dubs the hybrid style of his excursus 'the matrimony of Scarlatti and Brahms.'

Though it vaguely follows the classic sonata form, to Ángel María it seems more akin to a Debussy tone poem, with the amorphous vignettes unreeling backwards. Riffling through various modes, chiefly the Lydian and Dorian, it portrays Sonata's buoyant return to the open skies, her sentimental dalliance with Alfonso, her miraculous recovery, her seizure and torment by dastardly boys, her early life foraging in the great outdoors, her narrow escape from a kestrel while still a fledgling, and the moment she hatches from one of her mother's two white eggs, nestled in a clump of hibiscus at the bottom of his garden—or so the old man fantasizes to his nephew. He claims that in all recorded history, no monument like this has ever been raised to a mourning dove.

Throughout their year of domestic bliss, Alfonso sleeps with the bird in his tall mahogany bed, enveloped by a silk canopy and a nylon mosquito-net. He surrounds himself with a hedge of bolsters, so he won't turn over and crush his companion during the night. — Sonata's never content unless she's lying on my chest, he murmurs, with her head snuggled under my chin. Sometimes she twists her neck around and looks at me with her blue-rimmed eyes. I swear to you, there's real love in them; you'd have to see that expression yourself to know what I mean.

Ángel María is willing to concede there might be something to his uncle's delusions. Every time they enter the front hall together, the dove greets her paramour with the same melodious phrase, before lunging to alight on his shoulder. It's unlike either of her usual calls: a special salute, intended only for him. The maids say she always waits like a sentinel when Don Alfonso is away, poised on a full-size replica of the Venus de Milo. 'How appropriate for a femme fatale...' Ángel María jokes, to the agronomist's delight.

When Alfonso is at home, Sonata careens in and out of a huge brass birdcage. He won't allow Parmelia and Aimée to latch its ornate door, despite the messes she strews: chalky droppings and food-debris. Lidia no longer has the strength to stagger downstairs and defend the maids from his outlandish whims; but they squawk so much he gives them a raise so they won't quit. 'La bendita tórtola,' they called Sonata—'the damn pigeon.' She sticks her beak into everything edible, from mangú, concón, and mofongo to ripe zapotes and nísperos. To top it off, 'la bendita tórtola' sheds more profusely than an Angora: tufts from her breast-feathers cling to the tablecloths, curtains, and rugs.

It seems strange to Ángel María that the dove has become so housebound; after all, she fended for herself until her run-in with the mean little scamps. In the first weeks after she heals, Alfonso dutifully carries her to the farm's far-off corners in his jeep, and tosses her into the air. But whether she starts from the coot pond, the packing shed, or the cedar grove, she always makes a beeline for the mansion. By the time he reaches home, he finds her pecking at the windows, rapping till he lets her back in.

The months of Sonata's convalescence have been a respite for Alfonso, a vacation from his worries over his wife. If Lidia has no prospects for improvement, maybe this mourning dove does. Naturally, the dogs and cats aren't allowed into her private rehabilitation room, a vacated pantry. While her wings are mending, in the miniature splints he's devised, she can only hobble around on the floor. She coos sharply at the approach of maids, nurses, or other trespassers, to warn them she's underfoot.

Alfonso has to call Sandra to order several times, when she complains that he's neglecting his wife for a pigeon. 'Aimée might as well cook the squab for lunch,' Heroina sniffs; 'she's never gonna fly again.' She beats a hasty retreat when her employer informs her, with unaccustomed gruffness, that she can either mind her own business or pack her bags.

He's sure Sonata has grasped the ethical abyss between him and those midget thugs she encountered. Though she resists at first, she soon yields to his care with stoic meekness. Her small body and deceptive simplicity recall the manner of his idol, Domenico Scarlatti, so he names her after the maestro's compact sonatas.

In these days, Alfonso still owns more than half his mother's estate, which means his nearest neighbors are a long way off. But that doesn't stop the social-climbers of Cuesta India from trying to get a foot in the door. The most assiduous, Dr. Ventós, a knock-kneed dermatologist, brings Sonata along in his station-wagon: he shows up on a winter afternoon, crisp by Caribbean standards. 'Your farm has gained quite a reputation as a refuge for wounded animals,' he begins with a simper, a perforated box under his arm.

Alfonso nods coldly, but doesn't reply.

The doctor persists. — What magnificent weather! Just look at the cordillera. We hardly ever see it, for all the humidity. Today it's sharp as a razor.

Alfonso quashes the chitchat. — Hmm—a female; know how this happened?

Officiously, Ventós says he chanced upon the bird on his postprandial walk. He pried her miserable story from the boys who tortured her, before they scurried off to catch another victim. First, they stunned her with a rock from one of their slingshots; then they turned her into a living kite, by tying a long string to her feet. She flapped round and round in circles, till she fell to the ground from sheer exhaustion. — Now both her wings are broken, as you can see.

Alfonso brushed the interloper off. — I hope you'll excuse me, Doctor; I have to make some splints for this dove. Thanks for your trouble. — When he glances through his workshop window a minute later, Ventós is hastily driving off, miffed by the rebuff.

In an early exchange with his nephew, Alfonso denounces Canuban children for their cruelty to birds. — It's a national disgrace.

Later he'll realize that his uncle is always right; but at this stage, Ángel María dares to disagree. — Take it from me, Tío, boys are bullies everywhere. I went to summer camp in Wisconsin when I was ten.

Alfonso shakes his head somberly. — You're right. All humans are bullies.

Even before Sonata's treason and Lidia's decline, he espouses what he calls a 'Schopenhauerian stance,' a gloominess that also tinges his compositions. Every evening after dinner, he trundles to the music room, props up one of the lids, and annotates morose pieces of his own invention. For the harpsichord, he devises neo-Baroque concoctions in stately tempi, sarabandes with poignant titles like 'Jadis,' 'Wenn Nur,' and 'Ubi Sunt?' On occasion, he pens a late-Romantic elegy for the piano, modeled on Rachmaninoff or Scriabin—a 'Dirge for the Misbegotten' or a 'Plaint from the Tomb.'

Condescendingly, Canuban mélomanes like Horacio speak of his efforts as 'lovely throwbacks.' In the end, he shares them only with Ángel María, for lack of any other friends—until Chiara comes along. 'La nostra principessa dilettante,' he likes to call her, in his Vivaldi-era Italian. If his nephew is a surrogate son, he soon adopts her as a daughter.

Flying Backwards

Entering from the left, Chiara is hoodless; she slides the title Flying Backwards *into the black rectangular frame.*

The Male Reader: This is the Fifteenth Reading.

For most of Alfonso's life, Lidia has been his confidante. But from the onset of her dithering illness, she barely utters a word. The painkillers leave her almost comatose, and her hospital-quality bed, with its levers and dials, seems to have swallowed her whole. He tries to attend to her himself at first, but he finds the task too disheartening; he can't bear to see her lying there day by day, with no cure in sight.

Here, have a spoonful of habichuela con dulce. — She shakes her head. — Why not, Lidia? It's your favorite dessert.

Maybe because she senses his desperation, or maybe out of feminine modesty, she insists that he hire the nurses. Sandra and Heroina crank out a steady, dignified patter—but they can't coax many answers out of her, either. They hoist her out of bed once a month, for her doctor's appointment at the Clínica Mejía in Zarzuela, the Belle Époque neighborhood where she grew up.

After the nurses' arrival, for about a year Alfonso pursues his one-way sessions with his wife, reminiscing in a headlong monologue. Looking back on their marriage, there were a lot of happy times, he sums up one morning. It wasn't all disappointing; as in Händel, the 'Penseroso' was preceded by a cheerful 'Allegro.' — Ma non troppo… Lidia quips, out of the blue: this is her final spark of wit.

He retires as soon as she's diagnosed. By this time, Puerto Indio has already spread like an oil slick, oozing to the western edge of the estate. Slice by slice, he sells off half his holdings to developers, for prices that seem absurdly bloated. He curses each check he receives; but like it or not, the escudos keep piling up in his accounts at the Banco Cipango.

Alfonso always hoped his children would construct houses near his own, with stone from the nineteenth-century quarry beyond the cedar grove. To his disgruntlement, they prefer their trendy apartments in the Brickell-like center of town, and seldom look in on their parents. — My kids don't care for what you Americans call 'the sticks,' Don Alfonso comments dourly to a college classmate in the States.

Why should he go on farming, if nobody will ever build on what he's achieved? By varying his crops, he's become the leading supplier of fresh produce to the city; restaurant owners swear by his broccoli, artichokes, and arugula. When he dines out with Lidia, they hail him as a hero. Where his father planted the usual eggplants and beans, or left the fields fallow for decades, Alfonso lays out plots of exotic squashes, Italian melons, blue potatoes from Peru, black-eyed peas from Louisiana—you name it. That's how he wins Espinosa's approval. In his first years out of the Ag School at LSU, the Canuban government showers him with awards for his 'signal advances in horticulture.'

Not to forget the animals… Sonata isn't the only patient who's thrived under his care. Grunting and puling in sympathy, he feeds the injured victims with a dropper, a bottle, or even with his moistened fingertips. Unless he's rescued them as babies, he has to grapple with their terror and rage; his hands, arms, and face often bear the marks of their first reactions to his help. He soothes his charges so thoroughly that even ferrets and mongooses sit calmly on his lap. But instead of creatures from the wild, people usually bring him pets who've been run over, or who've hanged themselves unwittingly on a barbed-wire fence.

Over the years, he's saved thousands of mutilated dogs and cats. The maids refuse to clean up after the beasts in his menagerie, and Lidia reads him the riot act: he has to consign them to the garage, or else. — There's plenty of room in there for your veterinary ward. — In his heyday, Alfonso hires Pedrito, a deaf and dumb assistant, to hose down the filthy floor and dole out the rations of food. Lidia never sets foot in the 'zoo,' as she calls it, but she's a good sport about leaving her sedan parked outside.

Alfonso's fondness for animals has always been more general than hers. A trained ornithologist, Lidia focuses exclusively on birds. She keeps a meticulous log where she enters every sighting of hundreds of species, even the most common. The Berridos property brackets the Río Fernando, named for the Catholic King by Columbus himself. From the marshy riverbanks, broad bottomlands swell toward the orchards; springs bubble through thickets of scrub; copses dot the foothills of the cloud-walled sierra. Like Chiara and her lover Amado in Barlovento, Lidia glories in all these ecotones, which allow her to track an enormous range of birds.

Jumpy and shy, she resembles a heron herself, with her arched neck, cautious gait, slender legs, and inquisitive eyes. Her husband has perfect pitch and a talent for mimicry; he can tweet, caw, whistle, cheep, hiss, chur, twitter, pipe, chirp, wheeze, and cluck. She likes to take him along as a decoy on her early-morning field trips. To cap their outings, at eight o'clock they drink coffee from a thermos, among the rushes or under the trees. By that time, within an hour or two, they've spotted five to ten Caribbean endemics— the ground-nesting brody; the sociable bamboo chit; the 'four-eyed' tanager; the red-capped woodpecker, with its green-checkered back; the miniscule hummingbird, no larger than a bumblebee; the mango cuckoo, its hollow call knocking like a xylophone; or at daybreak, the tiny Antillean swifts, darting through shoals of gnats.

Lidia learned her avian lore from the taxonomists at LSU, renowned for its vast collection of specimens. As an undergraduate, she dreams of joining their annual expeditions to the Amazon—but even then, her delicate health stands in her way. She often discusses her plight with Alfonso; their courtship has slowly blossomed at the university's Club Canubano. The two of them stroll for hours under the live-oaks of Baton Rouge, with their extravagant, moss-swagged limbs, which Alfonso compares to the turns, mordents, and trills of Baroque sonatas.

While he's working on his B.S. degree at Tulane, he begins his harpsichord studies with a German-Jewish refugee in the French Quarter; he commutes across the swamp for lessons twice a week. Dire circumstances have baked Fräulein Lotte Fischbein (AKA Miss Charlotte Smith) into one tough cookie. First she flees from Berlin to France, and then from occupied Paris to New York. Nine years before Alfonso meets her, she's settled in New Orleans, and there she's legally changed her name to an English proxy. As she explains to her pupil, she wants to erase as much of her past as possible.

He understands her, but claims he'd much rather dwell on his own, 'weird' as it has been. — You'd be shocked if I told you.

After Berlin and Paris, I sincerely doubt it. — Miss Smith rolls her world-weary eyes. — Besides, I live in the Vieux Carré.

She reminds him of his mother, a cultivated woman who taught him the piano; even now, after all these years, he still thinks of her every day. He was an only child, and he often talks to his teacher about his parents, who died in a car crash when he was fifteen. Patriotically, he praises Canuba as the finest country on earth, thanks to its benign climate and fertile, well-drained soil. He can't wait to wrest the family farm away from the no-good overseer, a crook who robbed his father blind.

Not that his Papi deserved any better, Alfonso confides. He grieved for his 'querida madre,' his dear mother; but not for that 'dumb bastard.' At least their death had put her out of his reach. Pérez is a common surname in Canuba, Alfonso sneers; so it suits the shiftless paternal breed to a tee. — 'Poor whites'—or worse—Southerners would call them.

The Berridos estate has belonged to his mother's people for many generations. Pérez was a womanizer and a drunk, and Alfonso can't conceive what such a refined young girl could've seen in him. He inherited his own stocky frame from his father, who might've posed for an illustration of Sancho Panza. But he owes his aquiline face to the Berridos lineage; he's especially vain about his nose, straight and narrow as a flume. His slightly crazed, nut-brown eyes mirror his moods, mostly bleak—though when he rails at the evils of mankind, he can let out scornful hoots that betray a ferocious mirth.

In high school, his fellow students at the Colegio Jesuita don't know what to make of him: of all the guys, he's the most standoffish. He offends them by doing every iota of his homework; since he keeps up as he goes along, he doesn't even have to cram for tests. He never engages in sweaty sports or raucous parties like the other teens, brain-dead 'jevitos' or wealthy punks. The one time he'd comes back at night for a mixer, with those stuck-up girls from the Colegio Santa Ana, he makes a complete fool of himself. His father forces a half-pint of rum down his throat, to 'buck up his courage'; and then he waits outside the door, eager to see if his son can 'make it' with a chick. No surprise: woozy as a June bug, Alfonso paws a frantic wallflower till she screams.

The big man on campus, Pablo Cruz, shouts her down. — Don't worry, pendeja! He won't rape you: he's such a loser, he can't even jerk off!

For six years, Pablo and his sidekicks hector Alonso unrelentingly; the Spanish and Irish priests ignore their 'high jinks'—cowed by the hooligans, too. The razzing starts in the first week of seventh grade, when they find out Alfonso doesn't masturbate. — What's that white stuff? — He's never seen the creamy gunk before. Pablo and his pals are clowning around in the restroom—a little contest in a circle—and he barges in right when two of them uncork.

Alfonso is grateful his mother insists on home-schooling till he's twelve. — It's too far to go into town. What a waste of time! Besides, you have to practice the piano every day— two hours at least.

Animals are kinder than humans, Alonso tells Mingo, his imaginary friend; they only kill when they need to eat. He dotes on his dogs, cats, and parrots. No, he never clips their wings; they stay with him out of loyalty, out of love. Watching from the deep-eyed, ochre house, he's angry at how the campesino boys hunt grackles, kingbirds, and cuckoos. They even go after defenseless warblers and bananaquits—anything that moves. He hates the pebbles they sling, the stolen BB-guns they pop.

His mother doesn't let him mingle with riffraff like them; she entertains him with her art books, her orchids, and the Czerny piano drills. Their household instrument is only an upright Baldwin, but she frequently has it tuned—a necessity in the humid climate. One morning, in a spiteful rage, his father smashes the keys with his shotgun butt.

At the time, Alfonsito is nursing a rooster who's been ripped in a cockfight, healing his breast and neck with homemade salves. He rubs the same ointments on himself when Papi beats him with razor strops and knotted canes. His father gags him with a torn pair of boxer shorts, and the blood trickles down his legs and back. 'Mujercita'—'little woman'—the fat man calls him; or sometimes, when nobody can hear: 'maldito pato'—'goddam queer.'

For the life of him, Alfonsito has never been able to learn to shoot. — 'Si no sabes disparar, no eres hombre,' his father liked to repeat, slurring his words. 'If you don't know how to shoot, you're not a man.' Finally, he gives up dragging the pouty brat along the cool, fresh-turned furrows in the late afternoon, his favorite time to hunt. By then, Pérez has already screwed one of the farm girls down in the woods; the cedar-smell always sets him off. Ripe with liquor, now he's looking for partridges, quail, and doves.

Alfonso can spot them from a mile away; but he won't let on. Don't kill them for nothing, Papi! he pleads.

You'd think he's a girl the way he holds his ears when the escopeta goes off. Can't even clean a bird, he gets so sick at the sight of guts. And it's all your fault, you Berridos slut. You're all a bunch of perverts. You might as well dress him up in high heels and a skirt.

Alfonsito can hear them fighting night after night—but when his father hits her, his mother never makes a peep. The only giveaway is the thump, thump, thump of his fist; or the loud slaps, kapow, kapow, kapow, on her cheeks and thighs. Sometimes she moans later on, and so does he; but those noises are different: panting and excited, headed for a goal.

He wonders what his father would do if he ever found out she's sewn him a dancing dress. — It has to stay under your bed when El Gordo's home. — That's their secret name for him: The Fat Man. — El Gordo might kill us. — But Alfonso takes out the dress while they're asleep, when the house falls silent at last. The blue satin is as smooth as her skin. — Blue for boys, she told him. Why can't they just be alone?

I don't care about him, corazón. But I had to look after you when you tripped and hurt your forehead; we couldn't stay in the car. — His mother has always spoiled him, even mashing his hard-boiled eggs with a fork, so they wouldn't feel rubbery in his mouth. Yes, he's her precious one. For the Carnival parades, she decks him out like a little angel, with a gold-foil halo bobbing above his head.

In the twenties, a good Catholic can't evade her husband for long, so she returns to Pérez after only a month. Five years into the marriage, she realizes she's thrown her life away—and all of a sudden, she panics. Stuffing the small boy and a carpetbag into her Ford, she absconds to the eastern part of the country. In her restlessness, though she isn't a hiker as a rule, she backtracks to the foothills of the cordillera. — You like birds so much, Alfonsito; we'll track one down you've never seen before.

Her Model T doesn't make it very far on the pitted trails, so they continue by mule. The owner of the guesthouse in Milfuegos shows them a guidebook before they set out. — This is trogon country. You've heard of the quetzal in Central America; well, we've got one, too. Green back, red belly; the male has white bars.

They spend several days with a toothless campesina in her yagua-roofed hut, subsisting on rice and black beans. They roll off the prickly straw mattress at dawn, when greyish light stripes the floor. His fondest memory is knowing they're lost, in the sun-speckled woods. But it doesn't matter; he always feels safe with his mother—even when the accident occurs.

First they hear the loud *cok-craow*. She freezes in place. — Look, Alfonsito. On the jobo-tree. No bars; she must be a female. — The green bird is too large to miss, and too afraid to budge. She doesn't flip from her perch till the moment he stumbles and hits his head.

As he passes out between the keyboards, crushed by the pillow pressed down on his face, he sees her wheel off the branch in a flash of red—briefly flying backwards.

Reshuffling the Deck

Entering from the left, Diana is hoodless; she slides the title Reshuffling the Deck *into the black rectangular frame. Entering from the right, The Trans Reader replaces The Male Reader at the lectern.*

The Trans Reader: This is the Sixteenth Reading.

Alfonso's death is a heavy blow to Chiara; he's been more of a father to her than her own, who never bothers to call or write. As she surveys the dwindling circle of her closest friends—reduced not only by the deaths of Catulo and Virgilio, but by Horacio's Trappist vows—she finds comfort in the buoyant vitality of Leandra. Ángel María's wife could easily have joined the same cohort as Lamia, after the cellist's disastrous concert: the matrons who while away their days noshing chocolates and watching the soaps. Volunteering at her children's schools has kept Leandra's mind nimble; and like her willowy mother, Carolina, she has eluded the ravages of time.

Leandra has borne her husband three boys and five girls, providing employment for a constant stream of nannies. Though he's always taken pleasure in his progeny—during the few hours he spends at home—their mother grants the children her undivided attention. She often professes that she's learned more from them than from her academic discipline, the philosophy of art. But once her brood begins to leave the nest for boarding schools, colleges, and internships abroad, she returns to her former pursuits on a grandiose scale.

Frederica's latest initiative, the International Music Festival, scores a stupendous success for the Countess Fund. In memory of her terpsichorean days with the choreographer, Catulo Miranda, Carolina sets up a parallel foundation, the Del Río-Miranda Fund for the Development of Canuban Dance. Like the other endowment, it's quickly boiled down to a shorter moniker, the Carolina Fund. The two institutions often work in tandem, and by the late nineties and on into the noughties, Canubans are applauding such artists as Emmanuel Ax, William Christie, Christoph Eschenbach, the Three Tenors, Misha Baryshnikov, Pina Bausch, Joshua Bell, Merce Cunningham, and Christoph Eschenbach. Conveniently, Leandra becomes the Minister of Culture, in one of Espinosa's frequent reshufflings; it's all thanks to Ángel María, of course, who now holds sway as Chairman of the Presidential Cabinet. She offers Chiara an open invitation to use her loge at the theater, so her Italian friend always has the best seat in the house.

In New York, London, Paris, or Milan, Chiara would never have been so lucky; for premier events like those she attends every week or so, tickets would've been exorbitant, if available at all. Her friends in all four cities often ask her how she can bear to molder away in the 'tropical boondocks.' They never understand that there's enough going on to keep her satisfied, with none of the wear and tear. Most people who endure the ceaseless grind of a metropolis are too worn out to avail themselves of its resources. They like to be 'where everything is happening'—though only in the sense of proximity. The calendar of events is more restricted in Puerto Indio, but Chiara has it at her fingertips. Celebrities who remain aloof in major capitals mingle freely with their admirers on the island, and often comment that the Caribbeans' nonchalance soothes their jangled nerves.

Besides toiling with the Countess on the Festival, Leandra also serves as Assistant Director of her mother's nonprofit. In her multiple positions, she enters a frenetic spate of activity, as the new millennium advances. This is just as well, since she wants to keep busy. Plopping another egg in her basket, Ángel María has her named Minister of Education as well. She handles all her tasks with the selflessness she developed as a mother of eight. She often jokes that two foundations plus two ministries adds up to only half her previous load: the eight-ring circus she juggled before.

Given his ascendancy over the President, the Peralta Del Ríos now need Ángel María more than he needs them, to duck pesky labor and fiscal laws. He's always plied the philandering bent of the Canuban male; with a fortune of his own, he no longer keeps the same address as his wife. He buys a penthouse in one of the high-rises on the Malecón, where security is tighter than in a house with extensive grounds. Cool-headedly, Leandra files for divorce; in earlier years, she would've held back for the children's sake, but now they're old enough to take it in their stride. The divorce is easily obtained, since Ángel María already cohabits with another woman: Palmoliva, the flirtatious teenager who joined his whale-watching jaunt, way back in the eighties.

Fourteen years his junior, she promptly becomes his second wife—and then he ignores her, just as he did his first. Like Leandra, she can't compete with Carolina, his former mother-in-law. Though Ángel María doesn't depend on the Del Río millions anymore, he continues to trust her as his closest adviser. After a lengthy stint in Luxembourg at a tax-evasion bank—thanks to the good offices of the Canuban financier, Isabela Burley Luna—Palmoliva returns to the island with a platinum bob, a waif-like Audrey Hepburn air, and a smattering of several languages. Leandra once provided her husband with deep pockets and serial babies; Palmoliva's role is less exacting. All she has to do is look chic, greet the guests, say a polyglot word or two, and send the hors-d'oeuvres on their rounds. She does a top-notch job for Canuba's kingpin, who crafts its foreign policy with precious little input from the ancient 'demotator.'

As for internal affairs, Espinosa still wields power through his network of informers. To keep his subjects in line, an occasional murder 'happens' to take place—committed by covert operatives, and billed as an accident or a fugue. There's the usual catalogue: an armed robbery, a mudslide on a country lane, a freakish coronary, a defenestration while abroad, a furtive elopement to St. Bart's, or even a flight to the 'Bermuda Triangle.'

Despite almost winning several times, Milady never succeeds in her bid for the highest office of the land. She blames her recurrent failure not only on chicanery, but also on Canuban 'colorism,' whereby social acceptance diminishes as the gradations transition from white to black. By circulating false reports about her 'Bonaventuran pedigree,' the canny tyrant has clinched his stranglehold on the nation. Sadly, Milady's choice of partners reveals her own ambivalence; she consorts exclusively with semi-Caucasian men, the lighter the better.

She's paid a steep price for her political ideals: by arranging for her 'unfortunate mishap,' Espinosa almost rubs her out. When that attempt backfires, her limitation to a wheelchair garners sympathy, but not enough to break the hold of the 'demotator' on the voting booths, by hook or by crook. To cap her troubles, the car wreck damages several of her vital organs, which gradually decay. In early middle age, these afflictions eventually hasten her death; she faces it with stoic calm. At least her ending frees her from her painful years of paralysis. The last time Chiara visits her, Milady wheezes out her testament with quiet abnegation. — Maybe our Transformation Party will prevail only when this so-called 'Bonaventuran' is no longer in charge. I already know who will succeed me...

She doesn't disclose the new leader's identity—not even his or her gender. If she weren't so young, Verbena would make the ideal candidate. Since Virgilio's suicidal 'artwork' and Horacio's retreat to the monastery, she's led the painter's widow, Quilviria, a merry chase. At fifteen, she goes through a lad-mad phase, but then she becomes a dedicated activist, the unchallenged spearhead of the Transformation Youth Brigades. Though not biologically kin to her adoptive fathers, she's absorbed their example throughout her childhood, day by day. Now that all the 'Miranda boys' have vanished from the scene, she prolongs their mental and moral vigor, like a phoenix risen from their ashes.

When Chiara broaches this notion to Horacio, on one of his infrequent visits to the city, he scratches his tonsured head. — Yes, that's how I like to think of her, too. We palefaces are a sickly lot. Verbena is the vital shadow of our family, the spirit who will outlive us all. The white race, that stubborn cancer on the body of the world, can only be removed by blackness. Light and matter are just spinoffs. Why should we assume that they're felicitous? 'Dark light' and 'dark matter' outweigh them by far. On this island, we're returning to the cradle of humankind—to our distant origins in Africa. Soon we'll attain our ultimate goal…

And what is that?

He smooths the folds of his cassock. — Divine cessation.

Rooster Dreams

Entering from the left, Leandra is hoodless; she slides the title Rooster Dreams *into the black rectangular frame. She then joins the other bunraku puppeteers on the second-level stage. There, on the mainstage, and on the marionette stage, Leandra's play within the play affords an ample opportunity for mirror-imaging. Clarissa's final invective toward her parents and husband should be chanted as a Sprechstimme recitative, improvised by the actor playing Leandra on the mainstage. Accompanied energetically by the musical ensemble, the obscenities should be slowed down to the point of gibberish. Entering from the right, The Female Reader replaces The Trans Reader at the lectern.*

The Female Reader: This is the Seventeenth Reading.

Most Canubans would never have endorsed Horacio's view; they would've found it 'pro-Bonaventuran'—even traitorous. Though many things have changed during Chiara's two and a half decades in the country, the islanders' preoccupation with parsing 'Canubanidad' has not. Like negative theology, which defines God by what God is not, the debate seems to be conceived in contrary terms: 'Canuban-ness' is what's not European, not American—and especially, what's not 'Bono.' Canubans often dismiss their culture as a collection of 'idiosyncrasies,' underlining its whimsical side. Sardonically, they refer to their homeland as a 'paisito muy especial'—a very special little country. This tendency to mock their own identity is common among small, Third-World nations; but Canubans take it to an extreme. They often portray themselves as fickle nincompoops, fixated on sex and rum.

Why all this self-deprecation? Maybe Canuba's contrast with Cuba, and its similarity to Hispaniola and Puerto Rico, lies at the root of the phenomenon. Spain abandoned the three smaller colonies to their fate after the sixteenth century, reducing them to military outposts. Meanwhile, Cuba rose to preeminence as the crown jewel of the Spanish West Indies, 'la perla de las Antillas.' By the mid-nineteenth century, it was a cash cow for the motherland, producing sugar by the shipload. Like Hispaniola and Puerto Rico, Canuba remained a backwater, lagging behind in wealth, education, and prestige.

In Chiara's experience, Cubans are fiercely proud of their heritage, from Columbus to Castro, despite everything, while Canubans almost seem to apologize for theirs. This may account for their need to malign the 'Bonos.' The controversy about Canubanidad comes to a head when Leandra forces the issue on two different fronts, academic and aesthetic. As Minister of Education, she tries to guarantee instruction to all children, even those of Bonaventuran immigrants. And as Minister of Culture, she proposes an annual arts festival that would showcase the neighboring island, with joint sponsorship by the Countess Fund and the Carolina Fund. Behind the scenes, Ángel María eggs her on; but in the end, Espinosa overrules her 'dangerous' initiatives.

After five or six years of petty frustrations, she resigns from all her posts, public and private. When she announces to the press that she wants to make time for her writing, even her friends shrug their shoulders. Puerto Indio swarms with dilettantes, and Leandra's literary caprice would probably amount to nothing more than her nugatory *Études*, scored for coconuts and gourds. But to everyone's astonishment, she shifts the polemic about Canubanidad to a different sphere, from ethnicity and folkways to society and politics—and she pulls off the feat in an unexpected form: the theatre.

As it turns out, Leandra has far more in common with Ángel María than people surmised. Even before they fully part ways, she rivals him as the Canuban Proteus. Over time, she's been an aspiring philosopher, an avant-garde composer, a devoted mother, a workaholic volunteer, the driving force behind two major nonprofits, and the tireless head of two government ministries.

Now her play, *Sueños de Gallo*, which she shrouds in secrecy until the opening night, becomes a popular as well as a critical success—not to mention a 'succès de scandale.' It wins several international prizes, including Spain's award for the best Hispanic drama. In the magistral English version by Alastair Reid, *Rooster Dreams*, it rivets audiences from Broadway to Bangalore. Significantly, for the country as a whole, it alters Canubans' outlook on their past, their present, and their future. With audacity and ire, Leandra rocks the island to its core: she catalyzes the revolt that Milady, even at her zenith, had merely begun.

A thinly-veiled depiction of real events, the main action takes place in 1961—the year when Manfredo's henchmen killed his father, Papito Espinosa, bringing the geezer's coup d'état to a gory end. Ironically, Leandra could've steered a safer course by staging that gruesome chapter in the nation's history, too notorious to be denied. Instead, she chooses another episode everyone knows about, but no one dares to mention—at least not in public.

During the chaos unleashed by his father's bid to regain power, Manfredo rapes a fifteen-year-old girl in the countryside near Esmeralda; he also snuffs out her two elder brothers, when they rush to her defense. To shame the boys before their deaths, he orders several of his guards to slap them around, while he watches with sadistic glee. Shockingly, the parents have tacitly offered him their daughter, to keep him from confiscating their estate. Though they bartered her virginity for their lands, the heartless deal didn't include the slaying of their sons.

The pretext for Manfredo's threats of expropriation—and for his monstrous cruelty—is the family's abetment of Papito's insurrection. In those days, the younger Espinosa is still a vicious, flamboyant thug, not the frail 'demotator' of later years, with his professorial air and desultory gait. He reserves the right to deflower any girl who catches his eye; and his predilection runs to minors barely past the threshold of puberty.

Several fawners later pen novels about the era, gushing over the President's 'delight in feminine beauty'; in their mawkish yarns, these wretched decades resemble a ladies' tea. Partly to feather their own nests, and partly because they share the national state of denial, they gloss over the blood-spattered horror of the Espinosas' regimes. The atrocities flame up most drastically in the final struggle between Papito and Manfredo: during the dreadful months of that ordeal, father and son outdo each other in their savagery.

The victims of the triple assault—Celina, Antonio, and Juan Carlos—belong to the Orellana family, a clan intermarried with the Peraltas. Among the elite, behind locked doors, the story is often revisited, despite Manfredo's efforts to suppress it. Reportedly, he's committed many such crimes against humbler citizens, but their pitiful destinies have left no mark.

Leandra herself tells Chiara about the Orellana outrage during her first years in Puerto Indio, to cure her of any rosy illusions about the island's past. Growing up, her cousin Celina was her closest companion, and she learned every detail of the tragedy. Banished to a convent school, Celina never recovers from her trauma. At the age of seventeen, during the Christmas vacation, she hangs herself from a rafter—in the same stable where she and her siblings were defiled.

In her play, Leandra tricks out everyone with pseudonyms. The dictator, 'Blackstone,' is the sanguinary strongman of a small Caribbean nation. Celina becomes 'Clementine'; her brothers, 'Colin' and 'Wilfred.' Espinosa's father morphs into an elder brother named 'Brandywine,' who's just as barbarous as Blackstone himself. She rechristens the island 'St. Alban's,' a fictional enclave in the British West Indies.

Under these disguises, the underlying facts can be rehearsed, red in tooth and claw; and to thicken the smoke-screen, she retrofits the plot to the nineteenth century. There's a certain satisfaction for Canubans in seeing British rulers—their overlords from 1839 to 1880—

painted as dastardly villains, even if no one is fooled by the masquerade. Centerstage, the events unfold in a deep penumbra; but the ferocious acts leave no shadow of a doubt.

Relieved that she's scuttled her ministerial upsets, Espinosa doesn't inquire into Leandra's artsy endeavors. When her play premieres—at the National Theater that bears his name—he's totally taken aback by the furor that ensues.

A few months later, Chiara asks Leandra whether Clementine is an accurate portrait of her cousin. The dramatist shakes her head forlornly. — I only wanted to show the sordid underbelly of this island. My stick-figure Clementine disappoints me more than I can say. There were many more layers to Celina than I could ever capture on stage.

The next morning, Leandra invites Chiara to the mansion on Río Fernando, where she now resides alone except for the staff. In all these years, Chiara has never set foot in her bedroom, off limits to everyone but her smallest children. When Leandra ushers her into the sanctum, she understands why. Drawing back a curtain at the end of the room, she unveils a shrine in her cousin's honor: an oil portrait on the wall, silver-framed photos on several shelves, and a crystal casket full of letters.

The girl was a phenomenal beauty, whose guileless expression must've goaded the tyrant's lust. Leandra lifts a sheaf of papers from the box, and reads aloud from Celina's lyrical prose: memories of their walks along grass-fringed rivers, hand in hand; romantic trips to Paris and San Francisco; a notable lack of silly chitchat about boys; passionate yearnings to hold Leandra in her arms again. Chiara urges Leandra to publish the texts, along with some of the pictures. Everyone should know what her cousin was truly like, now that the tale of her abhorrent fate has circled the globe.

Leandra laughs derisively. — What a good idea! I'd end up under surveillance, house arrest, or worse. He'd find an excuse, believe me. I've already pushed the envelope, as it is. I could easily have an 'accident,' you know. Just think of Milady… — She lapses into despondency. — People are much too nosy. Nobody could ever understand what Celina and I shared: not only was it sacred, it was unique.

From Alfonso, Carolina, and many others, Chiara has heard how badly the landowners fared during the darkest years of the terror. But Luz Divina's reminiscences give her another slant on the period. It so happens that her housekeeper's uncle worked as the overseer on the Orellana estate, in the province of Cipango—not far from Esmeralda, the island's second largest city. When Celina was three or four, she was cared for by a trusted nanny, who'd been with the family for several generations; but Luz Divina served as her 'segunda niñera.' Only twelve years old herself, all she did was entertain the little girl, iron her clothes, and brush her hair. Luz Divina often describes her dense, straight tresses as 'Indian'—confirming Chiara's hunch that the Taíno genetic strain has never petered out.

Her bossy, loquacious housekeeper often prates about the carefree times in the country, before the 'rural exodus' to Puerto Indio. When her uncle gets hitched, the campesinos dance for three days in a row, only pausing to refuel on pork pilau and sweet-potato fudge. A year later, he steps on a nail, neglects to clean the wound, and dies of gangrene, his leg inflated to twice its normal size. Luz Divina always wraps up the anecdote—a set piece in her repertoire—with the same envoi. — He screams himself hoarse, and then he croaks! — Long before *Rooster Dreams*, Chiara relates the sylvan realm of Cipango to a sudden, brutal end.

Though the Clementine sequence lies at the crux of *Sueños de Gallo*, it's flanked by two other panels. The prologue harks back to the European conquest, when the Spanish enslave and decimate the Taíno. In Leandra's fable, the sinister Marqués de Cabrona, the first Governor of 'Santa Cruz'—later renamed 'St. Alban's' by the British— appears on stage in sixteenth-century dress. To Renaissance music—Victoria's dissonant 'Sancta Maria, succurre'— he ritually violates Guayacona, an Indian princess: it's a merciless display of European power. Donning beaked 'bautia' masks from Venice, his drunken lackeys cheer him on. When the girl entreats her parents to rescue her, Cabrona japes that they've sold her into bondage—in a futile attempt to save their own skins. Disconsolate, she leaps to her death from a lonely cliff, and the roiling waves wash her corpse out to sea.

In Puerto Indio, the upper crust are well aware that the Conde Del Río, the boon companion of Santiago Columbus, founded Carolina's lineage by wedding Casiguaya. She was the daughter of Synorix, the last Taíno cacique, who gifted her to the Spanish count. Despite the chieftan's pandering, he and the other nobles of his clan were burned at the stake by Santiago's successor. The grotesque auto-da-fé is pictured in one of the most celebrated illustrations of the Taíno codex, familiar to ordinary Canubans as well as to scholars throughout the world. By reenacting the Del Río story, Leandra has invested the island's history with all the poignance of a memoir.

The drama's epilogue is set in the late twentieth century. Two jaded sybarites, Georgina and Eustace, betroth their daughter, Clarissa, to an up-and-coming politico, whose complicity will help them amass even greater wealth. Marcus, the promiscuous mover-and-shaker, doesn't even pretend to love his wife: she's only a stepping stone in his career. On their honeymoon, he introduces her to sex with gingerly tact; but because their 'merger' has been so coldly arranged, to her the coupling seems as squalid as an assault. In an eerily illumined dream, after he ties her hands and feet to the four-poster bed, she fantasizes about her husband's behavior. Bizarrely, he's arrayed in camouflage fatigues, a red skullcap, orange gloves, and a yellow beak. With his claw-like fingers and rubber proboscis, he manhandles her body—discreetly clothed in flesh-colored tights onstage.

Undaunted, Clarissa bides her time. Instead of committing suicide, as her predecessors Guayacona and Clementine have done, she avenges herself by writing a play. Like Casiguaya, Celina, and Clementine, 'Clarissa' starts with a C—but now with the stern ring of 'clarity.' She exposes the misdeeds of her callous mother, her dilly-dallying father, and her dissolute spouse, who're colluding in a nexus of financial scams. Dreading imprisonment, they beg Clarissa not to mount the work; as they grovel and plead, she impassively looks on. Then, out of the blue, she blasts them with a five-minute torrent of pig-Latin obscenities, while the curtain gradually falls. Triumphantly, she frees herself from her marital yoke, her genteel bloodline, and the mincing hypocrisy of her class.

To the amusement or disapproval of the cognoscenti, Leandra caricatures the facial and gestural tics of Carolina, Adalberto, and Ángel María to a tee. To underscore her resentment, she specifies that the same older actors will take the parts of the parents in each segment. The same younger actor will portray the Marqués, Blackstone, and Marcus; while the same younger actress will interpret the roles of Guayacona, Clementine, and Clarissa. In the Canuban production, the thespians she selects bear an uncanny resemblance to their real-life models.

Leandra has lifted several pages from Jean Genet and Peter Weiss: instead of adhering to a stable chronology, she splices the three sections of the plot. Sometimes a persona will migrate from one epoch to another, in anachronistic dress. She also pays close attention to Catulo's approach in his last ballets: now and then, her players switch identities, blurring their gender and age. At her request, the designers of the Festival Catuli-ana return to Canuba, imbuing her drama with a hieratic, though natural flow. Most of all, Leandra's musical training shapes her work: as the title implies, *Sueños de Gallo* is an oneiric tone-poem, not a linear narrative.

To interweave the parallel stories further, her directions call for two ancillary stages, raised and recessed from the proscenium—where the Colonial pageant launches the show. In the central segment, as the primary cast enacts Blackstone's atrocity, a similar set of actors pantomime De Cabrona's masque on the second platform, in clownish costumes lit by blazing spots. On the same dais, above the modern-day coda of *Rooster Dreams*, the solemn jesters reprise Clementine's tale, in a rite both silent and subdued. Meanwhile, on the third scaffold—even higher and more withdrawn—marionettes limn the Colonial segment again, as a shadow-play behind a light-grey scrim. In a multi-layered 'Verfremdungseffekt,' Leandra removes the earlier vignettes to the level of myth: figments of a collective unconscious, they haunt the present all the more obsessively.

Entering from the left, Chiara is hoodless; she slides the title Chatter in the Wings *into the black rectangular frame. Entering from the right, The Male Reader replaces The Female Reader at the lectern.*

The Male Reader: This is the Eighteenth Reading.

To Chiara, the most striking facet of the play is Marcus's outlandish costume in the dream sequence. Taking their cue from the title, most people assume he's mimicking a rooster; but in that case, where's his coxcomb? As Chiara recognizes, the colors and markings are those of the Canuban woodpecker. When she quizzes Leandra, the author seems confused. — Oh yes, the bird theme. Well, Ángel María brought those beaked 'bautia' masks home from Venice when he went there on a business trip. They were already common in the sixteenth century, I've read.

A 'business trip' to Venice? How can she be so gullible? He must've gone there with one of his mistresses—or one of his male companions. — I guess your idea is that the 'gallo' is a 'pájaro,' a macho so potent he can easily flip from 'hetero' to the opposite. — Chiara bites her tongue; she's overreached herself.

Leandra seems unruffled, maybe because she's missed the point. — I found the costume in his bedroom one day, when one of the children hid in his closet. Human predators often use camouflage, and the beak and red cap reminded me of a gamecock. But what do I know? You're the one who's always toting binoculars around.

Nobody makes the link between the eye-catching outfit and the Taíno rite of passage depicted in the *True Relations*—much less the shaman's statue in the cathedral. Probably, Ángel María dons the get-up at his Mardi Gras 'areítos,' when the penthouse becomes a sandbox for his wildest experiments. Chiara is dismayed by his imprudence. Espinosa has outlawed any allusion to the final pictures in the codex, which he considers a national embarrassment.

Adroitly, she changes the subject to Brecht: she doesn't want to whet Leandra's dormant animus against her ex. Unlike many divorced couples, they haven't forced their mutual friends to choose between them. For all Chiara can tell, Ángel María might've been more 'innovative' with his wife behind closed doors than she lets on. Her vision of him as a raptor must've come from somewhere…

Predictably, the social elite care less about bird-lore and ethnography than the sensational 'who's who' of *Sueños de Gallo*. As for the pundits, they mainly question whether the work is faithful to the island's history—and to the all-important quirks of Canubanidad.

Leandra sidesteps such embroilments slyly and firmly. To the press, she avers her play has nothing to do with Canuba, much less with individual islanders. As someone who's been educated abroad from an early age, she's learned precious little about the country's past. She devised St. Alban's out of the whole cloth. Anyway, isn't Canuba itself—like any other place—an aggregate of each person's memories, illusions, and hopes? Don't all residents, and all visitors, conjure up their own distinctive island? She never meant to ground her drama in objective 'facts,' she argues; in the theatre, reality must always yield to the imagination. Leandra's youthful apprenticeship in 'la philosophie de l'art' supplies her with a stockpile of dodges and feints.

But unfortunately for her, nature imitates art. Celina hasn't told her cousin everything, as it turns out; and Leandra's account is more lifelike than she guessed. In the most harrowing scene of the drama, when the guards mistreat the boys, Blackstone guffaws so hard he has to slap his thighs and hold his sides. On a talk show, trying to ward off reprisals, Leandra cites the detail as proof that he 'doesn't correspond to any specific figure, despite what some gossipmongers have inferred.'

Indirectly, she draws a stark contrast between her brazen villain and the fussy Mr. Magoo she's dealt with in the government. But after reading her comments, a number of old-timers send anonymous letters to the papers, spelled out in block-letters they've clipped from magazines. Blackstone's hilarity echoes Espinosa's with chilling exactitude, they declare; in his salad days, he outstripped all his henchmen for sadistic mirth.

Leandra didn't experience the phase when Manfredo caroused every night with the top brass—when his cambucas sizzled the dance-floor, and he pawed every female in sight. That was when he'd strutted like the rooster of her title, the cock of the walk. She didn't stay in Canuba past the age of nine, and so missed the worst jag of his lechery; wisely, her parents enrolled her in boarding schools abroad, to shield her from the fate of Celina and countless other 'nymphettes,' as Espinosa liked to call them. In that horrific era, except for brief vacations on the Orellana estate, the two cousins kept up their intimacy by traveling in Europe or North America.

A year after the premiere of *Rooster Dreams*, Chiara is more than a little bemused when Leandra signs a film contract, though she's often inveighed that she would 'never agree to such a travesty.' It seems that even for her, Hollywood's appeal is irresistible. When the moguls finally get around to the project, at the start of the millennium, they distort the original work almost beyond recognition. Like the playwright, many of her compatriots deride the slipshod script, mediocre actors, and bland slickness of the cinematography. Adding insult to injury, the movie is shot in Bonaventura, not Canuba—for 'budgetary reasons,' or so the filmmakers claim. No doubt they suspect that Espinosa might sabotage their efforts, if they impinge on his exclusive game preserve.

Internationally, the movie's Anglo veneer allows the

tyrant to save face—an eyelash, at least. He takes comfort in the location: it resembles the lesser islands of the English Antilles, and diverts attention from Canuba. Like Antigua or St. Vincent, Bonaventura has a drier climate than Cipango, the lush region where Celina grew up. He also tries to score points by showing how unconcerned he is about the brouhaha. When cornered by a foreign correspondent, he quotes Leandra herself. — Señora Peralta Del Río has stated unequivocally that the drama, and therefore the film, has nothing to do with Canuba. At any rate, he goes on smarmily, though I'm well versed in the splendors of poesy, I'm unfamiliar with inferior arts like the theatre and the cinema.

Behind the scenes, he lambastes Ángel María for his ex-wife's 'overblown slander.' If he weren't so reliant on his protégé, he probably would've condemned them both to exile—or worse. He's never lost his capacity to maim and kill—though nowadays he executes his crimes by remote control, and without any laughs at the punchline.

In the clamor attending *Sueños de Gallo*, no one ever mentions the hoary 'demotator' by name. Broadly, the island analysts expatiate on 'caudillismo': the Latin American trend of dominion by strongmen—fascist, communist, populist, or all stripes rolled into one. Still, Leandra's sobriquets furnish a handy code for examining 'Blackstone' and 'St. Alban's,' and raking them over the coals: she's set in motion a groundswell that Espinosa can't check.

With new-found bravado, commentators point out that a caudillo's appeal springs from his presumptive virility. Blackstone humiliates the teenage brothers by proxy, to demonstrate that he's the alpha male; through his guards, he reduces them to a passive role. An editorial in the feminist weekly, *El Mujerón*, pushes the concept one step further: the fictive tyrant has emasculated all the men of St. Alban's; worst of all, the writer charges, they've renounced their own manhood without a peep. Unwittingly, they've whetted the Governor's appetite for the women he's demoted to sexual slaves.

In courtly language, but with gathering candor, elderly Canubans affirm that 'way back when, scoundrels like Blackstone' often violated under-age girls. Especially in the countryside, they report, many fathers 'offered their callow daughters to local nabobs' as a way of seeking patronage, privilege, and wealth. As for the unnamed 'leader of the pack' in the capital, he couldn't begin to accommodate all the 'tender gazelles' consigned to him by their parents, in return for preferment.

In a further sign of island glasnost, the *Clarín*, Puerto Indio's leading newspaper, sponsors a colloquy on *Sueños de Gallo*; it features the indefatigable Leandra, alongside Canuba's best-known talking heads. The symposium is such a watershed for freedom of speech that Chiara feels obliged to attend, though she's worried the panelists might miss the forest for the weeds—as at the earlier powwow on the *Verdaderas Relaciones*. In her lit-crit days, she heard enough pedantic blather at Padua and Princeton to last her for a lifetime. To hedge her bets, she sits at the back of the auditorium, so she can abscond should the need arise. And just as she foresaw, the seminar begins with some hairsplitting over 'a grave mistake, in the Prologue of the triptych, as to the number of sailors on the *Pinta*.'

But the temperature soon heats up, and she decides to linger for a while. Always irascible, Churchill Nuñez snorts that the dramatist's ruminations about the 'Clarissa syndrome' seem to come 'from another planet.' He's a chubby, punctilious little man, who dashes off articles about Canuban affairs for *The Tampa Bay Gazette*. — In your sallies to the press, Sra. Peralta Del Río, you imply that a male's amorous urges betray a wish to dominate females. — He snickers unpleasantly. — Quite the contrary, many women throw themselves at men. Everywhere in the world, every minute of the day, money, power, or prestige attract them to even the homeliest partner.

Pulling at his sparse tufts of hair, Plinio Shepard chimes in. — Of course. It's not always men who subjugate women—and adults of either gender don't always call the shots. In *El Elogio de la madrastra*, Vargas Llosa describes how a ten-year-old can manipulate a grownup erotically. He does it with a cunning motive: to have his stepmother thrown out of his father's house.

Marina Nadar, a literary journalist, seconds him. — Yes,

his title, *In Praise of the Stepmother*, is a bitter jibe. And what of the pubescent rent-boy in *The Prosecutor* by Roa Bastos, a fitting emblem of the corrupt Stroessner regime? — Nadar is a daredevil leftist; to most of the contributors, her remark seems a shade too parlous. Espinosa has often professed his fealty to the deposed ruler of Paraguay, his 'comrade in arms.'

A self-proclaimed 'anthropologist,' Udrilo Santana, is the last member of the panel to speak. He emits a weekly column called 'Island Days and Ways,' a pyrite-mine of apocryphal folklore. — You run into the problem of defining what a child is, within a given culture. When I was a lad, many found it normal for an old man to take a thirteen-year-old girl as his common-law wife. Despite your highfalutin education, Sra. Peralta Del Río, you shouldn't be so quick to denounce your countrymen. Virginia Clemm was thirteen, too, when Poe married her—and on top of that, she was his cousin. — He takes off his glasses emphatically, proud to have scored a point.

To Chiara, all this leering over relations with minors seems abject; she's equally repelled several years later, when García Márquez exalts pederasty with a fourteen-year-old 'whore' in his swansong, *Memorias de mis putas tristes*. Thankfully, Leandra challenges Santana on his own ground. — Poe lived in the mid-nineteenth century; but even so, most people were put off by his behavior. In my play, pedophilia is not the main point, 'denounced' or otherwise. I'm concerned with the craven behavior of the adults. No matter how you slice it, parents like Eustace and Georgina, who hand over their daughter to Marcus in the late twentieth century, are contemptible.

Lorenzo Díaz demurs. A prize-winning editor at the *Clarín*, he strokes his neat 'candado' goatee. — I don't know. Their strategem may seem less egregious in a culture where few taboos are attached to sex. Whether we like it or not, this is a selling point for tourism in Canuba, and the rest of the Caribbean. It's used by travel agents to lure their clients to our shores. By contrast, they never tout such 'exuberance' in the Andes or the Southern Cone…

A media consultant from Milan, Paolo Roncagliolo, suavely rises to the bait. As a tropical grace-note to his Dolce & Gabbana suit, he sports alligator flip-flops. — The Italian magazine *Turismo Sessuale* lists Thailand, Cuba, Brazil, and Canuba as its readers' top four destinations. Canuba consistently ranks high in the five categories of its annual polls, including 'nubile sex.' — He tosses this rubric off with a languid arc of his manicured hand. — These assessments have been reported in Canuban outlets many times over the years, without any protest. There are many countries poorer than yours, yet they don't flaunt their beachboy 'sanky-pankies'—an amusing term derived from the English 'hanky-panky.' I wonder, is this libertinism founded on economics, carnal generosity—or both?

Gabriel Llanos, a communications professor from the

Complutense in Madrid, draws a deep puff from his pipe. — Perhaps you Italians have more experience with that aspect of the islands than I do… But let's not fish for red herrings. I think Sra. Peralta del Río is decrying the evils of totalitarian societies, as *epitomized* by sexual exploitation. — He stabs the air. — For countries racked by oppression throughout the world, the worst nightmare has always been the torture chamber. As for child abuse, without naming names, many autocrats perpetrate it every day, by cutting funds for primary education, infant nutrition, and prenatal care.

Leandra rejoins the fray, deftly mitigating his risky words. — Some have berated me for studying abroad; but intellectuals like you have enabled me to view these issues in a wider context. It's ridiculous, as many have done, to pretend that I'm always referring to Canuba. As you've observed, Professor Llanos, I've simply tried to illustrate a general tendency. — She nods to him graciously. — Now, let's take some questions from the audience.

A gangly literature major from the University of Puerto Indio grabs a mike from one of the ushers. He reads an index-card that he's pulled from his pocket. — Hello, my name is Policarpio Reyes, and I have a comment—not a query. In *Rooster Dreams*, Blackstone's coercion of Clementine seems almost perfunctory. More revolting is his bestial laughter when he orders the guards to degrade her brothers—a heinous 'vaudeville' that lacks any aim, even the pretext of desire. Like their sister, they're treated as un-persons, toys of an indomitable will. All-pervasive, the dictator's ego abides no other. Only he—'Yo, el Supremo,' as another despot signed his decrees—has the right to be. Like a black hole, his radical negativity empties the space around him, till nothing is left but a void.

A commanding young woman takes the floor; she and the previous speaker are academic rivals—as Chiara can tell by the acid glares they trade. Not be outdone, she also comes armed with notes. — Sirena Kingston here. At the end of *Sueños de Gallo*, the catharsis of Clarissa's tirade doesn't flow from her filthy epithets, pointedly rendered in a childish pig-Latin. The clincher is the putrid subtext to which she gives voice. The victims of an overlord are always ingratiating; whether his oppression is 'hard' or 'soft,' they never say what they believe. In this as in all else, a dictator sets the tone, spouting euphemisms and double-speak, till democracy means autocracy, and the rule of law means the rule of one. — She pauses for effect, sucking in her cheeks. — But seen from another angle, maybe such strongmen are merely the pawns of history, the puppets of a bankrupt culture— figureheads of a people's inveterate sloth.

No one wants to grab that hot potato, to Leandra's relief. Hasn't the foolhardy young lady heard about Arístides Santos, an outspoken critic of the regime? After publishing two courageous articles, he perished from an implausible 'heart attack,' six or seven years ago. He was found beside a brothel, though this didn't jive with his habits. And every few months, other 'regrettable misfortunes' continue to occur…

As the afternoon wears on, the discussants get sidetracked again, chipping away at Leandra's faulty vision of the English-speaking Caribbean, or mocking her 'aversion to coitus.' One of them wisecracks that Andrea Dworkin's *Intercourse* must've been her 'bedtime reading.'

By now Chiara has had her fill of this flashback to her university past: the petty one-upmanship has degenerated into tedium, as usual. She's reminded of a former colleague, who punctuated his trivial coups d'esprit with the phrase: 'Kiss my brain!' Stealing away from the auditorium, she sees the Italian gesticulate grandly, just as he would've done back home. 'After all,' she hears him trombone, 'Columbus grew up in Genoa!' He and the Spaniard—wreathed in a Stygian mist of pipe-smoke—are boorishly ignoring their Canuban hosts. It's a fitting colophon to the rise and fall of Europe's empires, from ancient Rome to the present day.

Barataria

Entering from the left, Diana is hoodless; she slides the title Barataria *into the black rectangular frame. Entering from the right, The Trans Reader replaces The Male Reader at the lectern.*

The Trans Reader: This is the Nineteenth Reading.

Trudging home from the lecture hall, Chiara reflects glumly on the conniving ambition of Ángel María, the superficial complicity of his in-laws, and the feckless apathy of Canubans great and small. For such garden-variety turpitude, Leandra has identified a common gene. Espinosa has excoriated each and every mind, each and every heart—as surely as he once deflowered the 'gazelles' proffered by their parents. But brainwashing and browbeating aren't enough to explain the ruler's enduring popularity, especially with the working class and the country folk. In their insouciance, Canubans skip past every problem: evasion is an art they've practiced for five centuries, and which they've mastered to the nth degree.

The symposium's speculative mode is infectious; old habits take over, and she ruminates like one of the 'cultural journalists' herself. In Plaza Drake, she relaxes for a while, on her customary bench under the ficus trees. In this same spot, she's often daydreamed, while doing research on the Caribbean for her travelogues.

She remembers how the Taínos scraped together their annual tribute of gold for that first warlord, Columbus. Over time, the inhabitants of the archipelago learned to appease each successive caudillo—until obeisance, striking inward, has become a deep-seated need. *Sueños de Gallo* is a play about human rights, but not in a militant sense; despite the fierceness of Clarissa's harangue, the drama as a whole doesn't rant or proselytize. In the end, it enacts nothing more than a profound resignation: this, now this, now this—until the tyrant's subjects bow to every atrocity in advance, and self-abasement becomes their daily bread.

Chiara dismisses it as shadow-boxing when Canubans carp about Leandra's readjustments, as if she should've composed an encyclopedia entry. Why had she altered the scene to an English-speaking island? Why did the triple attack on the young people take place in the nineteenth century? Dyed-in-the-wool mythomaniacs, Canubans should hardly have balked at the blurring of fact and fiction, since this had always been their escape from a hostile world. What happens to Clementine and Clarissa could still happen to anyone in that waking nightmare, the tropical 'vida de sueño.'

Anguish instills the desire for a comforting blindness, a padding of vagueness. Maybe she's only being pompous—like the panelists—but she has to admit, to herself at least, that philology says it all. From Columbus to Franco, from Pizarro to Stroessner, from Cortez to Espinosa, Spanish has served Hispanic peoples as a dreamlike cocoon—wrapping all the Panzas and Quixotes, from generation unto generation, in a cushioning mirage. Born and bred in Sicily, nursed in its soft-edged dialect, Chiara can readily understand Canuba's dilemma. In a key passage of his novel, the Principe di Lampedusa—her cousin three times removed—spelled out her own island's comforting despair, its 'voluptuous immobility.'

Back in her sala, she inspects the obese tribe of lexicons; they line an entire shelf, sagging it down under their weight. Languages have always seemed to her like individuals, all with their own unique character. Like Italian, Spanish falls back on a foggy conditionality, an undulating bed of subjunctive and optative moods: everything may be, ought to be, might be, should be, could be, or might've been… But more radically than Italian, Spanish construes even the imperative as a subjunctive—as if no command, however urgent, could launch an action. At best, it might suggest a wish, a prelude to disappointment. So maybe we should tarry in the indeterminate, and keep adding other words.

The prolixity of Cervantes, that astonishing spinner of tales, whirls far afield from the jewel-like concision of Dante, with his stepped circles and interlocking spheres. Needless to say, there's a huge gap between Baroque open-endedness and Medieval order. But if the two literatures reached their acmes in opposing eras, there might be an underlying cause in the cultures themselves. Likewise, if Chiara elected to live on the floating island of Canuba, then this must betray an incurable ambiguity of her own.

Ineluctably, she reverts to the verbal plane. When translated, the same Thai or Urdu text is roughly a third longer in Spanish or Italian than in English or German. Both vernaculars of Latin seem to be whispering: Why not postpone resolution as long as we can? But again, the mother tongue of Cervantes surpasses that of Dante. As Chiara observed to Diana, on their way to Amado's grave: in Spanish, the same verb means 'expect' or 'wait,' since fulfillment may never come; the same noun signifies 'excitement' or 'illusion,' since every hope may be dashed; and again, the same term for a cherished 'dream' may devolve into nothing but 'sleep.'

The Hispanic temperament hovers in a cloud, where the feats a knight-errant longs to carry out—vanquishing giants, rescuing maidens in distress—become the ones he thinks he's achieved. A 'Cheapland' acquired for nothing, the 'Barataria' evoked by Cervantes is an island not unlike Canuba, modeled on the colonies of the Spanish Main. When Sancho Panza sets out to govern it, Don Quixote believes he'll set it to rights—just as Columbus speculated about his 'Asian' domain.

One day, after Don Alfonso's death, Chiara is shooting the breeze with her neighbor, Gisólogo. She alludes to Don Alfonso as a go-between, in the plot to assassinate Papito. Gisólogo winks. — Oh, sure—Alfonso Pérez Berridos… May he rest in peace. He wasn't in on that at all. But everybody let him talk, so he could feel important and brave. I guess we all want to be something we're not.

Chiara has long since lost her naiveté; she no longer takes anything for granted. Maybe her neighbor is only concocting a counter-fable, to salve his own conscience. He jerks his thumb toward the door behind him. — Papito's house was ransacked after his death, and his prize easy-chair ended up in my basement. This country is chock-full of bloody mementos, 'recuerdos de sangre.' Some of the old hit-men still rub shoulders with the families of people they killed.

As Chiara has learned, nonprofit foundations are often headed up by Espinosa's former accomplices; it's his preferred method of putting his henchmen out to pasture. Stranger still, no one seems to hold their crimes against them: you can see them making the rounds at every wedding, gala, or reception. In the same way, Sicily's mafia has always been in cahoots with politicians and the Church.

But as so often, Canuba outdoes her native island in nonchalance. The mafia's vendettas are never written off; the mobsters call each other to account, from generation to generation. More easily than Italian—and much more easily than English, German, or French—Spanish can turn any verb into a reflexive, so no one is liable for any act. Not 'I broke it,' but 'it broke itself.' Once again, Chiara shakes her head. 'Forgive and forget.' Canubans are often forced to forget, since only amnesia allows them to survive.

Ivanhoe's Den

Entering from the left, Leandra is hoodless; she slides the title Ivanhoe's Den *into the black rectangular frame. Entering from the right, The Female Reader replaces The Trans Reader at the lectern.*

The Female Reader: This is the Twentieth Reading.

Fed up with all the fracas, and wary of Espinosa, Leandra decides to move to Switzerland, where her youngest boy is attending Le Rosey. There's little to keep her on in Canuba. She's hardly on good terms with Carolina and Don Adalberto, after vilifying them in her play. Her older children side with their grandmother, the goose who lays the biggest golden eggs.

Ángel María, the dexterous alchemist, transmutes the uproar. When all is said and done, the roasting he's received in *Rooster Dreams* cements his rapport with Espinosa more firmly than ever. 'After all,' he commiserates with his boss, 'we're in the same boat.'

Leandra redoubles his luck by trading her mansion on the Río Fernando for his penthouse downtown—less in contrition than practicality. From now on, his low-upkeep apartment will be her pied-à-terre in Puerto Indio; but for most of each year, she intends to travel, ticking off the planetary sights on her bucket list. Between Petra and Angkor Wat, Antarctica and Mt. Denali, will she ever find time to write for the stage again?

Politically, Ángel María continues to maneuver in the background, undermining the 'demotator' from within. Though on the whole, his cabal proceeds smoothly, there's a pratfall now and then.

During one of Chiara's visits to her decrepit cabin on Playa Grandota, a weary stripling canters up on a bedraggled bay, its hooves trembling from exertion. 'A long trip, Señora.' He hands her a hastily scrawled letter. In rambling French, disjointed by emotion, Diana tells her that she fears for Ángel María's life. Through the grapevine, she's heard that their Italian friend is in Barlovento; she beseeches her to rush to Espada del Sur at once.

The next morning, Chiara thumbs a ride to the entrance of the estate. Thanks to a road recently built at the behest of the President's Advisor, Ángel María Domingues, the trip can now be made in less than an hour. How convenient for 'Osorio,' Chiara chuckles to herself; it's useful to have a Doppelgänger scratching your back...

She fords the river, holding her clothes above her head, and returns for the first time in several years to the earthly Eden of the 'Otters.' As she approaches the wooden house on the sweeping meadow, everything seems unchanged. The mambo is waiting for her on the verandah, as if they'd made an exact appointment. Chiara crumples beside her on a blue rattan settee, in an exhausted heap.

Diana's burnished skin and sensuous curves are as

enticing as ever. She kisses Chiara on the mouth. — I knew you'd come.

And also, exactly when.

Yes, Radio Bemba, we call it: the lips of gossipers.

What a sleuth! You follow my every move.

Diana sighs, and Chiara detects the suffering in her eyes—a silt of accumulated sorrows. — I've learned to collect information. You have to watch your back in a country like this.

'El Viejo' is a cat with nine lives. — Chiara lowers her voice. — But even he can't last forever. The question is: who's next?

Oh, I tried to start a Vodou revolution in Bonaventure, when I was young and heroic. But I was defeated by the bloodsuckers—the vampires who drain the people dry. That's why I can't go back.

I never go home, either—if it's any consolation.

Home… But do we have one? You know, I'm beginning to think the whole world is a prison, run by madmen of one kind or another. This island, first of all. — Her volume dwindles. — I always dreamt this country might become a utopia, once El Viejo was gone. Now I wonder whether the next dictator isn't just around the corner. — Her face is as unreadable as the Benin bronzes she always brings to mind.

Whatever she means, she won't elaborate. But at least they're circling back to the subject at hand. When Chiara speaks, she sounds hollow and remote, even to herself. —

Osorio. Where is he? You told me he's in trouble.

Strangely, the bogus name makes Diana start—or is it the person behind the name? She frowns. — It's an irony, isn't it? The man who'd free all the others, dragged off in chains.

To jail? On what charges?

Jail? Him? Don't be silly, Chiara. He's been kidnapped. There's a two-bit drug-runner in this province called Ivanhoe, who holds people for ransom as a sideline. Since he's the biggest landowner around, Osorio has challenged his stranglehold on the region.

So, there were turf-wars here, too—as in Sicily. Chiara recalls that the last time she chatted with Ángel María on the phone, he mentioned that 'Osorio' was going through some rough times. — Did he suspect this might happen?

Yes, a storm has been brewing for several months, and we've trained some of our helpers as bodyguards. But despite the danger, Osorio came down two days ago, hoping to surprise you. I was going to ask you to spend a few nights with us here. Well… Ivanhoe has ruined our plans. His goons forded the river, and galloped in like bats out of hell. They tied up the farmhands, wrapped Osorio in chains, and pistol-whipped his face. Then they strapped him onto a horse like a sack of coconuts. It was awful… — She quavers from head to toe. — Right before they gagged him, he told me to get in touch with you. He said you could pay them off by alerting his family. Of course, *I* can't do that. I'm nothing but his *mistress*…

From her acerbic tone, Chiara gathers the last word stands for a cruder one. — I guess he'd like to keep El Viejo in the dark.

Of course. Bien entendu. — She's almost inaudible. — This is Osorio's power base for the movement, and he can't blow his cover. He took a week's leave from the government to do some planning sessions with us here. He told his office personnel he was going on a hike in Mexico, without leaving an address. He said he wanted to be completely out of reach—to escape all the pressure for a while. If you can arrange to get him released over the next few days, nobody will notice what happened.

It makes no sense to Chiara. She whispers, too. — Won't the kidnappers look at his ID card when they empty his pockets? That will 'blow his cover' for sure.

For any eavesdropping ears, 'Rebeca' replies loudly. — Yes, he always carries his 'cédula.' You know what his full name is: Osorio Sapronilo Santos Rodríguez.

As the virtual head of state, Ángel María ordered the ID division to produce an 'alternate card' for him—an 'extra security measure,' he called it. From the sound of it, the kidnappers are petty crooks who might take his alias at face value. In Barlovento, far from television and newspapers, few people know what the eminent statesman, Ángel María Domingues, actually looks like. Despite her reluctance, Chiara acquiesces to Diana's scheme. Given her closeness to them both, what other choice does she have? Wads of money might set him free right away, and Espinosa—as well as the media—would be none the wiser.

She flies by charter plane from Barlovento to Puerto Indio, where she meets hurriedly with Palmoliva. Assuming she's never heard of 'Osorio,' much less 'Rebeca,' Chiara asks her for a loan of fifty thousand dollars to buy some land. If she waits for a bank transfer from Italy, she explains, she'll miss out on a marvelous deal. Her sisterly bond with Ángel María is enough to persuade his wife, so she doesn't need to embroider on the lie. In the munificent island tradition, Palmoliva accompanies her to their bank and withdraws the funds, without even asking for a promissory note. On top of that, since Chiara's in such a rush, she insists that she borrow one of their cars.

Now comes the hard part: finding Ivanhoe's redoubt. This Chiara can do only through some unsavory contacts 'Rebeca' has provided, and by greasing a series of palms. After a tense couple of days, holing up at Torsten's inn in Palma Verde, she's summoned to an obscure cove at Punta Tiburón, the western tip of the peninsula. She stows the bulk of the cash in the hotel safe before she sets out, and takes the added precaution of disguising herself. In her own opinion, unlike Rosalind in *As You Like It*, she doesn't look very convincing as a man; but 'all the world's a stage,' and she must press on. The campesinos who give her lifts on their horses don't seem to catch on that her whiskers are fake—or if they do, they shrug them off as a crazy gringa's caprice.

Punta Tiburón is the last untamed territory of Barlovento, with no paved roads at all. Though slash-and-burn farming has destroyed the original forest, the secondary growth is already mature. The immense cedars and samáns attain a girth of six feet, and the fig-trees trail like leafy cataracts from the mouths of limestone caves. But her pleasure in exploring this scenic frontier is undercut by her anxiety, and ominous thoughts parade through her head. What if Ivanhoe imprisons her too? Or worse? Maybe she's only walking into a trap. As she clings to her Samaritans' raw-boned waists, plodding through salty marshes and loping past waterfalls, she wonders whether she's taking friendship too far. Loyalty is one thing, but self-destruction…?

Near the meeting point, she has to fend off Ivanhoe's guards by repeating the password he sent her. The last horseman to offer her a ride is one of the capo's most shameless toadies; he refers to him only as 'The Great One'—'El Grande.' He brags that his jefe's main competitor was 'corralled' a few days earlier: from now on, Ivanhoe will go unchallenged. Thanks to the numbskull's palaver, Chiara gathers that Ángel María is still alive—not a foregone conclusion in Barlovento, where violence has spiked along with the tourist trade. When she encounters 'El Grande' later on, she has to smile at the oaf's unconscious humor:

'big' as a provincial caudillo, Ivanhoe is anything but when it comes to physical size.

The drug-lord's headquarters impress her more than she foresaw. Twisting upward from the rocky inlet—ideal for 'shipments and deliveries'—a tortuous path leads her past roughneck hoodlums to the vestiges of a Colonial fort. Behind it looms an ample cave, overgrown with vines and linked to the crumbling masonry by an iron palisade. The hideout might serve as a film-set for a B-rate spoof of *Heart of Darkness*; but Chiara hardly feels like laughing. She can anticipate what lies ahead of her: bowing and scraping, at best; rape and murder, at worst. Her only consolation is this: as a gringa, she might be worth more if she's still kicking—and still in one piece.

She navigates some hair-raising interludes, especially when one of Ivanhoe's Praetorians mistakes her for a hermaphrodite. 'I had a freak like you in the capital,' he rasps, keen to relive the thrill. But in the nick of time, the password works its magic, just as he's about to grope her.

After hours of waiting, she finally gains an audience with 'The Great One' himself. Like a bank manager, he labors at his metal desk in an anodyne cubicle, neither cave-like nor Colonial. When he stands up to shake her hand, he's barely five feet tall. His stalk-like neck doesn't seem strong enough to support his spherical head. Not one for small-talk, he mutters dryly: 'Señora Chiara, please remove that moustache.' Then he enjoins her to sit across from him while he 'does a few figures'—the weekly haul from ransoms and cocaine deals, no doubt.

They quickly arrive at an agreement. Osorio will buy no more land in the area; above all, he'll stop interfering with the local agriculture. Ivanhoe hails from a farming family himself. — My relatives are mad as hell with Osorio, and that Bono hooker he lives with. The men in our neck of the woods aren't used to taking orders from a... *black female.* — He spits out the final two terms, to underline that he could've phrased them far less politely.

So that's it: a backwater gripe, tinctured with the usual macho-racist cyanide. Osorio's cover would remain intact—for Chiara, it's one point scored.

Then the other shoe falls... — I only had that damn do-gooder picked up to teach him a lesson. But I can't let him loose unless he defrays the expenditures he's caused.

Would ten thousand do for now—then forty thousand in Palma Verde?

El Grande acquits himself in flawless bureaucratese: 'That will be quite satisfactory.'

Within an hour, Osorio is spewed from the compound like Jonah from the gut of the whale; its digestive juices have bleached him a sickly white. Chiara always assumed his 24-carat tan was natural; but in fact, it's from playing tennis and swimming outdoors. His clothes hang in tatters from his emaciated frame. Used to gourmet dishes and Château Latour, he hasn't stomached the grub in Ivanhoe's oubliette.

Diana was right: he's undergone a severe thrashing. Livid welts disfigure his swollen face, some of them badly infected. His steel-blue eyes blink vacantly in the noonday light. During the bumpy trip on horseback to the town, and from there by car to Puerto Indio, he never utters a word.

The next morning, Ángel María tells his staff that some bandits waylaid him on a back road in Mexico. They beat him up and held him captive in a jerrybuilt shack, without food or water; but after four or five days, they drank themselves into a stupor, and he escaped through the ramshackle floorboards. Some vacation, but thank God for cheap tequila! No, the Ministry of Foreign Affairs needn't file a formal complaint; after all, he went to the country incognito. Besides, he doesn't want his chums in the Mexican cabinet to know he didn't even call them. Bum luck, that's all. And now, let's get back to work.

Last Night on Earth

Entering from the left, Chiara is hoodless; she slides the title Last Night on Earth *into the black rectangular frame. From the words 'We're all fresh' to the words 'with our tears,' Ángel María's account should be chanted as a Sprechstimme recitative by the actor who pantomimes him on the mainstage. It should be accompanied by the musical ensemble. Entering from the right, The Male Reader replaces the Female Reader at the lectern.*

The Male Reader: This is the Twenty-First Reading.

He tells Chiara the inside story three weeks later; by this time, his face has almost healed. As a 'small token of thanks,' he invites her to dinner at the Mesón de Piedra, the most exclusive restaurant in Puerto Indio, housed in a restored Colonial palace. Amid the fishtail palms and coral-stone arches, the Ángel María she loves seems to bloom again. Setting aside his public persona, he speaks from the heart—about his children, his pet projects, his amorous entanglements. Now and then, Chiara detects a tremor in his virile, grainy voice.

After the meal, he takes her hands in his. The restaurant is well-nigh deserted, and they're ensconced in its quietest nook. — I'd like to tell you about Punta Tiburón, if you don't mind.

Of course, I don't mind. I spent so much time in the 'head office' there, I'm curious to know about the entrails down below...

He arches an eyebrow. — Curious, as always. — Turning earnest again, he goes on. —Well, it was a horror show—a thousand percent. But somehow, it was a breakthrough.

During the whole ride to Ivanhoe's hangout I was blindfolded, gagged, and trussed up in chains. Once we ford the river and they dump me off the horse, they jag through hairpin trails I never knew existed, unless they were faking them. It takes us forever to get there. That cruddy jeep of theirs doesn't have any springs, and I'm knocked half-senseless. For the final trek through the forest, they sling me over a horse again, like an animal fit for slaughter.

When we reach the fort, they take away my watch, my shoes, and all my clothes. They lock me up in an underground pit. It's more of a cave than a prison—just a dank, dirty hole, stinking of sweat, piss, and vomit. There isn't any light, except what comes through a narrow slit, high overhead. Once my eyes get used to the dimness, I can make out three other men lying on the floor. They're buck naked, just like me.

For a long time, nobody talks. Then one of them starts telling his story. His name is Reynaldo. He organized an illegal trip to Puerto Rico in one of Ivanhoe's boats—for himself, his wife, and a dozen other people from Cipango. But the 'damn pipsqueak' betrayed him: he stole everybody's money, and dumped Reynaldo in the clink. The other two guys, Daiyan and Corbis, are small-time pushers who've horned in on Ivanhoe's racket.

We're all fresh arrivals, and nobody can guess how long we'll stay in the pen—or if we'll ever make it out at all. Rey is a Protestant preacher, an Evangélico, and he quotes verses from the Bible to console us. Ten or twelve different Psalms, and whole chapters from the New Testament. He reels them off, and then he leads us in prayer. When he rises to his feet, we stand beside him. And while he's praying, we throw our arms around each other's shoulders. We pull together in a circle; we feel helpless and afraid, and we all started hugging.

I don't remember who gives me the first kiss, or if I can tell in the dark. All four of us are kissing, and crying like babies. They're long, deep kisses, and you feel like the other man's soul is pouring into your body. You're drinking him, and he's drinking you. We keep on for hours, sobbing, till the whole floor is wet with our tears.

The next morning, the guards find us sleeping, huddled together. They don't want us to be so friendly. Queers, they call us, kicking us in the head. Just jealous, I guess… After that, they drag us off to separate parts of the brig.

I'll never see those three men again; but this was the most awful, most beautiful night of my entire life. We're totally in the present, because none of us can predict what might happen to us next… — Ángel María leans forward confidentially. — People disappear on this island, you know. And that night could've been our last.

Overwhelmed, he pauses for a while before he goes on, still clutching Chiara's hands. He tells her about the drudgery—and the danger—of his next days in Ivanhoe's fort. Mostly he's bored stiff, counting the empty minutes until his release. He clings to the hope that Chiara will find some way to save him, without spilling the beans to Espinosa.

On and off, violence erupts: as his cellmates change, several times he's almost knifed. The guards traffic in food, girls, alcohol, drugs, or anything else the inmates can buy. Relatives send them a steady supply of dollars or escudos; the ones who're on their own have to beg, or provide 'special services' of the most degrading kind.

Punta Tiburón lies outside the judicial system, a law unto itself. Since Ángel María is effectually running the country, Chiara asks him if he plans to bring gangsters like Ivanhoe under control.

His voice diminishes to a thread. — There won't be any change until it's a total transformation. But that may happen sooner than people think…

She doesn't delve any further.

Higher Degrees

Entering from the left, Diana is hoodless; she slides the title Higher Degrees *into the black rectangular frame. Entering from the right, The Trans Reader replaces the Male Reader at the lectern.*

The Trans Reader: This is the Twenty-Second Reading.

A few months later, Ángel María rings her up around lunchtime. At first, he breathes huskily into the phone, like a stalker. She's not amused. — Cut that out, Angel Face. Or I'll hang up on you.

He laughs boyishly. — How did you guess?

Because nobody else would be so sophomoric.

Right! And to prove your point, I want to tell you all about my latest kick. I've turned into an addict! — He urges her to join him right away at his house in Cuesta India. He's decided to take the afternoon off—an unheard-of luxury for him—to acquaint her with his 'virtual pursuit.'

He can picture her sassy smirk at the other end. — Let me guess. Virtual—but not virtuous?

With his inimitable charm, he's always stood by her through thick and thin. For a decade, his lawyers have fended off Chiara's eviction by Lamia, the notorious cellist. Though the two ex-girlfriends have made up, the has-been musician still needs to sell the house, to pay the nurses and operations for her ailing relatives.

In return for his many kindnesses, Chiara has indulged Ángel María as his patient sounding board. She takes into stride whatever he cares to disclose, no matter how repugnant—though he rarely uncovers his darker side. Not that pornography, his latest fetish, offends her per se: people have to make their own choices. It's simply that like most women, she finds such films downright pedestrian. 'Sausages in motion,' she calls them; 'and a lot less exciting than choucroute.'

Inexplicably, most of her men-friends can never pile

their plates high enough. They always mansplain that males react more strongly than females to visual stimulation. Then, too, they want as much 'action' as possible; the emotional side hardly signifies—it's 'chick feed,' to hustle the partner into bed. More than once she's heard their corny quip: 'When it comes to sex, *she* asks: Why? But all *he* asks is: Where?' And when two men share a woman—or possess each other—their libidos flip into overdrive.

Hooking his computer to a wall-size screen, Ángel María fills her in: the age-old art form has been through some novel twists. Since the early nineties, 'cyber-porn' has mushroomed in North America, Europe, and Japan. Yaoi cartoons pioneer the theme; their depictions of ambidextrous eroticism are hugely popular among Japanese girls. Nipping at their heels, hendai animations—unhampered by laws about persons—allow for anything and everything.

By the end of the decade, 'educational' websites have sprung up like crazy, dedicated to the thesis that all humans are polysexual. American and European outlets, well-funded by bourgeois subscribers, have amplified the Asian prototype into a classic genre, less violent and more realistic. Their films feature human tyros in the pink of youth, expanding their appetites on the worldwide web, step by methodical step.

According to Ángel María, always a buff of financial details, the recruits who sign up are well-rewarded for their efforts. The 'impresarios' don't hurry them along, and the faint of heart can withdraw at any time. Using a nom de guerre, most trainees appear in three to a dozen episodes, lasting roughly twenty minutes each.

'This all sounds like grooming to me,' Chiara objects.

'It's more like coaching,' he counters.

While the European males look more epicene, the Americans come across as manly and clean-cut. Judging by their mannerisms of dress, gesture, and speech, they stem from middle-class backgrounds. In their initial interviews, they chat about their coursework and summer jobs, their dating habits and girlfriends. Once they get down to business, they do a solo scene, often set in a sauna or weight-lifting room. In the next few chapters, they can opt for other film 'firsts'; and in parallel sites, the girls follow a similar pattern. While the 'dudes' engage in a lot of rough-and-tumble, their feminine counterparts stick to the dreamy, soft-core mode that Chiara dislikes the least.

Like their masculine equivalents, some of the gyno-centric sites refer to themselves as 'universities,' and to the skills they teach as 'disciplines.' These institutions are a far cry from the milquetoast Princeton Chiara experienced, much less the uptight wasteland of Padua. After learning the rudiments, thousands of apprentices engage in same-gender sex for the very first time—and for a global audience. What's more, both males and females participate in cross-gender sex as lustily as before.

Ángel María is triumphant. — They're proof positive of what you and I have always known! It's not just Canuba anymore. The rest of the world has caught up with us…

Yes, the message is loud and clear. Unadulterated 'straightness,' like monotonous 'gayness,' is contra naturam.

He's baffled. — Oh, Chiara, I love it when you talk dirty.

Despite the excerpts he trots out on his giant TV—the before and after—she still balks at the concept. — Aren't these 'freshmen' and 'freshwomen' more experienced than they let on? Maybe the ingenu bit is just a pose.

Come on, I'm not that gullible. Awkwardness and bad technique are very hard to mimic. They'd have to be bang-up actors.

I couldn't have put it better myself.

Pachyderms

Entering from the left, Leandra is hoodless; she slides the title Pachyderms *into the black rectangular frame. Entering from the right, The Female Reader replaces the Trans Reader at the lectern.*

The Female Reader: This is the Twenty-Third Reading.

By chance, she's able to do some follow-up in Tanzania, while reporting on a photo-safari for *Travel Unlimited.*

A few days into the trip, she befriends one of the eco-tourists, Philippa Bracegirdle, a lecturer at the University of Sussex. As a self-proclaimed 'socio-sexologist,' Philippa is conversant with the websites. 'Oh, yes, they're all the rage,' she chats with Chiara over a nightcap, bobbing her curls and swinging her hobnail boots. 'Several articles about them have come out in the scholarly journals. If somebody wanted to revamp *The Way We Live Now*, this could really spice up the farce.'

Glad to have a listener, she takes issue with an essay in *Psycho-Salus Sexualis*, the foremost publcation in her field. The author, Fenshawe Gill, theorizes that affluent hetero youths don't engage in these self-exhibitions for money, or even for physical pleasure. Their unconscious motivation is the quest for male-male companionship, just as in ancient Greece and Rome. He cites a long list of learned examples to buttress his notion, comparing the mores of Western Antiquity, Persia, Japan, and China with those of certain Native American tribes, only to circle back to the esprit de corps of the films.

Shades of Horacio Miranda, Chiara says to herself… She jots down Philippa's remarks on several of the camp's paper napkins—grey, recyclable, and shaped like elephants.

Gill's onto something, at least, Philippa allows. Forty years ago, a popular book made quite a splash: *Men in Groups*, by Lionel Tiger. — Noting Chiara's ironic expression, she hoots. — I know, his name sounds like a joke, especially here in the Serengeti! But I swear it's bona fide. The work was an international bestseller, so academics didn't pay it any mind. Now all my colleagues admire it, with twenty-twenty hindsight. Tiger coined the term 'male bonding,' crucial to assessing 'bands of brothers' like soldiers, priests, and athletes.

As Gill points out, the websites couch their most daunting hurdles in terms of team spirit. The amateur 'models' are sportsmen by definition—otherwise their physiques wouldn't qualify. By invoking lacrosse, baseball, or rugby, the fraternal approach defuses the strangeness; playing around with men is just another game.

Chiara has already covered five or six pachyderms with wrinkly lines. Still longing for her classroom captives, Philippa forges ahead. — You may be wondering where I differ with Gill. Well, I'm sure camaraderie is part of the equation, but sensuality is based on instinct, after all. There may be a threshold to overcome, and comrades can help each other to cross it; but then gratification has to kick in. No matter what the lover's gender...

Chiara betrays no emotion, but Philippa waxes more intimate.

Hmmm... heightened endorphins. There's nature in all this, along with nurture. Tons of studies prove that bisexuality embraces a wide range of species; and also, that it's hormonally based. Gender isn't a fixed quantity, but a series of gradations. Look at our fellow primates, the bonobos. Apparently, they're almost as ambiguous as man. And woman.

She unfastens the top frog of her Cantonese shirt. Ignoring the hint, Chiara trundles off to her camp-bed alone.

Inscribed on Vellum

Entering from the left, Chiara is hoodless; she slides the title Inscribed on Vellum *into the black rectangular frame. Entering from the right, The Male Reader replaces the Female Reader at the lectern.*

The Male Reader: This is the Twenty-Fourth Reading.

When she gets back to Puerto Indio, she hands Ángel María her scribbles. He glances at them briefly, then tosses them in the trash.

Thanks a bunch, but you know I don't like that egghead stuff. Remember, I've been on plenty of athletic teams. I'm a jock myself.

You used to be. But your quarterback days at Texas A & M are ancient history. By the way, are you still indulging in—what should I call it?—'body-art'? — She sincerely hopes his fascination with web erotica has only been an 'Alterserscheinung'—a transient sign of aging. She hates to think of her friend as enslaved to adolescents of any kind, like so many men when their temples turn grey.

As to the websites themselves, she's come around to his viewpoint. These teenagers must've begun as blank slates, even if they'd ended up as textbooks. Philippa stressed the masculine 'learning curve'; but the Tiger principle governs the distaff side as well, Chiara reflects. Female bonding has been essential to all kinds of groups, from Sappho's circle to Ottoman harems; it still cements college sororities and Women's Institutes—not forgetting the 'jolly hockey-sticks' of girls' athletic leagues. This atmosphere of 'jocks on a lark' is the most appealing trait of the films Ángel María showed her, though she'd quickly tired of the beer-and-babes claptrap of the 'dudes,' and the fatuous shyness—or grating swagger—of the 'chicks.'

Still, one facet of what she saw that afternoon would haunt her for years: the conversion of the skin into a page. In the last decade, along with internet exhibitionism, 'ink' has also burgeoned. In her youth, as she recalls, only the lower rungs of society sported tattoos. Stevedores and factory-workers might've flaunted them, but not the sons of 'respectable' families. And a woman who wore one, no matter how discreet, would've stood out as a rank vulgarian—even a 'puttana.' The same was true in Anglophone countries. Nowadays, to judge by the online evidence, ink rates as 'cool' in the middle classes, for females as well as males.

Iconographically, the gender distinctions are marked. The girls prefer small flowers, hearts, and endearing animals—butterflies, teddy-bears, robins, and the like. Tucked away on their buttocks or breasts, they can only be glimpsed when they shed their underclothes. The boys, on the other hand, plump for bold typography, injected across large swatches of their skin: screeds that transform them into the flesh made word. The texts they favor take Chiara off guard: quotations from English authors, aphorisms in other languages—and above all, credos from every major faith.

Ángel María sets the speed to slow motion, so she can read each letter. In one of the clips on his screen, Shakespeare unfurls across a young man's lats and traps: 'The course of true love never did run smooth.' Somehow, as he and his 'best bud' share a voracious nymph, the warning loses its edge. In another scene, on a sinewy forearm, Tennyson mourns his Arthur: '…better to have loved and lost / Than never to have loved at all.' But the gyrations of that phrase, flexing up and down, declare the opposite: love is readily available, and no pudendum should go to waste.

Latin is the foremost foreign tongue, perhaps a throwback to high school days—though who studies it anymore? A football-player, 'Veni Vidi Vici' banding his chest, accomplishes several splashy goals; in this as well, he mimics Julius Caesar, that reputed bisexual. 'Aequitas' and 'Veritas' adorn a wrestler's thighs; a gymnast proclaims

'SPQR' across his scapula, in blue and black.

Other languages also light up the screen. A 'Midwestern meathead,' self-professed, pairs 'Heimat' with 'Gott' on his bulging calves: 'Homeland' and 'God.' At Camp Darby, outside Pisa, an army brat has ordered 'Fratello in braccia' scrawled along his ribs: a 'fraternal embrace.' Not to be outdone, a discus champ from Athens vaunts a full Psalm in Greek, tattooed in green across his back. As he launches into action, the verses quiver with a vigor all their own. They invade and inspirit his sheet of skin, that frail piece of vellum that time will grind to dust…

Some inscriptions are even more exotic: Chinese ideograms for the Taoist Dragon and Tiger, Japanese kanji for 'Beautiful Mistakes,' or Sanskrit devanagari for 'we die to be reborn.' Despite the earthiness of their couplings, the messages these champions convey are more sacred than profane, as sutra grapples with canticle, and koan makes love with Upanishad. A practitioner of martial arts spells out 'BODY' on his left digits, 'MIND' on his right. On his thighs, a pole-vaulter brags he's 'Hell-Born' and 'Heaven-Bent'—a pilgrim's progress in four words. From a bronzed washboard of abs, a portly Buddha admonishes: 'You only lose what you desire…' Each seeker of truth is a holy writ incarnate, a muscle-bound book.

An Irish Catholic from Boston—or so he claims, and his accent doesn't belie him—is the last parchment unscrolled for Chiara that afternoon, before she rushes off. Looping around his torso, a rosary in russet ink glistens with his sweat. Coursing up and down his spine, the images on his back ripple like a Titian come to life. On the nape of his neck, in shimmering robes, the Star of the Sea dances on her crescent moon, haloed on his flesh.

What's his intent, Chiara wonders, worship or blasphemy? For the youth of today, does either notion still exist?

The Sad-Faced Knight

Entering from the left, Diana is hoodless; she slides the title The Sad-Faced Knight *into the black rectangular frame. Entering from the right, The Trans Reader replaces the Male Reader at the lectern.*

The Trans Reader: This is the Twenty-Fifth Reading.

During these years, Chiara becomes acquainted with another view of youth, diametrically opposed to Ángel María's. Whereas the politician glories in the physicality of his 'champions,' as he calls them—whether female or male, on- or off-screen—Count Gustavo is even more extreme than Horacio in his 'noli me tangere' approach. The two were companions in their adolescence, when Gustavo would visit Puerto Indio to spend the summers with his great-aunt Filomena.

Whereas Horacio invited 'pulchritudinous exempla of all genders to disrobe for his delectation,' in his Latinate lingo, the Count could only abide the most beautiful. He was so aesthetically demanding that once they took off their clothes, he always found some flaw—a pimple, a mole, a hair—and summarily rejected them. This was the origin of their nicknames for each other: 'Omnilia' and 'Nihilia.' All the same, Gustavo wasn't a valetudinarian like Horacio; he often went on camping trips with Catulo in the seventies, especially along the southeastern coast of the island.

When he returns to Canuba at the dawn of the millennium, Gustavo has 'frittered away' thirty years studying in Europe, much to the disgust of his mother, Gräfin Frederica. Since the Countess is so energetic, constantly multiplying her 'boarding houses for young ladies,' such a lackadaisical son clearly disappoints her. But his laziness is trumped by his most grievous crime: he could've reaped the Del Río millions, simply by agreeing to wed Leandra. Aber nein! But no! She falls in love with him for life at the Universidad de Granada, during their daily strolls around the Alhambra Gardens. He rejects her proposal because of his 'unapplied same-sexuality,' an ideal he calls 'homo-spirituality.' For Leandra, her subsequent marriage to Ángel María has 'always lacked any intellectual core,' as she often repeats.

Frederica's disdain for her son is mutual. When Chiara first meets him in 2003, she tells him she dined at his mother's house the night before. Gustavo corrects her. — Please don't use the word 'mother' in reference to that unnatural woman, who's never felt a maternal emotion in her life. I call her my 'progenitrix.' My real mother is my great-aunt, Filomena, with whom I have the privilege of residing. I can't stand the tasteless barn of that strumpet who married my father.

Courtly and cordial, except towards the Countess, Gustavo is as lethargic as a boiled asparagus. Because of his tall, bony frame, his long, doleful features, and his chimerical views, Chiara dubs him 'the Sad-Faced Knight'—'el Caballero de la Triste Figura,' Don Quixote's main epithet. Rumor has it he's only come back to Canuba because he's squandered every last schilling of the Austrian fortune his father, the Graf von Gesichtseck, left him in 1970. Now over fifty years old, with Frederica cutting off the funds she sometimes doled out, he's forced to look for employment: a prospect far beneath his dignity. Mirabile dictu, a friend of Horacio's offers him a teaching post in philosophy at the Pontifical University in Puerto Indio.

There, he quickly hoists his oriflammes as a quixotic knight. His grand airs make him a number of vindictive enemies, especially when he denounces his fellow-academics as 'ignorant frauds.' He's taken countless graduate courses at Salamanca—the venerable university cited in *Don Quijote*—and he considers himself far superior to the ordinary professors, with their silly doctorates. 'I simply didn't bother to get one of the stupid things,' he says, without a trace of irony. The vengeful 'frauds' slip the police a bribe to search his rooms at Filomena's, where they unearth a few seeds of marijuana.

Fortunately, Gustavo's crusty Tía rescues his most prized possession, a cache of early 'physique magazines.' Tipped off about the raid by some of her sister-gossips, she rushes home in the nick of time. Later, she comments on the incident to her nephew. — I wanted to save you any embarrassment I could, my child. Some people might not understand, as I do, that your interest in boys is purely aesthetic—an appreciation for the beauties of Creation. — Ever since, he uses her euphemistic phrase as a tag for handsome youths.

His opponents merely meant to harass him: once he spends a few nights in jail, they file to have the charges dropped. The government would also prefer to keep the matter hushed up. After all, the Countess is a fixture of Canuban society; and the pious ladies of Puerto Indio view Filomena as a saint. But out of 'overriding principle,' Gustavo insists on staying in prison and going to trial. Taking his own defense, in the months-long proceedings, he advocates for the legalization of marijuana, and upholds it as 'an essential tool for developing mental clarity.' He claims that the THC in grass has helped him comprehend Fichte, Kant, Hegel, Schopenhauer, and Nietzsche; he also testifies that 'unlike the lightweights in my department, I've read all these authors in German.'

Predictably, the case causes a sensation; the papers run banner headlines, on the order of: 'Professor Weed,' 'Highbrow Flies High,' 'Philosopher's Stoned,' 'Count Hemphead,' and 'Prominent Family Goes to Pot.' When Frederica verbally pummels him on the phone about the 'unnecessary scandal,' he archly points out that he's shown tremendous restraint in court. After all, he hasn't mentioned his frequent use of mescaline, LSD, and mushroom tea to 'scale even loftier heights of contemplation.'

Like Don Quixote combating the windmills, Gustavo enjoys the thrill of opposing his enemies. But in the fray, he's lost his professorship, and so he goes back to drifting along. Since Frederica certainly didn't need it, his father, the Graf, left him all his fortune, in addition to the title. It wasn't a large sum, by European or American standards, though it would've been more than enough to live on in Canuba. Knowing his son's spendthrift ways, the Graf apportioned half the estate for his education, and the other half 'to be disbursed to him at his mother's discretion.'

Once she's obtained a notarized promise that he'll stay on the island, Frederica duly releases the remainder. But instead of leaving it in the sound investments she's chosen, Gustavo sinks everything into a small property on the southeastern shore, not far from Playa Cerrucho. He calls it 'Knossos,' in honor of Crete—'Canuba's Mediterranean twin,' he enthuses. 'I mean Knossos the way it was in ancient times, with swaying trees and babbling brooks—and not the ruin it is today, crowded with tourists.' In a lofty grove of hardwoods, beside a private beach, he builds a small but luxurious pavilion in what he calls a 'Minoan' style, inspired by his taste for the 'sublime' novels of Mary Renault.

In the end, Gustavo spends only a single weekend in his 'Cretan palace.' From his bedroom windows, he can detect the far-off wing-lights of airplanes, approaching the mega-resort up the coast: this spoils the archaic effect he's tried to create. Worse still, some Dutchmen appear on his doorstep; armed with survey maps, they announce their plan to build a casino and hotel next to his land. They advise him to sell, while the selling is good. Gustavo gullibly signs the papers, and vacates the premises that afternoon. Soon a huge parking lot replaces both the pavilion and the grove.

In the process of buying, building, and getting swindled, Gustavo has lost most of his 'meager half-fortune,' as he airily dubs it. He's also violated Frederica's financial precepts so flagrantly that she disinherits him once and for all. He's unrepentant. — Good riddance. I fully identify with Mary Stuart, who condemned her mother-in-law, Catherine de' Medici, as 'nothing but a Florentine merchant'—even if she was the Queen of France. I aspire to be as aristocratic as my father, and as retrograde as my great-aunt. Thank God Tía Filomena is here to take me in again.

Gustavo's arrogance stems from his peculiar upbringing. Much like his Aunt Filomena, his doting Austrian grandmother—his 'Oma'—satisfies his every whim. She even learns Spanish, so she can chat with him more freely. The more his mother Frederica embraces the Viennese dialect, the more Gustavo rejects it. Like his Hapsburg ancestor, Charles V, the Holy Roman Emperor, Gustavo scorns spoken German, the 'barbaric tongue of the Goths.' He reserves the written language, Hochdeutsch, which he masters to perfection, for parsing 'Teutonic thought.' From an early age, he insists on attending boarding schools in Spain, with a heavy emphasis on English. He especially favors monastic outposts with a sprinkling of North American priests, who instill in him a love of their continent's literature. Whenever she can afford it, 'Oma' sends him to New York and New England, to improve his fluency in the language.

As a result of all this pampering by his paternal grandmother and maternal great-aunt, the 'Sad-faced Knight' remains forever frozen in a state of childishness. Like an infant, he only eats a few familiar dishes; he prefers to go hungry, rather than to sample something new. It behooves Canuban hostesses to serve him one of his three favorite foods—red beans, chicken pilau, or thinly sliced Virginia ham—or else he'll gaze, through the entire meal, at an empty plate. On a higher plane, it's less irksome to pander to his pet doctrines than to question them: he's determined to be right, no matter what. Gustavo's many friends adore him because he's very affectionate to those he loves, but only if they recognize his absolute dominion.

One morning, Gustavo invites Chiara to visit a curious chapel he's discovered, in an obscure street of the Old Quarter. Built in the sixteenth century, and now absorbed into a private house, its stone carvings combine several Catholic saints with the signs of the Zodiac—a clear intrusion of humanist trends. As they turn north into a crooked lane of crumbling stone cottages, he's reached the end of his limited energies, and apologizes for his increasingly slower pace. She suggests that they should part ways, so he can go home to rest, but he dictates otherwise. — I *am* home, and you're invited to have lunch with me and my great-aunt.

He opens a tiny, wrought-iron gate and knocks on the door of the smallest house, overgrown with white thunbergia. A young woman, Bondadosa, instantly lets them in; she's dressed in an everyday cotton dress. — No uniform, like the ones my progenitrix makes her servants wear, he whispers to Chiara. — Bondadosa leads them into a miniscule parlor, where an erect old lady sits upright amid a Victorian décor, its accoutrements unchanged for a hundred years. Chiara has no trouble in identifying her as Tía Filomena; despite her stuffy demeanor, she insists that her guest call her that, too. 'Everyone does,' she states with a sweep of her hand.

She avidly enquires about their visit to the chapel,

which interests her for religious reasons, not architectural. Her own parish church, San Lucas, is just around the
corner. But when Gustavo begins waxing lyrical about its
'barrel-vaulted simplicity,' she cuts him short. 'The building
may be lovely, but its spirit is dead.'

Gustavo raises his eyebrow. — My aunt is a firm critic of
Vatican II, and she's right. Any liberalizing movement is for
the birds, as far as we're concerned.

Filomena's face is pallid as a sheet, and dusted with tal-
cum powder; her question-mark ears stand out coyly beneath her upswept, ivory hair. Chiara gathers that she always dresses as today, in sober black, with a tall collar and
long sleeves. The repast of chicken pilau and salad is spartan enough to begin with, but she and her nephew only eat
a few mouthfuls; no wonder they both look like wire sculptures. Filomena can't see well, and her hearing has waned;
but her memory is sharp as a tack, and her sense of humor
hasn't dimmed. After Gustavo retires from the table for his
siesta, she turns downright chatty, delighted to have a new
ear for her time-worn stories.

Still livid with disgust, she tells Chiara about the 'deplorable case' of her sister, Gustavo's maternal grandmother,
who ran a dubious boardinghouse just off Plaza Catedral.
Cursed with a portentous name, Afrodite, she fell in love
with a young rapscallion from the wrong side of the tracks,
who chiefly excelled at showering women with compli-
ments. That 'wretched little man' gradually degraded her

sister from a decent girl into a charwoman, who cleaned the rooms of ne'er-do-wells and loose females. She never finished her schooling, and could barely read.

Living on her meager wages, the sleazy Romeo lazed about in bars and 'other places of ill repute,' as Filomena primly puts it. Chiara has never heard a more precise definition of a pimp, without the term being said. She doesn't confirm the rumors about her sister having served as a 'sex-worker' herself, and then a madam; but they must've reached her ears in a city like this, which gorges itself on gossip. At any rate, the identity of Frederica's father remains unknown; she was Afrodite's only child, and she left the island for Austria with a 'ski bum' when she was only sixteen.

'Oh, my sister was a goddess of love, all right,' Filomena sums up, pursing her lips. 'Unfortunately, Frederica has followed in her mother's footsteps, only on a grander scale. No amount of money or fancy titles can cover that rottenness up. As they say, you can't make a silk purse out of a sow's ear.'

The Virtue of Idleness

Entering from the left, Leandra is hoodless; she slides the title The Virtue of Idleness *into the black rectangular frame. Entering from the right, The Female Reader replaces the*

Trans Reader at the lectern.

The Female Reader: This is the Twenty-Sixth Reading.

Countess Frederica often poses as a 'Communist,' though she's a hard-working capitalist at heart. Gustavo takes the opposite tack from hers, in this as in all else; if she's a 'Leninist,' then he's 'a Czarist.' Provocative fictions aside, he does personify a uniquely Latin American trend: even nowadays, the outmoded cultivation of fin-de-siècle poets like Rubén Darío. Gustavo's melodious Spanish, rolling from his lips like waves of gold, transports the devotees of Carolina Del Rio's tertulia to the era of Enrique Rodó, the palladin of idleness.

In an influential essay, the Uruguayan condemned Anglo-Americans as technological, money-grubbing Calibans, while exalting Latin Americans as graceful, impractical Ariels, destined for leisure and the arts. This thought still comforts those who fatten on ill-gotten loot—such as corruption or narco-trafficking—in a region racked by poverty. Their privileges bespeak an innate superiority, they assume: far be it from them, for heaven's sake, to lower themselves to mundane toil. Essentially, this reflects the Spanish grandees' disdain for demeaning 'trade,' archly transposed to the New World.

In his talks at Carolina's homegrown Atheneum, the listeners can never predict where Gustavo will take them next. As an offshoot of his series on Plato and Plotinus—

whom he calls the 'twin pillars of philosophy,' pointedly snubbing Aristotle—he embarks on a month-long tangent about Greek incursions into Bactria. He bases the lectures, in part, on his own travels in the area, where he allegedly came across 'whole tribes of fair-haired people, known to be descendants of Alexander's troops.' Privately, he confides to Chiara that he only spent a few days in Afghanistan, 'what with the Russians and all,' and invented most of his account out of whole cloth. To underpin his assertions, he relies on the outdated research of a Cambridge don, Sir W. W. Tarn, and a raft of other scholars from the turn of the century.

Gustavo always prefers to cite old-fashioned historians like Faure, Macaulay, Parkman, or Michelet as his sources. 'Who cares about the 'accuracy of their data'?' he's fond of exclaiming. 'It's the elegance of their style and the breadth of their vision that count. Scientific exactitude, my friends, is nothing but cant.'

His disquisitions mirror this credo. His series on Hellenistic civilization ends with a grand, two-hour peroration on the figure of Isis. Tracing her various avatars throughout the Mediterranean, where she's often depicted with the baby Horus in her arms, he stresses her many links with ancient myths of baptism and resurrection. In a rhapsodic voice, he identifies her as 'none other than the fountainhead of all mercies, the Virgin Mother of God we still revere, hailing her in our litanies by Isis's holy name: Stella

Maris, the Star of the Sea.'

From Hellenism, Gustavo zigzags forward to the Roman Empire in the second century AD, 'when the greatness of the Occident was balanced by the greatness of the Orient: the Han Dynasty of China.' This is the epoch when he would've chosen to live, he tells his audience, under the reigns of Pius Antoninus, Marcus Aurelius, or their 'sublime predecessor, Hadrian.' He consecrates a lengthy excursus to the cult of Antinous, who was deified by the enamored emperor, after the youth's mysterious drowning in the Nile. In addition to a musty tome by Francisco del Risco y Caracol, a forgotten Spanish historian of the twenties, he draws on Marguerite Yourcenar's *Memoirs of Hadrian*—'a fiction, but truer than truth.' He also exalts Royston Lambert's 'ineffable paean to Antinous,' *Beloved and God.*

Leaping to the Middle Ages, a few months later, Gustavo analyzes the rise of monasticism and the introduction, around the year 1000, of required celibacy for priests. In a further lecture, he evaluates the differences between Western and Eastern concepts of chastity, defending virginity as a necessary component of religious life. 'The world will crumble,' he inveighs, 'when the Catholic Church permits nuns and the clergy to marry. They shouldn't submit, like ordinary riffraff, to the bestial call of the flesh.'

After this lecture, still smitten by unrequited love, Leandra asks Chiara: 'Do you suppose Gustavo is celibate, himself?'

Chiara pauses a moment, before answering. As everyone's sister confessor, she's heard about the orator's peculiar habits in detail. On the rare occasion he finds a 'nearly flawless ephebe, or close enough to bother with,' he never needs to touch him. Since no physical contact occurs, in these once-in-a-blue-moon trysts, Chiara can reply to Leandra in good conscience: 'Celibate? Oh yes… I think he is.'

Gustavo Cast Forth

Entering from the left, Chiara is hoodless; she slides the title Gustavo Cast Forth *into the black rectangular frame. Entering from the right, The Male Reader replaces the Female Reader at the lectern.*

The Male Reader: This is the Twenty-Seventh Reading.

After selling his beachside 'Minoan palace' at a cut-rate price, the Count's resources dwindle to nothing, and his sybaritic mother angrily refuses to 'subsidize his indolence,' as she puts it. For over a year, his long-suffering Aunt Filomena keeps him clothed and fed, on the meager income from her savings. But then abruptly, at the age of ninety-three, she dies in her sleep. As expected, her will names Gustavo as her universal heir; and as expected, he promptly empties her bank accounts. He also sells the trim little Colonial house where he's spent so many months. No one who knows him attributes his disposal of the property to callousness. Estranged from Frederica, bereft of his beloved aunt, Gustavo feels cast forth into a hostile world. Spoiled by his Viennese grandmother as a child, babied by Tia Fílomena as an adult, the fifty-something Count has become an overgrown orphan, mourning for his cosseted past.

Gustavo elevates his sense of vanished, infantile ease into a cultural value. When Filomena, Canuba's last Victorian, passes away, he's convinced that 'the country's quintessence has perished with her.' In a natural reflex, he flees to an earlier womb of safety: his childhood haunts in Europe. At first his paternal cousins in Salzburg and Graz receive him cordially; but soon they tire of his petulant demands. He offends his family by addressing them in English, instead of his father's native German, which he speaks fairly well when he wants. In a huff, he reverts to Spain, where he went to boarding schools from an early age. These are monastic institutions, in isolated settings; but the nearby villages are too remote for his current needs.

In the end, he rents an expensive flat in the familiar city of Granada. He did his first degree at the University there, before switching to Salamanca, for the Master's he 'never got around to finishing.' In this familiar collegiate atmosphere, the 'droves of handsome youths'—as he reports to Chiara— provide an added fillip. Then, too, he wants to imagine the bygone pageants and masked balls at the palace of his ancestor, Emperor Charles V. Fired by anti-Muslim zeal, he's always disdained the Alhambra's Moorish architecture; he much prefers its Renaissance wing—especially the pillared, circular courtyard.

For several weeks, he repairs to that spot each day; after lunch, he also takes a stroll around the Generalife Gardens, where he and Leandra used to chat, now 'rife with the plash of fountains and warbles of spring.' But one afternoon, as he gazes from a flowered walk at the snowy peaks of the Sierra Nevada, he slips down a treacherous, inward slope. He's reminded of a Hopkins line he learned in secondary school: 'Oh the mind, mind has mountains: cliffs of fall…' Those he finds inside him don't lift their summits to the sky, like the Sierra's; they tumble down, cliff after cliff, to a bottomless abyss.

As he describes it to Chiara later, he suddenly realizes suicide is what he most desires: it's the only conclusion that makes any sense to him now. He decides to spend every peseta in his account on a final voyage, and then to 'bid the world farewell.' Coldly, dispassionately, he'll do away with everything he has, capping the spree by expending life itself.

He breaks the lease on his apartment, and forfeits five months of rent. In first-class, he flies to Rome, where he takes a suite at the Bernini-Bristol. He dawdles all day at the Vatican Museums, contemplating the statues of Hadrian and Antinous; he whiles away his evenings at a high-end brothel, splashing Madeira on the 'flanks of ravishing ephebes.' Restless again, he sails across the 'sapphire Mediterranean' to mythic Byzantium, and disembarks in the tumult of a modern Turkish city. Amid the 'junk construction' of Istanbul, as he calls it, a few patches of tesserae, like Hagia Sophia, are all that remain of his mosaic-encrusted dream. Despairing of any relief, he 'disavows both the Empire of the West and the Empire of the East,' and returns to the New World.

Installed in a room at the Mark Hopkins, he finds that San Francisco 'strangely uplifts' his disintegrating mind. He strolls for hours along the Marina, watching the multicolored kites as they soar and plunge. But just as he regains an even keel, he notices his funds are running short; in a matter of months, he's exhausted Filomena's savings of seventy years. All the same, he's stopped slipping deeper into the abyss. If he continues toward the West, till the sun flips sides and shines on the East, his balance might be restored. He presses on to Thailand, by tourist-class airfare—all he can now afford.

In Krung Thep—known to outsiders as Bangkok—he succumbs to his usual illusions, seeking by turn the elusive spirit and the distanced flesh. In the brothel district, he's amused by several well-lit shows, where boys dance in bikinis to hawk their wares. Each one sports a number on his translucent scrap of cloth. Clients ask for 'number 12,' or 'number 34,' and take the hustlers to convenient upper rooms. Flirting with some of them, Gustavo learns they alternate their sex-work in Bangkok with sojourns as novices in rural monasteries. Their offhand attitude, 'sanely removed from Christian guilt,' inspires him; he decides to follow their example, hoping that meditation will soothe his nerves.

At Khu Khan Temple, the largest in the city, he asks the priests to recommend a devotional retreat. The smiling clerics confer in their irrepressible idiom. Their best English-speaker enthuses: 'We've got just the place for you. It's run by British monks, though some Thais live there, too. The rituals are in Thai and Pali, but the everyday language is English. It's called the Bamboo Monastery, in the northern hills near Lom Sak.'

This news cheers him up; but then, without warning, he plummets from his inner precipice again. Almost penniless, he's staying in a fleabag hotel. The dull aimlessness of his wanderings; the struggle of tying his shoelaces in the morning; the intractability of the 'vile matter' composing the world; the squalid buzzing of the fan; the tense ticking of the clock; the meaningless patter of unknown words on every tongue—there seems to be no end to the tedium of life, and the hollowness of time. All colors, all dimensions, fade into nothingness.

Early one morning—after lying in bed for several days, without budging an inch—Gustavo fills the bathtub with tepid water, eases himself in, and slits his wrists, with a pearl-handled penknife. He feels no pain of any kind. Calmly, he watches the mirrored surface germinate, sprouting scarlet tendrils. They curl around him like liquid smoke, expanding into ribbons of pink. The table of water under his chin has turned bright red, a sunset on a lake, when he pleasantly passes out.

He wakes to find filthy rags wrapped around his wrists, and a rust-stained sheet tossed across his damp, naked body. The Chinese innkeeper is haranguing him in fractured English, his pudgy face enraged. 'You stupid a foolish man! Why you such a foolish man?' By an amazing stroke of luck—or was it misfortune?—he'd come to pester his deadbeat guest about settling the bill. Clients have to plunk the cash down in advance, and Gustavo hasn't renewed his deposit in several days. Receiving no answer to his angry knocks, the hotel-owner unlocks the door with a master key. By the time the Count comes to, an irate maid is mopping up the bloody water, and scrubbing the stains off the tub.

The innkeeper says his assistant will take Gustavo to a nearby clinic to get his wrists properly bandaged; after that, he'll have to make good on his debt, or leave right away. The Count listens passively, his sunken eyes in a total daze. But once he's been cared for by a nurse, and released from the clinic, he leaps into action. He realizes he doesn't have enough money to pay what he owes the hotel; he slips down a side street, when the assistant isn't looking. A minute later, he can faintly hear him shouting after him: by crouching down, Gustavo has blended into the crowd.

Better to lose his suitcase, than land in jail for defaulting on his debt… But where will he go? All he has are the clothes on his back, and a thin sheaf of baht in his billfold—his last remaining funds. The people on the street are staring at him, with undisguised curiosity. The innkeeper's makeshift tourniquets leaked on the way to the clinic, and the Count's shirt-cuffs are stained with blood. Nervously, he sticks his hands in his pockets. Asking directions from an English-speaker, he weaves his way toward the central bus station. He still remembers the name of that town near the Bamboo Monastery: Lom Sak. It's the only goal that occurs to him now.

At the terminal, the ticket-seller tells him it will take seven or eight hours to reach his destination, 'depending on the weather'; but luckily, the bus will be leaving in twenty minutes. The one-way fare costs him the rest of his baht: he's exhausted Filomena's legacy, down to the last satang.

The Bamboo Monastery

Entering from the left, Diana is hoodless; she slides the title The Bamboo Monastery *into the black rectangular frame. Entering from the right, The Trans Reader replaces the Male Reader at the lectern.*

The Trans Reader: This is the Twenty-Eighth Reading.

The farther he travels from the hubbub of Bangkok, the better Gustavo feels. As yellow morning molts into blue afternoon, he takes a numb, simple pleasure in the vibrant green of the rice-paddies, where slender peasants toil in conical hats. Towards evening, the bus careens along looping roads, as the landscape turns a bit hillier, and clumps of trees loom darkly at the edge of radiant fields. The bus-driver conscientiously reminds the Count to get off, when they finally reach the bustling town of Lom Sak, an island of tawdriness in a sea of rural tranquility.

To his surprise, Gustavo finds a ramshackle taxi at the station, right away. The driver understands the English words, 'Bamboo Monastery'—and away they speed, with only a hiccup or two from the ramshackle car. But when ten minutes turn into twenty, then thirty, the Count fears the driver has misconstrued his destination. Even if he hasn't gone astray, how can Gustavo pay the fee for such a long ride? He's fretting about this, when the man pulls over, seemingly in the middle of nowhere. He points to a raised path that leads across the somnolent valley, into a glistening forest of giant bamboo. 'Monastery,' he says, with a triumphant grimace. If that's true, it's certainly well hidden, the Count reflects.

Now comes the embarrassing moment: he shows the driver his empty wallet, and turns his pockets inside out. As a propitiatory gift, he hands him his Seiko watch; he pawned his Cartier in San Francisco. He adds his cheap sunglasses, too. The makeshift barter gratifies the man, who laughs and nods his head. Practiced in self-observation, Gustavo notes that he's just experienced a mild sense of relief: a positive emotion, at last—however weak. It might even be a sign of healing. He waves good-bye to the driver, and sets off down the narrow path.

Sunset is tingeing the flooded plain with pink—a gold-streaked coral that quickly deepens to red. It's a sinister reminder of his suicide attempt. But as soon as he enters the broad stand of bamboo, at the end of the causeway, Gustavo feels his cumbrous past drop from his shoulders. The stillness of untouched nature envelopes him. The winding path skirts massive clusters of tilted green poles, some as large as tree trunks; their roots trip him several times, until he learns how to detect them, under the carpet of brittle leaves. As he walks, his eyes grow accustomed to the dim, slanting light—first, from the sun's last rays, and then, from the rising moon. After he's meandered for half an hour, he catches sight of a distant beam, playing hide-and-seek behind the bamboo.

Eventually, he emerges into a long, rectangular clearing. On the far side, he recognizes the source of the will-o'-the-wisp: a bronze lantern, stocked with a chunky red candle.

It hangs at the entrance to a low, wooden building, over-flowing with the singsong chant of evening prayers. This is more like it, he sighs to himself. Instead of the clanging gongs and traffic noise that jarred him at Khu Khang, here's a peaceful, wavelike swell: a chorus, singing a cappella. It's almost Gregorian, though esoteric, too. He stands outside, a shadow among shadows, drinking in the sound, till the voices trail away. Then he taps, softly, at the frail wicker door.

He knows he must look frightful to these monks, in his blood-stained shirt. He's appeared on their doorstep like a beggar, without even a knapsack. But they don't ask for ex-planations of any kind. They simply offer him a bar of soap, an outdoor shower, a clean robe, and a place to sleep: the floor of a modest hut. The three other occupants help him lay out his mat, alongside theirs—murmuring a minimum of words, all in English, with varying accents. There's no time to find out where they're from, or who they were in their previous life, since the lights go out promptly at nine. Gustavo dozes off, and doesn't wake till the monks rise at four, to begin their next meditation: a session of Thereva-da breathing, followed by the brief, concluding chants. The breakfast at eight is eaten in utter silence.

After that, the abbot invites Gustavo to his study, 'for a little chat,' while the rest of the brotherhood do their chores. Abbot Ralston is New Zealander of fifty-odd years, with a high, marmoreal forehead, and an unruly mane of greying hair. His eyes, of an indeterminate hue, don't penetrate the Count's: they accept him—whoever he may be. His expression conveys patience and good will—a lucid awareness, incapable of shock. Gustavo tells him everything, down to the last detail.

The cleric takes such things as bikini-boys and slit wrists for granted; he later alludes to them, not without a touch of humor, as 'follies of the flesh.' The upshot is this: he welcomes Gustavo to the Bamboo Monastery, with open arms. He can stay indefinitely—as a potential novice, or merely as a guest. He's invited to participate in meditation, as well as the workaday tasks; but he isn't obliged to engage in either one. The most important job for him now is to regain his equanimity...

'Equanimity' is the abbot's favorite word, and it best describes the atmosphere of the enclave as a whole. Its fifty inmates are half Thai, and half from English-speaking countries—not only Anglo-Canada, but also Australia, Britain, Ireland, South Africa, and the States. Gustavo never finds out much about them, since they're instructed to use as few words as possible. Their lives are measured out in a perpetual round of religious practices and manual duties, on the model 'laborare est orare.' To his chagrin, Gustavo discovers that the eight o'clock breakfast—after four hours of chants and work details—is the only meal of the day. He has no appetite that early in the morning, especially for stewed vegetables over rice, the monks' staple diet. He's never believed in vegetarianism before, and these pure vegan concoctions, plunked down before him in gargantuan bowls, only confirm his distaste. He feels starved most of the time.

As for the rest of the schedule, he adheres to it vaguely, according to his moods. He can never adapt to folding his legs in the lotus position, despite the monks' encouragement. After a month, they let him sit on a miniscule bench throughout the meditation hours. He doesn't try to learn the words of the droning, sinuous chants, though he knows the language is Pali. The choruses flow by him, soothingly and superficially; quiet as a lowland brook, they eddy here and there, in distinctive melodies.

Once a week, Abbot Ralston delivers a dharma talk, on an adroitly sidestepped topic. Occasionally, he takes Gustavo to his study, for another private chat. Earlier, he was an Anglican priest: while not an expert on Plotinus or Bactria, he's delved deeply into comparative religion. With him, Gustavo can discuss Nietzsche's theories about Buddhism and Christianity, or contrast the 'Fire Sermon' with the 'Sermon on the Mount.'

Otherwise, the gaunt Canuban guest is largely left to his own devices. He gives up all pretense of meditation, which he inwardly discounts as painful and tedious. He prefers to saunter around the vast grounds of the monastery, especially the giant bamboo grove. In a quiet nook, where it borders on the foothills, he comes across a cobwebbed, older temple. There, for hours and hours, morning and afternoon, he daydreams in solitude.

As for the chores required by the rule, he's never done a stroke of manual labor in his life, and doesn't propose to start now. The most he manages is to sweep the meditation hall, from time to time, as a special concession. But none of the brothers ever complains about his shirking: apparently, the more they can serve him, the better—a principle the Count exploits to the full, as being only his due.

In the serenity of the monastic precinct, Gustavo recovers his equilibrium, slowly but surely. After six months, he feels well enough to get in touch with Puerto Indio again, by telephone. That noisy, new-fangled device is banned at the monastery; but the abbot agrees to drive him to town, on one of his occasional errands. At the public 'communications center,' he'll have a chance to call collect. The question is: call whom? Chiara may be traveling, or camping at the cave in El Silencio. Besides, since Filomena's death, what Gustavo most needs is an older female to pamper him, like her or his Viennese 'Oma.'

The senior woman in his life is now his mother, the 'progenitrix' he's always despised. But in the rosy light of retrospect, from the cushioning remove of Thailand, her harsh outline has lost its edge. Then, too, she's taken on a gilded haze. Gustavo would never admit it to anyone, above all to himself: but now that he's squandered two legacies, his father's and his aunt's, Frederica's filthy lucre beckons temptingly. In his vegan prison, behind thick bamboo bars, he longs for Virginia ham—not to mention other delights…

Far away, in Puerto Indio, the Countess sounds overjoyed to hear his voice. — Um Gottes Willen! We feared you were dead! Gustavo, my darling, mein Liebchen! — He tells her the monks have saved him from self-destruction, and that he plans to stay with them forever. — Nein, nein! You must come back. At least for a little visit, querido! She offers to pay his airfare to Puerto Indio, then send back him to Thailand, whenever he feels like returning. — Everything is different, now! Filomena turned you against me, but at last we can be mother and son! I'll treat you like the prince you are!

As Gustavo later describes it to Chiara, he now commits a 'monstrous error,' merely by saying yes. He's lured by the prospect of seeing his friends again, and of reveling in the lap of luxury. Through the local outpost of Western Union, Frederica wires him more than enough for a ticket home. Coincidentally, Abbot Ralston is slated to fly to Bangkok the following week, so Gustavo does that leg of the journey with him. Like the other monks, the equanimous New Zealander seems neither happy nor sad to bid farewell to his guest. At the airport in Bangkok, Gustavo manages to reroute his itinerary through San Francisco, instead of Los Angeles. With the funds left over from Frederica's money order, he wants to spend a few days in his favorite city, 'just to break up the long trip.'

Entering from the left, Leandra is hoodless; she slides the title Death Is a Stone *into the black rectangular frame. Entering from the right, The Female Reader replaces the Trans Reader at the lectern.*

The Female Reader: This is the Twenty-Ninth Reading.

By the time he reaches San Francisco, Gustavo is already dreading his reunion with Frederica. She incarnates everything he hates: vulgar busywork, half-witted pretension, backstabbing greed. He stays in a cheap, frilly bed-and-breakfast in the Castro, full of witty queens; but they fail to amuse him. Even the Marina with its soaring kites, the 'green island of the Angel,' and the bridges spanning the mist don't quell his waves of anxiety. After the sedative lull of the monastery, the bugbear of futility begins to haunt him again.

The gorgeous panorama of the Bay threatens to shrink, to become 'a diminished thing' —as in that wistful poem by Frost he often quotes. With furious, unaccustomed energy, he scales the hills, trying to recoup the ebbing splendor. But it sinks lower and lower, like iridescent water down a drainage pipe, leaving nothing but the crude, oily mud of the mundane. Consciousness becomes unbearable again.

On the streets of the Tenderloin, he amasses a large

quantity of valium. When he buys the first vial, he still tells himself it's only to calm a temporary panic; but soon he gives up that delusion. On his fifth night in San Francisco, he calls Chiara collect, amazed to find her at home; he chatters excitedly, without mentioning his plan. A half-hour after hanging up, he takes two grams of valium in a single dose—enough to kill a horse—and rejoices that he won't wake, ever again.

He blacks out little by little, settling into bliss. After a long stretch of darkness, he seems to start dreaming—a nightmare more vivid than day. He lies prostrate, in a sterile room somewhere, and strangers are marching in and out. He's too tired to complain, or even to lift his head from the pillow. Everything goes totally blank, for an even longer time; and then, to his immense regret, there's an orderly, and an intravenous pole.

Slowly, dreadfully, it dawns on him: he must've come back to life, though he was clinging to death. It was the stratum where he was at peace, a bedrock deeper than earth. He recalls a phrase from Stevens: 'Death is a stone.' The doctors and nurses are prying him out of the rock, wrenching him into the world like a terrified mole, unused to the light of day. Forty-eight hours later, they release him from the hospital, advising him to seek psychiatric help.

He learns the backstory from Chiara. The brief conversation with him alarmed her—more because of her friend's overwrought tone, than what he actually said. Just in case, she calls the reception desk, about two hours later, and asks to speak to the Count; the bed-and-breakfast is so simple, it doesn't have extensions in the rooms. Despite the insistent knocks of the gay couple who own the place, Gustavo doesn't respond. Frightened by Chiara's hunch about their Canuban guest, who looked very depressed that day, they resolve to open his door with an extra key. At first, they try to shake his inert form awake; but when they notice the empty vials on the night table, they realize why he isn't reacting.

In their horror and distress, they start shouting for someone to call an ambulance. Soon the whole house is in an uproar; but finally, someone has the presence of mind to dial 911. In the bedlam of people trooping in and out, Gustavo has roused slightly, enough to open his eyes for a few moments. With no-nonsense alacrity, the paramedics rush him to the hospital, where his stomach is pumped out. Hours later, when he can mumble something about the valium, the doctors marvel he's survived such a massive overdose. They call him 'a very lucky man'; but of course, he doesn't share their view. Paradoxically, he feels too morose to try to kill himself again; and so, heeding Chiara's anxious pleas, he returns to Puerto Indio.

Even boarding an airplane is a tremendous effort, at this point. When Gustavo arrives, Chiara is shocked at his condition. Bereft of his former eloquence, he searches haltingly for words, and his diction sounds as slurred as a drunkard's.

He has no option but to yield to his mother's tender mercies: now he's her captive, at last. She displays him in a canopied four-poster, like a Fabergé egg in a silk-lined box. Regrettably, Frederica takes a perverse pleasure in his misfortune: his friends can't help noting how she lords it over him, urging him to adopt 'a humility as deep' as her own. Needless to say, they have to smile at this skewed self-portrait.

Shortly after her baby's birth, the Countess effectively abandoned him, in her zeal to expand her business empire. Gustavo's paternal grandmother gladly took him in, providing him a home in her decayed Viennese 'Palais.' Unfairly, Frederica always resented that kindness, claiming that her mother-in-law, 'die alte Hexe,' turned her son against her. Later on, Aunt Filomena perpetrated the same crime as Gustavo's 'Oma, the old witch.' The Graf tried to make his son independent of Frederica, by leaving him a small fortune; but now she has him in her clutches at last. He begs her to send him back to Thailand, but she reneges on her promise. 'For your own good, 'Liebchen'!'

Mobile again, after his long convalescence, each morning Gustavo filches a little cash from his mother's purse; at compliant pharmacies, he acquires an arsenal of sedatives, tablet by tablet. Then he takes a bus to the southeast coast, to a low, seaside cliff near Playa Cerrucho—not far from where he built his 'Cretan palace.' He strips off his clothes and downs the pills with a quart of water; as soon as he starts feeling drowsy, he topples off the cliff into the waves.

Entering from the left, Chiara is hoodless; she slides the title Posthumous *into the black rectangular frame. Paragraphs five and six, and paragraph three from the end, should be chanted as a Sprechstimme recitatives by the actor who pantomimes Gustavo on the mainstage. They should be accompanied by the musical ensemble. Entering from the right, The Male Reader replaces the Female Reader at the lectern.*

The Male Reader: This is the Thirtieth Reading.

He should've drowned, or been shattered on the rocks. But at dawn, the next day, he finds himself lying on a beach, unharmed. Did he swallow seawater, after blacking out, and throw up most of the pills? Why didn't the currents carry him out farther, past salvation? An awesome, implacable force has willed him back to life again, he concludes. In a fit of primal fear, he clambers up the path from the beach, stark naked, and hails a passing car. The astonished driver gives him some work-clothes and rubber boots he keeps in the trunk; and leg by leg, the Sad-Faced Knight hitchhikes to Puerto Indio.

This time, he doesn't go to Frederica's house; instead, he knocks on Chiara's door. When he's had a few days' rest in her guest bed, she invites him up to the terrace on the roof, with its view of the cathedral. Point blank, she asks him: Shouldn't he seek some counseling, as the doctors in San

Francisco suggested?

Obviously, I'm despondent, he shrugs. But my problem isn't psychological, it's metaphysical. It's not for nothing I chose that specific place to try to end my life again.

Why? What did it mean to you?

His eyes glow. — There, many years ago on LSD, I had the most extraordinary vision of the sea. I'd been contemplating the waves for hours, and gradually moving to a new level of awareness. I could see each wave and swell as individual, all the way to the horizon, and I could hear each wave as a separate voice in an endless polyphony—millions and millions of independent strands, that also formed a whole. Suddenly, the sound stopped—the motion stopped. There was only a hum… and finally, total silence. And then an opening, a crack or fissure in this level where we are, so I witnessed the divine… an infinity of light that never blinded, that was lucid and still. It was the 'música callada,' the 'silent music' of St. John of the Cross…

He flaps his long arms, languidly. Despite herself, Chiara is reminded of the captive albatross in Baudelaire. — The divine does exist. That's the one thing I'm certain of: the divine is absolutely real. The problem is transcendence itself. I can't make that vision harmonize with this world where we live. — He gazes for a moment at the sky. — You see, Chiara, I'm a failed saint—the most useless creature that can possibly exist. I could renounce everything, if only renunciation would lift me to the heavenly sphere. I wish I could be an atheist, but I can't… That vision has cast everything else under a long, crushing shadow. In a true sense, the divine is the source of my suffering. But I'd never wish not to have known it: it's the only thing that gives meaning to my life. My gratitude for that is what keeps me going, between the wretched bouts of hopelessness.

He reaches over, and presses her hands with his. They watch as the mellow light of late afternoon creeps down the grey, crinkled slope of the weathered apse.

Chiara attempts to encourage him. — Some might say your revelation by the sea is how your particular soul apprehends God. We all conceive of him in a distinctly different way. My old friend Father Flores tells me that's only natural. After Gaza, Paul doesn't cease to be Saul. With all his hankering for laws, his wish to make others conform, he still belongs to a Hebraic tradition. He changes his aspirations, but not his fundamental being.

Gustavo takes up the point. — Yes, what a contrast we find in St. Francis… No rules and prohibitions, only a kinship with Creation. Bellini captures it so wonderfully, in the painting at the Frick, where the saint contemplates an endless landscape, at the break of day. Not only the world at dawn: the dawning of the world, in all its immensity… to spiritual eyes.

She latches on to that remark. — Clarity gives us distance from our pain. I imagine that's what you were trying to achieve in Thailand. Not necessarily through meditation.

Just through reflection on your life from a far-off place. It's like what Henry James says in a letter to Grace Norton. The wave of sadness crashes over us, it threatens to drown us: but at least, now it's transparent, now we can *see*.

You recognize my vision for what it was: a lucid perception of the true reality, not a drug-induced hallucination. — Still, Gustavo notes a certain doubt in Chiara's face. — Yes, my one great moment, and the preludes leading up to it, were all linked to drugs. But they were not illusions. I had one of those once, by a river in the mountains. I had taken acid then, too, and at one point, the boulders in the water started moving like jelly, shaking this way and that. I simply denied that silliness. I said to myself: I'm not here for psychedelic nonsense, crass tricks of the mind. And it all disappeared. You can't have these deeper insights on command, just by taking drugs. You have to prepare yourself, as the Taíno shamans did, or the Indians in North America, with purification, fasting, and concentration.

Chiara is beginning to grasp what he means. For Gustavo, drugs weren't at all 'recreational,' even when he sparingly used them to read books. Mainly, he limited their consumption to a religious context, like the Shuar-Ashuar in the Amazon, or the Crows in Montana. She remembers how Catulo once called her in a similar state of exaltation. Gustavo mentioned 'preludes' to his revelation by the sea; she asks him about those.

Again, his eyes glimmer. — My second most powerful

session occurred in the same place, along the coast near Playa Cerrucho. That's why we always called it the 'Sacred Grove.' On my vacations in Canuba, Catulo and I often went camping there, in a clearing near the road. From there, it was two or three hundred yards to the sea. Because of the way salt air stunts their growth, the tallest trees were the ones right around our camp, the farthest from the ocean. After he set up our tent, Catulo and I took some LSD one night, and suddenly it seemed like a long, long way through those big trees to the coast.

We felt like we were walking miles and miles, but we weren't tired, we were in bliss, with every sensation magnified. We took off our clothes, and peed into the underbrush, the two streams side by side. Talking about it later, we realized we'd both had the same feeling, exactly—the impression we were far above our bodies, with our minds touching the firmament. Those bodies down there no longer belonged to us; they were just tiny mechanisms, making water, like distant faucets in a sink.

He pauses, reaching back into his memory. — There was total stillness, not a breath of wind. But it was unseasonably cool, and there were no mosquitoes. We clung to each other, the effects were so strong, and we lost track of time and space... to the point when much later, we looked across the bay to the east, and saw a gleam growing there, we thought it was already dawn. Nothing surprised us. The sun was rising in the middle of the night... But it was the moon, of course; we'd forgotten there was even such a thing as the moon… And just as it started peeking over the great mass of trees, on the inlet's other shore, the wind rose precisely at that moment… so it seemed like the light was being blown, blown toward us by the breeze. The light was palpable, like wind, and the wind was shining, like light…

Just as in the 'Ode to a Nightingale,' Chiara. You must recall the words: 'But here there is no light,/ Save what from heaven is with the breezes blown…' Again, it was odd: we both felt the same sensation. And after the 'moonwind,' we were carefree, no longer afraid of the power all around us. We spent the whole night leaping on the jagged rocks, beside the sea. It hardly seems possible, but I assume we must've been levitating off the ground. We were barefoot, but the rocks didn't leave the smallest nick on our feet, after hours of running along the cliffs.

Gustavo is joyful now. Chiara has never seen him like this before. But then a shadow edges over his eyes, and he looks like the 'Sad-Faced Knight' once more. — There you have it, he says. It's the curse of having known such moments… They make the rest of your life seem empty, by comparison. Since those times, I've only led a posthumous existence. I've been dead for many, many years. My physical death will merely be an insignificant detail.

Entering from the left, Diana is hoodless; she slides the title Many Mansions *into the black rectangular frame. Entering from the right, The Trans Reader replaces the Male Reader at the lectern.*

The Trans Reader: This is the Thirty-First Reading.

Soul-searching doesn't alter one basic fact: Gustavo has no place to live. Luckily for him, Chiara has to leave for several months on magazine assignments, and he stays on in 'their' house, grumpily attended by Luz Divina. She's known him from way back, as a childhood friend of the Mirandas, long before Chiara 'inherited' her from the family. Supposedly, Gustavo plans to look for employment, while she's away; but as she helps her pack, Luz Divina scoffs at that idea. — Gustavo, work? He'll just lie around in bed all day, and live off you. He's nothing but a sponge.

At first, the Count does find a job, but only because it lands in his lap. A matronly friend of his late aunt's, who's founded an exclusive private school, hires him to teach philosophy and literature to the senior honors class. Though these are his favorite topics, and though his schedule only runs from ten to twelve AM, Gustavo soon tires of what he calls 'dry academic rigors.' On a phone call to the Outback, where she's writing about the kangaroos, he complains to Chiara about the 'gross imbecility' of his pupils. — It's disgraceful! They're more interested in Michael Jackson and Madonna, than Palestrina and *the* Madonna. — To the embarrassment of his patroness, he summarily resigns, a month after he starts. She stuck her neck out, by hiring the infamous 'Professor Weed'; now she explains his departure to the bewildered pupils, and their skeptical parents, as 'sick leave.'

From then on, as Luz Divina predicted, Gustavo idles in bed like Oblomov, reading or dozing, and employment is heard of no more. Since Chiara pays the rent, utilities, and maid service, all the Count has to provide is a little food for himself—grudgingly prepared by Luz Divina, who also does his washing and ironing. When the savings from his short-lived job peter out, he discreetly pockets contributions from his friends, broaching the topic with loud protests against his stingy 'progenitrix.' — I would never accept a penny from that woman, as much as she insists! — Having discovered his systematic raids on her handbag, Frederica is hardly likely to offer him a centavo. They revert to their former standoff, sundered by a frigid wall of silence.

This puts Chiara in an awkward position. In her absence, Gustavo has usurped her bedroom as his own. 'Their' house has no guest room—only a small maid's room at the back of the kitchen. It doesn't measure up to Gustavo's taste, and he finds it 'extenuating' to sleep on a narrow mattress. — Alas, this sublunar world has become too much of an effort for me. I feel like a Romanov in exile, utterly at sea in the grim, Darwinian struggle for existence. — To translate: he expects Chiara to stay in the kitchen, while he continues to occupy her room. He often implies that she should be grateful to maintain him. After all, isn't he descended from Charles V, the 'greatest Emperor since Hadrian himself'?

The Count's suicidal urges seem to have lapsed into a vague lassitude: that worry, at least, retreats from Chiara's mind. But Luz Divina's rage steadily mounts, day by day. — All that lazybones does is flop around. From the bed to the armchair, from the armchair to the bed. He makes me cook the same thing, over and over: chicken pilau. 'Arroz con pollo, arroz con pollo.' Aren't you sick of it Doña Chiara? That's all he ever ate when he was a boy, and he hasn't changed one bit since then.

Before long, when she comes back to Puerto Indio, Chiara feels like an interloper in her own home. With lordly benevolence, Gustavo allows her to sleep in the kitchen, like a servant who's outworn her usefulness. Now she understands why his other friends never offer to put him up, even for a night. To the most sympathetic, she suggests they should take their turn; but they always practice the Canuban art of shifting, step by step, to another subject. It's up to her, and her alone, to find another berth for him; meanwhile, he makes it abundantly clear that she's disturbing his noble routine.

As in a children's book she used to love, 'just then, something happens.' Her deliverance takes the form of a priest:

Padre Flores. She made his acquaintance long ago, and often contributes to his charities in poor neighborhoods. Earlier, he was the Canon of the Cathedral; but lately, his life has taken quite a dramatic turn. To start with, he dares to criticize the Archbishop publicly, for his deplorable role in the Fifth Centennial hype. As a result, 'White Batman' exiles him to a minor church, with only a few parishioners, where he often denounces the 'modernizing arrogance of certain Pharisees, placed far higher than they deserve.' At the end of the nineties, his estrangement from the Canuban hierarchy widens; he resigns from his duties, once and for all. To mark his independence, he grows a glossy black beard, sown with silver highlights.

To top it all off, he joins a renegade order—dismissed by the Vatican as an 'antediluvian sect'—the Brothers and Sisters of the Saints. In many ways, it's more traditional than the Church of Rome, with which it still maintains tenuous—though rocky—relations. The congregation declares itself 'the true Catholic faith,' and doesn't recognize the papacy of John Paul II as legitimate. In fact, it disavows all Roman popes since Pius XII. At the latter's death, according to the order's doctrine, their young founder assumed the triple tiara himself. Father Simon Peter wasn't elected by the College of Cardinals in Rome, of course: it was God in person—or in three Persons—who chose him directly, as the 'one, holy, catholic, and apostolic Mystical Pope.'

The only proof of this was a vision experienced by the

cleric himself—known as Pope Simon Peter I to his flock. As a Benedictine novice in Quebec, on the very night of Pius XII's demise, he was purportedly elevated into heaven, and crowned with a burning diadem of thorns. To his followers, his searing coronation symbolizes the 'agony and ecstasy' of his appointed path, in this degenerate world; despite herself, the phrase reminds Chiara of Charlton Heston, painting the Sistine Chapel in the melodramatic film. In Simon Peter's view, the reforms of Vatican II clearly prove that 'John XXIII and his wicked successors' are anti-popes. Since their 'usurpation,' the Fellowship conserves the true faith in its Mother House on the Gaspé Peninsula, as well as in its outposts throughout the globe.

Though minuscule, these convents and monasteries flourish in a score of countries, from India to Mexico—and among them, Canuba. Essentially, they compete for the same cohort as the evangelical sects: rustic, narrow-minded fundamentalists, distrustful of change. Like his papal rival at the Vatican, Simon Peter is fond of traveling to the far-flung corners of his ecclesiastical domain. One afternoon, in Puerto Indio, Padre Flores calls to invite Chiara to 'an audience' with the 'Mystical Pope,' who's deigned to bless the city with his presence. In the home of a dentist—who claims to be Moses reincarnate—the chubby pretender to Peter's throne holds forth to a sparse, but fervent, band of fanatics. Though Chiara can't imagine what a refined intellectual like the Padre sees in him, she can readily understand how this wall-eyed apostate might appeal to naïve souls with a martyr complex, who long for the simplicities of the Primitive Church.

A curious portrait of his order emerges from his fiery diatribes, skillfully interpreted from French to Spanish by Padre Flores. Pope Simon Peter I complains bitterly of a 'vicious campaign of persecution' by the government of Quebec. The courts have ruled that the order's schools don't meet basic educational standards. Why? Because they completely omit the sciences, contemned as a 'snare of Satan.' The observations of so-called 'astronomers' are indecent lies, Simon Peter blusters, to the delight of his adherents. In one of those frequent visitations with which she favors him, the Virgin herself has told him the moon is only a few miles away. 'Biology' propagates even more heinous heresies, with its 'ungodly' theory of evolution and its 'perverted prattle' about sex. Only the Lord comprehends the fearsome, miraculous conundrums of the body. Like Mary Baker Eddy, Simon Peter believes in no other doctor than prayer. The only exception, Padre Flores later confides to Chiara, is when he needs medical care himself; in that aspect, too, he resembles the Boston sibyl.

The order finds favor with gullible country-folk, in backwaters throughout the world. Here's the old-fashioned Catholicism, they assume, on which their ancestors thrived. The Brothers and Sisters of the congregation don't run around in jeans and T-shirts, or skirts and blouses, as many 'liberated' religious began to do after Vatican II. They wear traditional, ankle-length habits, hardly different from medieval garb. Full-bearded, the monks keep their tonsures neatly shaved, and the nuns never appear without starched, spotless wimples. Whole families from remote rural areas join the order—some spurred by dire poverty, as much as belief, Father Flores intimates to Chiara.

Once they enter the fold, the parents have to abjure matrimony, and live in separate cloisters, divided by gender; males and females aren't allowed to meet in private. If their paths cross in the course of their chores, former spouses address each other by their new monastic names, as though their past life together never existed. Their children become oblates of the order, brought up collectively with the orphans and runaways who swell their ranks. These 'captive minors,' as prosecutors term them, trigger many disputes with state authorities—and not only in Canada. To worldly accusations of 'child abuse' and 'school deprivation,' Simon Peter opposes 'signs of God's grace.' 'Why do the statues in our chapels weep real tears?' he asks, in one of the congregation's pamphlets. 'Why did the Virgin's image fly from Montréal Cathedral and land on our altar in the Gaspé, where she lives with us to this day?'

To Chiara, the main interest of the 'Holy Father's' talk is his colorful French; as pungent as a 'dizain' by Maurice Scève, it derives from ancient Normandy by way of his native Quebec. Just as Elizabethan English survives in

Appalachian enclaves, Renaissance French persists in the backwoods of 'la Belle Province.' For example, Father Simon Peter pronounces 'nuit' just as she's seen it written phonetically, in sixteenth-century Norman books: 'nuitte,' with a short 'i,' and a sharply sounded 't.' As for the heavenly visions, weeping statues, and flying pictures, she has her doubts: is the 'Mystical Pope' a madman, or a charlatan? Either way, she's astounded that Padre Flores—who holds a 'doctorat canonique' from France— feels drawn to this oddball, retrograde order.

Apparently, he delights in its antiquarian features, perhaps because he's something of a relic himself. His mother, a professor of literature at the Sorbonne, is related to Guadeloupian planters, cousins of the poet, Saint-John Perse; through them she met the Padre's Canuban father. She wrote her dissertation on the Christian epics of the medieval author, Chrétien de Troyes. In the controversy over Vatican II, she espoused the cause of Archbishop Lefèvre, the Swiss prelate who spearheaded a stiff resistance to the Council's reforms. His followers continue to defend the preservation of the Latin liturgy, and the maintenance of time-honored, clerical dress. In an aristocratic mode, their separatist movement parallels the peasant order of Simon Peter, and the two factions periodically flirt with a merger that might lend them greater clout in Rome.

Naturally, the sticking point always remains the same: Father Simon Peter's papal pretensions. No doubt, he values Padres Flores as a formidable tool in winning support for his global dominion—especially among upper-class, female donors. The Canuban's tanned baby-face belies the severity of his tonsure, incised like the imprint of a coronet on his salt-and-pepper hair. His amber eyes emanate kindness, and his raspberry tongue darts coyly from the neat, silky crop of his beard. In part, these traits explain why society ladies like Carolina and Frederica, who avoid 'populist cults' like the plague, dispense generous alms to Padre Flores. They relish his monthly visits to their boudoirs, hanging with pleasure on every word from his lips. On a deeper plane, they sincerely admire his selfless ministry to the destitute, in the slums of Puerto Indio. They also dispense funds for his latest project, a bee-keeping cooperative in a neglected valley, managed by an Abbey the Padre has founded there.

Chiara chalks up her meeting with the 'Mystical Pope' to the inexhaustible eccentricity of Puerto Indio. She would've dismissed it from her memory entirely, if Padre Flores hadn't appeared on her doorstep to borrow a book. In the ensuing conversation with Gustavo, it turns out the cleric shares his enthusiasm for English poetry. Striking on a Machiavellian plan, Chiara invites the good father to have lunch with them every Thursday, the day he comes to town on errands and fund-raising rounds. Despite his dubious quirks, at bottom he's driven by a genuine altruism; she only hopes he'll shed a bit of his selflessness on Gustavo, and take him off her hands. Sure enough, over the next few months, the two men's acquaintanceship evolves into an ardent friendship.

Besides Greek sculpture, the friends have in common a predilection for Church history and Palestrina. Best of all, they both incline to monastic life: and here lies Chiara's path to freedom. Gustavo balked at the Bamboo Monastery's veganism and stringent schedule; but perhaps he could adjust to the Padre's looser regime. Father Flores serves as Abbot to the order's modest confraternity, a mixture of Quebecois farmers and Canuban campesinos. From the Count's perspective, the Abbey's picture-book site should make it highly attractive, she wagers: the bee-keeping cooperative nestles in a fern-lush, river-fed valley, with a sheer, lacy waterfall at its head. Isolated for centuries, the hideaway still preserves its 'Taíno-Hispanic heritage'—as Padre Flores calls it.

When she broaches the idea of Gustavo joining his community, in a private tête-à-tête with the Padre, the big-hearted priest is frankly overjoyed. Among the rank and file of the Fellowship, he confesses, he often feels that he's 'wandering in a cultural wasteland, like the Hebrews in the desert.' It's all part of his spiritual discipline, and he's been content to 'slough off the need for intellectual, as well as material, possessions.' But at this point, after years of self-deprivation, he'd be delighted to bask in Gustavo's camaraderie. Chiara has to bite her tongue to keep from replying: Lovely, then he's all yours!

Given their friend's sloth-like inertia and childish aversion to change, she realizes only a well-concerted diplomacy will bring the move about. Fortunately, she can rely on the Padre's suave courtesy to back her up. Before long, he suggests that they visit him at the monastery, and Chiara seizes upon the offer right away. As expected, the Count balks. — It would be a trauma to travel that far. Remember what happened to Proust: he voyaged to Venice, and all he felt was disenchantment.

Padre Flores arches an eyebrow. — Ah, but life in this world always disappoints us, ever since the Fall. What does it matter where we are? Still, every now and then, the remnants of Paradise beckon—beauties of Creation that merit your gaze… I often watch them bathing, near the Abbey.

Gustavo's nostalgia is enticed. — It's been a long while since I've observed our riverine tritons, fugitives from the sea.

It's your duty, my dear friend, to go and pay them homage.

Like a three-year old on being sent to bed, the Count fixes on other objections. — I'm afraid I'd be offended by the fittings of your monastery. I went on a retreat to the Trappists once, but I didn't stay long. They used an electric bulb to light the ciborium, instead of a candle. It was atrocious!

You forget how old-fashioned our order is. We do everything by candlelight… everything but needlework. For that, we add a gas lantern.

You mean embroidery, like my grandmother in Vienna used to make?

Nothing that ornate, as a rule. We make our own habits, and patch them up when needed. But I did stitch a gold and crimson border on our festive altar-cloth. It's a floral pattern my Tante Isabeau taught me… handed down in my mother's family, ever since the Renaissance.

Hmmm… You're not vegetarians, are you? If we visit you, can I expect three meals a day? I mean, what I call 'food for Christians'?

The priest has lunched at Chiara's so often, he knows Gustavo's routine. — Oh, the Quebecois brethren like their Norman cuisine, heavy on cream. But our Canuban novices hail from the countryside here, and their favorite dish is chicken pilau. They'll gladly serve you as much as you want—two or three times a day.

Gustavo can think of no more obstacles; his curiosity is piqued. The following week, Chiara rents a car, so she can drive him to the monastery in style. Predictably, on the morning of their departure, he pretends he's sick; but she won't take no for an answer. During the entire trip, he frets about whether the monks will be clean, whether the abbey has proper bathtubs, and so on. After all, Padre Flores sometimes arrives at 'their' house all sweaty and 'odoriferous,' after laboring with his 'city flock,' in shantytowns like

Quita Sueños. For the Count, charity has to stop with the perspiration glands.

Still, once they reach the verdant valley, and he inspects his tidy cell, with its private sink and shower, he begins to warm to the Abbey. The older Quebecois brothers are dignified and silent. The Canuban novices hardly rate as 'beauteous ephebes,' but they're eager to please; sensing the Count's superior origins, they wait on him hand and foot. Above all, throughout the week, he wallows in the Padre's constant devotion. The priest indulges him so much, it almost makes Chiara laugh. At one point, she takes him aside and tips her hat to his performance. — This is just how I hoped it would turn out. You're a Viennese 'Oma'—with a beard.

Like any infant at Grandma's house, when it comes time to leave, Gustavo won't budge. — I can't bear the thought of going back to that vile city. Here, the air is pure, and I can go for long treks in the mountains.

Chiara smiles. His 'treks' are snail-like strolls of a hundred yards or so along the riverbank, till he finds a strategic bush. Hidden by its leaves, he spies on the 'peasant youths' at their evening bath, 'kouroi who stream and glisten in gilded light—living statues, you might say.'

Well, she inquires, how long would you like to stay?

I'd gladly remain forever.

If you really insist, she sighs. All right, then I have a surprise for you. Remember when I let you out of the car, and circled back to the house, just before we drove out of town?

Yes. But I've forgiven you. You left me looking at the Cathedral for a while, and that was entrancing as always.

You never asked me what I went back to fetch. It was the rest of your belongings! Luz Divina and I stowed them in the trunk, in three boxes.

How wonderful! You're absolutely telepathic. You knew I'd adore it here.

Yes, I knew… and as we speak, the Canuban brothers are taking your things up to your new room.

Fray Gustavo

Entering from the left, Leandra is hoodless; she slides the title Fray Gustavo *into the black rectangular frame. Entering from the right, The Female Reader replaces the Trans Reader at the lectern.*

The Female Reader: This is the Thirty-Second Reading.

Light as a feather, the Count's duties at the Abbey are never menial: no one dares to demean such a gentleman with dirty toil. He gives simple lessons to the novices, an hour or so a day: for these unschooled campesinos, any crumb of knowledge proves a novelty. When he feels up to it, he also aids Padre Flores with a monumental translation from French to Spanish. The priest does all the donkey-work of preparing the drafts, while Gustavo has the task of correcting his Castilian, with subtle stylistic tweaks. Needless to say, he's never learned to type—much less to handle a computer, 'that infernal machine.' So he dictates his nuances to the Padre, who enters them with angelic patience, despite his myriad other duties.

The object of their labors is a voluminous treatise of well over a thousand pages, written by Mother Lucy Paul, the Abbess at Simon Peter I's 'Holy See' in Quebec. It claims to prove, though inscriptions and documents spanning the history of Judaism and Christianity—and even remounting to Babylon, Assyria, and Ur—that God has chosen the 'Mystical Pope' as his Vicar on earth, from time immemorial. He's always been predestined to sit on the throne of the Vatican, 'now usurped by the Anti-Christ, whom the Devil has christened John Paul II.'

Innumerable prophecies have foretold the Apocalypse, and the febrile religious warns the awesome days of doom will 'begin to unfold very soon, perhaps tomorrow.' As a prelude to Armageddon, 'Pope Simon Peter I' will receive a revelation concerning the Trinity, which will 'turn the universe on its head.' The Blessed Virgin Mary will then transport him in her arms to Rome, and install him as Pontifex Maximus at the Vatican. In a simultaneous move, the Archangel Michael will snatch up the 'Polish impersonator' or his successor, and cast them down to the lowest ring of hell.

When quizzed about whether he believes these ravings, on his visits to Puerto Indio, Padre Flores always replies: 'Of course, every word!'—though with a winsome twinkle in his eye. Gustavo, questioned by phone, stonewalls: 'We're not writing the screed, Chiara, only translating it.'

Sotto voce, he tells her that the Quebecois monks are 'a study in primitivism.' — Imagine returning to the Middle Ages, in a time warp, swamped by childish superstitions. They counter any statement based on science or logic with the same refrain: 'It's a trap the Devil has laid in our path!' — Gustavo and Chiara conclude that like bigots everywhere, the friars oppose evolution, astronomy, paleontology, and other such 'delusions of Satan' because it makes them feel superior. Above all, they look forward to the afterlife: they relish the sadistic joy of sending themselves to paradise, while damning the rest of mankind to perdition.

Of course, the Count is only a would-be monk: a new circumstance shows he hasn't given up the 'things of this world.' In the nineteenth century, a precursor of the Espinosas despoiled many 'latifundistas' of their estates, and one such property belonged to a great-great uncle of Frederica's. This semi-mythical fiefdom buttresses her pretense of descending from a lineage as illustrious as her husband's. On a lark, the Countess sends the deed to her son, hoping to soften his heart. In fact, as she admits to Chiara, she considers the document worthless—and she's right.

A couple of years after Gustavo moves to the abbey, one of his distant cousins—a half-baked law student—proposes to recover the demesne. He's writing a paper about the case for one of his courses; leading Gustavo by the nose, he persuades him to do all the foot-work and research. For several months, the Sad-Faced Knight takes the whole matter very seriously. He stays with Chiara now and then in Puerto Indio, and spends hours rifling through moldy boxes at the Land Court. He unearths nothing more than two useless scraps of paper; the strongman's henchmen have destroyed everything else.

After that, for almost a year, Gustavo refuses to budge from the Abbey. — Puerto Indio has become such a dreadful place, he tells Chiara on the phone. I love only nature now. Who cares about all those thousands of acres we lost? The monastery is enough of an estate for me. — While the novices and friars labor in the apiary and kitchen garden, the Count strolls about like a country squire, whiling away the hours—just as he did in Thailand, amid the rice-paddies and giant bamboos.

In the late afternoon, his walk always takes him to the riverbank. Padre Flores alone divines his aim: to watch the local peasants as they bathe in the stream after their chores. To reach that 'scenic spot,' Gustavo has to cross a pasture, adjoining the abbey grounds. There, a broad, piebald cow grazes on crunchy stalks and succulent tufts. At first, her isolation strikes Gustavo as odd; but such is her placidity, he dismisses his misgivings. He even grows fond of her: like a dog or a cat, she seems to await his arrival eagerly. As time goes on, she positions herself closer and closer to the path; affectionately, he rubs her forehead as he passes by.

Frequently, the cow hinders his progress out of sheer excitement—just as smaller pets can get underfoot, when their master is climbing the stairs. But one day, she refuses to stand aside, so he has to sidle past her as best he can. This awkward ballet continues for a week or two—until one afternoon, he realizes she's baiting him. She won't let him squeeze by, no matter which way he dodges; every time he moves, she makes a counter-move.

Absurd though he sounds to himself, Gustavo reasons with her jestingly. — Now 'vaquita,' let me by. What are you doing to your friend? Come now, little cow.

But the more he cajoles her, the more overwrought she becomes. She presses her muzzle against his chest, several times; and finally, she deals it a sideward blow that sends him reeling onto his back. After that, she won't allow him to rise again. Crouching over the astonished Count, she uses her prickly chin to squash him down—nuzzling him with an impetus more lovelorn than aggressive. She stares at him with her huge, liquid eyes, their pupils dilated by her longing.

As from a distance, he hears some dull, cracking sounds: with a strange disinterest, he feels his ribs snapping like sticks under her weight. Only by straining against the halter around her neck can he prevent her from crushing him flat as a pancake. He spends an hour like this, thwarting her advances while night falls, and gazing surreally into her face. Degree by heated degree, the frustration of unrequited love seems to enrage the cow.

But is this love or hate? Lost in his musings about these twin emotions, he slips into a meditative funk. In her own way, so does she: her stomachs churn and her udders swell in a ruminative weir, a lactic sinkhole of emotion. His arms and chest ache, even as his mind threads a fathomless loop, beyond all space and time. Bizarrely, this most carnal of embraces culminates in an out-of-body experience.

When he's exhausted all his strength, and can't tug on the halter anymore, he starts yelling for help. Some of those same yokels, whose rinsings he's so often glimpsed, hear his hoarse, frantic cries as they finish their ablutions. Canuban country-folk don't honor animal rights, even those of their dearest mascots. They don't think twice about beating the lovesick cow with the broadside of their machetes. Finally, she turns on her attackers in fury. They yelp gleefully as she charges them, laughing at her clumsiness. Then they carry the hapless friar back to his hortus closus, safely shielded by a cinderblock wall.

The piquant story of the amorous cow and the aristocratic monk takes the media by storm; journalists interview Gustavo several times, in his private room at the Diplomatic Hospital in Puerto Indio. At great expense to the order, and under the good Padre's watchful eye, that top-notch facility keeps him interned several weeks for CAT-scans, monitoring, and initial rehabilitation. Frederica doesn't fork over a centavo for his care, and never visits her son—not even once. This willful offspring of hers, she rails, who's already disgraced her as 'Professor Weed,' can now add other sobriquets to his credits. The yellow-press headlines paste the new scandal onto the old: Pothead Priest Cowed, No Ac-Count Can't Take Heat, Beefy Mama Steams Egghead 'Fryer,' and so on.

The Schism

Entering from the left, Chiara is hoodless; she slides the title The Schism *into the black rectangular frame. Entering from the right, The Male Reader replaces the Female Reader at the lectern.*

The Male Reader: This is the Thirty-Third Reading.

One morning, while Gustavo is convalescing at the Abbey as slowly as possible, Mother Lucy Paul telephones from Quebec, to extract a pledge of dogmatic solidarity from Father Flores. She fully expects him to knuckle under, so she can glory in his submissive tones over the phone.

It seems that in the most recent conversation of the 'Mystical Pope' with the Holy Virgin, she has revealed her elevation to a higher rank. She has now been ensconced as the fourth member of the 'Quadrinity.' All the 'Cardinals' of the order, including Abbot Flores, must now formally confirm the new doctrine. In earthly terms, in her own estimation, this will allow the Abbess to inherit the tiara from Simon Peter I, and reign as the first female Pope since 'Papess Joan' in the Middle Ages—a legendary figure by whom she firmly swears.

Padre Flores repeats her assertions in a doubtful but polite voice. Overhearing the discussion, Gustavo wrenches the receiver from the Abbot, and the Count is anything but compliant. — I speak for Cardinal Flores, when I state that there's no room whatsoever for a gynecological ward in the Holy Trinity. Besides, the Padre is leaving your absurd order, forthwith. — He hangs up, before the imperious nun has a chance to reply.

In fact, the Sad-Faced Knight attaches the same emotions to Padre Flores he's invested in the other feminine figures of his life. In one version of the Count's inner script, he worships the Abbot for satisfying his every wish, like his grandmother in Vienna—or later, his Tía Filomena in Puerto Indio. In another, modeled on his mother, he resents Father Flores for any form of 'betrayal'— which means the slightest opposition to his whims. The ultimate treason—as with Frederica, in his infancy—would be abandonment.

When it first arrives—a fustian screed in fractured Latin, calligraphed on pseudo-antique parchment—Gustavo greets the Cardinals' *Doctrinalis Declaratio Unitatis* with delight. Here's the perfect excuse for Padre Flores to break with the ludicrous order of the Brothers and Sisters of the Saints. Not that he disrespects the BVM: quite the contrary. But like any other female, she has her rightful place, and it is a lesser one compared to that of the Trinity.

All the same, as staunchly as Padre Flores, Gustavo applauds the old-fashioned traits of the order: its insistence on medieval tonsures, cords, wimples, sandals, and cassocks; or its rebuff of Vatican II's encroachments on the Mass. As the Sad-Faced Knight likes to say, only 'Montini, the swine'—Pope Paul VI—would've stooped so low as to dispense with Latin, instruct officiants to turn their backs on God, or permit that 'abomination' known as the Kiss of Peace. Human contact during the liturgy is sacrilegious.

But to the Count, as to the Abbot, Father Simon Peter's novelties have also become increasingly irksome. How can the 'Mystical Pope' tolerate distaff priests, or allow equal votes to nuns in the General Chapter? All this smacks of modern feminism, an anathema to both of them: in their view, equality for women runs counter to Christianity.

On a visit to the Abbey, Chiara argues in vain for a more enlightened approach. After all, why shouldn't our concept of God include a feminine element? Why should we anthropomorphize him as a masculine persona? Obviously, the Godhead isn't male or female.

Padre Flores laughs her off. 'You're beginning to sound like Frederica.'

The mere mention of his 'progenitrix' sends Gustavo into high dudgeon. — The Word was made flesh as the Son of Man, he thunders; the Apostles were all men, and every Pope for two thousand years has been of the same gender—except the chimerical 'Papess Jeanne,' an invention of Protestant propaganda. He dismisses the Gnostics, the apocryphal gospels, Mary Magdalen, and all of that: only males can speak with authority, in heaven as on earth. On all these points, the Abbot and the Count politely disagree with Chiara. The 'Quadrinity' proposed by the *Declaratio*, they conclude, with the Blessed Virgin Mary as the Fourth Person of the Godhead, is an arrant heresy, an untruth.

There's no question of continuing with the order, the Count avers, tossing the parchment to the floor with contempt. Like all religious absolutists, he dreams of founding his own congregation, which would restore rigor and purity to a wayward world, and he assumes that Padre Flores concurs. Together, they'll declare their independence from both deluded Quebec and misguided Rome, and return to the authentic tenets of the Church.

But there's a basic hitch in Gustavo's deliberations: he longs only for Catholic orthodoxy, whereas the priest believes in Christianity itself.

To the Count, the creed consists of ancient precedents,

encrusted into a golden mosaic over the centuries. Paraphrasing Tertullian, he considers their irrationality a proof of their validity. Floating high above the quaint marquetry of dogma and tradition, he admits a few sparks of divine illumination, granted to a spiritual elite. The great mystics—Eckhart, Ruysbroeck, the 'Doctor Mysticus,' and the rest—have attained the equivalent of Buddhist nirvana: the West's 'cloud of unknowing' equals, more or less, the East's 'generative void.'

For Padre Flores, in addition to the time-honored canon and the 'unio mystica,' Christianity imposes an ethical teaching, enshrined in the Ten Commandments, the lessons of Jesus, and the injunctions of St. Paul. Gustavo appreciates the Mass as a sublime set of lyrics for Dunstable and Josquin Desprez; whereas the priest, when he celebrates the Eucharist, never doubts the Reality of the Presence he holds in his hands. Above all, he clings to the conviction that every Christian must imitate Christ, first and foremost: his benignity, his altruism—and his truthfulness.

The fundamental difference in their attitudes soon comes to the fore, when a final decision has to be reached. No, Father Flores will not sign the Cardinals' affirmation of the 'Quadrinity'—but in practical terms, what next? After consulting with Sandro Silva—the same crooked lawyer who's evicting Chiara from her house in the Old Quarter— Gustavo seizes on a double solution. By means of some bogus legal documents, it will be child's play to divest the order of its monastery in Canuba. Silva's scheme would award that property, lock, stock, and barrel, to Padre Flores and the Count.

After all, hadn't the Abbot headed up the construction of the edifice? Under the island's laws, whoever roofs a building of his own accord has become its owner. The Order might've originally bought the land, but by erecting a shelter, Padre Flores has taken possession of the parcel. Moreover, Silva brainstorms, the congregation still owes Gustavo fifty thousand dollars for his translation of Lucy Paul's book into Spanish, as the Abbot can corroborate. Since the Mother House in Quebec never paid him for his work, the Abbey and its land can be adjudicated to the Count in compensation. All the Padre has to do is put his signature to both the lawsuits which Silva has drawn up on the pair's behalf, and the attorney will take the matter from there, in the convoluted entrails of the courts. A couple of corrupt judges, who stand to gain by receiving a portion of the acreage—like the crafty lawyer himself—will sew up the deal.

As soon as Padres Flores returns from ministering to the poor in Puerto Indio, Gustavo proposes his machinations with unbridled glee. He's dumbfounded when the priest objects to such chicanery, on moral grounds. 'The other day you announced to Mother Lucy Paul that I'm leaving the order,' he goes on, in a small, tremulous voice. 'Didn't I have some say in the matter?'

You know very well you left that idiotic mafia long ago, in your heart and mind.

But where will I go? What will I do?

These are petty questions, unworthy of a daring intellectual, the Sad-Faced Knight points out. After all, he himself has repeatedly shown the courage to throw all caution to the winds. He's spent his inheritances, broken off relations with his family and friends, and strenuously tried to kill himself. Besides, those queries are answered by Silva's juridical strategy. It doesn't matter whether the Quebecois and Canuban brothers leave the premises. 'You'll stay here with me, as co-owner of the monastery and grounds,' the Count assures him. 'And we'll make do.'

It's clear to Padre Flores, even in his distress, that Gustavo would never lift a finger, and the back-breaking toil would fall to him. At best, the Count would peruse the *Georgics* for poetic aperçus on apiculture. 'I don't think I can do all the work alone, and we don't have the money to hire field-hands.'

'Then if worse comes to worse, we'll just sell the whole estate, and live off the proceeds,' the Sad-Faced Knight nonchalantly replies, with a careless wave. 'We could find another hillside somewhere, or move to Amalfi—who cares?' He's beginning to grow weary of the Padre's cavils. 'So just sign the papers, and let's set the courts into motion.'

The conscientious priest never dreamed he'd be faced someday with a vital choice between practical survival and basic honesty. As he realizes in a flash, Gustavo has placed him in the seat he himself loves to occupy: on a canoe rushing down a river of no return. Padre Flores can turn his back on the order, but he can't reject every ethical principle he's ever cherished.

I won't endorse those trumped-up documents, he meekly declares. No cash payment was ever offered to you for the translation. In any case, I never took my vows with an eye to amassing wealth: just the opposite. We have no right to this property. What you're saying is simply a pack of lies.

He doesn't care about a comfortable home or a carefree future, he continues, warming to his theme. Tempted with riches by the Prince of Darkness, our Lord said: 'Get thee behind me, Satan.' Proclaimed as the monarch of the Jews, he demurred with the Padre's favorite phrase: 'My kingdom is not of this world.'

Wretched disputes ensue, in which the Count derides the Abbot's right to any moral pretensions, after adhering to an 'illicit cult' like the order, all these years. 'A witches' coven of women's libbers!' He marshals the full force of his philosophical training to demolish the priest's jejune qualms about Silva's plan. If he can't understand the complexities of logic, Gustavo sneers, perhaps he should cede to a superior mind...

When his high-handed browbeating produces no result, the Count switches to sentimental wheedling. Why should Padre Flores discard the quiet life he and his followers have led in this idyllic setting, with its meadows along the riverbank?

What of his charming conversations about literature and art with his aristocratic friend, an authentic descendant of the Holy Roman Emperor, Charles V? How can the 'bearded grandmother' deprive the Count of his pleasant nest, where humble novices wash his clothes, clean his room, and cook his pilau, so he lives like the landed gentry—to which, by hereditary right, he belongs? Padre Flores can't conceive of such niceties, perhaps; but he should strive to maintain them for more sensitive souls.

Paralyzed by indecision, the harried priest extemporizes. He yields to one of Gustavo's lesser demands, and sends him to Quebec as his emissary before the 'College of Cardinals.' Though the Count prides himself on his diplomatic skills—'second only to those of Talleyrand'—Padre Flores has little confidence in his success. What Gustavo really seeks is a schism between the Canuban Abbey and the order, not a rapprochement. He's already started referring to their retreat as 'Avignon by the waterfall.'

In Chiara's view, the Padre merely wants to rid himself of his overbearing friend for a time, so he can reflect in peace about his future course. Only extreme desperation could induce the father to immolate a hefty portion of his meager budget—which normally would've gone to assisting the poor—on first-class airfare for Gustavo, who objects that he 'can't conceive' of traveling in a tourist cabin, 'with caged turkeys and screaming babies.' Turkeys, Chiara muses, on Air France? Maybe the human variety...

The Mother House

Entering from the left, Diana is hoodless; she slides the title The Mother House *into the black rectangular frame. Entering from the right, The Trans Reader replaces the Male Reader at the lectern.*

The Trans Reader: This is the Thirty-Fourth Reading.

Predictably, the Count finds the Mother House in Quebec repellant. He later describes it to Chiara as a cluster of unpainted cinderblock bunkers, about twenty miles west of Gaspé, the principal town of the region. As soon as he appears on the scene, the President of the 'College of Cardinals' coldly informs him of two unimpeachable truths: one, there can be no compromise on the *Declaration of Doctrinal Unity*; and two, the Count is possessed by devils, and must submit to an exorcism, straightaway. To Gustavo's horror, three of the toughest priests—former convicts, he wagers—tie him down to a table, and summon forth his demons. Because he screeches and writhes, chafed by the tethers they've tied to his wrists and ankles, they eventually claim he's been healed.

As the Count soon ascertains, the Mother House is renowned for its exorcisms. The vole-like Guest Master, Père Lazare, who shows him to his room in a moldy trailer, brags that 'millions of demons' have issued from the mouths of the local inhabitants. — I've seen people who're so fat from all the devils inside, that as soon as they rush out of them, their stomachs collapse until they're skinny as beanpoles. — He never tires of describing the gruesomeness of these fiends, as they issue screaming from the mouths of the possessed—scraggly and sinuous, humpbacked and slack-jawed, lupine and bristling, or leprous and obese. One day Gustavo asks him if he's ever, just once in his life, sensed the presence of an angel. When he replies that he hasn't, the Count cryptically observes: 'As they say, birds of a feather flock together.'

Gustavo also converses, in a mixture of English and pidgin French, with some of the shy Quebecois and Indian children whose impoverished parents have left them to the mercies of the order. These are the controversial 'oblates,' who've caused such a furor in the Canadian press, bringing down official sanctions on the Mother House for physical and mental abuse, and near-emprisonment for Father Simon Peter. The Count notes the welts on the orphans' legs: 'It's because we've been bad,' they murmur, with frightened eyes. He confirms the anti-scientific slant of the education meted out to them, which has been severely criticized by the Ministère de l'Éducation of Quebec. These pupils believe the moon is made of silver, and that the sun revolves around the earth. 'The nuns told us so,' they stammer timidly.

The formidable sisters are clearly in control, drilled into

fighting mettle by their headstrong Abbess, Lucy Paul. Despite their liberation campaign on other fronts, the nuns keep the cooking all to themselves. Mother Lucy Paul commands her subordinates to refuse Gustavo any form of nourishment, unless he punctually attends all the Masses celebrated during his stay—four a day, at 7 AM, 11 AM, 3 PM, and 6 PM. These are near-pagan rituals, in the Count's portrayal, each with twenty celebrants, both women and men, so that all the priests in the order can officiate several times a week. — With the huge altar laid out, and the forty hands moving up and down to the clang of gongs, it seems like an Aztec sacrifice! — Chiara reflects that he may be mixing cultures—though not metaphors: the Eucharist is also a sacrifice.

The priests chant in Latin, of course, but interpolate 'deviant, delusionary' passages into the usual liturgy, based on Father Simon Peter's near-nightly chats with the Virgin. Gustavo is 'honored' to dine several times with the 'Mystical Pope' himself, much diminished since his most recent visit to Canuba. He gabbles in his old-fashioned French, peppering it with bits of American slang, picked up from the cable channels he watches most of the day. Mother Lucy Paul, whose English is cuttingly precise, insists on joining them 'to translate.' She tartly cuts off the Count's attempt to plead the Padre's cause. 'His Holiness is with us a thousand per cent on the *Declaratio*,' she asserts, glaring at Father Simon Peter to make sure he holds his tongue. 'Father Flores is a blot on the order; if he doesn't sign the parchment, we will have no choice but to expell him.'

Though the ambience of the mother house is highly unsettling, almost an oxymoron of Christianity, Gustavo can't help but admire the fervor of Simon Peter's followers: the childlike sincerity of their faith disarms him. He recounts to Chiara that in their old-fashioned habits, the nuns and monks look like throwbacks to the Middle Ages. Distanced from modern times by elaborate starched coifs or well-trimmed tonsures, their solemn faces further stress their archaic air.

These religious don't stroll up to receive the Host in the palm of their hand, with the blasé gesture of most modern Catholics. Without exception, they kneel at the altar rail to take Communion; the priest places the wafer directly into their mouths, so that only consecrated hands touched it. 'I'll never forget one young monk,' the Count enthuses. 'His stark profile was plucked from an illuminated manuscript. He always dropped his head in ecstasy as soon as the Sacrament passed his lips, like a martyr decapitated for his creed.'

Throughout the lengthy Masses, the full-throated chorus never flags, belting out antiquated melodies with ardor. 'No Broadway show-tunes sully the air, like those that mar most services nowadays,' Gustavo notes with satisfaction. At the end of every Eucharist, a porcelain figure of the Christ Child is held out to the communicants, so they can kiss the hem of its garment. The inmates of the Abbey have survived Protestant iconoclasm, unchanged: when they pray to an image, they never doubt that it's actually listening—attentive to their plea, and ordained to grant it.

But that's where the sinister side of the Fellowship's atavism also creeps in. Not only does the crucifix behind the main altar of their church repulse the Count on aesthetic grounds, it weirdly embodies the cult's persecution mania. As one of the 'Cardinals' tells him, the religious fully identify themselves with this garish sculpture of a mutilated Christ, covered by putrid wounds, and with blood dripping down His limbs. 'We have been vilified, like Him,' the bearded partisan tearfully pronounces. The order's megalomania flows from a heavenly sanction, the palm of martyrdom.

In their conflicts with the Vatican and the Canadian authorities, its members never accord an iota of validity to their opponents' points of view. By celestial revelation, they simply knew that our planet is the center of the universe, the earth is flat, the world was created four thousand years ago, and so forth. Copernicus and Galileo, with their 'diabolical views,' burn in hellfire, they assure Gustavo; and as for Darwin, he slinks in the bowels of Hades, almost on a par with Lucifer himself.

All the congregation's delusions spurt from a copious source, the fertile brain of the 'Mystical Pope' himself. To curry favor with the order, the Count has to listen to tapes of his homilies, mishmashes of shopworn piety, false humility, and fervid hallucination. He also endures a surreal film that depicts Simon Peter's hagiography: his childhood in the remote countryside of Quebec, his foundation of the Order, and his subsequent rise to the 'Papacy.' He's caused statues to weep, cured invalids with a pat on the head, and conjured visions his companions could see. His certainty the House of Loreto will fly from Italy to Gaspé, on the day of the Second Coming, inspires the friars to build a cement plinth near the chapel, as the pedestal where it will land.

'His Holiness' often goes on about his chats with the Virgin, or other assorted saints. On one occasion, he tells Gustavo that an obscure figure named St. Alexander importuned him early that morning, while he was brushing his teeth. The apparition complained that the order has neglected to hang his picture on the walls of the Abbey, a grievous offense. He reminds the ersatz Pope that centuries ago, in his Italian pilgrimage on earth, his irreligious parents made him live under a stairway and drink from the gutter. Father Simon Peter commands his underlings to rectify the omission right away—and somewhere, in their files, they find an insipid portrait of St. Alexander. More than ever, the Count can only attribute the 'self-abasing loyalty' of Father Flores to a 'spiritual masochism.'

Philippe Égalité

Entering from the left, Leandra is hoodless; she slides the title Philippe Égalité *into the black rectangular frame. Entering from the right, The Female Reader replaces the Trans Reader at the lectern.*

The Female Reader: This is the Thirty-Fifth Reading.

On his return to the Canuban Abbey, Gustavo condemns the order with even more zeal than before. Now he's seen with his own eyes, he trumpets, what a devious cabal it really is. Within the ranks of the monastery by the waterfall, two distinct factions soon square off: while the Quebecois monks support the 'College of Cardinals' back home, the Canuban novices side with Padre Flores and the Count against the 'feminist heresy.'

The theology behind the wrangle means little to the campesinos who take up their cause. They simply feel more faithful to the kindly priest and his sidekick than to the foreign interlopers, who've come from God knows where. The Abbot may speak foreign languages, just like the Count—but at least both of them are half-Canuban, and both understand the customs of the country. Gustavo in particular convinces them of his authenticity. Doesn't he stroll along the river each afternoon, to enjoy the company of the local men when they bathe? And doesn't he call for plate after plate of chicken pilau, turning up his nose at that rancid

French garbage? Putrid cheese and bitter grape-juice: it's not fit for humans.

When Padre Flores refuses to support Silva's maneuvers, Gustavo takes his cue from the Canuban novices. He'll enlist their backing to make a direct appeal to the people. The simple folk in the surrounding villages will rise up in arms to prevent the order from dismissing the Abbot, whom they idolize for his unstinting charity. For years, he's provided them with much-needed medicine or food; and often, he's literally given them the clothes off his back. Faced with a popular outcry in his defense, and moved by the peasants' need for his continued aid, surely Padre Flores will change his tune...

Admittedly, the Count has never envisaged himself, even in his wildest dreams, as a rabble-rouser. And yet, as he looks back over history, there was at least one blueblood who adopted a populist stance. In his fantasies, he begins to identify with 'Philippe Égalité,' a duke of royal lineage who embraced the cause of the French Revolution, despite his cousinship with Louis XVI. The more the Sad-Faced Knight considers the present pass, the more he deems it right and just he should defend the one true Church, and rouse the peasantry to her sacred banner. After all, hadn't there always been a natural alliance between the serfs and the lords who protected them? In feudal times, all would've condemned new-fangled shams like the 'Quadrinity.'

Riding forth to battle on his own two legs, he convokes

the campesinos from the surrounding countryside. They've often seen him intone the readings in the Abbey chapel, and at times even deliver a sermon, so they think of him as a priest. Little do they know that while he does believe in a Supreme Essence, he doesn't believe in its incarnation. He's less a Christian than a Platonist—in love with the Idea, not its earthly simulacra.

The local farmers know nothing of that; to them, he's simply the right-hand man of their benefactor, Padre Flores. If he's rushing now to the father's rescue, they can only join his campaign. A thousand of them converge on the monastery, where Gustavo—standing on a table, under a luxuriant ficus tree—harangues them about the dastardly designs of Mother Lucy Paul, lambasting the 'Mystical Pope' into the bargain.

'I'm here today to warn you,' he declaims, swinging his lanky arms. 'The entire order is a snake-pit of heretics. These evil foreigners came to us from a Satanic land called Gaspé. They fooled Padres Flores and me for a while, but not anymore. There's no room for them in our Holy Church. The good Father and I are Canubans, here to defend our island from these devils.' Inflamed by his rhetoric, the crowd rampages through the Abbey; terrified, the Quebecois monks scatter into the hills. But unlike the mobs of the French Revolution, these insurgents don't do any physical harm to the clerics, or vandalize the building itself.

In his tirades, Gustavo emphasizes that Padre Flores is

the only member of the confraternity who's tried to keep it Catholic, with the aid of himself and the other Canubans. Inspired by the fraud Attorney Silva is poised to commit, he insists that the Padre will always be the rightful Abbot, whether the evil Mother House acknowledges him as such or not. But owing to the flamboyance of his exploits, 'Friar Gustavo' quickly becomes the spokesman for the monastery, and poor Padre Flores doesn't have the gumption to raise his voice.

Once again, the media has a field day with the Sad-Faced Knight. No longer 'Professor Weed'—or more recently, the 'Heartthrob of the Lovesick Cow'—he suddenly morphs into the 'Terrorist Count.' To his friends' amazement, over several months, he organizes ever-larger riots, in the backwater towns closest to the Abbey. Hoisted by strapping lads onto a makeshift dais, composed of rough-hewn tables or chairs, he incites the masses to expel the order from Canuba, without delay.

Television crews regularly film his inflammatory speeches. With his neck-tendons strained like cords, his sentences cresting in barely controlled shrieks, and his hands chopping the air spasmodically, he resembles a tall, gangly Hitler. Glued to the screen in awe, his friends can hardly recognize their lofty, mild-mannered companion of so many years. 'We must remove these monsters, by any means, legal or illegal!' he howls. 'They are the imps of the perverse, the agents of Satan on earth!' On late-night talk shows, more urbane in diction and gestures, he engages in tonier philippics.

On the sly, Gustavo has photocopied some articles from the Canadian press kept by Padre Flores; they appeared during various skirmishes between the order and the government. Anti-clerical journalists made hay of the successive scandals, diffusing whatever rumors landed on their desks; the more sensational media spiced up the stories with embellishments ad libitum. The result was a dossier that reads like a churchy version of a thriller, with a paranoid 'Pope' neglecting under-age oblates, dastardly nuns hatching conspiracies, and 'Cardinals' raving about houses propelled through space.

'Fray Gustavo' often draws on these materials as 'objective sources,' when he appears on the Canuban interview programs. The ecclesiastical starlet hasn't commanded such a wide audience since his debut as 'Count Hemphead,' during his trial for drug possession, when he defended the use of marijuana for 'contemplative purposes.' Like a latter-day Savonarola, he profits from his renewed notoriety to rail against the vanities of our time, and to call for a return to the 'childlike devotion of yesteryear.'

Much as Chiara distrusts 'Pope Simon Peter I' and his domineering henchwoman, Mother Lucy Paul, she can't agree with the Sad-Faced Knight about the Quebecois monks at the Canuban Abbey. When he decries them as vipers, he willfully ignores their sincere good works, in helping Father Flores minister to the needy. She's also troubled by his unconcern about getting the Abbot into an even deeper quagmire with the order. In his blindered view, Padre Flores wishes to deprive him of shelter because of 'obtuseness.' The Count fears losing a convenient place to live; he never stops to think that Father Flores stands to lose much more—a decade of his life, his moral compass, and maybe even his priestly vocation: his whole raison d'être.

When Gustavo visits Puerto Indio for a series of morning radio broadcasts—on a bigoted program called *Defensores de la Fe* (*Defenders of the Faith*)—he bridles at any word of sympathy for the cleric. 'Please do not attempt to excuse his idiotic stubbornness!' he exclaims to Chiara. 'He's nothing but a charlatan and a turncoat!' From her perspective, a charlatan and a turncoat are what he's refusing to become. Appealing to patriotism, in his public tirades, the Count often repeats that Canuba must eradicate the dire 'alien order' right away, if it hopes to remain the 'last island of unswerving Christians in a sea of pagan cant.' Again, it seems that he has lost his grip on reality.

Caught in the crossfire between Gustavo and the Quebecois monks, Padre Flores suddenly goes to pieces. The last straw breaks his back one morning, when Brother Jean-Marie and the Sad-Faced Knight confront him in the sanctum of his own spartan cell. The friar, Lucy Paul's staunchest supporter at the Canuban Abbey, waves the *Declaratio* in Father Flores's face, demanding he either endorse it today, or leave the order forever. The ferocious Count tugs him in the opposite direction, issuing his own ultimatum: either the Padre signs Attorney Silva's lawsuit papers forthwith, or he, Gustavo, will commit suicide by sunset.

Tussling, the two duelists stumble out of the room and down the stairs. The dithering Abbot, left alone, throws himself on his cast-iron bed and bawls like a baby; then he gets up, and starts packing his bags. When the Count sees him dragging his luggage toward the monastery jeep, he pulls at his arms and shoulders. 'You nincompoop, you gutless fool!' In the ramshackle vehicle, Fray Jean-Marie drives Padre Flores to the International Airport near Puerto Indio; at one point, he's heartened to overhear the priest murmur something about 'going to Quebec, to face the music.'

Practice

Entering from the left, Chiara is hoodless; she slides the title Practice *into the black rectangular frame. Entering from the right, The Male Reader replaces the Female Reader at the lectern.*

The Male Reader: This is the Thirty-Sixth Reading.

As soon as Padre Flores departs, the peasant rebellion led by Philippe Égalité grinds to a halt; the country folk no longer heed their firebrand, once their saint has fled. For a few more months, Gustavo tries to ward off the inevitable. Egged on by his lawyer, Silva, he fakes the Padre's signature, claiming ownership of the monastery by squatter's rights; but the land court quickly dismisses the lawsuit as invalid. Though the judges usually proceed with snail-like sluggishness, in this instance they speed through their deliberations, owing to the notoriety of the case. Since they take even more bribes and kickbacks than the other branches of the judiciary, they don't want the outspoken Count to lambaste them in the press. They make doubly sure of his discretion with a gag order: he will be jailed for forgery, if he dares to broach the subject in any public forum again.

As for the lawsuit seeking fifty thousand dollars for Gustavo's translation work, filed in a civil court, the magistrates pose the obvious question. Where is his contract with the order, to the effect he would receive those emoluments? Changing tack, his shyster attorney alleges that Gustavo is a paying lodger; and as a tenant, under one of Espinosa's vote-snagging laws, he's entitled to a year-long postponement of his eviction, so he can search for alternative housing. But the Quebecois monks readily puncture that argument, by testifying he's never shelled out a cent. On the contrary, the Mother House counter-sues him for the accumulated expenses of his room, board, and travel—not to mention damages, libel, court costs, and so on. In the end, the police remove the Count from the Abbey by force, and dump him and his belongings by the side of the highway.

Right on cue, someone named Ofelia—a 'distant cousin of Tïa Filomena's,' as she introduces herself—sends her chauffeur to collect the Sad-Faced Knight, his suitcase, and his cardboard boxes full of books. A miraculous coincidence... though much later, Frederica admits to Chiara that Ofelia isn't really related to Filomena at all. Behind the scenes, Gustavo's dread 'progenitrix' has hired the woman to take him in, for fear he'll stir up even more egregious scandals, if left to his own devices. As grandmotherly and affable as Padre Flores—but without the beard—Ofelia is a widow from Esmeralda, who belongs to a wide nexus of bourgeois matrons in the city. All of them hunger for culture, and gravitate to 'book clubs,' the latest fashion around the world.

A congeries of genders, age-groups, and social classes participated in the old 'tertulias,' traditional throughout Latin America. The audience listened politely to a purported expert on some topic, drummed up by the host of the gathering, and asked haphazard questions at the end. 'Book clubs'—at least, in their Canuban format—are less eclectic. They're mostly attended by ladies of a certain age, who vote by common accord to read a specific book; meeting once a month, they discuss the assigned text on an equal footing, for better or worse. In fact, the books are often merely a pretext for gossip, stiff drinks, and peccant desserts.

But in provincial Esmeralda, always plagued by an inferiority complex vis-à-vis Puerto Indio, the participants still feel the need for a mentor: an expert who can field all their comments and questions, and weigh their relative merits. This godsend, Gustavo, who's often starred at the famous 'tertulia' of Carolina Del Rio in the captial—and who can boast the mile-long pedigree of an Austrian count, to boot—answers their prayers. He refuses to read 'chick novels,' but for clubs that specialize in philosophy, history, or psychology, he deigns to serve as their well-paid tutor. Before long, he's earning pocket change as the moderator of these semi-serious conclaves.

After several uneventful months, Frederica rejoices that her ploy had worked: at long last, her son has come to his senses. She decides to reward him (again, she only owns up to this later) by having Ofelia hand him three thousand dollars, out of the blue. She hopes he'll use the sum to acquire something special: a high-tech stereo, or a decent wardrobe, or an up-to-date encyclopedia. The cash is wrapped in a note from an apocryphal lawyer. With remarkable succinctness, for a man of that profession, he advises Gustavo that Moninga Parra—whom Ofelia identifies as an even more distant cousin than herself—has left him a small legacy, in acknowledgment of his 'contributions to Canuban intellectual life.'

When the Count phones to share his 'good tidings' with Chiara, she finds it odd that he has so many unheard-of cousins, who've suddenly taken an interest in his welfare. Still, this seems of a piece with the Sad-Faced Knight's checkered history; always battling with windmills in quest of his ideals, he's experienced reversals of fortune at every turn. Today, a Holy Roman Emperor, residing in a palace; tomorrow, a homeless vagrant, sitting by the road on a box of books. Today, a penniless pilgrim, begging for food at temples or abbeys; tomorrow, a sybarite, lavishing money on sleek 'ephebes' and grand hotels. As she goes through her final eviction proceedings with the Metaxas, Chiara is relieved Gustavo hasn't asked her for shelter. Given his high-handed habits, he would've banished her again to the cot at the back of her kitchen, while commandeering the rest of the house for himself.

When he does drop by to visit her, several weeks later, her melancholy friend wears a rare expression on his face: a carefree grin. Heartened by his sunny mood, Chiara hazards a daring jest. — You look so happy, you must've tried to kill yourself again.

The Count groans, with ghastly amusement. — How did you know?

She apologizes contritely. — Oh, I'm sorry! I was only joking. Dear Gustavo, what happened this time?

He seems eager to tell all. — Well remember, I called you about Cousin Moninga's legacy? You know what comes over me, every time I inherit a little bequest. It was only a few thousand dollars, and I said to myself: this is just what

I need to do it right, once and for all. So, I registered in that splendid new hotel, by the sea near Punta Rosada—the Palacio Sereno. It's superb, with vast terraces along the cliffs, and a regal staircase going down to the water. I calculated my demise very carefully, down to the last detail. In my sumptuous suite, I read my beloved Plato for three or four days, especially the *Symposium* and the *Phaedrus*. Of course, I wound up with the *Phaedo*—very appropriate, don't you think?

Yes, but the occasion itself wasn't appropriate at all.

Gustavo is undeterred. — In the wee hours of the morning, around five AM, I washed down a batch of sleeping pills with a bottle of madeira—the very best, of course—and crept down the stairs in secret. For a while, I just stood there in the dark, leaning over the ocean, waiting for the pills to take effect. At dawn, I felt very sleepy, and then I must've fallen into the waves. I lost all consciousness—but when I woke up, I was in a hospital room. Apparently, my body floated around for several hours... I ended up far away down the shore, on a deserted beach. An old fisherman called an ambulance. I was senseless, but still alive. The same old story, all over again. Hard as I try, I just can't die!

The way Gustavo recounts the events, almost with pleasure, makes them sound more attention-getting than pitiful. Chiara teases him again, but with his deeper welfare at heart. — You're so accomplished at tutoring your ladies, and so abysmal at committing suicide, why don't you stick to your strong suit?

Gustavo laughs. — The only positive result was that the hotel refunded my week's deposit to Cousin Ofelia, since I didn't stay but a few days.

Emboldened by his jolly tone, Chiara doles out another spoonful of medicine. — I wish you could be less of a perfectionist. You've spent several fortunes, and enjoyed everything the world can offer, but it's still not enough.

Oh, my friend, I fear the case is much worse: I can't condescend to inhabit a body. I remind myself of my collateral ancestor, Henri III. In his later years, he founded the 'Ordre du Saint-Esprit,' and traipsed through the streets of Paris with flagellants. Though he'd been King of Poland and then King of France, he expected much more, so he invented a new royal seal. It was adorned with three interlocking crowns. The legend underneath it said: 'la troisième au Ciel.' 'The third one in Heaven.' Now you have to admit: only an 'androgyne' could've come up with that.

It was Chiara's turn to chuckle. — At least he believed in an afterlife!

I don't believe in this life, much less an afterlife—whether it's grey Elysian Fields, or mansions of jasper and gold.

Things go downhill from there, when Chiara mentions Padre Flores. The Sad-Faced Knight bristles. — I can forgive him for what he did to me, but I'll always consider him spineless.

She can't help but think of the egotists in Lewis's *The Great Divorce*, who create their own hell by blinding themselves to others. The conversation limps on after that, as they carefully steer clear of Scylla and Charybdis: the noxious prelate and the fiendish 'progenitrix.' Another uncanny image flashes through Chiara's brain, when she sees him to the door. He steps into the crowd of the Carnival parade—milling across the plaza, that February day. Just before he turns away from her, an inner cloud darkens his eyes; and then he disappears, as abruptly as the souls in Dante, who've told their tale and melt into the throng.

A month later, Chiara reads his final comment: on the sublime and the ridiculous—but above all, on the mediocre and quotidian. Putting the hotel's refund to use, Gustavo signs in at the Palacio Sereno once again. In an overnight bag, he carries Plato's works and a single change of clothes. He repeats each stage of the previous scenario: the same dialogues, the madeira, the sleeping pills, the descent down the stairs at dawn. But there's one fatal difference: this time, he succeeds. The currents sweep his body out to sea; his bloated corpse drifts for days, till a trawler hauls it back to shore. He's left a sealed envelope in his room, neatly addressed to Chiara. She opens it on a sun-splashed morning, in the courtyard of her house, and finds three words: 'Practice makes perfect.'

Entering from the left, Diana is hoodless; she slides the title Perfect *into the black rectangular frame. Entering from the right, The Trans Reader replaces the Male Reader at the lectern.*

The Trans Reader: This is the Thirty-Seventh Reading.

When he comes back from Thailand, several years earlier, and seeks refuge in Chiara's house, Gustavo spends hours telling her about his misadventures in Asia. 'My life is so strange,' he says to her one day, 'I can hardly believe what's happening, most of the time. You're always writing articles about acrid wines, toadstool tarts, and bashed-up ruins. Well, why not memorialize my story instead? It's much more eventful. You have my full permission—more, my encouragement. I don't have the strength for such an exhausting ordeal...'

In feckless Canuba, the Count seemed like an interloper, almost a creature from another planet. But aren't we all a mixture, Chiara muses, part alien and part indigenous? For over five centuries, the island has been a crossroads for disparate cultures: Caribs and Taínos, Taínos and Europeans, Europeans and Africans, Africans and Arabs, Arabs and Asians, Asians and North Americans, the current influx of tourists and the fierce new Caribs yet to come—whoever they might be. This country has always been a seabound, windswept narration, with characters that have altered over time… or haven't changed at all, but only adopted an alias, and a different face to match.

The suicide note left by Gustavo didn't bring his 'practice' to a 'perfect' end. Like any performance artist worth his salt, he knew how to produce the most telling effect; and with that in mind, he adroitly sized up his audience. For his final stroke, he chose a single correspondent, robbing her of any power to reply—leaving her bereft, as well as bereaved. Of all his friends, Chiara would suffer the greatest impact from his swansong, since she was already laden with guilt: his remark, grotesquely amplified, would haunt her as long as she lived. Why hadn't she taken him more seriously? Why hadn't she housed him and coddled him like Padre Flores, Filomena, or his Viennese 'Oma'? Still, the Count didn't hate Chiara, not at all. His twin bêtes noires were Padre Flores and Frederica: in his vivid imagination, they alone deserved to suffer for his death. The problem was: he couldn't hurt them. They wouldn't be fazed by his gesture, for opposing reasons.

The priest, for one, doesn't believe in mortality: for him, the deceased only pass on to another life. As for Frederica, who could crack her carapace? Who could dint that self-appointed hubcap of the universe? Through his distraught acts over the years, Gustavo wrote her hundreds of 'suicide notes'—but even so, she doesn't feel the slightest compunction about his fate. A few weeks later, Chiara hears her grousing to a mutual friend. — Oh, that son of mine! Always so 'egoistisch'! I had to cancel a dinner party the night they dredged him up, and run to the morgue! Couldn't he think of somebody besides himself, for once! 'Geradezu typisch'! So typical!

As planned, Gustavo's note knocks the wind out of Chiara. The clearest sign of her despair is that she can't read anymore—not even detective novels, where the world is set to rights, a standard antidote for depression. Consequently, she turns to the next best thing: another literary genre—so-called reality. It just so happens that a momentous legal drama is underway in Puerto Indio, and she decides to attend the proceedings. After all, she reasons, a trial is the supreme fiction, with twists and turns that unfold at each successive 'hearing'—of words we usually pass over without a thought. The arraignment, as a matter of fact, is called a 'reading of the charges' in Spanish.

But in due course, this is followed by the testimony of the witnesses: voices that intertwine and confound each other—and that often, on cross-examination, contradict themselves. To her, the obfuscation becomes unbearable. In their different narrations, the prosecution and the defense are trying to place their characters within a cohesive plot. Unknown facts and incidents come to light, looping back into the story and reshaping it: the past becomes as impenetrable as the future. Despite all the talk, almost everything remains unsaid. The tale brims over with the 'dark matter' that we suspect is looming all around us, but which our limited insight won't allow us to discern.

To her immense relief, after a month or so, Padre Flores reappears on her doorstep. Seating him in one of the heart-backed chairs in the sala, she tries to strike a jovial note.

— From your 'brown wrapper,' I see you're still a renegade monk. How did they treat you in Quebec?

Well, after keeping me in solitary confinement for ten days—they call it a 'private meditation room'—the 'High Priestess,' Lucy Paul, and the 'Mystical Pope,' Simon Peter, realized I'd never, never recant. In good conscience, I simply couldn't join them in declaring the BVM the fourth member of the 'Quadrinity.' And so, they disowned me, once and for all.

What brings you back to Puerto Indio?

I had nowhere else to go, and the Franciscans here took me in. I don't want to sound pretentious, but I can only call what happened next a miracle. A few days later, I received a call from the Greek Orthodox Synod of Puerto Indio. They asked me to set up a mission to distribute food to the poor in Quita Sueños. They'd heard about my work in that neighborhood already, and here I am, taking up the challenge again!

Don't tell me you've managed to become an Orthodox priest that quickly.

No, but I'm studying to qualify. In the meantime, I wear a friar's habit, as before. Sr. Metaxa, the financial patron of the Synod, has been indulgent about that.

Chiara gulps. She's heard from Lamia that her father has turned devout in his old age. And after a bypass or two, he's doing remarkably well. But teaming up with Padre Flores? — Does he know about your 'proclivities'? she asks.

Oh yes, he's surprisingly conversant on the subject. He says I can think whatever I want, as long as I don't do anything with either a woman or a man. Amusingly, he goes on about how I shouldn't worry for my safety, in that rough-and-tumble part of town. Despite his repeated heart-attacks, he claims he's still a tough guy, a 'machote.' And he'll defend me with his own fists, if any of the hoods dares to harass me.

She smiles. — He seems to be forgetting you're a veteran of tough neighborhoods. There may be a few temptations of St. Anthony. But whatever goes on in your imagination, I'm convinced your sacred vows are more important to you than anything else. Though I'm sure you'll never neglect to admire the loveliness at hand—or in your case, beyond hand.

Padre Flores assents. — Why should I? Only obsessions that make us lose control are malignant. Misguidedly, Puritans tend to locate evil in the body parts, instead of where it's really found: in the soul. But what is 'evil' anyway, when you come right down to it? Nothing but a hollowness, a negation. Aquinas calls it 'the absence of good.'

Or as the Buddhist teachers say: it doesn't help us to

speak of good and evil; that just piles on the guilt. It's more a question of what's most useful. Would it help to get drunk, or to think things through? To fornicate, or to meditate? What would be more satisfying, in the long run?

We don't need Plato to realize that beauty is uplifting in all its forms—for the beholder, and for the beheld.

Chiara hesitates. — Then let's hope there's an escape clause for Gustavo, too.

You mean, in the beyond?

The wherever.

I'd call it a horizon, a door that keeps opening before us as we move, in this life or the next. All the more so, for Gustavo, because he's reached such an extreme. His dream is to be superhuman, to be an angel. To be absolutely perfect.

'Perfect.' Now Chiara feels compelled to tell the priest about the messsage the Count left for her. He consoles her by saying that what it really means is that no amount of 'practice' will make you 'perfect.' — The irony is that perfection is beyond 'works.'

That's why Zen painters leave a defect in every image.

It's curious to her, how Padre Flores often speaks of Gustavo in the present. Clearly, in a profound sense, they're wedded for all eternity. But she's puzzled. — I can't understand why you became a reprobate in his mind, when all you wanted was to look after him, for the rest of his life.

Oh, he set himself up as an arbiter, and his judgments were infallible. Palestrina composed the 'only real music,' and Bach and Mozart were merely 'heavy metal, the worst of pop.' Fra Filippo Lippi was the 'only genuine painter,' and Caravaggio was merely a 'crude degenerate,' who launched the decline of Western art.

Like you, Padre, I could never agree with that 'anathema sit.' Gustavo couldn't tolerate the idea of a painter bringing street people and peasants into his studio, as models for Christ and the saints. Not to deny the splendor of Lippi, but that's what I love about Caravaggio's work: it portrays true incarnation, in ordinary human flesh.

Flores agrees with her in a pensive voice, as though coursing quickly through remembered canvases: 'And the deeper the incarnation, the more the divine shines through…'

As you say, our friend wanted to be disembodied, like an angel.

That's why I tell you he has more hope than anyone. He's reached a pinnacle where death is all he wants. And self-inflicted death is what most isolates us from love.

You're forgetting that severe pain—and above all, mental pain—can make a person long for relief, no matter what.

Yes, Chiara, I know. That's exactly what I mean: the death-wish will bring him full circle, and he'll come out on the other side, the side of life. He's done it before, in his vision by the sea. One day he'll attain that clarity once more; and this time, his peace will last forever.

Pascal wrote that he who's never doubted his faith has

never believed.

The priest's face wears a knowing look. All he says is: 'Mysterium Dei...'

They fall silent. For their friend, they both desire tranquility in any guise, even what Horacio calls 'divine cessation.'

Samson Agonistes

Entering from the left, Leandra is hoodless; she slides the title Samson Agonistes *into the black rectangular frame. Entering from the right, The Female Reader replaces the Trans Reader at the lectern.*

The Female Reader: This is the Thirty-Eighth Reading.

She and Diana hit if off so well in Barlovento that Chiara longs to see her again. One morning, she stops by the mambo's temple in the slum of San Sebastián; she finds it locked and barred, converted into a warehouse. When she calls the telephone number for 'Rebeca,' the 'compañeros' promise to get back to her; but they keep putting her off till she gives up.

What's going on? Does Ángel María still resent their entente cordiale? Out of jealous spite, has he warned Diana to avoid her at all costs? This hardly seems to harmonize with his free-wheeling approach to friendship and love…

Over the years, Chiara bumps into the priestess when she's researching an article: about eco-lodges, handicrafts, or undiscovered beaches—the usual odds and ends. Diana always pops up in out-of-the-way places: in the shantytown of Quita Sueños, where Padre Flores ministers to the indigent, many of them 'Bonos'; on Carolina's sugar-cane estate near Playa Nieves, worked by farmhands from the smaller island; and on deserted Punta Ceiba, a well-known entry point for 'boat-people' crossing the channel from Cap-Joyeux.

Clearly, Bonaventura is the key: Diana maintains close links with her poorest compatriots, especially those who've just arrived in Canuba, the disappointing Promised Land. She never explains what she's doing in these localities; in fact, she reduces their chats to a minimum, shallow and brief. 'Comment ça va?' and a few chestnuts about the weather—that's as far as she'll go.

Chiara chalks up her secrecy to an obvious cause. Over the years, many NGOs have decried Canuba's treatment of Bonaventurans as neo-slavery; it's only natural that Diana's trying to improve their plight. No doubt she's covertly gathering info for Human Rights Watch, Amnesty International, or some other advocacy group. To support her efforts, she has to have an underground network at her finger-tips—another incentive for stealth. She's already declared that like Ángel María, she's angling for the victory of the Transformation Party.

Chiara could probably catch Diana off guard at Espada del Sur, if she dares to take that step. But she's under pressure just now from *Wide Wide World* for a piece about Mongolian herders, so she doesn't have time to make the trek to the Barlovento estate.

Maybe Diana is closer at hand—if not at her temple, then somewhere else in Puerto Indio. She'll have to worm her whereabouts out of Ángel María. At his seaside retreat, 'Osorio' can kick back and cohabit with 'Rebeca'—his lawful wife, as far as the campesinos know. But 'for simplicity's sake,' he's enjoined Chiara not to bring her up by either name in the capital. Well, she'll have to break her pact with him, like it or not. In a way, she welcomes the chance; his scruples about the mambo have always struck her as pointless. Palmoliva is inured to his extramarital affairs—and besides, she has plenty of her own to keep her occupied.

Conveniently, in a couple of days Chiara will attend a massive party at their mansion in Cuesta India, along with hundreds of other guests. The general melee, once he's gladhanded his acquaintances, will afford her the ideal chance to take Ángel María aside. Lately, he's had no time for her. Tipsy and sentimental, he'll recall their sojourns in Rome and 'on the coast,' and then she'll steer the conversation around to Diana. Like most social lions, Ángel María is at his most expansive in large-scale gatherings, where he can disburden his heart in some unheeded nook.

In the meantime, five of his eight children have returned to the island to launch their careers—a cinch where 'all the right people' have known them since birth. Each expects the usual perk of the jeunesse dorée, a suitable car: a baby Beamer, luxury jeep, or raffish convertible. Four double garages now defile the façade of Sosa's chef d'oeuvre, which *Architectural Digest* once extolled as the 'trend-setter of the new millennium.' These tacked-on bunkers enshrine Puerto Indio's latest god, the automobile.

When Chiara first appeared on the scene, almost three decades before, the city still drowsed in a Colonial siesta. An overgrown village, it resounded with the wrangles of Renaissance church-bells, the clip-clop of horse-drawn carts, and the sing-song of vegetable-vendors. On their turbaned heads, flower-ladies balanced buckets of calla lilies, fragrant azuzenas, and birds-of-paradise. Harmless scavengers, like those that Proust described, chanted their pleas for tattered clothes and dented pots to a cadenced, Gregorian tune. 'Rooopa, ropa vieeeja.' 'Ooollas, ollas usaaadas.'

Since then, Puerto Indio has metastasized into an ersatz Miami, with elevated freeways whooshing past office-blocks. In the interstices, hovels creep up the hills like a fungal growth. Hotbeds of gang-wars and drug abuse, these slums magnetize job-hungry peasants, eager to escape their hard-scrabble farms. The Barrio Antiguo, shielded by building codes, retains a modicum of its former charm—but only at the price of sterility. Family homes and grocery-stores have yielded to yuppy bars, where Katy Perry and the Backstreet Boys bellow so loudly that dogs a mile away begin to yowl.

Like the Old Quarter, Ángel María's house has partly survived. If time has disfigured the front of Leandra's 'wedding gift,' the terraces at the back remain intact. A hallmark of Sosa's art is to unfold many buildings from one. Monolithic at the entrance, the mansion features a two-story vestibule; from there, it fans out in seven levels, each of them painted a different, muted hue. Set at asymmetrical angles, they abut on patios of varied sizes and shapes, their sculpted gardens spilling down to the Río Fernando.

Carolina still owns the land on the opposite bank, and she has purposely left it undeveloped. Here the river seems the same as in former days, when Chiara contemplated its mottled back from Alfonso's aerie: now as then, the anaconda sluggishly uncoils, as if it has swallowed a tapir or a sloth.

On the night of the fete, the breezy season of Lent has desiccated the atmosphere; the air glows limpid and ultramarine, under a full, blazing moon. Far away, in another world, the sierra slices through the sky with its jagged blade. Chiara wears a simple black dress and a string of antique pearls, an heirloom from Sicily. The two guards at the outer gate have known her for eons; they don't ask for the printed invitation. Palmoliva and Carolina are receiving their long chain of guests in the lofty atrium, as pale and golden as a tall glass of Vouvray.

After a botched abortion in Luxembourg, Ángel María's second wife has ended up unable to bear him a child. Already a bit puffy with age, she's upstaged by Carolina, the statesman's inveterate sidekick. He's always found the socialite more entertaining than his wives; and since his divorce from Leandra, 'looking after the grandchildren' has given her an extra pretext for sticking close—even if most of her 'nietecitos' are well into their twenties. The Del Río fortune stands her in excellent stead with Ángel María's pampered offspring, who require a steady supply of lavish toys: plush apartments, surfing jaunts to Australia, state-of-the art skiing gear, and so on. In Cuesta India, she feels fully entitled to edge out Palmoliva, since she financed Sosa's masterpiece herself.

As though she's signed a Faustian pact, the Nipponophile matron waxes more girlish each year. By contrast, her husband Don Adalberto has rapidly declined; he never leaves the house on Plaza Catedral anymore, even for an event such as this. Carolina much prefers her suite at Ángel María's place to her own 'dreary clinic'—where a medical team looks after her husband around the clock. She only goes there once a month to reign over her lackluster 'tertulia,' which has long since fallen out of fashion. Respectfully, she acknowledges the hospitality of her daughter's ex by keeping to her own wing during Ángel María's private trysts. The separate planes of the house, the soundproof walls, and the dense hibiscus hedges sustain their concordat.

Palmoliva slinks off frequently to Quiquiricoba, Don Adalberto's coffee plantation in the mountains, where spirited rides—on horses or their grooms—console her for her husband's meager attentions. Her stepchildren also revel in the ranch: its colossal swimming pool and teakwood decks are better suited to 'wet-parties' and barbecues than the patios of Cuesta India. They've all been raised on American cable, piped into every bourgeois home for the past twenty years; and when they aren't aping South Beach, they're mimicking Malibu.

Carolina's delighted to leave Palmoliva holding the fort. — Oh Chiara, darling, what took you so long? There's someone I want you to meet. — She tinkles her hair-pins and straightens her obi, like a Kunichika concubine who's just stepped from his prints. Chiara scarcely has time to buss Palmoliva's cheek before the bossy geisha whisks her toward the lower terraces.

She speaks in a quiet voice as she trips down the stairs, hanging on to Chiara's arm. — Actually, he's someone I wish you didn't have to meet. I've never worried about Ángel María, in all these years. I've always thought he could take care of himself, if anybody could. But now he's teamed up with a person I find… well, unsavory. And I've also noticed that Angelito seems—I'm not quite sure how to put it—down in the mouth. Now, please help me figure out if the two things are related, and if there's anything you can do. On a matter like this, he doesn't pay me any mind; but he'll listen to you.

They pause to chitchat with several friends along the way. Among them are Héctor and his husband Bjørn, the Norwegian cetologist. Proudly, they announce they've just adopted two children, a girl and a boy. Chiara's happy her former contender for Amado's love has found such a stable partner. If only she'd been so lucky!

A half-hour later, she and Carolina emerge onto the patio where Ángel María is entertaining his special guests. It's a circle forty feet in diameter, and now the moon hovers straight above it, incandescent as a lantern placed there by design. The most desirable youths at the party—the beauties of the moment—have gravitated to this flagstone platter of light. In groups of three or four, they cluster appetizingly, like fresh hors d'oeuvres waiting to be consumed.

Those whose hour has passed lounge in the adjacent rooms, Ángel María's private apartments. All are stale morsels he sampled long ago, and would discard tonight with a careless squint. Through one door, Chiara catches sight of Lamia, daubed with clownish mascara. Her sagging skin is stippled by electrolysis, and she's recently dyed her hair a henna-streaked orange. Despite her alarming girth, she's trying to make a comeback, at least for tonight...

Through another door, Chiara glimpses Chuchu, lining coke from a low onyx table; her seven veils swirl around her, a Valentino dress that half-bares her skeletal limbs…

Ángel María's list of ex-paramours is long. Chiara counts over a dozen faded belles, arranged along wide plate-glass windows in a tutti-frutti frieze. Single, married, or divorced, all briefly sated his whims while their flesh was still lustrous and firm. None of them—except for Lamia, of course—'knows that Chiara knows.' But which of them, she idly wonders, found out about the others over a cup of tea, prepared like a cozy dose of hemlock by a 'fellow-victim'? Or confessed her affair to a blasé husband, who didn't give a fig? Their middle-aged hulls list in an alcoholic fog, shrouded by ennui and self-disdain…

Warming to her game, she peoples the rooms with vanished conquests, like Catulo—or Virgilio, whose 'bromance' never wavered. She realizes that most of her host's masculine paramours, even if they've survived, won't be present tonight. The Miranda brothers apart, they were generally from unacceptable milieus: impecunious artists, uncouth peasants, urban 'rough trade.' But there might be exceptions, Chiara speculates, as she suddenly beholds the great Casanova himself.

He stands on the threshold of his bedroom, with his arm stretched around Ciro's waist. Hmmm… here's a link she's never made. A Paleozoic lover of Lamia's, who once rated as an international polo star, he must've been attractive long ago. Too meaty a dish for Ángel María to pass up, back then… But these days, flabby and addled, Ciro is perpetually smashed. With a ruthless push, the statesman sends him tottering, as the two women sidle up.

Ebullient as ever, Ángel María gives his Italian confidant a bone-wrenching hug, while Carolina poises for flight. — Dear boy, don't forget to introduce Tango to Chiara. Your protégé should meet your soulmate, don't you agree? — Mission accomplished, she sprints toward the stairs to head off Frederica and the Archbishop, who've taken a wrong turn. No doubt she'll guide them to one of the larger courtyards, where dinosaurs like them are left to browse.

Ángel María glowers at her receding kimono. — She's obsessed with him.

No, she thinks you are.

There's still an edge in his voice. — What has she told you about Tango?

Nothing much—except one, he's a pal of yours; two, she doesn't like him; three, you're feeling blue; and four, he may be the reason.

Totting up the data as always, I see. In other words, she's told you everything. I can't pull the wool over her eyes, any more than yours. So, I'll be straight with you. I'm head over heels in love with him.

You, in love? People are supposed to be in love with you, not the other way around.

For many years, Ángel María has been a Dorian Gray,

outdoing even Carolina. Though his body has softened over time, he's kept it in shape by swimming and playing tennis. But now he's showing a slight inner-tube of midriff bulge; his handsome face has slackened somewhat, and his chestnut hair is streaked with white. He falters. — I guess I've finally met my match.

Don't sound so tragic. Some would say you've got the better part of the bargain. The lover is the one who feels the grand emotions. Sure, we've tried to keep an unholy vow: never fall in love. Lamia taught us that. I broke the rule with Amado. But if you're breaking it, too, I'll have to cheer you on.

No cheerleading—not yet. — He reverts to his usual bantering tone—and switches to English. He relies on it to mark his distances, when Chiara hones in on him too much. — As the Americans say, it takes two to tango.

Oh, I'm sure Tango will follow your lead before long. Where's he from, anyway? Argentina?

No, but he could pass. And he loves Gardel—that's how he got his nickname. Have you heard the latest Conehead joke? Why do Chilenos like tangos? Because at the end of every one, an Argentino bites the dust.

Through a peat-bog of exes, he shepherds Chiara to the shiny cohort on the patio. Canuba mints a yearly issue of youngsters like these. At this assembly of the upper crust, they're much lighter-skinned than the average islander. She easily guesses which one is Tango. He epitomizes the

Spanish ingénus in Pérez Galdós: hybrids of Adonis and St. Sebastian, carved in Carrara marble, with wide jet eyes and wavy, blue-black hair. Feeling a sudden chill, she remembers how the author depicts them: blind from birth, confined to a wheel-chair, sprawling half-drowned on a beach...

She pokes Ángel María in the ribs. — He's the one in the silver suit, isn't he?

It's 'grigio moiré,' according to the tailor at Cavalli's; but it does look silver in the moonlight… I gave it to him. Do you think it's too flashy?

No, not at all. It 'suits' him to a tee. And his bad-boy air keeps it from looking fey. You're right: he's the spitting image of Gardel at twenty or so. And you say he's not from Buenos Aires? Montevideo, maybe? Or Porto Alegre?

As soon as he opens his mouth, you'll know where he's from.

After the intros, when Tango begins to talk, what comes out is pure Cipango-ese. A drawl endemic to the mountains near Esmeralda, it substitutes *l* for *r*, so the word 'Señor' sounds like 'Señol.'

Chiara's tickled pink. — It's been quite a while since I've heard undiluted Cipangueño.

I'm not a clodhopper, if that's what you mean.

Don't get your hackles up. I'm an amateur linguist, and I enjoy accents like yours. In Italian, we have hundreds. For example, mine's from southern Sicily. In the last few decades, many of you have left your region. For Puerto Indio, Spain, or the States. Your dialect is disappearing fast. To me, that's a shame.

You're right about that. — Clearly, Tango is appeased by her concern. — I'm the only young guy left in Potros, my hometown.

Potros is one of my favorite places! When I first came to the island in 1979, I saw a cavalcade there. To my surprise, all the riders looked like Spaniards. They really knew how to handle their horses. It was like the Feria de Sevilla.

Now she's won him over. — That was the good old days. Our first settlers came from Andalusia. If you go back to Potros, you'll find mostly Bonos today. That's fine, but my folks feel kinda lonely. They're the only Spanish types still around. Me, I spend most of my time here in the capital.

Ángel María beams at him with a proprietary air. Ignoring him, Tango barrels on. — But every Easter, my pals come back from New York for Semana Santa. We go rambling in the mountains and swimming in the rivers. Like when we were growing up.

Ángel María throws an arm around Tango's ample shoulders. — This year there'll be a senior 'compañero' joining the pack.

Though outwardly amenable, Tango shivers at his touch. The politician is pushing sixty, and his crow's feet have multiplied. To seduce the teens on the terrace, he'll need to offer handsome gifts, and promises of more to come.

They can gauge exactly what they're worth, no doubt. As if reading Chiara's mind, Tango preens in his expensive suit, lifting his head to sip a glass of Taittinger. This is an acquired taste, no doubt—as Ángel María will have to be, for his courtship to succeed. Tango is hard and slim as a stiletto. In Spanish, the opposite of a firearm—an 'arma de fuego'—is an 'arma blanca,' a 'white-arm' or blade. Against Ángel María's flaccid flesh, this slender boy must glint like a knife…

Her fantasy's cut short by another apparition: dark as a thundercloud, Diana eclipses her pallid rival. He seems to have no inkling who she is for Ángel María—or by this stage, perhaps, who she was. Turning on his heels, Tango blends with the youthful set again, intent on resuming his flirt with a leggy girl.

The Bonaventuran priestess, still resplendent despite her years, hardly gives him a second glance. She only has eyes for Ángel María, and their jet-black pupils glitter with rage. Chiara has grown accustomed to her country mode, as the manager of the Barlovento estate; even when she's run into 'Rebeca' elsewhere, she's always been informally attired. Not since their chance encounter in Rome has she seen her decked out like this: her glossy hair is looped in a topknot, and a red taffeta frock highlights her curves.

Ángel María tries to ward her off. — Oh, what a pleasant surprise! Look who's here, Diana… our old friend from Italy.

She pecks Chiara on the cheek; but nothing can distract her from her prey. She bears down on him in strident, French-inflected Spanish. — Oh yes, 'Osorio,' you must be amazed to see me. You invited hundreds of guests, but you forgot about me.

He's floored. Under his breath, he reminds her not to use that name; out loud, all he can do is stammer. — W-well, you know how it is, with my w-wife and m-mother-in-law making up the guest list…

She scowls. — You mean they wouldn't want to rub shoulders with your negrita? — Canubans often use the diminutive for 'black girl' as a term of endearment, even to address whites. But Diana makes it sound insulting, like the n-word or even worse. — Are they afraid the shoe-polish might rub off?

Embarrassed, he whispers again. — Don't be ridiculous. You know everybody in this country is mixed. It's just that… you and I aren't married, and people might gossip.

The priestess grits her teeth. Melodramatically, she seems determined to defy every taboo. A hush has settled over the patio, and a wave of rapt attention ripples through the crowd. — Gossip? What could be more scandalous than this? The way you chase after these boys and girls! Some of them aren't even twenty! You won't be satisfied until they're drunk, drugged, or broke enough to go to bed with you!

Ángel María is speechless, for once in his life. Diana hurtles on, completely derailed. —And I know which one you want the most, this piece of trash you've dressed up like a doll! — She lunges into the clump of onlookers, and wraps her hands around Tango's neck. Drawing smears of blood, she digs into his throat with her red-lacquered nails. — He's just a peasant—an empty-headed loser. And he's a criminal, too: you'll find out soon enough. I've checked up on him…

She loosens her grip, mumbling incoherently. — I don't understand… I'm from one of the finest families of Bonaventure… I studied in Paris… We've just fallen on hard times, like everybody else on our island… — Her voice trails off, then rises again to a screech. — He doesn't love you… I do! The only reason you're with him instead of me is that he's white!

Tango wriggles free, fleeing from the terrace in disgust. His patron will have a tough time coaxing favors from him tonight, Chiara wagers. Livid with anger, Ángel María wastes no sympathy on Diana. His switch-hitting affairs are common knowledge, but you aren't supposed to ventilate them publicly. Her barbs about race don't outrage him, either—only the fact that she's aired them. On both counts, his future bedmates must feel the same instinctive malaise; unforgivably, Diana has flouted the sacred pacts of Canuban hypocrisy.

Though the island seethes with polymorphous love, poured out unreservedly, it's always concealed behind screens of deceit. Never mind that they dissemble as much as the Emperor's new clothes, given the national passion for klatch. Externally, face has been saved: Canuba's is a culture of shame, not of guilt.

As for the other dirty secret, here the cover-up is even more ornate. You can refer to racial prejudice, all right, as long as you qualify it out of existence. In Canuba, isn't everyone part white, part black, part Taíno, with a dash of Asian spice? Don't the country's lovers pursue their amourettes across ethnic lines? Aren't there twenty different terms for the rainbow of complexions? Don't Canubans joke about their color, and discount it as beside the point?

Diana has endured such indignities for decades. A mistress not accepted in 'good society'; a woman whose lover has jilted her for a boy; an 'African' from the lowly, lesser island—and hungry for revenge, she's finally vented her fury. Now she's sobbing uncontrollably, in an explosion of triumph and release.

But these are tears of overwhelming sadness, too: her longtime partner has dashed her hopes, whatever they may have been. As he scurries off to comfort Tango, she calls after him half-heartedly: Monstre de la nature! 'Monster of nature.' It's an outdated phrase for sodomite, one Chiara's only come across in history books.

Abashed, the adolescents shrink back into their reassuring cliques. Plastered or stoned, the frumpy ex-paramours—Lamia, Chuchu, and the rest—loll about as before, impervious even to their own disillusionment.

Chiara and Diana stand alone at the center of the terrace. The moon bathes them in its isotopic radiance, like the sole survivors of a nuclear blast.

Chiara decides her best course is to leave, and take the priestess with her. When she clasps Diana's hand, she doesn't resist. They slowly climb the stairs to the vestibule. The glamorous mambo's makeup has trickled down her face: she looks like a wreck. No one in the rest of the house has witnessed the scene, as humiliating for her as for Ángel María. The most prominent guests, consigned to the upper floors, have already slipped away in their chauffeured limousines; even Carolina has vamoosed.

The last guard posted at the front door bids good-night to Chiara, with a sly, conspiratorial wink. Inwardly, she has to laugh: no, the Canuban mind will never veer from its one-way track…

Hope Unmasked

Entering from the left, Chiara is hoodless; she slides the title Hope Unmasked *into the black rectangular frame. Entering from the right, The Male Reader replaces the Female Reader at the lectern.*

The Male Reader: This is the Thirty-Ninth Reading.

Once they've passed through the outer gate, Diana unsnaps her scarlet purse, shaped like a miniscule heart. She pulls out a cell phone, which must've been the sum total of its contents. After marking a number, she utters an order in Bonavent, and a bottle-green Mercedes wheels around the corner. Again, Chiara observes how far removed she is, here in Puerto Indio, from her rustic plainness at Espada del Sur.

I'm assuming you need a ride.

Chiara answers tacitly, by climbing into the other side. As they whip through the deserted streets, she wryly remarks: 'Last time it was a blue Lexus... Maybe you owe me a few explanations.' The priestess doesn't respond. She's regained her sang-froid, the cool aplomb that undergirds her mystique.

Unless Chiara's mistaken, the route they've taken doesn't lead to the Barrio Antiguo. When she objects, Diana replies laconically. — Didn't you ask me once about Esperanza, Amado's last girlfriend? It was a long time ago, but I haven't forgotten. We're about to drop in on her now. — After several twists and turns, they stop in front of a conventional townhouse in the well-off suburb of Loma Linda. Speaking in Bonavent again, she tells the chauffeur to wait for them a while.

As she unlocks the front door, she goes back to French. — Esperanza and I are such good friends, I even have a key to her place. Back then, Reina was right that I would know where to find her. — Yes, Chiara recalls: when Amado died, his wife claimed that Esperanza caused his accident, and that Diana could track her down.

They enter an antiseptic foyer, painted stark white: it could've been located anywhere, from Dallas to Istanbul to Mumbai. Chiara harks back to Catulo's account of Amado making love with his Esperanza, in this anonymous, upscale locale. She shudders to think how little of our life clings to things, once we're gone. Death wipes our surroundings spic and span, like a factotum with a sponge. Of course, that's the typical viewpoint of a rationalist, she reminds herself; Vodou would tell us otherwise...

Diana ushers her into a snug, luxurious sitting room, decorated in the trendy Belgian color-scheme: cream, grey, and beige. — Have a seat, and make yourself at home.

At long last, it dawns on Chiara: she's been an absolute cretin. — Thank you—Esperanza. — She perches on a chrome-plated chair.

I was wondering when you'd *finally* put two and two together. — Diana sniggers unbecomingly. — Amado and Ángel María kept telling me what a clever detective you are. I think you'll agree: you completely failed the test. I never believed those fairytales about you working for NATO, much less the CIA.

I guess I shouldn't feel complimented, but I do: the Langley clowns make more gaffes than anyone. They can't even tell you where the Chinese Embassy is in Belgrade...

Anyway, they're not the sort of company I keep. But how about you? Are you a spook yourself? Why do you have two names? Three, counting 'Rebeca.'

Oh, I've got more than that. You have to, in my line of work. Or I should say: lines…

Why the plural?

To begin with, I have a ceremonial name, used only in the Gagá. I'm a priestess, first of all: that's my real vocation. Once you've been ordained, your path is predetermined. My followers are very poor—Bonaventuran immigrants in Quita Sueños and San Sebastián, where you and I first met.

I looked for you there, not long ago. Now your temple has turned into a warehouse.

I was attracting too much curiosity. It's better to be a moving target…

Who's after you? Espinosa?

Yes, but he's not the only one. — Diana sighs. — To do more for my people, to give them food and shelter, I've always had to take on other jobs. Aid agencies in France know me as 'Sandrine.' For CARE, I'm 'Wendy.' As 'Rebeca,' I manage the Barlovento estate for 'Osorio.' And here in Puerto Indio, I'm Ángel María's assistant: 'Esperanza.'

So he's the executive Amado told me about, who keeps you in high style.

Now you're catching on. — She leans back in her chair. — It's a relief to give up the game.

What was the point of it, all along? There seems to be

more to this than helping Bonaventurans, or advancing Milady's cause.

Diana avoids Chiara's eyes for a moment, then looks her square in the face. — I've had my reasons. You're the only person who might've put the whole jigsaw together. When you and I shared him as a lover, years ago, Amado was afraid you'd match me up with 'Esperanza.' He didn't want you to make such a ruckus I'd lose my job—we needed the income too much. And Ángel María has always been wary of your international connections.

Amado could never believe that Chiara wasn't the jealous type, like Héctor Méndez or Reina. In his own way, Ángel María is just as naïve. Chiara throws up her hands. — Connections? I travel a lot, and I know a few ambassadors—but I only see them at parties.

What do I care? — Diana crackles her taffeta dress. — I don't have to listen to Ángel María anymore—not after tonight. I'm getting out of the whole ugly business. So you might as well hear the rest of the story… — She pauses for effect. — There's an odd coincidence in all this. Didn't it ever strike you? 'Esperanza'? It's the name of the Canal…

The Canal de la Esperanza is the channel that Canubans cross illicitly, on their way northwest to Puerto Rico. By now, Chiara has had enough of the cloak and dagger act. — Oh, Esperanza is a fairly common name. What I've always found ironic is that the 'Channel of Hope' destroys so many people's lives. Amado wanted to make the trip, as you know better than anyone. He told me you were planning to do the same.

That's what I led him to believe. Can you honestly picture *me* in one of those rickety boats?

No, I have to admit I can't. Then why would you encourage him to run such a risk?

Diana broods for a moment. — I expected to be living in the States—so I wanted to make sure he'd be there, too.

But you were going there legally—is that it?

Ángel María swore he'd arrange it. And I fell for his lies. He'd already taken me back to France, down memory lane, soon after we met; and then to Italy… And after that, to Chile…

Right, I remember. — Chiara fights back her annoyance. — I had to pay for Amado's phone-calls from my house to 'Esperanza,' when she went there with her boss. Without realizing it, I'd had her right in front of me, when we spent those days together in Rome with Ángel María. I still don't understand why he always clammed up about you here in Puerto Indio—or why you avoided me so much, except in Barlovento. I ran into you several times in other places, but you barely gave me the time of day. Did all that have something to do with the Esperanza Channel, too?

Now you're getting warmer. — Diana licks her lips, a mannerism Chiara once found alluring; but no longer… — That's how I met Ángel María in the first place, when he was working at the Central Bank on foreign relations. On behalf of several NGOs, I was trying to get a loan to assist the Bonaventurans in this country—in the sugarcane fields, and in the slums. The poorest of the poor. I was an idealist, and Ángel María made fun of me. But he also fell in love… — She flinches. — Don't look at me like that! Don't!

Chiara shifts in her chair, ill at ease. — I'm sorry, but that's what he'd say to any woman as good-looking as you.

I'm telling you, this was different. — Diana glares at her. — At first, I didn't give in to him. I was in love with Amado, the most sensual man I've ever known.

I can testify to that. — Chiara clears her throat.

Of course, his physique was impressive. But you and I don't care about that. His kindness, his charm, were as great as his… other gifts. He and I went a long way back, more or less to the time when he brought you to my temple in San Sebastián. The passion I felt for him was pure; after all, he was penniless. Ever since my family went bankrupt, I've been forced to catch as catch can. With him, I wasn't in it for the loot. He's the only man I've ever loved.

Then you fooled me tonight. Ángel María must've been a close runner-up.

What do you expect? A woman hates to be rejected.

Chiara has reached the boiling point. — Especially a kept woman. Amado bought you a lot of presents, too— though he couldn't afford them.

Only because he wanted to. Ángel María treated me to much more expensive gifts.

So you decided to have your cake, and eat it, too.

Yes. That's when I moved into this house. Paid for by my lord and master. — Diana clasps her hands, in a parody of gratitude. — Thanks to me, Ángel María has earned a lot of money. I'm not a parasite.

Oh no…

Listen! He's made millions off of me! It's because of all my work, and my contacts, that he's placed so many Bonaventurans in construction jobs and agriculture here, and sent so many Canubans to Puerto Rico and New York. That's why they gave me the nickname. Just like the Esperanza Channel: I've always been their last resort.

Chiara is dumbfounded. — All that's completely against the law. I can't believe that Ángel María, who wants to change this country for the better, would lower himself to human trafficking.

You don't know him as I do. He's more than two-faced, he's hundred-faced. Or maybe he doesn't have a face at all. — Diana's closes her eyes. — I know things about him that would really shock you. He's the ringleader of all the torture and killing that goes on in Canuba. That's why Espinosa gives him so much power: he's afraid he might be next.

There were some nasty rumors about Ángel María's role in Alfonso's death. The 'demotator' is so fragile, another pillow might do the trick… Still, Chiara can't accept what she's hearing.

Diana persists. — The way he's treated me, I'd like to see

him dead.

Her iciness sends a chill down Chiara's spine; later, those words will come back to haunt her. — You make yourself sound like a victim, but you've been working for him of your own free will.

Only at first. I ended up in this mess for my people's sake. My mother's Canuban, but only because she was born here of Bonaventuran parents. Like my father and me, she identifies with the smaller island. That's why she returned to Saint-François to marry him.

She explains that over time, as she assisted her fellow-migrants from Bonaventure, she befriended many poverty-stricken Canubans, too. More and more, they asked her to sponsor their crossings to the States. But Ángel María gradually turned the whole operation into a business—a lucrative scam. He and his henchman hoodwinked thousands of campesinos, stealing their life-savings and leaving them in the lurch. For years, he threatened to rub Diana out, if she confided in anyone.

When we ran into you in Rome, I was afraid he might suspect I'd already spilled the beans. That's why I pretended I didn't know you. I was terrified. On the beach at Espada del Sur, his doubts flared up again. He lit into me after you left, and I was afraid for my life. To top it all off, now he's ditched me. He figures he can run the show on his own, with the network I've put together. He used to feed me a line about divorcing Leandra, and setting me up in Miami as his wife.

Then, when he got rid of her, he married a two-bit blonde. What's her name? Palmoliva? And now this brainless kid, Tango, just because he's young and white. No, that's the last straw… — The tendons stand out in her throat.

Chiara takes it all in. — I suppose you were planning to 'help' the Bonaventurans in Miami, too.

I was. And damn him, I will.

Chiara hesitates for a minute, while the priestess simmers down. For her own selfish reasons, she's distraught at the turn things have taken. During the kidnapping crisis in Barlovento, Diana even kissed her on the lips… Now she seems utterly hostile. Maybe Chiara should try to grasp her point of view. — I'd like to understand, honestly. Why were you so intent on ransoming 'Osorio,' if he was exploiting you like this? Why didn't you just let him rot?

What if he'd escaped some other way, and I hadn't lifted a finger? There would've been all hell to pay.

Were you really so powerless? Couldn't you have 'removed your protection' from him, as you did with Amado? Wouldn't another accident have finished him off?

A Closet Case

Entering from the left, Diana is hoodless; she slides the title A Closet Case *into the black rectangular frame. Entering*

The Trans Reader: This is the Fortieth Reading.

Instead of answering, Diana makes a big to-do about her 'duties as a hostess.' An incongruous urge, in Chiara's opinion. She's leery of the rum-and-soda the mambo serves her, and only pretends to sip her drink. Is it poisoned? Anything seems possible now…

When Diana settles into her chair again, cradling a kir royal, Chiara returns to the matter at hand. — You used to hate me because of Amado, but I assumed we became friends in Barlovento. Now I suppose you resent my closeness to Ángel María. If what you say is true, then Amado was a saint compared to him.

Diana's voice sounds hollow, though she caresses Chiara's hand. — It's never been about you, only them. Amado was worse than you realize. He betrayed me, just like Ángel María. That bastard's two-timing with Tango isn't anything new. It started when he barged into this house one day, when I was in bed with Amado.

Catulo related the incident after Amado's death, but Chiara keeps that to herself. Omniscient or clairvoyant, Diana reads her thoughts. — I know you've heard about this; but not the whole story. I told Amado to hide in the bedroom closet. Just for a minute or two, while I sweet-talked Ángel María into leaving. But my 'boss' was overbearing; he needed me, the way an addict needs crack. I was desperate to send some money to my parents in Bonaventure. I couldn't afford to put him off. I'd planned to discuss a loan with him that afternoon, but he dropped by earlier than usual. It was awful. I had no choice.

She jumps up and leads Chiara to the bedroom. — Look, here's the closet. It happened so quickly, I didn't have time to think. All Amado had to do was lean at a certain angle: through these slits, he could watch everything. He was staring at our every move.

The narrow louvres are part of an ornamental tracery. For the life of her, Chiara can't summon any indignation: all three of these lovers were libertines. — So what? Amado could hear you, even if he shut his eyes. And knowing him, maybe he enjoyed the show. — As she listens to herself, she can't believe how jaded she's become, after soaking for decades in the Canuban marinade.

You're right. — Diana nods ruefully. — A few days later, I caught the two of them together.

Nothing can faze Chiara anymore. — By standing in the same closet, yourself?

No, I'm not like Amado. I couldn't have stomached that. If I'd been a man, I would've killed the sonofabitch who was screwing the woman I loved.

Diana—under any name—has always been prim and proper in her diction, if not in her behavior. The expletives are an index of her rage.

Chiara prompts her gently. — But Amado took it all in his stride. And you couldn't forgive him for that.

How could I? He even joked about it later, as though we'd played a funny prank. — She raises her glass in a caustic toast. — Ángel María always came by on Tuesdays and Saturdays. I couldn't visit him at home, the way his society women do, on the pretext they're 'friends of the family.' Not me, not a Bono.

Her acidity curdles the air; in all fairness, Chiara can't contradict her.

One Tuesday afternoon, when Amado knew he needed to stay clear, I went to the florist's at the corner. I wanted some lilies and chrysanthemums—don't ask me why; it was just a whim. As I left the shop, I caught sight of Amado a block away, on the street next to mine. He was talking to somebody who'd stopped for the traffic light. I recognized the car: it was Ángel María's black Jaguar. There's a parking lot off to one side, a little further down. When the light changed, he pulled into it, and Amado followed him. I lost track of them after that. Ángel María showed up at my house an hour late, and couldn't rise to the occasion for me.

Maybe they were discussing the problem, man to man.

You mean pervert to pervert… — The contempt in her voice is frightening. — I'm sure they were making some kind of date—if they didn't have each other right there. — She lingers over the notion, like a child toying with matches. — That same night, when I went to the temple in

San Sebastián, I lifted my blessing from Amado.

Chiara trembles all over. — Fate saved him from the boat trip—the one you dreamed up. But you weren't surprised when he was crushed in the wreck.

No, not at all. — She grins like a skull. — And I unloaded the guilt on you.

You've told me that before. But you used to blame it on the loas. — She shakes her head scornfully. — You give yourself too much credit, Diana. I was raised as a Catholic, like you. We're good at stacking guilt on ourselves, without any magic spells.

What about absolution? Is it normal for guilt to last this long—seventeen years and counting?

No, it's not. But even if what you claim is true, how can you be so callous about Amado? Don't you have a daughter, his child? And didn't she need her father?

She has dealt a painful blow, and Diana winces. — Lucita has no idea who her real father is. I pinned the paternity on Ángel María. Birth control isn't failsafe. He'll always support her from a distance. And she'll never even know that Amado existed.

Chiara is incensed. — How can you be so spiteful? You can't play God. You can't erase Amado from his own daughter's memory.

Lucita looks just like me. She's mine, not theirs—either one of them.

Where is she, then?

Diana's smugness crumbles; suddenly, she weeps. — She lives with a foster family in Puerto Rico. I haven't seen her for ages, but we write to each other every week. She's nineteen now, and studies nursing at a community college. Ángel María bought her false papers through our network when she was five, and sent her to San Juan. In the trade, we call it a 'macana': it costs a lot more than going by boat. But he wouldn't do that for me. Oh, no… he kept postponing the trip. He said he needed me here. He didn't want me to get sidetracked from my work—by raising our child! When he's had eight with Leandra. His white family is official, and we're not. Lucita's brothers and sisters have never even heard of her.

Overcome by her anger, she paces around the room. — He's the most heartless person I've ever known, and I'm totally at his mercy. I don't have anything of my own. I should at least get a salary for what I do. But I don't dare complain. Every now and then, in a mocking little voice, he reminds me: 'I can have you deported anytime, Diana— or worse…' He foots the bill for this house, the car, the chauffeur, my clothes, my food, the supplies at Barlovento, Lucita's expenses—all of that. But I'm his slave—just as we've always been, for centuries. He won't even let me be a mother.

Chiara can only manage a feeble response. — That doesn't sound like the man I know. Maybe he has his reasons?

Oh, you can't imagine how cruel he is. Sometimes he dresses up in a costume with a bird-mask, and ties me to the bed. What he does to me is unspeakable. — Diana buries her face in her hands, swaying from side to side. She doesn't look up again.

Chiara lets herself out, and gives the chauffeur her address. She needs to go home. After Diana's revelations, she can no longer vouch for anyone—the living or the dead.

The Untold Want

Entering from the left, Leandra is hoodless; she slides the title The Untold Want *into the black rectangular frame. Entering from the right, The Female Reader replaces the Trans Reader at the lectern. The Whitman verses should be accompanied by Tibetan bells, almost inaudible.*

The Female Reader: This is the Forty-First Reading.

Chiara makes a pilgrimage to El Silencio, and stays there longer than at any time since Amado's death. She sleeps in the caretaker's shack, and climbs to the cavern each day.

Sitting on the familiar rock, she writes page after page about her vanished lover—no longer a hero to her now: or a martyr, almost a myth. She means her words as a memorial; but she no longer feels the remorse that has plagued her before. Unintentionally, by claiming it for herself, Diana has delivered her of guilt.

Her notebook entries assume a mellower tone, as if she were saying a calm farewell. Whitman's verses echo in her mind, like quiet waves beating on a distant shore:

The untold want, by life and land ne'er granted,
Now, Voyager, sail thou forth, to seek and find.

The untold want, by life and land ne'er granted,
Now, Voyager, sail thou forth, to seek and find.

The untold want, by life and land ne'er granted,
Now, Voyager, sail thou forth, to seek and find.

She's sure she's learned a lesson from Diana, even if she hasn't absorbed it yet. Her image of the priestess has spalled into a thousand tesserae, poised to realign in some unpredictable form. A different icon is taking shape: she can almost see it glimmer in the darkened apse of the cave.

A Fallen Angel

Entering from the left, Chiara is hoodless; she slides the title A Fallen Angel *into the black rectangular frame.*

Entering from the right, The Male Reader replaces the Female Reader at the lectern.

The Male Reader: This is the Forty-Second Reading.

Chiara's hard-won composure is undermined on her return to Puerto Indio, the Tuesday after Holy Week. Since Maundy Thursday, when he'd set out from Cuesta India in his Land Rover, Ángel María has gone missing. Chiara didn't take her cell phone to El Silencio; she doesn't care for that intrusive device—and anyway, there's no reception at the cave in Barlovento. In the meantime, Palmoliva, Carolina—and even his timid mother, Doña Ramona—have left frantic messages on her answering machine at Plaza Drake. Does she have any idea where he might be?

When she calls them back, they all tell her the same story. Ángel María agreed to join his wife and some of his children at Playa Hermosa, after a two-day excursion to the mountains with some friends. But he never appeared at the beach on Holy Saturday; and if something had come up, it was unlike him not to let his family know.

According to Carolina, the 'friends' in question must've been Tango and his pals. — Remember, Chiara, they'd been planning a trip together during Semana Santa. Thanks to a tip from me, the police have grilled the little brat. He claims Ángel María never showed up for their rendezvous; but I bet he's lying…

Her instincts prove right. The National Police mounts

a countrywide search for Ángel María Domingues—the 'socialite, financier, and leading light of the Espinosa government,' as the media begin to chorus. Eventually, one of the search parties finds a male corpse in a steep ravine near Potros, Tango's hometown. The killers have mutilated the victim, disfigured his face, and smashed his head. If they hoped to impede his identification, they don't know much about forensics. His fingerprints and dental records are incontestable, not to mention the birthmarks on the torso itself. At the morgue, his mother Doña Ramona confirms them: a mole on his upper left shoulder; a tiny, port-wine patch on his lower back.

From then on, the detectives scour the vicinity for Ángel María's SUV. It isn't long before a campesino reports that he's seen a 'rich man's jeep' under a lean-to of fronds. He works on the family farm of one of Tango's chums, a Canuban-American whose parents live in Queens, like most 'Canubicanos.' Once the police retrieve the vehicle, their interrogations of the local villagers yield a trove of evidence. Tango is arrested, along with his alleged accomplices; although all four of his childhood friends are naturalized US citizens, they haven't bothered to flee the island.

The trial is held by magistrates without a jury, in keeping with the country's Napoleonic laws; it lasts for ten weeks, and is mainly attended by the families of the accused. To Chiara's dismay, she's the only member of Ángel María's circle who follows the proceedings in person.

Carolina and Palmoliva pretend that they're working nonstop to sort out his financial affairs for the probate court, without a moment to spare. To their amazement, they've discovered he owned a massive estate in Barlovento… Chiara makes no comment. Ángel María's children, as well as his cronies, drum up one excuse after the other: they just don't have time to swing by the court, even for a minute. It's the prelude to a broad conspiracy of silence about his death—and above all, about his life.

The four US nationals lounge in the dock with faces that are by turn cocky, sour, testy, or indifferent, depending on their moods. All of them embody a social problem often bandied about in the Canuban press: the criminalizing of 'Canubicano' emigrants. It has achieved greater currency through a flurry of articles by the Editor in Chief of the *Clarín Canubano*, the island's leading newspaper.

True, the 'Canubicanos' residing in the States send two billion dollars back to their homeland each year. These remittances provide more national income than the country's free-trade zones and sugar production combined; they're surpassed only by profits from the tourist industry. The 'absent Canubans,' as they're often called, invest their American earnings in all kinds of businesses, especially in Puerto Indio.

But the downside of the symbiosis is also undeniable. The cherished dream of going 'pa'llá'—'over there'—

discourages people from improving themselves on the island itself. Most of those who leave have no education or technical skills, so they don't represent a 'brain drain'; but since they're ambitious and tenacious, they do amount to an 'energy drain.'

Once they've made the perilous crossing to the Promised Land, 'Canubicanos' meet with a further set of problems. Faced with an extreme climate like New York's, they incur heating and cooling bills for the first time in their lives. The taxes they've often evaded on the island now hedge them in on every side. Food and lodging cost far more in the States, and the jobs for unskilled workers are scarce.

Their children undergo urban poverty, far more grinding than the bucolic simplicity they've known: in the first decade of the millennium, the slums of Puerto Indio are still largely peopled by campesinos, in close touch with their villages. Though immigrant youngsters attend better-equipped schools in Queens, they sit through classes in a language not their own. All too often, they end up unemployed, just like their parents. The financial prospects for most of these teens are scarce, unless they turn to the readiest source of cash: petty crime.

The anonymous streets of the North provide a college of mayhem that doesn't exist on the island—or certainly not to the same degree. The land of Tío Sam is known worldwide for its abundance of high-powered firearms; in Canuba, handguns are harder to obtain, and more carefully registered. Thanks to the tight weave of social integration, Puerto Indio's delinquency rate remains the lowest in the Western Hemisphere, for a city its size.

Often, the young 'Canubicanos' who get in trouble in the States haven't qualified for naturalization yet; after serving their sentences, they're shipped back to their country of origin. But by this time, they've taken graduate courses in malfeasance, at the 'US Prisons University,' as one journalist puts it: what they haven't learned in the 'hood,' they've learned from the older jailbirds.

Though Tango's chums are already citizens, and no longer subject to deportation, their trial shows how even a brief return to the island allows such kids to draw on their 'street smarts'—often the only training they've ever acquired. These greenhorns may have missed the mark on forensics, but not on the American art of legal sleight-of-hand. Collectively, they hire a clever attorney, Montorio Saragosa, notorious for getting guilty clients off the hook. His services don't come cheap, but his fees are paid by the parents of the 'Queens quartet'—as they're dubbed in the press—who cover Tango's costs into the bargain.

At first, the other defendants go along with Tango's story: Ángel María didn't appear at their rallying point, and so they never even met the man. They speculate that some highway bandits must've mugged him on the outskirts of Potros. But the evidence—eye-witnesses who saw all five of them in the Land Rover, traces of Ángel María's blood on their shoes, and so on—is incontrovertible. Despite all that, the Attorney General or Procurador General, Jaime Mora, appointed to this special case, has his work cut out for him.

Instead of challenging the obvious, Saragosa advances an array of mitigating factors, designed to reduce the sentences to a slap on the wrist. He begins by depicting the young men as victims of 'transculturation,' expatriates who've been uprooted by their uncaring families. He's biting the hands that feed him; but the 'Canubicanos' don't mind, if this will keep their sons out of jail. The rampant violence in North America, he goes on, where children are mowed down by shooters at school, has distorted his clients' psychology. This argument has a patriotic ring, but the magistrates soon make clear that it can't justify the perpetrators' acts.

Saragosa's next rationale also sounds a familiar note: when they assassinated Ángel María, the defendants were suffering from temporary madness. The older man's wicked influence turned them briefly into devotees of a Satanist cult that requires human sacrifice. His Bonaventuran mistress, a certain Diana, is painted as a scheming witch who converted him to her 'pseudo-religion,' with a view to subverting the Canuban state. No doubt about it, the wily lawyer has done his research, ferreting out some of the best-kept secrets of Ángel María's motley existence.

The priestess herself is unavailable for questioning; several weeks before the trial, she's dropped off the face of the earth. Saragosa deals the chauvinist card again, by stressing her Bonaventuran roots; and as so often on the island, a racist subtext interlines his comments. Ángel María told Tango quite a lot about Diana, Chiara gathers. Still smarting from her insults at the party, he tried to exonerate himself by slandering her.

But the District Attorney demolishes this tangent as hearsay: there's no corroboration of any such 'blood-cult' in Canuba. Besides, the 'cuarteto de Queens' had never been introduced to Diana, by their own admission. On the other hand, Jaime Mora has ascertained that they've racked up hefty records in the United States. The FBI has forwarded reports to him about their priors, such as armed robbery, fistfights in bars, driving under the influence, and possession of cocaine.

The last two points lead Saragosa to attempt another angle. As the defendants testify, just before the murder they ingested large amounts of alcohol and drugs: as a result, they're not accountable for their behavior. Ángel María himself induced the gullible youths, many years his juniors, to abuse these substances, most of them illegal. Sadly, the attorney concludes, the boys' alleged victim caused his own demise.

Once again, the tactic seems to backfire. In his cross-examinations, Mora elicits a wealth of details about what actually happened. The young men aren't as quick-witted as their lawyer, so Saragosa's coaching doesn't always work.

The prosecutor grills them relentlessly, assuring them he'll be lenient if they confess. The jumpiest of the five, Valdomero, finally breaks down and tells the whole story, and it isn't long before the others follow suit.

At the beginning of Holy Week, Tango travels to Potros to rat around with his childhood companions, as all of them affirm. Ángel María teams up with them on Thursday as planned, around five in the afternoon. They rendezvous at the farm where the Land Rover is later recovered, and then they hike to a solitary clearing in the woods, toting backpacks full of rum and other treats. They bring a hurricane lamp along, and sit around on big rocks and fallen logs. It isn't till after midnight that the gang polishes the older man off. Before the endgame, there's a lengthy minuet of cat and mice—until the mice turn into tigers, and tear the cat to shreds.

As Chiara listens to Valdomero and the others, she can reconstruct the scene from Ángel María's point of view. Though none of his pals can compete with Tango's beauty, they share his sultry Andalusian looks: alabaster skin, shocks of blue-black hair, and eyes that gleam like obsidian. Their slight admixture of African and Taíno traits makes them all the more appealing to a connoisseur.

According to them, the 'old goat' soaks up even more booze and drugs than they do. His Peter Pan syndrome pushes him to dizzy heights, as he revels in their coarse horsing around. Gradually, he tries to seduce them. Playing with fire, he starts stroking the virile cubs, who seem so enticingly amenable. Not only is Tango always game, but he's intimated that two of his friends went 'gay for pay' during their last vacation on the island.

Valdomero confirms this. — A couple of the guys did some of that stuff for money and Ex with some gringo creeps, back in July. Tango was dumb enough to blab about it to the lech, and that gave him the wrong idea. When we met Ángel María, he seemed pretty cool in a grandaddy kinda way. He was real nice, super-friendly, fallin' all over himself. Said he wanted to help us get good jobs, run with the in-crowd, hook up with rich girls. It was like a party, ya' know, everybody clownin' around and tellin' jokes. He brought us three liters of rum, and three of whiskey. The best. We already had a sack of grass—plus some meth and a few grams of coke. Also a bag of Ecstasy pills.

He smiles for a moment, remembering the fun. — Ángel María was a riot, man. He put on this crazy bird outfit and acted out those cartoons we used to watch on TV. Woody the Woodpecker. You know, da-da-dá-da, da-da-dá-da, da-da-da-da! I've never seen an old guy like him get so high. When we tore that dumb beak off his face, all he did was go on laughin' like a maniac. But then, I guess about a couple hours later, he got too palsy-walsy. He was, like, makin' passes at us. Puttin' his hands where they didn't belong, talkin' about how cute we are—things like that. It really pissed us off. But maybe he didn't mean it that way.

According to the FBI report, in the US the 'Queens quartet' practiced a hate crime unknown on the island, 'gay-bashing.' For Canuban purposes, a different term might be coined, Chiara muses to herself: 'bi-bashing,' maybe, since unadulterated gays are so scarce. As Jaime Mora mentions in passing, the bar-brawls the four started always involved an attack on a homosexual, which witnesses consistently declared 'unprovoked.'

Once she hears this, she can picture the situation near Potros with dreadful precision. To Ángel María, these young hoodlums all seemed typically Canuban, telling off-color jokes in Cipango dialect and hugging each other with abandon. In his enthusiasm, he doesn't pick up on the fact that a foreign virus has infected them. At some point, he pushes them too far, and their homophobia—widespread in North America—drives them berserk.

On one of his rare visits to Puerto Indio from the monastery, Horacio concurs with her: the pack's reaction must've caught Ángel María off guard. Home-bred Canubans would've put him off with a chuckle, or an affable poke in the ribs. Later on, individually—behind closed doors—they might've welcomed his advances, on the pretext of earning some cash. At worst, they would've treated his antics as irksome, telling him firmly to cut it out. To take homoeroticism to heart, you have to consider it a psychosocial force, not just a drunken caprice—and that runs counter to the island taboo.

As Valdomero and the others testify, Ángel María boasted he'd already 'done things with Tango.' He probably assumed this would wear down the others' resistance. But he must've been flying in the stratosphere by then, since by saying those words, he broke the oath of silence. It wasn't about what they'd done or what they might do: the outrage was to state it at all. Within his own cultural code, Tango was now obliged to turn on him with the rest. Initially, he didn't take the bait, until the others hounded him; and then he flogged Ángel María with a vicious chain of invective. Even so, he refrained from the first stages of physical assault—until a final stick of kindling made him ignite.

Around ten o'clock, the 'payback' begins in earnest. Verbal slurs turn into kicking, beating, and worse. Tanked on alcohol, weed, coke, meth, and Ex, they do it all in slow motion. Media-censors fail to grasp that brutality is far obscener than sex, and much more likely to spur imitation. The tormentors compete with each other, raising the ante. As the abuse draws to an end, they taunt Tango for not pitching in on the action. 'Maybe it's true what this guy says, huh man? Maybe he's been treatin' you like his little girlfriend?' That's the Canuban taboo of taboos: male passivity. They've laid Tango's best-kept secret bare. Shame drives him to grab one of the knives, aim for Ángel María's heart, and stab his lover to death.

By this point, it's past midnight—the early hours of Good Friday. In a dimwitted attempt to avoid prosecution, the boys crush their victim's skull with rocks. Under the back seat of the jeep, they find a tarpaulin and some rope; adding some tree-branches to the corpse, they stash the formless bundle in the trunk. Then they go on a joy-ride down tortuous mountain roads, searching for a remote ravine. Their minds are so befogged, they circle back to a gully not far from where they started out, and dump the cadaver there.

Twenty minutes later, they stop at a country store to pick up some much-needed munchies. The place doubles as a gambling den, and several crap-shooters see them clearly under the naked light-bulbs overhead.

The grizzly, gap-toothed proprietor, flattered by his new-found importance at the trial, jaws at length. — It's not every night we get five young fellers in a fancy car like that, ridin' around with blood all over their clothes. — He simpers idiotically. — They claim they just slaughtered the biggest hog on the farm. Funny time of day for it, I laugh! Why didn't you clean up, then? That's what we're gonna do now, one of 'em says, swim in the river and wash off. Sure enough, besides Pepsis, crackers and cheese, and plantain chips, they buy two bars of soap.

Face-Deface-

Entering from the left, Diana is hoodless; she slides the title Face-Deface- *into the black rectangular frame. The last two paragraphs should be a Sprechstimme recitative, accompanied by the musical ensemble, and sung by the actor miming Chiara on the mainstage. Entering from the right, The Trans Reader replaces the Male Reader at the lectern.*

The Trans Reader: This is the Forty-Third Reading.

In their piecemeal confessions, the other New Yorkers also admit that Tango didn't take part in Ángel María's mutilation. Standing to one side with his hands over his ears, he didn't even want to watch; he'd only intervened to 'put him out of his misery.' They comment that the dying man continued to stare at them, through every phase of his ordeal, as he slumped against the tree. Several of them make the same remark, even if phrased somewhat differently. One them goes a step further: 'He kept looking at us, even after he couldn't see.'

As Chiara listens to their statements, a strange link occurs to her. Uncannily, Ángel María's murder followed the artistic method of his boyhood admirer, Virgilio Miranda. She's always been haunted by that lapidary poem the painter liked to repeat: 'face-deface-efface.' She reproaches herself for thinking of it now, in such a gruesome context. But the words rustle at the back of her mind... sibilant as a ghostly voice, like the wind through murmuring leaves.

In the grim finale of his Don Juan's career, Ángel María confronts these young men with variance—nature's essential truth. The more she reflects on what happened, the more she realizes how much his polyvalence must've frightened them.

Humans are like sea-currents, leopards, minerals, or flying fish: no two are exactly alike, and all evolve with each tick of the clock, though at differing speeds. A lump of carbon takes a billion years to compress into a gem, but other alterations proceed more swiftly. A cumulus cloud rears up, collapses, and tears apart in a gale; a mango ripens on the vine, falls to earth, and rots... until the rains wash it away. Each person's internal gender shifts from minute to minute, hour to hour, month to month. As Kinsey observes, sensuality knows no barriers and no norms: in the actual world, 'only deviations are real.'

Since Ángel María transcends every cliché—every attempt to cram the heart into a pre-set mold—these cowards can't abide his unrelenting gaze. In his genial way, at the outset he must've told them about his businesses, his governmental ties, his family life, his wives, his children, his girlfriends, his travels, his favorite sports. In turn, he would've listened to their callow, checkered stories, with his usual sympathy and charm. 'What was it like to grow up in Queens?' 'Have you ever held down a job?' 'Don't you want to go to college?' He isn't putting on an act; he truly wants to know, and help them achieve their goals.

But then, when he becomes more intimate, when he expects pleasure from them—or worse, asks for affection—he swells into a force too potent for them to bear. Even in Arcadia, his protean nature must appall them. Swooping down like Zeus among the shepherd boys, he threatens to snatch them up, to bare their sensitive undersides, to illumine their hidden instincts—released by the unrepentant shimmer of his desire. How many people can one man be? How many selves, they must wonder, do I contain?

They have to shatter that mirror looking back at them, even out of death; they have to destroy that face elated by change, fierce with a freedom they can't control. They have to obliterate those defiant, limitless eyes, before they become their own.

-Efface

Entering from the left, Leandra is hoodless; she slides the title -Efface *into the black rectangular frame. Entering from the right, The Female Reader replaces the Trans Reader at the lectern.*

The Female Reader: This is the Forty-Fourth Reading.

'Jeder Engel ist schrecklich…' As Rilke wrote, every angel awakens our dread. If Ángel María committed even half the atrocities Diana claims, some might say he got his just deserts; but until she has proof positive, Chiara downplays her accusations as tinged with jealous bile.

For now, the trial engrosses her; all the more so, since no one else seems to care. To her chagrin, the grisly confessions Mora has drawn from the defendants redound to their benefit. All the magistrates hear is that Ángel María plied the young men with liquor, encouraged them to use illegal drugs, and then molested them. Though none of them is under-age, in his summation Saragosa vaunts them as 'chicos heróicos,' 'heroic kids' who thwarted a powerful, deranged criminal.

Thanks to a word to the wise from Tango, Mora shares some films with the judges, in a session closed to the public. From their final remarks, Chiara assumes they must've viewed some clips from Ángel María's video files, obtained by subpoenaing his home computer. After a brief deliberation, the magistrates rule that Ángel María 'indulged in his unseemly leanings, provoking the youths to involuntary manslaughter.' To them—as to most of humankind—homophile is tantamount to pedophile, though that was not her friend's tendency at all. Tango and his pals receive the lightest sentences possible; they'll be eligible for full parole within a year.

Chiara can only bite her lip. Five against one? They

could've easily resisted any advances her friend might've made, no matter how aggressive. Besides, his overtures were never heavy-handed, as his former lovers could've attested—if any had been brave enough. From the many stories that circulated on the grapevine, and from her own experience at Espada del Sur, she knows he could be insistent at times; but even when he didn't succeed—as in her case—he always remained polite. Needless to say, no one invites her or any other woman to testify: for a man to make a pass at a female is merely par for the course.

True, he was strung out on liquor and drugs, just like his butchers. But even if he'd lost his self-control, how could these delinquents have felt 'shocked'? All five of them had records, even Tango—Diana had been right about that. Three of them had already served as rent-boys, when the opportunity arose. As for the other two, their walks on the wild side included armed theft and battery; they could hardly pose as innocent lambs. Maybe they planned to add hustling to their repertoire, if they hadn't done so already. Since Ángel María fondled them unguardedly, Tango must've told him they were 'up for grabs.'

In the end, what sways the court against the victim is his frankness: Ángel María, not his killers, is condemned for their crime. His heinous offense, for which he deserves torture and death, is no more—and no less—than the transmutation of values. In the mountains that night, as plainly as Diana at the party, he challenged the dictates of hypocrisy. His murderers couldn't forgive him for that, and neither can his judges.

Like his barbarous defacement, the effacement that follows his trial is radical. The hooligans ditched his corpse into a ravine; in that inept cover-up, only five banded together. But the erasure carried out in this final phase, as summed up by Virgilio's dictum, is absolute: all of society expunges Ángel María from its memory, private as well as public. In the same way, ever since Catulo's death, people never mention its cause; the dancer's illness is referred to as 'cancer' or 'meningitis.' A ghastly irony of AIDS is that those two diseases have acquired a euphemistic ring.

The initial consternation over Ángel María's death engenders grandiose obits in the press, once his body turns up. When the hearings begin, Canubans eagerly debate the topics raised by the defense, such as 'transculturation,' Bonaventuran Vodou, and illicit substances. Even a 'black mistress from the neighboring island' might pass, as long as she's only that. But as soon as bisexuality comes to the fore, the politician's name evaporates like morning dew. It's all right to link him to teenage gangs, 'Satanism,' or cocaine and meth; the 'other thing' cuts too close to the bone.

Once the reality surfaces, his family hushes up the judicial procedures; deep pockets can go a long way in buying journalistic 'reticence.' Ángel María's sister flies in from Monaco to lead the whitewashing campaign—though she stubbornly refuses to organize a memorial service.

According to Carolina, who fetches her at the airport in her limousine, Begonia feels no regret about his homicide, only about the societal fallout. As the chauffeur drives them to town, she laments 'all this ludicrous outcry.' She's known her brother would disgrace them with some sort of scandal, sooner or later. To her, it seems, his final agony means nothing; her fund-raising for Opus Dei is all that counts.

Before he becomes a right-wing Pope, Cardinal Ratzinger heads up the Congregation for the Doctrine of the Faith, formerly known as the Inquisition. Under his influence, John Paul II, a kindly pontiff who will soon be canonized as a saint, labels homosexuality a 'dangerous disorder'—while allegedly soft-pedaling the more grievous transgressions within the Church's ranks. It's rumored that Begonia and her husband shell out large bribes to muzzle the Canuban press, lest they lose their prestige among the ultramontane in Rome. If so, they needn't have bothered: when it comes to this topic, everyone on the island always keeps mum.

In the last stages of the trial, the brief notices about Ángel María's murder merely state that the defendants admit to attacking the victim and stealing his car, as though these were the only salient facts. The journalists even have the gall to bring up 'doubts about the gang's culpability,' or point to 'extenuating circumstances…' Palmoliva, Carolina, the dead man's children, and the rest of the country fall in line with this sanitized version. After a month or two, no one ever alludes to Ángel María again; his oblivion is now complete.

A Message from the Grave

Entering from the left, Chiara is hoodless; she slides the title A Message from the Grave *into the black rectangular frame. Paragraphs four and three from the end of the letter should be a Sprechstimme recitative, accompanied by the musical ensemble, and sung by the actor miming Ángel María on the mainstage. Entering from the right, The Male Reader replaces the Female Reader at the lectern.*

The Male Reader: This is the Forty-Fifth Reading.

During her stay at the cave in Barlovento, Ángel María sent a letter to Chiara at her Puerto Indio address. Five or six days after her return, when his corpse has already been unearthed, Luz Divina digs the missive from a kitchen drawer. Grandly, she presents it to Chiara on a silver tray.

— I was keeping this in a special place. The messenger said it was urgent.

'Then why on earth…' But with Luz Divina, there's no point in asking. Chiara breaks off her question, and opens the envelope. Ángel María's round, flowing script greets her warmly. She can almost hear him speaking, with his customary nonchalance:

Chiara, querida amiga, the only real friend I have in this world—

I've been trying and trying to call you, but your housekeeper tells me you've left for Barlovento. By the time you come back, I'll be out of town myself—in the mountains, and then at the beach. You could try my cell phone, but I'll probably turn it off during the holidays. So I want to make sure you get this note as soon as possible.

I'm sorry you had to go through that nasty scene with Diana the other night. But I'm glad you found out about the strains in our relationship. Knowing how changeable I am, you must be amazed that she and I have stayed together all these years. Sure, there are lots of things I haven't told you. I didn't want to hold anything back, but there were business considerations—let's put it that way—that required a lot of restraint, even where you were concerned…

First of all, I'd like to thank you for persuading her to leave the house. It gave me a chance to clear the air with Tango—not an easy task, believe me—and put the party back on track for the late-night guests. That was the best favor you could've done me, and knowing you, I'm sure you didn't stop there. Diana's often told me how much she enjoyed those days we spent together in Rome, just the three of us. Your stay with us in Espada del Sur, too. So I imagine after you left the other night you had a nice, long talk, and you tried to calm her down. That's the second reason I'm writing you, to ask if you'll do me an even bigger favor, and keep up the good work. Every time I call her, she cuts me off before I have a chance to say hello. She keeps the door bolted shut, and she won't let me in no matter how much I knock.

There are lots of things I need to explain to her, but I can't do it if she won't let me; so I'm wondering if you could break the ice. She's angry at me now because of Tango, and I know he must have come as a shock to her. We don't move in the same circles, so she didn't find out about my 'other life' with him until now. I guess she started snooping around because I didn't invite her to the party. As far as that goes, she shouldn't have been surprised. I've never appeared with her anywhere in public. She seems to be blaming me, but it's not my fault if Canubans don't like Bonaventurans. She should know they feel invaded by immigrants from her island, and in my position, I can't afford to offend my countrymen.

It's kind of weird, but for them, me being with her would be a lot harder to take than me being with Tango, because it would be… well, more obvious, I guess. You know how Canubans pick up on everything, but with Tango they can pretend he's just a young protégé, and avoid admitting the truth. But Diana is a striking, desirable woman. As a Bonaventuran, she's not part of our set, so tongues would start to wag. People couldn't manage not to notice. And I just can't do that to my wife and children. Not to mention my high profile in the government. All around, I have to keep up appearances. If it were just me, I wouldn't care. But even more important: if she and I were too up front, we might run into trouble, because of the business affairs

I mentioned earlier. When it comes to them, discretion has to be my top priority.

What I want to tell Diana is this: she should accept me as I am, because I've accepted her as she is, much more than she's realized up to now. She has no idea I've been aware of her and Amado all along. And there's another secret I've been keeping—from her, of course, but even from you, and for the same reason. You didn't know I was a friend of his, any more than she did. Isn't it obvious to you now? In his heyday, he was the best-looking guy on the island, and I made sure to cross paths with him. I met him through Catulo, before you settled in Puerto Indio, when Amado was still Héctor's boy. We had fun with each other several times, way back then—but that affair was 'history,' as the gringos say, long before my relationship with Diana. I didn't want to fight over Amado with Héctor, like you ended up doing. Our art-critic friend loves to stir up trouble, and I had to worry about my career with the government. You know how it is here: nobody cares what you do, as long as it isn't public.

Then fifteen or sixteen years ago, I ran into Amado in Diana's neighborhood, and we got to talking, like in the good old days. He let me know he was also seeing her, and I was bowled over. But why? It wasn't just a coincidence. She's beautiful, and he's always had great taste in women— you included. Even that idiot Reina he married was a knock-out in her younger days. I couldn't be angry at him for wanting Diana, any more than he could be angry at me. We were old friends, and more than friends, and we started meeting again pretty often after that. We couldn't talk about it with her—we did everything we could to put her off the scent. But maybe she'll learn to understand us now. The main thing for us was our little girl Lucita, the daughter Diana had with us. Amado and I used to laugh, because she tried to make each of us believe we were the father. Lucky for her, Lucita looks just like her mother. She doesn't take after either one of us. What Diana needs to know is this: Amado didn't care, and I don't care, who the father is. He and I always liked to think of Lucita as belonging to all three of us.

I've explained it a million times, but Diana doesn't want to understand why I had to send our daughter out of the country. It was because her mother and I have been forced to make some risky moves, and I didn't want an innocent child like Lucita to pay the price. She might've been kidnapped and held for ransom, or worse. And the more Amado found out, the more he agreed it was best for her not to stay around past her early years. As it turned out, he was the one that died, not Lucita—and not Diana or me. That was just a stupid accident: it could've happened to anybody. But I'm glad we have our daughter now to remember him by.

I'd like for Diana to know Amado and I were lovers, and that I knew they were lovers too. We're all in this together, so there's nothing to forgive. I'm glad he made her happy, the way he made me happy—the way he made you happy, too. Can't she see Tango like that? I wouldn't mind sharing him with her, and her with him—and both of them with you, if you weren't so hard to get. I don't expect bourgeois society to understand. As I say, I keep up appearances for my wife and children, and for business reasons, too—not to mention politics. Everybody on this island knows bits and pieces of the truth, but nobody wants to accept the entire picture. Diana is different. She's too sophisticated to go on being so damn limited. I want to be open with her, just as I was with Amado—and just as I am with you.

So please try to make her come to her senses. Tango is no threat to her, any more than Amado was. Poor Amado—I'll remember him, in the countryside he loved so much. Long ago, we went together to those mountains, to the same village where Tango and I are meeting up tomorrow. Every time I visit the higher ranges of Cipango, my childhood comes back to me—the summers I spent there with my grandparents on their ranch, riding my sturdy little horse and swimming in the river. And over Christmas, you're in a different country. It's cold up there, not like the tropics at all. Sometimes an icy drizzle makes you shiver. And you're not eating the same old mangoes and avocados: you can get fresh radishes, and cherries— and apples, too. And that wonderful milk-fudge, wrapped in leaves. Only the local campesinas know how to cook it: 'cremadura,' they call it.

It's funny, lately I've been thinking a lot about Amado. It's almost as though he's been shadowing me. Sometimes I turn around and look over my shoulder, expecting to see him. It makes me wonder whether anybody is ever completely dead—or completely alive. Part of him is still with me. And part of me is already with him, already gone. I think it's really true we die each day, little by little, right from the moment we're born. It's almost as though death is filling us up, drop by drop. Then suddenly we're dead, before we know it. But death has been inside us all the time, like something dark that keeps adding up. Invisible, but there.

Sorry if that sounds morbid, Chiara. You know I'm no philosopher—I don't keep my nose in the books like you. This is probably the longest letter I've ever written, or ever will: take it as a compliment. Over a drink I like to shoot the breeze, but what I really love is action. And I'm hoping to get a lot of that with Tango, up in the mountains. He's handsome, isn't he? But he says I won't think so, once I've seen his friends. He says they're 'the best-looking dudes around.' I can hardly wait. 'And they're cooperative, too,' he told me last night with a wink. He also tells me there are some great horses on his parents' farm. I plan to do a lot of 'riding' with Tango and his chums, if you know what I mean… but only if they're up for it.

Well, as you say, I'm incorrigible. I'd be the last to deny it. Please tell Diana I know my faults—but tell her it's all right. There's room for everything in life. See you soon. For now, a big hug from your old friend,

Ángel María

Like the detectives, she tries her best to track Diana down. When she calls the 'compañeros,' they tell her 'Rebeca' has left Espada del Sur for good. Chiara doesn't have her cell or landline numbers, but she drops by her townhouse a dozen times, day and night—to no avail. Before long, the court issues a subpoena, requiring the mambo to testify 'about her alleged Satanist cult.' Reporting on the first phases of the trial, the papers confirm Chiara's suspicions: Diana has disappeared without a trace. And if the police and the journalists can't find her, then neither can she. She'll just have to wait till the priestess contacts her—but not like Ángel María, she hopes, in a message from the grave.

Archaeology

Entering from the left, Diana is hoodless; she slides the title Archaeology *into the black rectangular frame. Entering from the right, The Trans Reader replaces the Male Reader at the lectern. Except for the first paragraph, the actor miming Chiara on the mainstage performs this text as a Sprechstimme recitative, accompanied by the musical ensemble.*

The Trans Reader: This is the Forty-Sixth Reading.

What of herself? I haven't died, Chiara keeps repeating to the ceilings and the walls; I haven't died. Ángel María's letter has sparked a recurrent dream. Pages from the Taíno codex come back to her, flooding her sleep with their bright, colored panes. She moves through the verdant fields, forgotten hamlets, and jungles on a defeated island—

all peopled with figures as stark as stained glass—until she crosses the threshold of the last illumination…

I am the woman you see before you: for me there can be no escape. Behind me, grey clouds boil over into a storm. It might be a hurricane, the whirling dance of Yúcatu the sea-god, who will blast away our villages, and bend our forests to the ground. I don't know, and I won't find out. Our cacique bowed and scraped to the white men's god, but their mangled idol couldn't save him.

Here he is, dead from the spots, the smallpox they brought in their ships; our clansmen bear his corpse to the burial ground. Women and children, we follow them; we file beside the ocean in a rhythmic step, to the thudding of the drums. The broad red leaves of the manca-trees fall from their branches, plucked off by the wind. I have been a servant all my life. I was taken by my master as his seventh wife, when I reached the age of twelve.

There is a custom and a law, and the youngest of the wives must be sacrificed. The older women have spoken: I must join the cacique in his grave. In the upper panel, on the page that lies before you, I beg them to let me live… Our lord himself no longer believed in the ancestral ways. I will take care of your children, I promise with all my heart; I will never have children of my own… But hard of heart, they do not listen… Ungrateful, stupid little snake; you have the honor of eternal life, but you reject your good fortune… Trembling, I throw myself at their feet. All I can do is weep.

Look how I dip to the right, down to the corner of the page, where the men drag me into the tomb. I cry out… No, no, no… With his hatchet, the eldest son smashes my head. My shout is frozen on my face. My flesh will putrefy, my bones will turn to dust; but I will not serve my master in the afterlife…

Now I am Chiara again… that is only one of my names. I walk beside the sea in this same place—or a thousand places, all the same. The sky is encased in sheets of lead. The scarlet manca-leaves, sinking to the ground in the steady breeze, remind me of an autumn far to the north.

I pick one up: brittle and dry, it feels like a piece of painted vellum, a fragment of ancient skin. I inch down the dangerous walkway; the ocean has washed away a third of the primitive steps. I've come to visit a neglected monument, preserved by Espinosa decades ago. He set this site aside to prove that the Indians were savage brutes, justly slain by the soldiers of the Faith.

A low, tin roof shelters the excavation, though rising waves nibble at its edges. I brush the debris aside with a tool I find chained to the floor: a scraper, thin and sharp as a woodpecker's beak. There, at the bottom of the tomb, shrouded by a film of brine and mud, I discover you—my sister, my twin. You crouch in a corner of the grave, holding up your arms to ward off the blow. The stone ax has met its mark. A hole the size of a fist gapes in your skull. Your jaws stretch wide in a never-ending scream.

We look into each other's eyes—eyes that once were and now are not, eyes that now are and one day will not be. We see where we've come from, and where we must go; soon we will know who we are.

The Robe of Fire

Entering from the left, Leandra is hoodless; she slides the title The Robe of Fire *into the black rectangular frame. Entering from the right, The Female Reader replaces the Trans Reader at the lectern.*

The Female Reader: This is the Forty-Seventh Reading.

With Horacio cloistered at the monastery, and Padre Flores immersed in his Quita Sueños ministry, Chiara has nowhere to turn. She tries to find solace with Frederica, but she's too self-centered to understand, much less to empathize. When Chiara confides that all the successive deaths have been weighing her down, the Countess stares at her wide-eyed. 'What deaths?' she wants to know. The decease of Catulo, Virgilio, and Ángel María, with whom Frederica fraternized for decades, has left her unmoved. Most shockingly, the suicide of Gustavo, her only child, doesn't even cross her mind.

But to them, Chiara has to add two significant others, Amado and Don Alfonso. All these kindred spirits have preceded her into the grave, tearing gashes in her life. Month by month, she has sunk into the slough of despond—so deep by now that she can barely struggle forward, pace by weary pace. Despite her attempts to be courageous, the roll call of the dead has finally taken its toll.

Mutability has cut them down one by one—either through wasting away or sudden quietus. But the devastation also takes a wider form: the slow undermining of everything she cherishes. In that hourly attrition, she witnesses her touchstones fragment and dissolve. In Barlovento, crooks from the Calabrian 'ndrangheta'—at least they aren't Sicilians, a smidgen of comfort—have spawned the first resort hotel on Playa Grandota, selling single rooms for the price of doubles. Other monstrosities—time-share condos, tacky McVillas, honky-tonk bars, casinos by the sea—have quickly followed suit. Halogen lamps now blaspheme the beaches where she and Amado galloped naked under the moon on their headstrong mare.

In the capital, the tranquil riverscapes surrounding Puerto Indio have given way to wholesale suburbia: ranch-burgers, row after row, tinted in Florida pastels. At a distance, high-rise apartment blocks overshadow the Barrio Antiguo, annihilating any sense of scale. With his usual bad taste, the Archbishop has delivered the coup de grâce, erecting high-tension wires on an industrial scale for his needs. Their concrete columns and unsightly cables set a unique example of ugliness: in every other Colonial quarter in the Americas, the grid has long since been buried underground.

The 'Columbus donut,' a mausoleum with one or two of the Admiral's bones, continues to drain the nation's power by shooting a halo of beams against the clouds. Outdoing the Pope, White Batman wants to say his masses in an air-conditioned cathedral, with plate-glass doors like a bank's: 'St. Peter's can't compare for modern comfort,' he assures his diminishing flock. Meanwhile, even in the Barrio Antiguo, a stone's throw from the church, the city's destitute swelter in the usual blackouts, unaided and unpitied by His Eminence.

In Chiara's early years, the island seemed pristine, almost as untrammeled as when Columbus had first set foot on its shores. At the noontime of her voyage, it rose intact from the ever-shifting sea: a terra firma, an Eden on earth, where her happiness could finally take root. Its royal palms, gleaming and svelte, lifted their crowns to the bounteous sun; its cordillera shouldered and braced the sky, like the rugged backbone of eternity.

But that brave vision, sculpted in radiant light, now flickers with the transience of a mirage. Canuba's fundaments have shuddered, in shocks and aftershocks; inexorably, the island is sinking back to the ocean floor. On the surface of the waves, all that lingers is a fire-ship: the illusion known as memory. The past has merged with the mist that enshrouds the Caribbean night; dream-logged and muffled, the future is reduced to a blank.

In this ceaseless erosion, her toehold has faltered; she's slipping into a bottomless pit. The more she tries to climb back, the more precipitous the slope becomes. Loss after loss has whittled away her sanity, until she fears she's losing her mind. In despair, she consults a shrink, something she's always sworn she'll never do. His 'mood-enhancers' are so drastic, they drive her through the roof with anxiety. When he switches her to sedatives, they numb her into listless inertia. Meanwhile, monthly eviction notices remind her that soon her house on Plaza Drake will be swept away by the unstoppable tide.

She grasps at a few final straws. Her tried-and-true solutions might still work: travel, hiking, and meditation. If she combines them, the healing effect might be magnified. She decides to go to a region she's never visited before, far away from the island. But she longs for the solace of the familiar, too—and Quebec is dotted with Catholic convents, like the Sicily of her childhood. She flies to Montreal, rents a car, traces an itinerary on the map, and sets out to restore her inner peace. Naturally, she will avoid the Mother House Gustavo visited, with its exorcisms and bigotry. She knows there's far more to Quebec than that.

In the countryside, the lilt of the grainy French gives her a fillip right away: from the St. Lawrence to the Gaspé, 'le québecois' sounds like aural driftwood, washed up from the Renaissance. With growing contentment, she treks through several parks along the vast Lake St. Jean. On its southwestern shore, she spends a week with the Trappistine nuns near Roberval, inspired by their abstract church. The sweeping roof of the wooden nave reposes on a massive omega, carved in solid oak; but to her, it also stands for zero, a symbol of the generative void. As so often, she has to smile at her own grab-bag of religions. For the Salve Regina, the sisters light candles before a Baroque Madonna—the only vestige of their former chapel, demolished years before. On the winds of the unworldly, borne by her swirling robes, she seems to be taking flight.

It's high summer, and the weather is perfect. Chiara presses onward and upward, walking for several days along the craggy Saguenay, the southernmost fjord on the planet. In Tadoussac, she joins a cetologist friend on a whale-watching trip, to observe the humpbacks in their summer habitat; it cheers her to think that she's met a few of them in Canuban waters, many years before. At times she even identifies their markings—a black streak on a grey-white head, a charcoal flipper spattered with milky dots, a tail with a V-shaped notch on one of its flukes.

Near the border with Vermont, she goes on another retreat, at the opulent cloister of Ste. Marie-sur-Lac. Like the Trappistines, the Ursulines own immense tracts of land—and like all the orders, female or male, they attract few vocations among the young. As everywhere else, Chiara has to acknowledge, here the Church is in crisis: most inhabitants of the 'Belle Province' have jettisoned their custom of daily Communion. It's mainly the rural poor who cling to their ancient beliefs.

But whatever their leanings, clerical or secular, Quebeckers always impress her as the *other* Latin Americans—surviving against all odds in the 'Anglo-Saxon' North. Like their confreres in the Spanish Caribbean, they flourish on song, dancing, fetes, and drink; their joie de vivre skips to the music of their earthy Romance tongue.

Over the border, in New England, her pilgrimage reaches its final goal—at a Buddhist center, not a Christian enclave. A cluster of dorms and meditation halls, it recycles the house and barns of an abandoned farm. Though equally austere, it's unlike the Zen monasteries she frequented in earlier years. No dharma talks, no cryptic koans; here the approach is simpler and more visceral. The participants pledge to maintain ten days of utter silence. Vipassana, the breathing technique of Theravada—the Minor Vehicle of Buddhism—has but one primary aim: to quell the over-active psyche, the constant chatter of the 'monkey-mind.' In fact, this is far harder than it sounds.

Divided by gender into two separate groups, the novices can't introduce themselves to each other. Her inner monkey blabbing, Chiara promptly invents names for the women around her, even if she has to keep them to herself. Once she's identified them as 'Wellesley,' 'Fanciulla,' or 'Marie Curie,' she can't resist spinning a yarn around each one. She tries to squelch these tales and focus on her breathing, but they sprout, fork, and loop like jungle vines. 'Felicity' has an autistic brother, and she considers his disorder her fault... Flat-chested and mannish, 'Agatha' grew up on a dude ranch... The parents of 'Pixie' owned a restaurant, until they moved to a nudist camp in Boca Raton...

Since she's always been an avid reader, her penchant for fiction hardly surprises her; but her second compulsion does. Left to its own devices, her mental rain-forest overflows with architecture and decors. She lays out city after city, quarter after quarter, square after square, landmark after landmark, house after house, room after room—down to the Biedermeier furniture, the Mantegna engravings on the walls, and the Sèvres plates in the sideboard.

But like the characters she's devised, these places all succumb to ruin. Her personae come down with fatal diseases, tumble off mountainsides, or vaporize while strolling down a lane. Her train stations collapse, her churches catch on fire, her art galleries molder into dust. As in Canuba, a Ming vase 'se rompe,' breaking of its own accord; a magnificent concert hall transfers its location on a survey map, remaining half-complete. Disquiet pervades her universe: it's turned into a giant trap, a quicksand of frailty and doom.

There's one young woman she's nicknamed Beauty

Girl—not because she's pretty, but because she often primps at the washroom mirror. What for? The men lodge in another wing; and even if her taste runs to females, they can't look at her here—eye-contact is 'interpersonal' for the contemplation monitors, as frowned-upon as an exchange of words.

Typically, Chiara knits the woman's entire story from that single stitch, her habit of preening: Beauty Girl was orphaned at birth, with no one to love but herself; her self-adoration led to frigidity. Unable to keep a human partner, she's developed a mania for dogs; but as soon as they sense her neuroses, they go on the lamb. And so on… the ramifications burgeon day by day. As a last resort, Beauty Girl has turned to Vipassana for deliverance… but what will happen afterwards? Tune in…

The feature of the compound Chiara prefers is a trail along a deep, narrow ravine. At the bottom, emblematic of the 'monkey-mind,' a noisy stream gabbles nonstop; its gurgling is close, but not so close that it dominates everything. Mindfulness has removed the slimy rocks below to an almost harmless distance. By calmly placing one foot in front of the other, you can free yourself from vertigo. If you proceed step by step, you can stroll beside the brook and listen to its jabber, without being taken in. There's little danger you can stumble, and plunge into the abyss.

One morning, toward the end of their stay, she and

Beauty Girl happen to meet on that path. Down in the gully, they see something strange, so strange they can't believe it. By now, they no longer trust their capacity to tell the real from the unreal. After many days of sitting-practice, you settle into a trance, a state that magnifies the senses. In the absence of stimulants like alcohol or caffeine—excluded from the center's vegan diet—a cup of herbal tea seems as heady as wine. A birdcall hundreds of yards away, a warble so faint it would normally go unheard, startles you with its poignance—an outpouring more fervent than Brahms.

The two women lean on the guardrail side by side, staring down at the roiling stream. Lank and awkward, four furry animals lope along beside it. Their elongated shapes and elastic movements remind Chiara of Dr. Seuss, whose books she once read to a neighbor's children in Princeton. Breaking the rules in their excitement, she and Beauty Girl glance at each other with brightening eyes. Have they both seen the creatures? It's a 'misdemeanor' to express themselves, even without speaking; but otherwise, how can they make sure they haven't skidded from Theravada into lunacy?

A naturalist friend of Chiara's will later conjecture that the animals must've been a family of otters. They rarely leave the water; but when a stream becomes too shallow, they have to lurch forward along its banks, as ungainly as canoers porting from lake to lake. The two passers-by both believe they've imagined the beasts. The incident discloses how open they've become, how willing to let themselves riff on the fancy of the moment, without cleaving to their obsessions.

Now they're ready for the last afternoon of their training, when the teacher abruptly shatters the stillness. It's oddly jarring to hear a voice. Out of the blue, she tells the apprentices to single out the people from the past they hate the most, and to forgive them with the clear serenity they've stored away, like patient bees filling a honeycomb. She suggests that those they bitterly despise might well be themselves…

Forgiveness: it seems like a Christian notion, tailored to satisfy Westerners. Still, Theravada—like latter-day Nichiren—is closer to popular piety than the abstractions of Zen. And in all schools of Buddhism, the Bodisattvas emanate mercy, as full of charity towards mankind as Christ. Searching far within herself, Chiara pardons her father, Héctor, Lamia, Diana, Ángel María, and Amado. All have made her suffer in varying degrees—either directly, through callousness and scheming; or indirectly, through their own self-destruction. But as she plumbs deeper, she uncovers fear, not hate: not fear of others, but of life itself.

From what she's read about war zones, death is so common it becomes something expected, almost matter-of-fact—though traumatizing to the soldiers over time, if they survive. By contrast, the declines or eclipses of her friends have transpired against a background of vitality: that's what has made them so disturbing. Behind the flowering orchid, there lurks the lethal spider; beneath the luminous wave, the marauding shark. If this gathering malaise comes to a head, it might demolish her. To overcome her anguish, she must forgive the world itself for stealing everyone and everything she treasures—and finally, for robbing her of herself. Yes, she has to answer its indifference with detachment; but more than that: her disavowal has to equal the highest stage of love.

In Christian terms, though many would take it amiss, she has to forgive God for her crucifixion, just as Jesus did: when he said 'this is my body,' given up for you; when he accepted the cup in Gethsemane; when he assumed he'd been forsaken. In reality, hers has only been a 'cruci-fiction', nothing more and nothing less. Instead of taking charge of her life, she's blamed external forces; whereas the truth, as always, lies somewhere in between. Everyone is both the victim and the torturer, the endless weaver caught in the endless web. No, you never change; you repeat your themes with only the slightest of variations. The three or four personae in your puppet show might change their masks, but they remain essentially the same. At best, all you do is trace your familiar circle upward instead of downward—in a spiral of ascent, and of assent.

At the beginning of her voyage through Quebec, Chiara visits the Musée des Beaux-Arts in Montreal. She stands for almost an hour before a landscape by Poussin; later, she'll often remember the painting. A boy appears in the foreground, just when a snake is sinking its fangs into his heel. He shudders with pain, but also with foreknowledge; he has no doubt that he'll die. The image is so bold that viewers often overlook the other three figures. The more Chiara studies them, the more they seem to comment on the main event, adopting different postures toward the cruelty of fate.

In the background, a bearded man ignores the tragic scene; idly reclining on the riverbank, he fishes with a slack pole and dangling line. Though fully aware of the incident, a clean-shaven man follows the road ahead of him, refusing to swerve from his path. But on the left, a beautiful woman raptly witnesses the boy's misfortune, with an unflinching gaze. Clothed in a robe the color of fire, she gives herself up to the compassion that will ravage her; and she wears the flames with joy.

Leaving the House

Entering from the left, Chiara is hoodless; she slides the title Leaving the House *into the black rectangular frame. The chant about the Builder should be a Sprechstimme recitative, accompanied by the musical ensemble, and sung by the actor miming Chiara on the mainstage. Entering from the right,*

The Male Reader replaces the Female Reader at the lectern.
The Male Reader: This is the Forty-Eighth Reading.

Years later, when she sees the landscape again at an exhibition in New York, Chiara realizes she's recomposed it to fit her needs. The boy is only frightened by the snake, which isn't near enough to strike him. There's no man striding along the road at all, though she can still visualize his stolid face and resolute gait. The woman stands not on the left, but on the right, and she's staring at a point outside the canvas, not at the central figure.

Back then, Chiara turned the painting into the one she required. Did the dying boy symbolize her panic? Did the man display a stoicism she couldn't muster—that literally 'wasn't there'? Did the woman focus her whole being on someone else, as Chiara never could?

The pictures we've seen are superimposed; layer by layer, they accrete into a mental palimpsest. A similar Poussin in London shows the youth already dead, and the serpent entwining his corpse. In a Caravaggio a few rooms away, a lizard has bitten a child, who winces in pain. Another version in Florence is even more emphatic... A curatorial show-piece, it travels from exhibition to exhibition. She's come across it at the Jacquemart-André in Paris, and yet again in an odd potpourri at the museum of Ravenna, *Miseria e splendore della carne... 'Misery and splendor of the flesh'...* There's also the youth in a portrait by Cavalori, who pulls aside his flesh to reveal his heart… There's also… There's also… All the images have fused.

And so, she can't vouch for another 'souvenir' she's brought back from her trip. At the end of the cycle of meditation sessions, the leader sang an ancient chant in Pali, then in English. Chiara believes she's come across it later, in a book of monastic verse; in any case, she's translated it long ago into the fable that helps her survive:

Builder, I have found you out;
you will not build another house.
Your rafters have broken,
your ridgepole has fallen;
all desire has come to an end.

Whether she likes it or not, she'll have to give up her refuge in Puerto Indio, so she might as well do so with lightness in her step. She should welcome her departure as a liberation—a heaven-sent, magnanimous gift.

Like the Poussin in Montreal, the Buddhist allegory seems as many-sided as the 'lilies of the field' or the 'camel through a needle's eye.' But why not take up all the parables and tales again, she asks herself, going back to that of Gilgamesh? Foundational myths or lessons for living, they distill new meanings over time—like physical objects, from tables and chairs to galaxies. It's misleading to make false distinctions: in fact, the table is a composite of atoms, the remnants of extinguished stars. But it's also simply a table, where Love invites you to 'sit and eat.' Despite astronomy, we can still perceive the outlines of the gods in the sky; each time we presume we've grasped the universe, a breakthrough sends us back to reframe our quest again.

Yet there's no reason to reject our previous points of view. If nothing else, they create the history of our truth—or more likely, our truths. Chiara revisits the 'Prodigal Son,' a story that seems to dovetail with her half-imagined painting. Is there really a right and a wrong? She believes that sometimes there is—in an immediate, instinctive sense. But once the moment is missed, she doesn't have to wallow in guilt, year after year: she might become her own forgiving father, and dismiss her childish mistakes.

Her house is a house without walls, like life itself: the only house she can never lose, because she's already lost it from the start—second by second, hour by hour. And when she accepts this, she has shed her ultimate fear: the fear of death, which is only the fear of time.

Migration

Entering from the left, Diana is hoodless; she slides the title Migration *into the black rectangular frame. The last four paragraphs should be a Sprechstimme recitative,*

The Trans Reader: This is the Forty-Ninth Reading.

After Chiara's eviction, she's certain she'll say farewell to Puerto Indio: 'the world is all before her, where to choose her place of rest.' But in the end, she knows that place will choose her. Not only because of her travels, but also because of her wandering mind, she's always been a migrant... As a farfetched consolation, she envisages her uprooting on a vaster scale.

Like many sectors of the globe, the Caribbean is affected by increasing migration. In the first decade of the millennium, magazines around the globe are touting Canuba as the premier tourist destination of the archipelago, and the fastest-growing economy in Latin America. But the benefits aren't trickling down to everyone—and besides the vacationers, there are travelers of a desperate stripe. The island is well-placed to understand the problem from both sides, given the outflow of its citizens to North America and Europe, and the inflow of Bonaventurans to Canuba.

One reason for the meteoric rise in illegal voyages from Canuba to Puerto Rico is the confusion about a change in US policy. The federal authorities in San Juan suddenly offer amnesty to all 'indocumentados' who seek to regularize their status. But in Canuba, the proposal is widely misquoted as exonerating anyone who reaches the adjacent island on their own. Human traffickers encourage the fallacy in order to drive up demand for their services. Before long, the American Coast Guard is intercepting around nine hundred boat-people a month, and the Canuban Navy is staving off a similar number before they can leave the island. No one can guess how many thousands cross the Esperanza Channel without getting caught, or drown unnoticed in its chronic storms.

Unexpectedly, a story breaks that galvanizes attention to the crisis. The heroine of the saga is none other than Diana, who's disappeared from Chiara's radar after their face-off the year before. Suddenly she's a constant presence in the media, not only in Canuba, but also in Europe and the States. Thanks to her new-found fame, she has no trouble obtaining visas nowadays, wherever she wants to go.

Until she views the priestess on several American talk shows, Chiara has never realized she speaks English so well. She recalls that Diana did a stint in her youth as an intern for Oxfam in Ghana. Since then, she's probably improved her command of the language by collaborating with foreign NGOs, on behalf of the poorest Bonaventurans. In one of the interviews, Oprah Winfrey urges her to write a blow-by-blow memoir of her odyssey, and promises to feature it in her book club series. The upshot is that Diana receives an advance from Doubleday, and returns to Puerto Indio in triumph. She plans to amass the impressions of other illegal migrants, as counterfoils to her own experience.

Her ordeal begins shortly after Ángel María's murder; in the latest press accounts, she refers to it discreetly as 'the death of a close friend.' To Chiara's bemusement, she denounces another of her patrons by name: Filiberto Castañeda, Lamia's ex-husband. Diana fumes that he got her pregnant and then rejected her, after leading her on with promises of marriage. Was this a wily ploy to extort even more financial support for her daughter?

Chiara never guessed she was Amado's lover, 'Esperanza,' until Diana herself told her. It's astounding to learn that in addition to his and Ángel María's, she's also been Filiberto's mistress—the 'skank' often denounced by Lamia. Did he know about her other two lovers? Among her many professions, the mambo is an accomplished courtesan; with no effort on her part, men swim into her net. Like Balzac's Esther, she possesses a beauty they can't resist—and more than that, an intoxicating fascination. What sobriquet did she use with Filiberto? Aspasia, Cleopatra, Mata Hari?

Before long, she's able to ask Diana in person. A few days after her arrival at the airport, where her flight is met by thousands of fans, the priestess rings her up. — Could we meet somewhere, my Italian 'sorella'?

Mystified, but moved to hear her voice again, Chiara invites her to lunch. — Of course. Just the two of us, here at home. While I still have a home...

Oh no. From the sound of it, we have a lot of catching

up to do. — They make a date for the following Saturday, the only free slot in Diana's tight schedule.

The meal will cause trouble with Luz Divina, Chiara's crusty maid of all works. She won't be able to leave as early as she likes, at two in the afternoon. Worse, she'll have to wait on a 'Bono,' a 'prieta' even darker than herself. Trying to mollify her, Chiara touts Diana as a 'celebrity, famous around the world.' But no: though she's seen the priestess on TV, to Luz Divina she's just a 'hussy.'

To complicate matters, she's identified her as the same woman who consorted with Amado many years before; she's still scandalized by their comportment to this day. — He slept with *her* in your bed! — Chiara volunteers to cook and serve the meal herself. But Luz Divina relishes self-sacrifice: her employer has to behold each moment of her agony, as she wins the martyr's palm.

On the appointed morning, they wage the usual battle of wills. Luz Divina complains that she's run out of propane gas. 'Why didn't you say so before?' Chiara sends an errand boy to refill the tank. Predictably, other snags ensue. They're out of parsley. Pepper. Cilantro. Chiara doesn't cave in. 'That's all right, Luz Divina; we'll have to do without them.'

When the lunch hour rolls around, the housekeeper glories in her suffering. She glowers, sighs, and curses under her breath; as she serves them, each gesture seems like a herculean task. Backstage, in the kitchen, she maniacally clangs pots and pans, scrapes chairs across the floor, and rearranges the cupboards.

It's a huge relief when Chiara and Diana finally escape to the rooftop terrace with their coffee. Fifteen minutes later, they hear Luz Divina slam the front door, and then they watch her stalk across the Plaza. A Bonaventuran doesn't need to ask the whys and wherefores; Diana has been through all of this before...

The women slalom in a lingo of their own, an amalgam of French, English, and Spanish. They make fun of Diana's 'Adventures in Medialand,' holding hands now and then. And when it comes to Filiberto, they can't contain themselves.

What did you make him call you?

He didn't want to know my real name. To him, I was 'Mamacita.'

'Hot Babe'? That's pretty lame.

Oh, the harder they try, the dumber they get...

Spoken like an expert... Well, he was already tamed by Lamia. You're meek as a lamb compared to her.

I've never met her. Ça va sans dire. All he ever told me was: 'I hate that bitch.'

She does take some getting used to!

They marvel at the 'sintonía' they've reestablished; their effortless rapport takes them back to their halcyon days in Espada del Sur. They even joke about the prickly aspects of the past.

Chiara proposes a 'Lovers of the Beloved League,' in

honor of Amado; but Diana protests. — We'd need a super-computer to store all the names.

Not as big as the one we'd need for Ángel María…

Diana is deadpan. — I don't have any room to talk. What's the expression? Glass people throwing stones…

What has transformed her? Chiara wonders. The days at sea?

The bougainvillea, hibiscus, and jasmine hover around them, a mottled cloud of magenta, purple, coral, yellow, and pink. They fall silent; but there's no discomfort in the air, only a sense of expectancy. After a long pause, Chiara can't avoid asking. — Did you do the same thing to Ángel María you did to Amado? Did you 'lift your protection' from him, too?

No, no… — The question startles Diana; but she continues without spite. — I learned my lesson from Amado. When Ángel María turned his back on me, I left it at that. He didn't love me anymore—that was all.

But he did love you, for heaven's sake! You priests are as bad as doctors. You think you're all-knowing, but you're not. I've been waiting to show you this for over a year. — She pulls his letter out of its envelope.

Diana reads it intently; and then she begins to weep. When she lifts her head, she faces Chiara squarely. — I've been a fool all along. I heard that Ángel María died a terrible death. But I didn't know he and Amado were such good friends, and for so many years. I loved them both—

too much to see them as they really were. If only I'd had more time, maybe I could have gotten used to the idea. All right, I think I can say it now: used to the fact they were lovers as well as friends. The line is so thin, why not erase it? It's amazing that two machos like them could agree to share a child.

I'd say it's a tribute to you as much as to them.

A spark of fire dances across her eyes. — I was furious, when Ángel María took up with Tango. His letter explains one side of how he felt; but it can't change everything he did to me. To all of us, including himself… — She takes a deep breath. — I was right about that scumbag Tango, anyway. He got off the hook this time, but he'll self-destruct sooner or later. And so will his pals.

She goes on to say that long before the murder, she was warned by her sources that Tango was a thug. She wanted to contact the cops, but they already suspected her of abetting illegals; if she'd come forward, she would've ended up in jail. For a Bonaventuran woman, prison in Canuba is worse than capital punishment. The guards would've abused her over and over, till she died of AIDS or exhaustion. She had no choice but to go underground. Ditching everything she owned, she left the apartment just as it was. In any case, without Ángel María, she couldn't have paid the rent.

Chiara's voice betrays no malice. — Didn't Filiberto chip in? He should have.

Oh, his motto was always 'a pay for a lay.' He's an

accountant: he figured out what method would cost him the least. No loans, no regular support. Only 'piecework.' He's the one I'd hate now, if I could still hate anyone; but he's just a little idiot.

For years, Diana plays a double game with him, hoping he'll free her from Ángel María. But she never loves him; she only exploits him, just as he exploits her. Several months before she leaves Canuba, she finds out she's pregnant with a second child. This time she knows whose it is—Filiberto's—since she hasn't slept with Ángel María for a year. She never imagines that at over fifty, she's still fertile, so she's been fairly lax about taking the pill. Filiberto uses condoms, but one of them must have leaked.

When she tells him the 'good news,' the bean-counter panics. He's terrified of Metaxa, his father-in-law. He makes the mistake of fessing up to the old man, who screams at him from his wheelchair. — Having a child with a Bono will cause a scandal! And betraying my daughter Lamia? It'll hurt the entire company!

Filiberto tells Diana he'll call the police if she ever comes begging him for a hand-out. He wants her to have an abortion, but she refuses. According to Vodou, it's a mortal sin; the loas never forgive a crime like that. They would've mounted her without mercy; they would've ridden her like a nag till the end of time... — Her eyes lose focus; she's roving far away.

Chiara prompts her. — Where did you hide?

Filiberto said he would hunt me down. I took refuge in a Bonaventuran batey, deep in the cane-fields near Coyambaya. My people rescued me. They never pried, they never asked me who I was. I wore ragged, second-hand clothes, just like the other women. If I had to talk, I only spoke in Bonavent.

When the Canuban foreman questions her, she says she comes from a faraway village; her husband disowned her, and kicked her out of the house. In the batey, she cooks for the bachelors, washes their clothes, and tidies up their huts. She's always aided others in their poverty, but now she's become dirt-poor herself—going on, day after day, with no hope of betterment... After a while it becomes hypnotic, almost like a litany. At her convent school in Saint-François, the nuns always repeated: to work is to pray. Laborare est orare. She finally understands what they meant.

But after the trial, when things calm down, she has to make her move. Who's looking after her daughter in San Juan, now that Ángel María is dead? Did he make some provision for her in his will? Once the monthly payments stopped, did the girl's foster parents put her out on the street? How would she complete her college education? Diana is seven months pregnant, but she feels compelled to search for Lucita right away.

No matter what, she has to leave the island. She lives in constant dread of being recognized. Not only is she afraid of Filiberto, the investigators of Ángel María's murder have now connected the dots, linking her closely with human trafficking. The government has issued an all-points alert, with pictures of her at every police station. She expends her last money—3,000 escudos she's kept in a torn felt cap—to buy a passage on the cheapest boat. Her contacts push her to the top of the list; in a matter of days, she embarks in a rundown trawler.

The afternoon light is beginning to mellow; through a filigree of climbing vines, it gilds the crooked buttresses of the cathedral apse. — You set out from an inlet near Playa Nieves, didn't you? That's what I read in the papers.

Yes, at a cove a good ways from the town. I've said all that to the press, but I've never owned up to the worst of the story.

The engine stops working when they're only a few kilometers out. At first, no one touches the boat's radio, to keep the signal from being picked up. As the crew gets desperate, and tries to mayday the coastguard, they realize the batteries have rusted into junk. The small, overcrowded craft tosses uncontrollably under the blazing sun, in heavier and heavier seas. There are forty-five people on board, maybe fifty. About half die the first week, including the captain; diarrhea and sunstroke do them in.

Nobody has to push the bodies off the boat. After a while, a big wave washes them away, dead or alive. — The tallest waves are like that, Diana says; the crew calls them 'marullos,' and you can't resist them when you're weak. One young man holds his lover in his arms for hours, trying to keep him safe; but in the end, a giant marullo sweeps them off together. It's the same for a family of five: the mother, the father, the two girls, the little boy. All in a single wave.

In the second week, the sea turns calmer, and it starts to rain. The survivors capture water in a tarpaulin, so they no longer suffer from thirst. But their supplies have run out, and their hunger is unbearable. That's when the most horrible phase sets in…

Two men, a Canuban and a Bonaventuran, are still in fairly good shape. Like the other campesinos, they've brought their machetes along. Every time one of the sick succumbs, they chop off pieces of the arms and legs while the meat's still fresh. They tie the corpses to the gunwales till they're through with them, and only shove them overboard when they get too ripe.

Yes, that was reported in the media. It must've been awful.

Diana wavers for an instant; then she bursts out. — Yes, Chiara, yes. But here's what I've never told anybody else.

When the men see she has a chance to survive, they feed her, too. They won't take no for an answer. She chokes on the raw human flesh, but some of it goes down.

You can't imagine how dreadful it is, she says, to spend weeks on the open sea. Without any shade, under the limitless sky. The rain comes and goes; but the sky is always there. The day-sky and the night-sky. An enormous eye that changes color but never shuts.

Before people breathe their last, they start raving. They think they're walking down the street in Puerto Indio, or making love with their wives, or taking their First Communion, or drinking rum and playing dominoes.

The whirling glare of the sun hits you from every side, bouncing off the sea. But the moon is what really drives you mad—watching you night after night, while you slide up and down on the waves. It's the face of death closing in on you, a relentless, flattened skull.

Diana pauses. — And I'm the same as everybody else. Some are willing to go, and some aren't. With my beliefs, I always thought dying would be easy; but I was wrong. You have to be ready. It's not a question of faith. You can't be released, if you're bound by hate and love.

Self-hate and self-love.

Yes, most of all. To me, hate and love will always taste of human blood—sickly, salty, and sweet. One night, I have a miscarriage: it happens while the men are stuffing more meat into my mouth. As the unblinking moon stares down, all I can think of is blood. Blood flowing into me, blood flowing out of me.

The men throw the foetus overboard instead of eating it—a last nod to decency. I'm too exhausted to object, or even to say a prayer. Thick clouds bear down on us, and everything goes dark. The sea gets rougher and rougher; the waves are like high, collapsing cliffs.

Without the moon, the ocean is black as night. Night is all around us, up and down, so I can't tell which way we're heading. I long for the baby I've just lost, and then I feel a warmth in my breasts. There's milk trickling out, dripping down my belly to my thighs.

The men creep closer, and I know what they want. I let them suck my nipples like baby boys, like black and brown twins. We keep on that way for three or four days, and I lose my strength bit by bit. But it doesn't matter. I can't stand the taste of blood anymore—the taste of hate and love. I'm ready now, ready to leave this life behind. Ready to go to Guinea, where I belong.

The last few passengers stop breathing, and the men shove them into the ocean. They don't cut them up anymore. 'We never wanted to, we never wanted to'—that's what they say over and over, crying like little children.

I put my arms around their shoulders. They suck on my breasts and kiss me, suck on my breasts and kiss me, so some of the milk flows from their mouths into mine. That's how I survive, whether I like it or not.

And then in the dead of night, the boat falls apart. There's no moon, no stars: the sky hangs so low, the clouds are like an iron lid. Our voices are too weak to call out.

We float in the water... We drift away from each other, into the dark... I'm alone, and I'm nowhere. I can't see, I can't hear. There's only the softness of the water, and the salt in my mouth...

After a while, that ends too. I'm totally numb. I can't tell if I'm still alive or already dead. There isn't any difference anymore. I wish I could call it peace. But it's nothing. Not even nothing…

And I'm less than that. Less than nothing…

Lucita

Entering from the left, Leandra is hoodless; she slides the title Lucita *into the black rectangular frame. Entering from the right, The Female Reader replaces the Trans Reader at the lectern.*

The Female Reader: This is the Fiftieth Reading.

All three survivors lose consciousness—each of them sure that death has come. They've never guessed how near they are to shore. Shortly after dawn, the sea coughs them up at Piedad Bay—a deserted arc of sand near Playa Nieves, not far from where they embarked three weeks before. Unconscious, their bodies are tumbling in the surf, twenty or thirty meters apart.

A few local fishermen are standing on the beach. Earlier, the fitful sky threatened a storm, and they hesitated to launch their boat. But now the clouds begin to break; and in the light of the early sun, they catch sight of the three heads bobbing offshore. Revving up their outboard motor, they're determined to bring them in—dead or alive.

By pressing their chests and puffing into their mouths, they restore their breathing to normal. The medics of the Canuban Navy, who arrive at the beach an hour later, take care of the rest. Lurching down potholed roads in military vehicles, they rush Diana and the two men to a clinic in the town of Nieves, where they remain in critical condition for several days.

As soon as her companions are able to talk, the story of Diana's altruism emerges. Loyally, they never speak of how they crammed human flesh down her throat. They only tell about their own dilemma—and how by offering her milk, and draining herself of resilience, she risked her life to save theirs. Far from hiding their cannibal acts, they detail them to the press, though they express the deepest guilt for what they've done. Thanks to the priestess, they recount, they weren't tempted to defile the last passengers on board...

For Diana, her charity in extremis means not only fame, but also security from bureaucratic harassment. Her equal treatment of the Canuban and the Bonaventuran becomes a byword—an emblem of racial and national harmony— and now no immigration official would dare to deport her, much less accuse her of human trafficking. Under the spotlight of the media, any such move would unleash a global uproar; the NGOs she's worked with over the years would also staunchly rally to her defense.

Once her US residence visa is approved, she intends to settle in Miami, a city with a huge Bonaventuran community. For the time being, she sets up house again in Puerto Indio; her daughter Lucita comes from San Juan to join her, and continue her studies in Canuba. As it turns out, she need not worry about the girl's financial welfare. Ángel María created a generous trust for her, shortly before his decease—'in memory of Amado Paniagua,' the legal documents specify.

This was something he wanted to tell Diana in person; but his horrifying murder thwarted his aim. To avoid any further disrepute, Palmoliva and Carolina concealed the legacy, even from Chiara—though they duly mete it out. But Diana doesn't want to profit from her daughter's wealth. If all proceeds as planned, her book about migration will more than tide her over, at least until she finds a stable livelihood.

Even so, she confronts a different kind of quandary. She's read a great deal, but she's never written anything before. How should she go about it? On the day she has lunch at Chiara's house, she seems totally at a loss. Her hostess takes a positive tack. Jot down some notes, she suggests; and then keep plugging away.

An Inside Narrative

Entering from the left, Chiara is hoodless; she slides the title An Inside Narrative *into the black rectangular frame. The penultimate five paragraphs should be a Sprechstimme recitative, accompanied by the musical ensemble, and sung by the actor miming Chiara on the mainstage. Entering from the right, The Male Reader replaces the Female Reader at the lectern.*

The Male Reader: This is the Fifty-First Reading.

As soon as Diana leaves, a smile crosses Chiara's lips. She hasn't really answered her question. How can she? She's only published articles, shorter or longer, in travel magazines. But her desk-drawers and closets are full of notebooks—multiple versions of the same reclusive person, her other self. She sometimes regards them as brothers and sisters, hypocrites who can never be appeased. They keep her going, but they won't let her end.

For twenty years, they've been her solace, her medium of contemplation. They always verge on becoming a book, but never do. At the eleventh hour, they warn her that writing a narrative is like building a house. As you live inside it, more and more—first as a dream, and then as a finished construction—it changes everything about you: your habits, your character, your very being. Like it or not, you become the prisoner of your own creation. The novel is a labyrinth—and finally, a mausoleum.

Despite everything, she wants to go on living; and so, she scribbles and scribbles, week after week, with no conclusion in sight. The tropical island she invents grows more and more luxuriant, extending thousands of pages from shore to shore. It swells into a continent; but then it buckles, dissolves, and spills beyond the map. Like the Ocean Sea of the Admiral's charts, laced with monsters and mermaids, it falls off the edge of the world.

Even so, she has a sextant and an astrolabe. Long ago, she adopted two basic rules of narration. The first is simple enough: linear progression; though like memory, it can also run in reverse. The second is this: you can fracture a story as much as you like, even to the point of breakdown, as long as you kept shifting it from within. You can make the account double back on itself by subverting the plot, the personae, the underlying meaning, or all three.

This can happen in unexpected ways, as her favorite tale proves. The last third of *Genji* has nothing to do with the prince himself, either in development or in atmosphere—not on the surface, at least. Genji is already dead, and he's rarely evoked in the rest of the account. Now his 'son' is the protagonist, a character who appears to be his opposite. Their bogus kinship is a fiction within a fiction, like a play within a play.

Genji excels at womanizing, martial prowess, and the arts. Young Kaoru, timid and unassuming, dithers at every turn. The religious theme, muted in the first two thirds of the work—a few Shinto rites, devoted to the Emperor—now moves to the forefront, as the entire Court adheres to the Buddhist creed. Genji glories in fleshly pleasures, from the most straightforward to the most refined. Kaoru abjures the senses, striving to evade the snares of desire.

Their false blood-tie brings out their spiritual link, stretching the plot beyond its material skein. The 'son' is as obsessed with love as Genji, though his passion occupies a different register. The three sisters he woos accept him as their husband—not as the spouse of their bodies, but of their souls. Two of them die young, and the third becomes a nun. Kaoru seduces them more radically than Genji could ever have done. What seems at first like a departure from the narrative is really its fulfillment: or in fact, departure and fulfillment are one.

The narrative serpent circles back to bite its tail. It doesn't matter whether Murasaki finished the book; her authorship of the coda has often been disputed. By this point, as in Homer, the epic has created its own world, and generates itself. Though advancing in time, the second yarn is sewn backward into the first, like the somber lining of a bright kimono. A celebration of shadows undergirds the saga of Genji, throwing his radiant tale into high relief. When a black cloud looms behind a light-struck landscape, it chisels the hills, meadows, and brooks far more sharply than the sun.

In his essay on darkness, Tanizaki describes a sight once common in Japan: beautiful women with blackened teeth, seated at the end of an enfilade of screens. In the candle-light of winter afternoons, they embody a lustrous dimness, an aesthetic of obscurity... Light doesn't exist without a counterfoil; Chiara learns to accept this, when Amado dies. As she lingers alone on the roof that night, she carries the notion one step further: thinking of Diana and the men at sea, she gives up her belief in detachment.

Can she restore it at a further remove? The moon is in its invisible phase, and ponderous clouds have buried the stars. She can't see the light, but it's there; a reassuring metaphor, but only for a moment. The truth is much more terrible than that: without suffering, there would be no compassion; without grief, there would be no love. Behind the clouds, the faceless moon: is anything left? On a night as black as this, the only moon still shining is the wayward moon of words...

She thumbs through some of her notebooks. They seem to reminisce on their own, telling her about their memories. You've spent so many months with us, they murmur, speaking in various voices. Together, on a cliff above the sea, we've watched the choreography of light and dark. Day by day, we've seen the wind shatter the watery plain, blowing the waves white and black.

We've seen the ocean rage like a tortured elephant, or rest on a shelf like a looking-glass of bronze. We've seen it turn to milk, to steaming sweat, to curdled blood. We've seen it streaked with ribbons of conch-shell, lilac-grey, and copper-green, or swept with whitecaps like flurries of snow. We've seen the clouds float over it like red balloons, banks of purple sage, curtains of yellow and orange, rainbows arrested in mid-flight.

Rainbows—we've seen them by the hour. Aerial oil-slicks. Patches of iridescence. Sundogs chasing fogdogs. Cirrus ribs with rainbows crouching inside, till they lose their shyness and swing from cloud to cloud. We've seen the sunset cordon the earth with fire, like a supernova swallowing it whole. All these lessons have been good; but none is better than a simple ray of light, when it pinpoints a branch or rock.

At night there is the moon, always unpredictable; and sometimes there are moonbows, the rainbows of the moon. In Chiara's time at the mouth of the cave, they descend from the dark like curving stigmata—in limpid mist, or after several days of rain. As in an ancient myth, the moon lifts up her hunting horn of cloud; she wheels away, her profile half-concealed. And then her moonbows tauten and span the sea, vaults of silver and ash that tunnel through the sky.

On other nights, the moon mounts the thunderheads like a rider changing shape, transforming and transformed. Cascades of blindness, twisted organ-pipes, swirling garbage, tattered pages, plovers veering from coal to chalk, shipwrecks and landslides, herds of horses slashed by cobalt blue… Windows that open on battlegrounds, on walls of hopelessness, on dead-ends beyond salvation…

What is it about the moon? A union of extremes: a Janus of pitch-blackness and dazzling light. A glitter all reflective: a giant mirror, not a source. It never flares, never radiates; it only gathers, impassively, the afterglow of day. A walking death that imitates the paces of the sun. A graveyard in the sky, as bleak as the flower-seller's call: 'flores para los muertos.'

When the moon scatters its snapshots through the clouds, they gleam at a second remove. When the pictures glimmer on water, glass, or polished stone, they shine at a third remove; and on and on, into the abyss… The shadow of the tree becomes a razor, more incisive than the tree. Moonlight is final darkness, resurrected from the tomb. The moon is our vicarious life, the life of words.

The notebooks are waiting. Left to themselves, she knows they'll spin and weave, stitch and unthread, fraying the story into silence. Once upon a time, the cosmos was made of matter and light, scattered through empty space. Now the void is full: darkness is the essence of the universe. For a decade or two, that might be our narrative—until we tell the tale again…

The next morning, Chiara calls Diana. — I'd like to help you with your book. — She can't bring herself to say more; no, not yet.

The Mariner

Entering from the left, Diana is hoodless; she slides the title The Mariner *into the black rectangular frame. Paragraphs eleven through thirteen should be a Sprechstimme recitative, accompanied by the musical ensemble, and sung by the actor miming Chiara on the mainstage. Entering from the right, The Trans Reader replaces the Male Reader at the lectern.*

The Trans Reader: This is the Fifty-Second Reading.

That evening, one of the notebooks trudges into her study, unannounced. Dog-eared and worn, he has a haggard look; he must've spent too many months at sea. Defiantly, he tosses a manuscript on her desk.

Lately, she's taken to writing on a laptop at the back of the house; she's almost abandoned the large front room. When the intruder barges in, she's grappling with another kind of notebook—staring at the screen, racked by a spell of self-doubt.

She'll never understand the island: it will always be an enigma—a low-hanging cloud... tantalizingly close, but just beyond her reach. All she can do is shuttle through her fantasies, trapped inside a mirage. They seem to have no bearing on her own experience—much less anyone else's. Her only consolation is this: the longer you walk in circles, the more likely you are to find what you've missed.

Don Quixote's adventures reach their climax in part

two, when his chivalrous romance has finally come to life. Instead of a scarecrow or a vagabond, an actual Duke has welcomed him to his palace—an edifice of marble, no longer a haystack or a barn. Instead of being rebuffed by a peasant girl, he's honored by a Duchess. Even so, he clings to his illusions, unable to comprehend where he is; he throws away the only moment he can't afford to waste.

There are times when we should drop our masks, and step away from our roles; times when the play becomes the real. Times when the erosion of the world will settle in our hearts, if only we consent to be the heart of things…

But is this fair? Maybe our illusions *are* reality, much harder than any castle of stone…

Notebooks are stubborn: no doubt about that. The mariner waves toward the stack of paper he's brought along. — Glance at this later, if you want.

She recalls that manuscript from decades ago, all in verse. Lines bar each page like the rungs of a lopsided ladder. Couplets, tercets, septets. Numerology: do not enter here.

He challenges her. — Why don't you take a little break? It's a lovely evening, one that will never return.

'I can see that for myself.' From her desk, she looks at the terrace through the wide-open doors. 'All the more reason…'

In the late afternoon, awareness seems to collect in scattered pools, to coalesce the fragments left by day. Light clings to the walls and plants, questioning each speck of paint, pondering each stem. It gingerly unfolds the leaves of the bamboo, and reads the fronds of the motionless palms.

There is a time in the intervals of time, when dusk is like a morning flowing backwards; when knowledge still hangs golden on the tree—no longer forbidden, but granted before you ask. In this daily equilibrium, twilight dawns. Abstractions lie before you like objects on a table, and even their shadows are luminous.

The transparence is the mystery itself: as might be suddenly a place you've known for many years—a place so familiar, you can picture it from memory without a fault. But what of it now… and now again? What seems like an island by day, turns into a cloud by night.

Here you are, a reflection on the screen; and also a ragged notebook, waiting in front of the doors. Your face retreats into the counter-light, but your outline is clear as a bell. That faulty image of life—that metaphor, forever mixed—ripples through the room and into the garden, visible as sound…

She puts the laptop aside, not bothering to shut it down. The screen will continue to glow as darkness gathers—just as late at night, in forgotten churches, a few candles burn for departed friends… In the gloom where she sees them flicker, she hears the old, implausible words: Let the dead bury their dead.

Not resisting any longer, she follows the notebook to

the roof. They settle into their chairs again, exactly where they've always sat, between the hibiscus and the jasmine. Framed by a tangle of vines, the cathedral apse rears above the plaza like a cliff, a gravestone at the end of space. It has to happen, sooner or later. She must give up her lovers for lost: that is the 'heartlessness' of love.

'How is your book going?' the mariner asks. 'If that's what it is. Or would you rather keep talking to me?'

Where You Live

Entering from the left, Leandra is hoodless; she slides the title Where You Live *into the black rectangular frame. The last two paragraphs should be a Sprechstimme recitative, accompanied by the musical ensemble, and sung by the actor miming Chiara on the mainstage. Entering from the right, The Female Reader replaces the Trans Reader at the lectern.*
The Female Reader: This is the Fifty-Third Reading.

It's tempting to comfort a neglected friend; but this time, you won't be sidetracked. The next night, you climb up to the roof alone. Here, and nowhere else: this is the only place you can be found.

It's not true what the notebooks say. They're just being selfish, keeping you to themselves. The book isn't a tomb;

it's a house you build, room by room. Like a nautilus shell, chamber after chamber. Once you move away, someone else can walk inside, and listen to the murmuring surf.

As a girl, turning pages in Sicily, you're Nausicaa when the hero swims to shore; dripping wet, wreathed in juvenescence, he glistens in the sun. By accident, he stands beside a ruined temple to Poseidon—not the god who favors him—its architraves and columns just a rubble on the ground. Across the bay, caught in another time-warp, a Norman fort crumbles into ruin…

One day you begin in medias res; you tell your tale to Dido, watching her love for you weigh her down. You ride out hunting together. In a cave, she's the quarry you wound, as a storm rages outside. You set sail, and then you loop back. You become her: you meander in a maze of grief. You can't absolve him; you have yourself immolated on a pyre, so he'll see the flames from the sea…

The darkling woods. The hybrid lonza, the lion, the wolf. You're rescued by your guide; you follow him, step by step. Pausing beside him, you breathe the trembling air. You pity Brunetto; you weep for the lovers and their interrupted book. Drawn by the beloved's cart, you ascend from dawn to dawn. The seraphim revolve in light, wheeling to obscure the eyes of God…

Quijote to the core, you fail to come to grips with any rock or tree—to clasp any hand outside of words. You struggle to disband the myths and walk on bare earth.

But all you ever do is rehearse an endless romance. You expire in a room full of islands never ruled, dominions never conquered, virgins never saved… your head is full of worm-eaten plots, rusty ideals, broken mirrors, tarnished swords…

The sea will call you many names, till you almost sink with your ship. You pose as a husbandly savage, an unhinged captain, a questioning first-mate. You meet the gamesome whale, the fin, the right; but the sperm whale rams your hull, tumbling your forecastle into the brine. A phantom in the hinterland, a Pierrot Lunaire, you thrive on greyness, on ambiguities—never confronting the prison guard, yourself…

In the stifling dark, you sit with Rogozhin near the low, shrouded bed. You listen, but with the blankness of the pure—with their terrifying innocence. So, he killed her? Infantile, you want the deck of cards they played with the night before. A memento to keep her alive, or a distraction from the thought she ever needed to exist... Is there a reason, beside a grave, for children to sing?

At the head of a valley, you stop: a woman preaches under a tree. You set out with a stalwart carpenter, the unfallen Adam of this pastoral world; in the greening shire, you ride to the gates of a country house… In another era, you're Romola, drawn into the bonfire of the vanities… And in another, you're captured by Deronda, safe within the fiction you inhabit side by side…

With a subtle change of voice, you enter the portrait of a lady. You learn to accept the uncertainty of endings, the humor of burning furniture, the taunt of love-letters in a silting lagoon. You follow a trilogy that opens to the sky. You revisit a landscape through a picture frame; you sigh, renounce, and fold your wings without despair; an Olympian quartet sculpts a frieze on a golden bowl...

Others, still others... You glide or stumble from shelf to shelf, not asking for rules or revelations. The years solidify, thicken as you read through layer after layer. Suspended in amber, Françoise pulls back the curtains. The Duchess gabbles in her peasant brogue, and you tap on your grandmother's wall. Albertine plummets from the clouds: a woman, a man. You rewrite your pages one by one, as patient as Céleste...

The boys in Lezama's paradise are brothers of your own. On puffs of charcoal dust, you bisect a man who wears a mask. You drift through Havana, unstable as the weather, precarious as love. A cook, a vase, a melomane trapped in glass, you march in a Roman general's parade. History loses its bearings, but the hours glow in a single line. Whitening, day breaks, beyond the foam of time...

Words are always saying: you must eat my flesh and drink my blood. John eats the book from an angelic hand. Mary is reading a book when Gabriel appears. She looks up, and conceives what the scroll from his lips will mean. The letters stir inside her, the embryonic Word. They rend her as seven sorrows, seven glories, seven joys. She's the mother to her father, the mystical bride of her own son…

Magnificat. The swords strike inward, water to wine. Communion is a spoken spectacle, the staging of the real: eating and being eaten, seeing and being seen. The Taíno codex blazes before your eyes, a people devoured by their images. Pages embodied and disembodied. Scriptures written each and every day on our youth; on our middle years; on our fragile vellum of old age…

A pillar of salt, you stand before the plains. The deluge of flames leaves you unharmed. The rows of books immolate you, quietly impenitent. You beg to be consumed by their vision, their memory, their fire. On the tables are seven lamps you made from shells; you turn them on, one by one. The room floats upward like a raft on streaming shadows, a language half-dark, half-light.

You remove your face, your final disguise. The reader inside you speaks from the surrounding air, externalized: a necessary angel, your guardian. The books, the shells. The light pouring through them. If you've ever been alive, this is where you live.

The Heart-Shaped Chairs

Entering from the left, Chiara is hoodless; she slides the title The Heart-Shaped Chairs *into the black rectangular frame.*

The Male Reader: This is the Fifty-Fourth Reading.

She would use these months as best she could; she would revisit each scene until she reaches the end. Single-mindedly, she colonizes the archipelago all over again. Catulo told her the truth: 'All you found was what you were looking for. Canuba is you.'

The third night, she tosses and turns as if her sheets were sails, her bed a spar—where a loving, merciful captain would hang her at dawn. She gets up, unable to sleep, and goes back to the roof.

The island rings her horizon, and Diana rises above it like the moon. All these years, the priestess has attracted her by a force as strong as gravity. But now, Chiara is overcome by the fullest surge of all, rushing like the spring-tide—the flood of equinox. At times, Diana's luminosity has filtered through; at other times, her darker side has trumped it. Of all the orbs Chiara has tried to chart, she's the most inconstant: Diana, Rebeca, Esperanza. She rules the crossroads where all must part; seemingly indifferent to justice, she chooses who'll prosper and who'll die. She hounds her friends and lovers without remorse, hunting them down where they feel most secure. In her bounteous phase, she fosters seedtime, fruition, and harvest. But then she pivots away again—cold and unattainable—and hides her Ocean of Storms, her Sea of Fecundity.

Ángel María is inchoate—a nebula of unformed stars. Chiara can't fathom him, can't pin him down. If what Diana recounts is true, Chiara has misjudged him naively. Despite all his talk, did he buttress the dictatorship? Or did he undermine it from within? Ángel María betrays no contrasting quarters: in him they overlap, an indistinct penumbra. He switches his costumes hourly, always with the same aplomb. But someday, he might lead you into a labyrinth; as you turn the next corner, he might lunge at you like the Minotaur. The prologue to a seduction killed him; but if given the chance, he might've murdered someone else. Chiara has reached the point where she stands back from his polyvalence, without defining what it entails. Most of all, he's fooled himself: he has no idea who he really is.

Solar and expansive, Amado captures each of them in turn: Dulce, Héctor, Reina, Catulo, Diana, Ángel María— Chiara most of all. His countless lovers orbit around him like planets. As he illumines them from different angles, he brings out every shade of gender, every nuance of need. They're like shirts he tries on, testing their fit, their weave, their endurance. He uses them; but unlike Lamia, he never misuses them—even when he rips them apart. His abruptness is that of the giver, not the predator. Nothing intrigues Chiara more than the danger of those moments, when she reels on the brink of annihilation. She can never forget that at the apex, he always wears a far-off smile of… what? Where is she going with that ellipsis? As far as her courage can take her, no doubt…

With Amado, she never wants to hold back. Transcultural, translingual, trans-erotic, their love always hinges on metamorphosis—barreling toward the West instead of the East. They leap beyond the self, not through nirvana, but through a restless blurring; through a ripple of evanescent havens; through an insatiable want.

Amado isn't alone in bringing her under his sway. Her other characters, too, materialize, then vanish: they disappear from chairs, slip behind doors, jump out of windows. Why are they so volatile? Like him, they wander in and out of her for years. They pass through her like light through a crystal lake, or mist through the boundless air… And though all of them are ghosts—Chiara first of all—they're illusions who can touch and be touched. They meet in the crooked valleys of sentences, the unraveling streams of the island. Scarred and eroded, 'these mountains are my Beloved for me…'

Why pretend she isn't pretending, minute after minute, phrase after phrase? She's given up on continuity. Her 'memoir' resembles the shredded yarn Canuba has made of 'Maria de Oro'—Mary good as gold, or Mary Worth. The plot has been tying and untying, knotting and unknotting, for seventy or eighty years. But on the island, the senile matron has lost her grip. Each morning, the episodes appear in the newspapers out of sequence—totally at random. No temporal succession, no narrative flow: everything is happening at once.

And so, the story isn't linear. Why should it be? Chiara wonders. Humans always zigzag, doing their best to muddle through. Only angels move in strict trajectories: this is what astounded the prophet most of all. 'They turned not when they went,' Ezekiel says; 'they went every one straight forward.' In his book on the heavenly hosts, Dionysius explains that their unswerving gait is a sign of their perfection; angels are untainted by weakness, forever and utterly the same.

Like Diana, Chiara has convinced herself she caused Amado's death. The last time she tells him good-bye, she nudges him aside, pushes him into oblivion. But all three of them are only links in a twisted chain of causes: an endless chain, frighteningly commonplace. It takes valor for Catulo and Virgilio to persevere, knowing their hours are numbered—to keep working at their art, to stay on the side of creation. Alfonso, too, prevails, despite the withering of everything he loves. And in his final moment, Amado flashes like a sunburst, rescuing someone else with no thought for himself.

When she considers herself, Chiara is tempted to resort to the island ploy: as she's often noted, its ethos is based on shame, not guilt. In the Canuban code—a Taíno throwback, most likely—you never apologize. When you call a spade a spade, a club a club, a heart a heart, the offender is aggrieved. Now you're the one who's injured her or him, and everything is canceled out. The double trespass is doubly pardoned. As Canubans always assure you: it's already been forgotten. 'Ya se olvidó'. Maybe that's healthier. A tabula rasa absolves your conscience—absolves you even of your consciousness.

In order to be forgiven, you have to forgive. Nobody is right; but then, nobody is wrong. Is that enough to grant you release? If so, then how far can the code extend? Could it condone you when you've slain a defenseless child? Of course, she didn't kill Amado, any more than Diana did. And Amado wasn't a child—much less defenseless. He was light-years ahead of her when it came to experience; already, in his twenties, he was ancient.

Who is the parent in this story? There are many sons, many daughters, many mothers, all interwoven by the web of birth. But for her, there's only one father, and he is remote—of that, Chiara is sure. Fleetingly, Amado becomes him: but this was only an illusion, the more so because she's made the same mistake before.

Her own father dominates her childhood even now—a childhood she'll never outlive. She mourns the sadness of his faults, the poignance of his absence, as if he might still love her one day across the void. The gift was bestowed on both sides: he gave her the freedom *not* to believe in him;

and she gave him the freedom *not* to exist. In this contest of hide and seek, they've arrived at a draw.

She's delirious now, but eerily calm. She listens to her voice as it threads through the night sky—heard only by herself. And also—so she hopes—by him. Maybe 'Thou,' 'God,' and 'Our Father' are merely 'notnames' for an artist who ruthlessly destroys all his works. Children are always drastically unfair to their progenitors, blaming them for their inability to be. She doesn't believe in her own complaints; but for that very reason, she feels compelled to repeat them one last time, and let them go.

Searching for a greater dimension: only a battered child can dread the father and still long for his embrace. Her standard Pater Noster exalts him, no matter what he does. Halfway through, she implores him for a crust of bread; then she beseeches him to pardon her mistakes. Worse, she begs him not to lure her into sins—sins he'll later condemn. What kind of father would make his children wheedle him for food, or damn them to suffer for what he's tempted them to do? What kind of father would send his son to be mocked, flogged, crucified? What kind of father, after that, would expect to be loved? And yet we love him anyway, beyond all reason.

In the starlight, she picks her way down the stairs. She strolls under the arch into the library, and pours herself a glass of wine. Leaning against the window-sill, she raises a toast to Luz Divina. This is the room where they faced off, in the rocking-chairs with heart-shaped backs When she stole the clothes, had she been 'bad'? Or by losing her patience, had Chiara been a 'monster'? No, in their predetermined script, they were only saying their lines. Of the two of them, who's more at fault? It doesn't matter. They've received each other's forgiveness in advance: each other's 'fore-giveness.' It's written into their names, like the upper clarity of the firmament.

A breeze furrows the air: a fish-tail palm sways slowly under the lanterns of the square. For her, too, it's simply a question of growth, of serenely accomplishing her death. Here she's lingered in a hideaway—a child's drawing of an inner house, where she talks to friends who aren't there. Where she invents a family meal, grateful to her father for never coming home. Thank you for putting these hearts in our chests, and thank you for tearing them out. For making them as hard as wood, for carving them into chairs. For leaving them empty, for axing them to pieces, for burning them to ash. But all that's only make-believe: it's said and then undone.

She's nowhere for a moment, and everywhere at once. And all this time, she's still in the silent room, as if she's never left this world, and never will.

Entering from the left, Diana is hoodless; she slides the title Fireship *into the black rectangular frame. Entering from the right, The Trans Reader replaces the Male Reader at the lectern.*

The Trans Reader: This is the Fifty-Fifth Reading.

Chiara is haunted by the Sacred Mount, the Sacro Monte di Varallo, with its throngs of life-size wooden figures, depicting biblical scenes. It's a pilgrimage site in Northern Italy her godmother took her to when she was a child, and despite her wonderment at these painted sculptures, she was left with a sense of unease. Beyond their deeper significance, these were human beings converted into puppets, threatened by mold, insects, dismemberment, sudden fires—though as she was also convinced, this is where faith enters in.

For the island, the first decade of the millennium brings welcome news: the death of Espinosa, at the age of ninety-six. But that blissful deliverance is overshadowed by the wider catastrophe. It's one of Chiara's pet jokes to refer to horrific goings-on—earthquakes, famines, pestilence—and then turn aside with a sardonic sigh. 'It's too awful to think about; let's go back to the real world: books.'

When 9/11 and its vengeful sequel unfold, she chokes on the flippancy of those words. There's no way she can ignore the horror, and she responds with opinions so strong they astonish even herself. Canuba has always been a fastness where she can ride out distant storms like these. Now she watches them in far-flung places as if they were happening in her mind, a nightmare from which she can't awake.

The terrorist acts are dreadful enough, but the wrong-headed resolve of the Americans and their allies to invade Afghanistan—and even worse, Iraq—multiplies the disaster a hundred-fold. To Chiara's disgust, Italy also runs with the pack; Berlusconi and his Mediaset hyenas bare their fangs. Every morning at breakfast, the pictures explode from the newspapers like land-mines: innocent civilians massacred or maimed, whole populations forced into homelessness, ignited oil-wells polluting the atmosphere.

To some, Chiara's reactions seem extreme; but she can hardly control her outrage. Against this gruesome backdrop, Espinosa affords a dose of tragicomic relief. To curry favor with the gringos, he belatedly sends two hundred ground-troops to Iraq: fittingly, it's his last major initiative. At the eleventh hour, he's found a new adviser to replace Ángel María; but he's only a yes-man, mealy-mouthed and clueless.

The rickety geezer has been obliged to re-assume his full presidential load, and he no longer sleeps at all. One night, around four o'clock in the morning, he undergoes a massive stroke, while working alone in his office. At dawn, his assistant finds him sitting at his desk with his eyes wide-open—not purblind anymore, but sightless once and for all.

Stranded in Iraq during the limbo of Espinosa's final months, ill-equipped and under-trained, Canuban soldiers become the laughing-stocks of the allied 'crusade.' Their plastic boots aren't suited to the desert heat, and melt on the tarmacs; all too often, they get stuck in them, like the mice on Luz Divina's sheets of glue. Photo-journalists regularly snap them in awkward poses, ungainly as the Statues of a childhood game.

In fact, most of them are hardly more than boys, lured from the slums of Puerto Indio with 'visa guarantees' by the US Embassy—commitments that will never be honored. Their madcap pictures, diffused by Reuters, AP, and France Presse, don't inspire Chiara with hilarity—more like nausea. Despite the grins on their lips, their eyes stare back from the page with bewilderment and apprehension. They remind her of the teenage warriors in the Taíno codex, about to be killed by the Caribs.

Those who survive the IEDs and friendly fire are repatriated by the Spanish; the Americans paid for them to come to Iraq, but not to leave. They return just in time for the festivities over Espinosa's demise. Cowed by the general jubilation, his few remaining followers cancel the state funeral he planned for himself. No longer waifs of the Iraq War, the veterans receive a rollicking welcome— as picaresque anti-heroes, but heroes nonetheless. 'Hacer el Amor, No la Guerra,' hand-painted banners proclaim:

'Make Love, Not War.'

Oversize effigies of sizzled boots, on floats or dangling from telephone poles, symbolize the people's liberation: they will never be squashed by the tyrant's heel again. Canubans might be hit-or-miss at martial rigor, but they always know how to party. Bars offer cut-rate prices, and revelers flaunt their Carnival costumes out of season, despite the summer heat. A month-long blow-out fills the streets of the capital, and spreads to the farthest crannies of the countryside.

The only successor Espinosa groomed was Ángel María, so no one is on hand to perpetuate his 'legacy.' Power-shy for decades, the opposition is now obliged to take the helm. Milady's widower, Pipi Balboa, the candidate of the Transformation Party—is clearly a cipher; but to satisfy racists, subliminal or otherwise, he has the advantage of being white. On the election posters, he chews his lips with a quizzical smirk, insipid as an iguana basking in the sun. Sensibly, the politicos choose Verbena as his running mate, though she's only in her twenties. The soul of the youth movement, the Bonaventuran heir to the ultra-Canuban Mirandas, she personifies the island's future.

Upstaging Balboa, she smiles majestically from the billboards, her round black face and expansive Afro wedging him into a corner. Though she was adopted by a clan of intellectuals, she identifies with her humble roots as much as with the elite. The lower classes see her as theirs and theirs alone, the emblem of their aspirations. According to legend, God and the loas rescued Verbena from poverty and malnutrition. Now she will answer the prayers of the destitute, and aid them in turn. 'Saved, she will save,' rings the popular chant. In a special election, several months after Espinosa's death, the Transformation ticket wins in a landslide.

Privately, Chiara reflects that Virgilio's daughter is his utmost creation. She's superseded his lugubrious poem, 'face:deface:efface.' As her image beams from every wall, every bumper, every TV, she recapitulates his work, soaring from childhood obscurity to international fame. But despite this cause for rejoicing, havoc continues to beset the rest of the world, like brimstone falling on a distant horizon. Chiara fears that eventually, the firestorm of 'terrorism' and 'counter-terrorism' will swallow the Caribbean as well; but for the time being, uncontrolled 'development' appears more subtly insidious.

Large hotels now encroach on the Peninsula of Barlovento, sucking up its aquifers with their wildcat wells; cut-rate whale-watching trips disturb the mating cycle of the humpbacks off its coast; slash-and-burn farming razes its few remaining virgin forests. The sex-tourism discussed by the panel after Leandra's play has become more and more rampant in the region—just as elsewhere on the island.

Honing back to an even closer view, a sea-change is already lapping at her door: she has formally agreed to vacate her house within three months. She won her suit in the Appeals Court; but then Metaxa's lawyers took the case to Cassation, the supreme tribunal of the land, where Doña Grecia's second cousin presides. Chiara keeps an attorney on retainer, Osiris Lama, and she confers with him quite often—or in fact, the other way around.

Osiris drops by every day, to keep her abreast of 'procedural complications.' Gawking at her through his pebble-thick glasses, he spouts an endless stream of jargon, waggling his Easter Island head. One morning, he latches onto her knee and whines pathetically that he's fallen in love, scrabbling for her waist like a weasel. As soon as she spurns him, he sticks her file on the back burner; even Carolina, who recommended him, can't light a fire under him now.

Finally, at her counsel's insistence, Chiara throws in the towel. She later learns that he accepted a tawdry bribe from Metaxa, in return for giving her that sage advice. What's left to her now? She has to break free of the island, or stay trapped in a world of 'what might've been': it's a clear-cut choice. Once she abandons the house, she'll never set foot in Canuba again. Consigning her books to storage, she'll travel forever, stopping nowhere for more than a month.

Return to Dawn

Entering from the left, Leandra is hoodless; she slides the title Return to Dawn *into the black rectangular frame. The last two paragraphs should be a Sprechstimme recitative, accompanied by the musical ensemble, and sung by the actor miming Chiara on the mainstage. At the end, the curtain above the marionette stage is drawn back to reveal the puppeteers, who seem superhuman by comparison. Entering from the right, The Female Reader replaces the Trans Reader at the lectern.*

The Female Reader: This is the Fifty-Sixth Reading.

Stopping nowhere... That's the theory; but after a year in Asia, she gravitates back to the Caribbean. A magnet pulls her irresistibly to Puerto Indio: several days before her departure for Cambodia, she meets someone in Plaza Drake. He isn't the usual boy in search of an author, but an adult of thirty-eight, and mature even beyond those years. His name, Constantino, has been shortened by his family to 'Tino'—which in Spanish, also means 'knack.' The son of well-off campesinos from the mountains near Esmeralda, he now lives in the capital, where he owns and manages a construction firm.

As a teenager, he alternated between barnyard antics and baseball, and sacred processions he staged with a group of friends. These were organized at the behest of his father, the local Deacon in an isolated village. His parents sent him to the Salesians at age sixteen, to train for the priesthood; but soon enough, he traded the seminary for women and drink. 'Dejé a Roma para buscar a romo,' as he puts it; 'I left Rome to chase after rum.'

Latinisms from his early years lodged in his mind, and they surface every now and then. One afternoon, he casually refers to a sunlit cloud as a 'monstrance,' and he mocks Chiara's laptop as her 'ciborium.' His next phase, teaching primary school, must account for his crisp diction and stolid patience. After that, he does a tour of duty in the sports squadron of the army; he even bags the gold medal for discus-throwing at the Pan-American Games. Back in civvies as a hotel handyman, he starts building extra rooms for the boss; and that's how he embarks on his current career.

Like most Canubans, he's a jack-of-all-trades, a chameleon—in more ways than one. In the armed services, he slept with a man. He only did it once, but that was enough to establish his 'open-mindedness': being 'abierto de mente' is a quality he values as much as Chiara. 'Wholeness,' he calls it. Before she knows it, Chiara finds herself lodging more and more often at an inn in the Barrio Antiguo. Conveniently, Tino has settled right around the corner with his third common-law wife, who never asks any questions. She seems content to have a couple of evenings each week with her friends, several of whom are part-time lesbians.

Such flexibility might have provoked Chiara's habitual phrase: 'it's all in the island air.' But as she knows from Ángel María, the rest of the world has caught up with Canuba by now. Inwardly, she chuckles at her own abstruseness. Ambivalence has always appealed to her mainly as a metaphor, a founding charter of liberty. But as much as she tries to withdraw to a second remove, she always needs to anchor herself in the middle ground. In the end, there's no way around it: only an individual can exist; only a person—that inextricable paradox of grandeur, mediocrity, virtues, and faults—can be worthy of love.

Tino is both earthy and down to earth; he reminds her of Amado, without his self-destructive yearnings. He isn't quite as handsome; but at her age, that doesn't matter anymore. His skin is smooth as polished rosewood, hairless except for the down along his calves. Rounded and firm, he emanates goodness and health, like a loaf of multi-grain bread. 'I don't have to leave this island to be a man of the world,' he boasts. His grandfather was Chinese, and it shows in some of his features; those of his siblings reflect the usual mixture of Afro-European and Taíno genes.

Above all, Tino bears the traces of his Arawak descent: he recalls the natives Columbus and his nephew Santiago encountered on the island, half a millennium ago. Chiara nicknames him 'Tino el Taíno.' Sometimes they visit the consecrated haunts in Barlovento together, and stay at Torsten's hotel. A hurricane has blown away the ruins of the cabin at Grandota, and Palmoliva has sold Ángel María's estate to the Club Méditerranée. But the cave at El Silencio endures unchanged, and Chiara plans to keep it that way. Artlessly, Tino has rekindled all her familiar obsessions. Framed by the mouth of the cave, gazing at the sea—not unlike a watchman from the *Verdaderas Relaciones*—he seems to be awaiting the caravels from Spain.

If 'Tino el Taíno' is marriage material, then so is Diana. Writing for the magazines, as usual, Chiara ricochets across the globe. Between trips, she often sojourns with her former 'rival' in Miami; an exotic hybrid of activist and mambo, she's as striking as ever. With her, Chiara relives the dewy, sisterly Eros she'd shared with her cousins in Sicily, long ago. There are no somber phases in Diana now, only a warm, continuous glow. Her book has made her a star in the field of human rights; acknowledged as a leader of the African diaspora, she champions the dispossessed on every continent.

Over the years, something deep and enduring has grown up between them, all the stronger thanks to the rift they've overcome. Diana's apartment in North Beach is almost as much a home to Chiara as her former house on Plaza Drake—though she's sworn she'll never cling to any one place again. Miami is underestimated, she comes to realize; the city offers more than glitzy marinas. In its tremulous blueness, you can feel as if you're nowhere, adrift at sea. It's calming to stroll along the boardwalk near sundown, absorbed by the flat, uneventful horizon where a sailboat wavers, at the planet's edge.

But before she falls off, she always returns to her cornerstone, the island of her memories. Did she 'find' it, like Columbus? Or does she only imagine it? If Asia was the Admiral's delusion, maybe the Caribbean is hers. In the end, she wonders, are 'finding' and 'imagining' the same?

No, reality can't be uprooted, as the Spanish were forced to concede. The colonists borrowed many place-names from the Taíno tongue, and even from Carib, the language of the 'cannibals'—though the worst 'man-eaters' had been the Europeans themselves. When they overran the archipelago, they did their best to obliterate the past. Abolishing the heathen gods, they christened Canuba the 'Isla de San Tomás de Aquín,' and baptized the smaller island 'San Bonaventura.' To Chiara, it seems like a map straight from Dante's *Paradiso*, where Dominicans and Franciscans are reconciled by their two great saints; as in Cantos XI and XII, across a narrow gulf, they embrace for all eternity.

But evangelizing monks, even backed by swords and guns, could never budge the pagan bedrock. Santiago, the defender of the Indians, tried to shield them from the 'Domini cani'—the mastiffs of the Inquisition. Eventually, the tides washed the very name of St. Thomas away: and so, the bigger island endures as what it has always been—for the Taínos, Canuba; and for the Caribs, Moriqueya. The native terms signify the same: Great Earth, the Mother of the Clans. Puerto Indio is a monument to the slain, who only survive in the bloodline they founded—the almond eyes, the Arawak hair, the honey-colored skin.

Sometimes she doesn't come back to either of her lovers for months on end: she almost spends more hours in the air than on the ground. Out there somewhere, far beyond Florida and Canuba, cruising between Chile and China, or Iceland and Nepal, she wings through an indeterminate space—a world that is also the worldless... But she's equally enmeshed in Diana's public campaigns. Hoisting banners in front of consulates and embassies, she protests the plight of refugees. At her friend's request, she also writes reams of petitions against torture, human trafficking, the death penalty, the petroleum wars, and on and on.

She's comfortable merging with either Tino or Diana; that's appropriate for a ghost, since phantoms are porous by definition. But there are limits, too: close though she is to them, she keeps a certain distance, in the farthest recess of her mind. She continues to go on retreats in convents and meditation halls; and without even noticing at first, she's undergone an autumnal reawakening of her inner strength. She wants to be free—but free to be attached.

On her most recent visit to Canuba, Tino is busy with a building project, so she travels to Barlovento by herself. At the end of her stay, she flies back to the capital in a chartered plane, instead of going overland by bus. In the Cessna, she sits next to the pilot; they depart at first light. As dawn expands, she looks down steadily until they land in Puerto Indio. Bays, hills, rivers, mountains, plains, palm-groves, orchards in bloom: the landscapes that unscroll remind her of Virgilio's final portraits, in their dense profusion of detail. But instead of his understated sepias, the colors that meet her eye are greens and blues, yellows and pinks—the rainbows of a covenant, the signs of a promise we can only make to ourselves... or to others. A father is among them, and a mother and son who intercede, granting redemption.

The towns she recognizes are like mismatched, well-thumbed beads, ticking off the names of their patron saints: Juan, Ana, José, Clara, Jacobo, Francisco, Bárbara, Ambrosio, Magdalena, Sebastián... And there are other places that spell the rosary of nature, once unfallen and pristine. Idly, at the back of her mind, she translates from Spanish into Italian, into French, into German, into English. Emerald, Forgotten Woods, and Silver Cove; Lost Rivers, and Savannah-by-the-Sea; Wandering Stones, Nest of Vultures, Whaler's Point, and Stolen Time; Savior, Golden Shore, and Desolation Cliff.

The plane swoops over the city in a wide, lazy arc; it skims so low that she can pick out the neighborhoods, can see the people as they mill in the streets, with their rolling island gait. She can even glimpse the smiles of the joyous and the mad, the frowns of the valiant and the depraved. At corner bars, the dancers sway to a soundless beat, their palms raised high to receive the light. But to her, these aren't just pictures anymore, or words on a silent page. They're bodies, and minds, and spirits, their faces unrepeatable, turned up one by one like nothing but themselves, as she circles out of the clouds and back to earth.

Afterword

As I related in the 'Foreword,' Return to Dawn *owes its origins to a scuffed, leather briefcase packed with notebooks. Artemisia Vento, a Sicilian travel writer, entrusted them to me in 2016. Familiar with my efforts as a translator and editor, she'd sent a message to my website, shortly before she moved to Asia. She took it as a sign when she discovered I was living on her native island, in the historic center of Palermo. She was there too, by chance, at an elderly aunt's palazzo on the Via Paternostro. On a radiant day in early October, we met at a sidewalk café, shaded by the towering trees of the Giardino Garibaldi.*

This would be her 'last week in the West,' Artemisia confided. She'd already made a farewell visit to her parents, south of Siracusa, as well as a final pilgrimage to her favorite sculpture, the extraordinary Dancing Satyr *of Mazara del Vallo. On a whim, she'd decided to leave me her 'scribbles': for many years, she'd been drafting a lengthy narrative. 'It's not exactly a grab-bag, but the three divisions differ widely. If you care to give them a glance, you'll see what I mean. Who knows? Maybe you could turn them into a trilogy of novels.'*

Was it her reassuring gaze? Her even-tempered charm? Whatever the reason, I took to her on the spot. As I skimmed through her manuscript, I quickly perceived that it was sui generis, to say the least. Among her other jottings, mainly aphorisms and short poems, I found the three-part narration she'd mentioned.

In the course of that unforgettable week in Palermo, I asked her a number of questions, as we strolled through the city or met at our habitual café. Though she'd split the narrative of volume one (which I later entitled Sailing to Noon) *among nine different voices, wasn't her sequential approach a bit old hat? 'Do you teach creative writing?' she joked. Jetting around the globe for her travel articles, she'd read tons of novels on her endless flights, so she was well aware of shifting trends.*

When she'd started her project, in the late seventies, straightforward plots were still the rule; but then they'd morphed and morphed again, as in a hall of funhouse mirrors. 'Some might say they underwent a metastasis,' she quipped. 'Clearly, the fade-ins, fade-outs, and parallel stories are copied from the visual media: well and good.' But in her initial phase, she'd merely tried to portray the world 'as she found it—or misconceived it.' She loved insoluble mysteries, temporal ricochets, myopic details, alternate endings, molting personae, and metafictions. But why retrofit them like hidebound rules?

Even so, why had she opted for a blow-by-blow chronology? Despite some flashbacks, she replied, her linear structure flowed from the daily entries in her journal. After accumulating a series of segments, she'd toyed with stringing them in reverse, from the future to the past. 'Forward or backward, the whales appear at the center, and that's where they belong.' But given the event-driven tenor of the first book, she'd decided that the backwards movement would be more appropriate for the sec-

ond, since it's grounded in memory. The five main voices tell their stories in retrogressive order—which she considered the fundamental flux of reminiscence. 'Tragedies and comedies take place over time,' she clarified; 'at some point, they happen to us all. But they're never the final chord: we constantly revise and transform the past. Our dead survive within us in the present. Memory is the surest form of resurrection.'

At a pomegranate stand near the Palazzo dei Normanni, she shrugged disarmingly. 'As to the first section, label my technique "archaicizing," if you like; or call it the "New Simplicity," if that rings up to date. I couldn't care less. The next two panels are more contorted; they warped organically as I wrote them, to fit their misshapen themes. Anyway,' she added, 'a thousand modes of story-telling can coexist. Isn't eclecticism a hallmark of the "postmodern"? Sorry to use such a trendy term!'

I pressed on. Wasn't her mimicry of 'Spanglish' or 'Germglish' condescending, even offensive? 'I don't see why, if that's how some of us actually talk. Isn't your question patronizing in itself?' No social circle is inferior, she went on—and no speech-pattern, either. From the dawn of humanity, translingual hybrids have been the norm, not the exception. Like the Sicilian 'dialect' of her childhood, she considered them fully-fledged languages, equal to any other. 'Oxford English,' 'newscast American,' 'peninsular Spanish,' 'Hochdeutsch,' 'Parisian French,' and 'standard Italian' are variants, too. As an amateur linguist, she'd always aimed for accuracy; she'd even made tape-recordings of her principal models. But she doubted that they revealed any universal traits. 'We all develop an idiom of our own, as unique to us as our fingerprints. More than anything, we need to listen to each other, with sympathy and respect.'

In the second part of her manuscript (which I later entitled Midnight at Sea), Artemisia retains no more than four of the narrators of Sailing to Noon: Lamia, Horacio, Amado, and Catulo. But she adds a fifth chronicler, the painter Virgilio, who is only briefly evoked in the previous book. Chiara, a Sicilian travel journalist (whose thoughts may mirror Artemisia's own, much as she denied it), figures here as their interlocutor, the 'sister confessor' whom they all address. Did this reflect a systematic shift from the first to the second person? I asked my new Italian friend.

'Aha, you've found me out!' she laughed. 'No doubt you've also noticed that my last block of notes is in the third person.' This section would eventually complete The Caribbean Trilogy, as the novel Return to Dawn. She conceded that this trinitarian structure of 'three persons of the same narration' (rather than 'nature'), reflects a theological subtext. 'What can I say? Once a Catholic, always a Catholic. But I don't believe anyone can accuse me of being dogmatic! Quite the contrary. Some might complain that I treat sacred themes with too much flippancy.'

As to flippancy, hadn't she overdrawn her protagonists, verging on parody? 'You don't know the Caribbean very well! In fact, I toned them down.' From early on, the characters in Dickens, Trollope, or Balzac (and later in her reading life,

Goncharov, Vargas Llosa, or Galdós) had amused her with their zany tics. All the same, satire should never be dismissed as reductive; members of a class, nationality, or any other cohort are individuals, not stereotypes. 'Who's to dictate how others should sound and behave, much less think? Doesn't this depend on factors like their age, education, and experience? Don't Anglos vary widely among themselves, and Italians, too? On the other hand, foreigners often understand us better than we pretend. It might be a matter of distance—the greater inclusiveness of a panoramic lens.'

Why had she created Canuba, instead of depicting an actual place? In her case, she felt, 'hyper-realism' made little sense. She'd spent her youth on several continents, never staying put for long. As a reporter, she'd crisscrossed the planet—though the Caribbean had always lured her back. Her emblematic island was an amalgam of Venezuela, coastal Colombia, Hispaniola, Cuba, and Puerto Rico, with other elements thrown in. Canuba's creole was a potpourri; its flora and fauna, too, sometimes wryly bogus. It even had its own dance, the 'cambuca.'

Readers could liken the island to their own countries, or reject any similarity; in either case, they'd be right. In its humble way, Canuba resembled Macondo or Yoknapatawpha: both 'there' and 'not there.' She'd never presume to carve a local backdrop in stone, even 'Nodica,' her alias for her hometown; her subjectivity would interfere. Her sister Nina's 'Nodica' was contrary to hers, though they were raised side by side.

I tried to pin her down: wasn't Chiara her alter ego? 'No, not at all! I'm too much of a prude; besides, she's hooked on romantic illusions. I fused several friends to write her script—just as I did with the rest of my vaudeville troupe.'

When I smiled, she explained: 'Throughout my notes, especially in parts one and two, Catulo, Lamia, and Horacio are performing artists, don't forget. Amado and Reina boogie for the disco crowd in the first section. Ángel María wears many masks to attain his goals, which culminate in part three. Luz Divina stars in her own domestic skits. Frederica impersonates a grande dame. Even the cat, Cirenea, poses as a virgin. Chiara projects her "pathetic fallacy" towards nature, but also towards mankind. Far more deeply, as a consecrated mambo, Diana enacts religious rites... To top it all off, the final division is imagined as a multi-staged "spoken opera" with music—almost a secular oratorio.'

Then all your characters are playing roles? 'Oh yes, unconsciously or consciously, to the point of "camp." Drama: in the Caribbean, it's everywhere—even more than in Italy, and that's saying quite a lot! Each island is a small proscenium, where the actors loom larger than life. They stylize themselves into caricatures; they emote at a histrionic pitch. Once you're addicted to that intensity, the outside world seems drab... But after four decades, I've had enough. For me, the show is over.'

Ironically, by now we'd meandered to the Teatro Massimo. 'Baroque playwrights knew exactly what I mean,' Artemis-

ia summed up, waving toward the colossal facade. 'My Nodica might be Noto or Modica, under the twilight of a scrim. My Tragusa rhymes with Ragusa, where a Deus ex machina might lurk behind the Duomo's crimson drapes. But if you climb the hill and open them, there's nothing there!'

She gave me a brusque, double kiss on the cheeks. This would be our last conversation, she announced. 'Do as you please with "our" notebooks; it's entirely up to you. My only request is that you burn them in the end.' We said good-bye on the theatre's steps, between the two huge lions cast in bronze; their Art Nouveau riders, Opera and Tragedy, had never looked more precarious. With profound regret, I watched her stride down the Via Maqueda, unswerving and determined. Her flight was due to leave in several hours; I'm convinced I'll never see her again.

Artemisia's firmness of purpose had inspired me: I accepted her challenge then and there. Sifting through the welter of pages, I perceived how her trilogy might fit into a well-established scheme. At the antipodes of Canuba, Samuel Butler welded New Zealand into a dyad: itself but also Erewhon, a faulty palindrome of Nowhere. During our chats in Palermo, Artemisia adverted to Barataria, the 'insula' Sancho Panza misgoverned—as ineptly as Columbus ruled the Spanish Main. Prospero's island, where he demotes Caliban to the status of a Taíno slave, is cut from the same bloodied cloth. As these works affirm, while we'll never expiate our colonial past, we can disavow its triumphalist screeds. Humanity's anchor, too heavy to raise, drags destructively across the ocean floor. Seen through a whale's eye, every corner of Europe has also been a colony, even if the overlords have switched command.

Beavering away, I perceived another dimension in the tripartite arrangement of Artemisia's notes. The book I would later entitle Sailing to Noon *focuses on primal nature and untrammeled love. The second volume of the trilogy,* Midnight at Sea, *is dedicated to the visual and performing arts: painting, cinema, music, and choreography. The third novel,* Return to Dawn, *examines society and politics, acted out as a poly-traditional drama on a three-tiered stage.*

As I translated and edited the opening section, I began to wonder whether Artemisia's ostensibly 'quaint' techniques weren't ahead of their time. Strangely, they combined the outmoded and the avant-garde. Horacio's Latinisms look backward to Montaigne, but forward to Bolaño's Xosé Lendoiro, who quotes from Roman authors in Latin. Catulo, Lamia, and Frederica, with their jumpy antics and hard edges, their capitals, hyperboles, and exclamation marks, cavort like cartoons from a manga. In another twist, the idyll between Chiara and Amado blends a romance—bodices and trousers ripped—with a nature documentary. When extreme opposites attract, they couple like separate species, defiantly belying our practical age. Yet despite all their passion, they can't swim upstream to the Taíno past: its environmental harmony has dwindled to an obsessive mirage. They self-identify with an-

imals, in their longing for that primeval oneness; but like the rest of us, they're swept down a river of change.

In the tongue-in-cheek 'seminar' at the crux of the tale, library shelves bookend a mock colloquium. Ruined civilizations coalesce within the island's seabound edges, compressing and compressed. Amerindians, Africans, and Europeans honeycomb its restless population, constantly transformed. Like Castilian itself, the Canuban language recycles borrowed words. Ancient Greek, Latin, Hebrew, and medieval Arabic jostle with imported slang, just as they do in the Spanish classics. The erotic analogues of Middle Eastern cults implicitly undercut the biblical Song of Songs. Defaced by Christian bigotry, pagan columns can barely uphold the Church's fissured roof. The gender-blurring of the novel fleshes out these metamorphoses in the most blatant terms. The only 'orientation' is disorientation. Personality can alter at any moment: the self is a circumstance.

Generalizations swirl and clash, but no one takes them seriously—much less abides by them. 'Hypertexts,' like the one I'm writing here, gratefully collapse.

From its inaugural bars, Midnight at Sea, the second book of the trilogy, is permeated by music. In Palermo, Artemisia suggested that my editing of this section might trace a quadruple arc. Ideally, its four monologues should echo the tempi of a Late Romantic chamberwork—especially by Brahms, her musical lodestar. Lamia's narration corresponds

*to an allegro ma non troppo; Virgilio's, to a ponderous ada-
gio, or even a largo; Horacio's, to a quirky scherzo; and Catulo's, to a breathless presto. As in a composition, leitmotivs
assert themselves and reappear, while other themes are developed with variations. Adhering to the melodic paradigm,
I've left such reprises intact: like iterated melodies, they nurture a poignant familiarity. This vantagepoint chimes with
the personae themselves. Lamia and Horacio are profession-
al musicians, and Catulo's choreographies jive with extensive scores. His backdrops are provided by Virgilio, whose
ekphrastic descriptions of artworks almost slow his soliloquy
to a standstill.*

*Lamia, Virgilio, and Chiara undergo episodes of synes-
thesia, which combine the auditory and the visual. Cinema
unites those two parameters par excellence: tributes to the
seventh art crop up often in these pages, particularly in the
Lamia and Catulo segments. American and Italian films pre-
dominate, from the Tarzan movies,* Gone with the Wind, *or*
The Wizard of Oz, *to the commedia all'italiana,* Una gior-
nata particolare, *or* Un borghese piccolo piccolo. *A curious unicum is the Japanese cult-classic* Demon Pond, *which
virtually grafts itself onto the plot. Apart from recurring ci-
tations of* The Tempest, *linked to the Miranda brothers' surname, the one performing art that gets short shrift is theatre.
Artemisia's annotations reserve it for the undergirding of
book three—along with opera, the apotheosis of stagecraft.*

Midnight at Sea, *as its title implies, may be the most som-*

ber volume of The Caribbean Trilogy: *three of the narrators, Virgilio, Catulo, and Amado, reach out to Chiara from beyond the grave. Still, true to Artemisia's tragicomic bent, humor is added to the mix: a mock academic conference, or Countess Frederica's acerbic spat with the Polish Baron, Valentín. The gritty comments of the Asociación C y E, along with Amado's streetwise grace-notes, recall the folk or Gypsy fillips that leaven Viennese quartets.*

Zestfully, Amado and Catulo no longer suffer from their misfortunes on earth, whereas Lamia's lovelessness and Virgilio's self-abnegation seem to leave them in limbo, helplessly straddling life and death. Painting is an art of contemplative visual stasis, however animated its subjects may be; dance thrives on motion and communal patterns. To some degree, the marked disparity between the narratives of Virgilio and Catulo springs from their chosen métiers. A testament to unity, the latter's final anecdotes subsume Chiara's memories as well, exalting the symbiosis of friendship.

In all the narratives of Midnight at Sea, *arcane cultural allusions abound—a salute to the choreographer's 'latest theory.' Rightly or wrongly, he deems such flourishes a trademark of Latin American writers: correctives to unfounded self-doubts that they're viewed by Paris, London, or New York as limited provincials. He detects this trait even in the most eminent authors, such as Lezama Lima and Borges. Anachronistically, he might've applied his notion to the dense intertextuality of Roberto Bolaño.*

As Artemisia's translator and editor, I've resisted the temptation to 'correct the correctives,' or 'Hemingway-ize' her baroque extravagance. Catulo jibes that his principle comes to the fore in the Miranda brothers themselves, 'archetypally' prone to erudite nods and winks. For example, in the after-life, he claims that he and Amado are reveling in cherubic minglings of 'pneumatic sensuality,' quoting John Milton as his authority. He might also have cited the explosive congress between a woman and a seraph in Laura Restrepo's novel, Dulce compañía, or the similar scene between a man and an angel in Tony Kushner's epic play, Angels in America.

In Palermo, I discussed the topic of sexuality with Artemisia at some length. Though she called herself 'priggish,' and did seem rather nun-like, why was there so much eroticism in her texts, down to the most scabrous and granular details? She threw up her hands. 'Hahaha, you can't tell a book by its cover—or a monk by his habit, as we say in French! I've spent time in Asian temples where the sisters alternate their retreats with bouts of "street-walking," unperturbed by the slightest pang of guilt. In the West, we might harken back to the ambiguous mores of the Abbaye de Thélème in Rabelais, where the "coed" cloister encourages amorous dalliance. All the same, I need not remind you that my characters have nothing in common with myself. Or who knows, maybe they created me, so I'd create them!'

It would be easy to conclude that Artemisia was striving to overcome the age-old Italian dichotomy of the Virgin and the

Whore, which admits no gradations between the two poles. But surely, there's a theological aspect here as well. During our visit to Santa Maria dell'Ammiraglio, with its Byzantine mosaics of brilliant blue and gold, she affirmed that she took very seriously the 'twin doctrines of the Incarnation of the Logos and the Real Presence in the Host.' In a key passage of volume one, Chiara attends a Mass. Of the words at the Elevation, 'Hoc est corpus meum'— 'This is my body'—she declares that they are 'simple and magnificent. They say nothing more—and nothing less—than the mystery of life itself.'

By extrapolation, it might be supposed that the more radical the fleshliness of experience, the more intensely spiritual it becomes—though the Propaganda Fide would scarcely condone such a view. Yet the Doctor Mysticus of the Church, St. John of the Cross, repeatedly invoked in The Caribbean Trilogy, couches the marriage of the soul with God in vividly carnal metaphors. These derive from the Song of Songs— the subject of impassioned glosses by numerous saints, from Gregory the Great to Bernard of Clairvaux.

Another issue I broached with Artemisia was 'cultural appropriation.' In his musings, Virgilio outlines many of his artworks, whether actually executed or not. He's haunted by the seduction of the image, convinced that only a picture can draw us in, expand our vision, freeze the music of time, remove us from ourselves—and in the process, turn us into ghosts. Controversially, he also embroiders on illuminations from 'the Taíno codex,' an indigenous manuscript from the *early sixteenth century. In that apocryphal tome, the last Native Americans of Canuba have assembled an album like the Aztec or Inca exemplars, with pictorial panes scattered through the narrative.*

Since the Taíno left no such record, as far as we know, Artemisia's account is fictitious: as elsewhere in her trilogy, she aligns this First Nation with her own thematic ends. Even so, as Virgilio observes, the healer with his brother-husband is consistent with the 'Outsider' of the Guayakis—an Arawak tribe akin to the Taíno. Carib cannibalism, a persistent trope of Spanish propaganda, is embodied in the ritual consumption of the enemy's manhood; similar practices have been documented in various corners of the world. The graphic portrayals of alien fertility rites—unthinkable from a Western perspective—reinforce Artemisia's thesis that theology and sexuality are interrelated languages, which ultimately converge.

Appropriation—a 'cosplay with others' identities'—has become a highly suspect endeavor in our time. Given the abuses of the past, we're leery of misinterpreting societies, genders, or cultures not our own. A fortiori, by blending dozens of dissonant voices in her notes, Artemisia seems to have amassed a chorus of appropriations. Was such an exercise well-advised? As she and I agreed in Palermo, we constantly have to interrogate who is appropriating whom, and with what intent: from derision to empathy, and all the nuances in between. If the 'crazy quilt' grows too distorted, it can de-

bouch in a self-defeating labyrinth—though that very maze may spark a sudden breakthrough, a sloughing-off of toxic illusions.

This comes home to us in Appropriate (declared from the outset as both an adjective and a verb), a recent play by an African-American about a family of déclassé whites in the South, squabbling over the legacy of a country estate. The author, Branden Jacobs-Jenkins, boldly jettisons the speech patterns and behavior 'appropriate' to his subjects; he 'appropriates' his foul-mouthed personae into a historical nightmare, where all their words and acts are 'inappropriate'—from their origins in the slave economy to the inevitable collapse of the plantation house.

The sarcasm of Lars von Trier's Manderlay seems to haunt this corrosive agon. Significantly, Artemisia's characters sometimes make comparisons between racism in the American South and similar tendencies in the Hispanic Caribbean. But as they imply, the latter hinge on a pseudo-playful 'colorism,' not a stark antagonism between black and white; accordingly, they're harder to pinpoint with any cohesion. Lamia in particular finds herself caught up in a fruitful, complex anomaly. Though often offensive to our Anglophone ears, her ritornello-like rants highlight both the strengths and the challenges of ethnic intersectionality.

While Lamia, Amado, Chiara, and the Miranda brothers all contend with ambient biphobia, the story of Ángel María in the third volume of the trilogy, Return to Dawn, *demonstrates how an unconscious self-contempt can lead to political violence. The arriviste's family background of sensualists and wastrels spurs him to multiply his amorous encounters, and to use them to scale the heights of fortune and power. His collusion with the dictator, Manfredo Espinosa, proves the depths of his depravity. His macabre murder at the hands of gay-bashers, while extreme, might seem to some like a just retribution for his torture of the tyrant's opponents, while dressed in the portentous insignia of the Taíno's woodpecker clan.*

Here history doubles back on itself, linking the machismo-ridden 'rooster dreams' of Return to Dawn *with the Native American sculptures of* Sailing to Noon *and the Amerindian codex of* Midnight at Sea—*not to mention the 'waterboarding' or 'tortura de agua,' used early on by the Inquisition. Much like Kaoru in the third book of* Genji, *Chiara's literary touchstone, she maintains her fraught kinship with Ángel María, despite their differences. Her 'shining Prince' will never become the emperor, despite his dashing attributes. Shallowly, she even seems to condone his addiction to pornography as a devotion to sacred writs on fresh vellum, soon to shrivel and wilt—a memento mori preserved on film.*

Meanwhile, the frustrated desire for monkish detachment of a newly introduced character, Gustavo, runs up against his aesthetic excess and 'metaphysical' self-denial. He's forced to rehearse his suicide four times before it succeeds, on the fifth attempt. It's no coincidence that the operatic tinge of the scenes featuring him and Ángel María is augmented by their enactment in a tri-level theatre, to an exotic musical accompaniment. All the same, the main text of the 'secular oratorio' is fairly conventional in style, a third-person account—even if it's recited like a specious gospel and pantomimed by puppets, whose masters are finally unveiled. With that coup de théâtre, Artemisia underlines that we're all hapless marionettes of forces beyond our control. Of course, this entire novel is a modest offshoot of 'closet dramas' like Samson Agonistes *or* Faust, *principally meant for reading—though sections of it could conceivably be performed.*

The only survivors of the trilogy are a trio of women: Chiara, Leandra, and Diana. Paradoxically, Leandra writes a play-within-the-play in which she unmasks the patriarchy and the corrupt regime by disguising them, much as Hamlet *does. Diana becomes an unwitting 'cannibal' on her failed escape by boat from Canuba; yet she exonerates herself by saving the lives of a Bonaventuran and a Canuban. Their maritime saga heralds an era of entente between the two adjacent islands, not unlike the concord between Dominicans and Franciscans in Dante's* Paradiso, *as Chiara points out. Still, she brings the narrative down to earth—literally, as she circles over Puerto Indio in a cub-plane at the end, observing its citizens as unique individuals, their faces raised upwards to the light. This is the lesson that Diana and Chiara, the faithful lovers of an open marriage, will impart to future gen-*

erations—as personified by Lucita, the 'collective daughter' of the trilogy.

While not wanting to tamp down Artemisia's frankness on an array of topics, I've espoused a more cautious stance than hers, and I hope this will be sensed by other readers than myself. In editing her pages, I've steadily consulted Hispanic-Caribbean, European, and Pan-American friends, to gauge whether the attitudes of her dramatis personae are credible. Besides moral values of all stripes, I've been obliged to map the byways of gender. Here, too, I've sent the manuscript to representatives of diverse identities. In his study of Jean Genet, Sartre dissects sexuality as a parabola of possibilities, where each person lands at some point along the curve. But what if the spectrum shifts from moment to moment, as in Canuba, and gender—like ethnicity—is iridescent rather than fixed?

The larger conundrum is whether any place, any culture, or any individual can truly be defined. Artemisia was raised on an island known for its quaint folkways and turns of speech, not unlike her composite Caribbean enclave. Because of education, employment, and her innate sense of rebellion, she left her native Sicily early on. Over the decades, she has adapted to many languages and cultures around the globe. As she told me in Palermo, her universalism persuades her that foreigners can learn to grasp her birthplace as she does: from the inside. Utopia, dystopia, or both at once, she gladly gifts it to others—all the more freely, since for her it only sub-

sists in an unredeemable past.

With equal honesty, she has faced the dilemma from the other side of the looking glass, as a longtime resident of 'Canuba.' She and her friends in the Hispanic Caribbean often wonder how they can continue to inhabit islands that are no longer what they once were. Above all, how can they save their Atlantis from the tourist tsunami, exemplified by the mega-resorts where Catulo grudgingly works? How can they reclaim their traditions, when even their most treasured memories are mostly myths?

Of the many uprooted souls I've encountered over the years, Artemisia alone has sailed beyond the 'untold want' of a permanent home, greeting each successive harbor as her Ithaca. But by incurring so many displacements, by enduring the pains of so many rebirths, she has only made her longing more acute. As she acknowledged in Palermo with a melancholy air, her nostalgia has finally evolved into a yearning for nowhere. This is what John Crowe Ransom calls a 'cry of absence, absence in the heart'—or in the words of Gabriela Mistral, a 'país de la ausencia, extraño país.'

In all three books of The Caribbean Trilogy, *the characters voyage through an 'archipelago of mind.' As I've attuned myself to their unquiet voices, I've pondered whether such concepts as the 'other' and 'othering' might be amplified. In any given group, aren't its outlying members the 'others' in relation to the core? And doesn't that nucleus often implode, so that the excluded become the included? Most of Artemisia's characters have revolted against paternalism, the family, and the Church—though only seemingly, perhaps. Adamant non-conformists, they're 'othered' within their own societies. Their 'mother tongues' have lapsed into a delta of peregrine idioms.*

Could this be 'the way we live now,' socially as well as linguistically? More than a two-way street, tolerance may be a multi-vectored thoroughfare. We often forget that to the 'other,' we are the 'other,' too. Temperamentally, the warring forces within our personalities seem to 'other' each other, even to cancel each other out. We never know one another fully. But do we even know ourselves?

Biology tells us that sexuality is not a stable quantity, and that physical organs don't determine instincts, much less roles. As to 'race,' it does not scientifically exist. There's no such thing as a single ethnic origin: we all stem from a meshing of myriad strains—no matter how our secondary features may turn out, in the throw of the genetic dice. Our cultural strands are as reticulated as our chromosomes, thanks to our constant interweaving through immigration and exchange. If divergent narratives of the world can cohabit, perhaps 'appropriation,' 'intersectionality,' and 'otherness' can be energized through a fusion—rather than a fission—of clashing ontologies. Such an experiment, parlous in daily life, can best be conducted in the cyclotron of art.

This essay might serve as an afterword to my rereading of The Caribbean Trilogy, *or as a foreword to someone else's perusal of the work. Between them is the 'interword,' the pres-*

ent that shuttles back and forth—veering through our memories and our hopes. While Sailing to Noon *propels events towards the future,* Midnight at Sea *deflects them towards the past.* Return to Dawn *portrays them as a triple unreality, where 'all the world's a stage.' In all three books, Artemisia invites us to explore her chapters in every direction, or to skip around them at will, as in the random daydreams of a balmy afternoon. If we follow her hint, we'll embark on a reverie that each of us has known—careening from trepidation to joy, and from anguish to confidence.*

We often walk a tightrope of dread: stretched across Pascal's 'two infinities,' it hovers between the atoms and the stars. Yet no man is an island—and no atom, no star. When our commonality with the universe seems to recede beyond our reach, we're tempted to seal ourselves off: no keys will unlock our solitary door. But this is precisely when we should open ourselves to grace—however we construe that word—and thankfully begin again. Our one essential task is to confront reality with courage. The 'divine light' we ignore, fear, or praise may simply be a benign ordinariness—an unblinking acceptance of the here and now.

A Note on the Type

Return to Dawn is typeset in Minion, which was designed by Robert Slimbach in 1990 for Adobe Systems. Minion was an early member of the well-regarded Adobe Originals program: it featured a set of type families derived from classical typographic styles. Minion is based on typefaces such as Jenson and Bembo that appeared in Venice in the late sixteenth century. It exhibits the graceful proportions, harmonious contrast between thick and thin strokes, and sculpted serifs for which these typefaces are known. Despite its venerable lineage, Minion works well for contemporary typography, and is widely used in current book design.

Hoyt Rogers has published his fiction and poetry in a wide range of periodicals, including *The New England Review, AGNI,* and *The Fortnightly Review.* As a prize-winning translator, novelist, editor, and essayist, he has worked with Viking, Knopf, Farrar Straus, Yale, Seagull, and various presses large and small. He has collaborated with Paul Auster, Yves Bonnefoy, Lincoln Kirstein, Philippe Claudel, and many others. He is the author of a poetry collection, *Thresholds,* the novels *Sailing to Noon* and *Midnight at Sea,* and a study of the Late Renaissance. Please visit hoytrogers.com.

Artemisia Vento is the pseudonym of a travel journalist whose work appeared in countless magazines from 1978 onward, under different bylines. She specialized in writing about islands, above all in the Caribbean and Mediterranean, with a focus on village traditions and nature. At the end of 2016, she abandoned her career and withdrew from the world; she now lives a cloistered existence somewhere in Asia. The location of her community, and whether it is Buddhist, Christian, Vedic, interfaith, or secular, are secrets she keeps to herself.

Frank Báez has published eight books of poetry, as well as fiction and non-fiction works. In 2006, he received the Short Stories Prize of the Santo Domingo International Book Fair for *You'll Have to Pay the Shrinks Yourself*; and in 2007, the Salomé Ureña National Poetry Prize for *Postales*. He was selected for the Hay Festival in 2017 as a member of Bogota 39, the best Latin American writers under forty. From 2023 to 2024 he was a Mellon High Impact Scholar, at the University of Texas at Austin. His latest books include *What the Sea Brought Ashore, Dismantling My Father's Library,* and *The End of the World Came to My 'Hood.*

Mary Heebner's artworks belong to many collections both private and public, including the British Library and the Getty Center. Her numerous books combine her paintings with her writing, or pair her art with authors ranging from Shakespeare to Eshleman. Harper Collins published two volumes of Pablo Neruda's poetry accompanied by her paintings, with translations by Alastair Reid. Her fascination with antiquity informs her artworks and artist books on Lascaux, Angkor, and Classical sculpture. Please visit maryheebner.com.

Joan Tapper was the founding editor of *National Geographic Traveler*; she then moved on to *Islands* magazine, which she headed up for thirteen years. She is the author of *Island Dreams: Caribbean*, a comprehensive work on the archipelago, with photographs by Nik Wheeler. She has written many other popular books on travel, culture, and history, working with such publishers as Thames & Hudson and Random House Penguin. She is also a well-known editorial consultant, for writers of both fiction and non-fiction. Please visit joantapper.com.

John Balkwill, our late and much-regretted friend, was a book designer, publisher, and artist. He studied with the master printer Gabriel Rummonds, as well as with the wood engravers John DePol and Akira Kurosaki. He collaborated with various authors on edition projects, including Gary Snyder, Daniel Boorstin, James McPherson, and Wole Soyinka. He produced artist's books with Jacquelyn McBain, Mark Ryden, and Peter Goin, among many others. His books and prints, amply exhibited, figure in both private and public collections. Please visit luminopress.com.

Still in mid-career, **Isa Benedetti** has shown herself to be a versatile designer, not only of books but of visual media, such as feature films and television series. In those fields, she has displayed the ample range of her creative capacities. Her past credits include *The Stork, Tabula Rasa, Hotel Cocaine, Road House, Books & Drinks, Are You Afraid of the Dark?, Insular, Croma Kid,* and *Holy Beasts* (starring Geraldine Chaplin). Her forthcoming projects continue to mirror the extensive scope of her interests: *The Queen's Jewels, Minotaur: Picasso and the Women of Guernica, That Night, Melodrama,* and *The Short Life of Flowers.*

The Caribbean Trilogy

But this new world here sought, is stranger far
than his, who stretched his vans from Palos.

— Melville

Though it stands fully on its own, *Return to Dawn* is the third volume of *The Caribbean Trilogy*, three novels by Hoyt Rogers (with Artemisia Vento and Frank Báez). The first book, *Sailing to Noon*, was published by Spuyten Duyvil in 2024: it garnered a number of literary prizes, including the 2025 Independent Press Award for Hispanic/Latin Fiction. Setting a record, the second and third novels, *Midnight at Sea* (2025) and *Return to Dawn* (in review copy, slated for publication in 2026), are the joint recipients of the 2026 Independent Press Award for Hispanic/Latin Fiction.